THE

PASSED

GENERATION

THE *PASSED* GENERATION

A compelling saga of families in disarray,
peppered with pride, upheaval, and unity

Dave Echols

© 2020

THE
PASSED
GENERATION

Executive Editor: Elaine Lindsey

Editors: Gloria Jean Pennington & Howard James

Cover design: Darcel Pugh

Reviewers: Allen Richards & L. E. Lopez

ISBN: 9781735873220

Library of Congress Control Number: Pending

Published in the United States of America

Dave Echols
PO Box 5355
Laurel, MD 20726

Family, friends, and acquaintances with whom I've ever shared a kind word, smile, thought, or a pleasant experience – this one's for you –

Preface

Prior to the start of, during, and now on the other side of writing The *Passed* Generation, I sometimes think about how to answer an important question: "Why the heck did I write this book?" Well, the answer lies squarely on the shoulders of others, as they provided the impetus to tell a story. Let me elaborate.

First off, beyond the influence of family, TV, and Hardy Boys novels I devoured while young, I must specifically mention one of my elementary and middle school studious and insightful classmates, Neil Lavender, who unknowingly helped me work on my creative talents. He had a way of looking beyond the obvious to find aspects of things I didn't recognize at first. I followed his various trains of thought and caught on to his perceptions. A seed had been planted.

I also need to give a shout-out to the memory of my 8th, 9th, and 10th grade English teachers. (Sorry, I don't recall their names). The 8th and 9th grade teachers boosted my desire to create when each accused me of plagiarism after I turned in compositions and poems I wrote during class. The 10th grade teacher prodded me to be more insightful when she explained what no one in the class recognized as "the sick soul of Beret" portrayed in the novel "Giants in the Earth." Her explanation and my instant "Ah ha!" understanding of what she'd said gave rise to my wanting to always try to watch for signs that a character has remained true to their character.

Then there was the military experience. Meeting all sorts of people from all over the USA certainly helped to round out my perception of individuals. It was quite an experience to walk into a controlled environment with many others who'd also been ordered to report and join a tossed salad of humanity. I had to quickly learn to deal with multiple personalities from a plethora of different guys and gals. Fellow soldiers, I'm sure you know what I mean.

Post-military, there have been many folks outside of family that gave rise to my wanting to put pen to paper, with the emphasis on those I've worked with. The problem is remembering everyone. Some that came to mind yesterday are not necessarily ones I remember today, and I guarantee I'll remember {and likely forget) others tomorrow. Note, there were co-workers for whom I don't recall last names or don't wish to individually state redundant last names for those with the same first name. Here are some, in no particular order:

Tim, George, LD, Vic, Joe, Milt, John, Ron, Ras, Rudy, Faye, Mike, Howie, Charlie, Bede, Bob, Steve, Alex Nobile, Pete Setaro, Elise Taylor, Al Tanko, Bill Rathsmith, the guys in the work crews I supervised, and folks who supervised me. Following that last thought, a pair of my supervisors quickly come to mind, Pat Wendrzycki and Jack Edwards.

Pat was a great person to work for. She seemed to always exude a calming force and had an easy way about her. I appreciated her managerial style. Those few years with her and the others in the office (Joan, Marie, Edie, and Betty) were memorable, purposeful, and heavily tilted toward fun, no matter how busy we were.

I also need to say a little about Jack. He was the type of person who was easy to like and actually *want* to have as a supervisor. While working for him, it was always as if he was helping you work, even though his actual contributions were those of allowing you to work, expecting obtainable results, and honestly considering his subordinates' points of view.

Beyond folks I've worked with on a 9 to 5 basis, I've also interacted with a diverse horde of musically talented people. Believe me when I say that singers can be extremely touchy about any sound emitted from the throat. That's not necessarily a negative observation - I've sung with some solid vocalists. The M.U.S.I.C Inc chorus, Barbershop choruses, and Gospel choirs I've dealt with immediately come to mind. Those groups are examples of how individuals can to get together to enjoy harmonious harmony, if you will. Surprisingly, egos were not left at the door. Instead, they were brought in to help bolster the sound without crushing other egos.

I've also dealt with many R&B groups. That's where the ability to work with other personalities has proven to be a blessing. Rather than dwelling on difficulties, I need to state that I've worked with some really wonderful folks. If I had to pick one from the cream of that crop, it would be Keith Matthews. He and I have shared numerous stages for years, and I wholeheartedly give him 2 thumbs up. Not only is he a great singer, he is also great to work with. He is undoubtedly talented enough to have his voice known 'round the world. Hopefully, that distinction will come one day.

Sports have also played a part in the development of my appreciation of synergetic allegiances. Teammates and opponents from basketball, football, baseball, softball (fast pitch was great!), and racquetball – those folks represent another great source of observing and dealing with personalities.

It's impossible to overlook Dr Jonathan Mandras as someone who helped inspire this book. His professionalism and his personality are top notch in that he always makes you feel that he is truly *your* dentist while he tends to you. Please pardon this digression - his wife Erin wrote a book, "Austin's Allergies", about their son's food allergies. It's a really good read for a youngster and I'd recommend it to anyone. I found it enlightening.

Back on point, I wanted to write a book. To get it done, I simply plucked the main thrust of the book out of my wondering mind. Applying personalities was fairly easy due to the individuality of folks I've dealt with. I simply designed characters unlike anyone I've ever known or heard of to fill in the blanks. Imagination poised on a tangent angled far from life's experiences helped to expand the scope of the story. It became a teeter-totter of real vs imaginary things. The overriding thought was 'if *that* particular incident happened in real life, then *this* particular incident could happen within a fictional tale'.

Bottom line, I had a story to tell and I wanted it to include scenarios that pose "if I could have, I would have, and maybe I should have" points to ponder. To spice things up, I tossed in unusual circumstances to parallel coincidences that dreams (or maybe nightmares) are made of. It was quite interesting to maneuver personalities and situations around a plot that began small but was then expanded. Later on, I developed the plot further to create a climactic soul-searching and gut checking web of intermingled lives.

My overall feeling is that writing the book has been a topsy-turvy experience. I could further describe it as the output from a whirlwind of emotions derived from observing, living, and treasuring memories of things encountered while traveling down the road of life. That said, it would have been great if life's speed bumps, black ice, and potholes along the way had been avoided. A mystical solution would have been for fate to have dragged those obstacles to the side of the road and dumped each one into a deep ditch before I had to deal with them. On the other hand, pesky intersections have been easier to successfully manage. They only require courteous adherence to rules and tactful maneuvering.

By the way, I can't help but assume that you also have a story to tell. Please do it. Let your imagination run wild. Just remember that your unusual and far-fetched ideas and coincidences are fine as long as characters remain true to themselves.

Contents

THE *PASSED* GENERATION

Prologue

Life is full of surprises. Most surprises hinge on elements rooted within people, places, things, time, or by phenomenon far beyond the scope of human ability to understand. However, no matter where one's belief lies, big and small surprises have always been a part of life.

Surprises affecting lives lurk within this story. Folks become wrapped up in what starts as a somewhat insignificant thing that eventually expands to inject massive changes into multiple lives.

That's how it goes. Surprises, or more succinct and to the point, unusual happenings, begin with the simple act of interacting with others. Those simple interactions eventually become manifested into multifaceted surprise packages, one day, one action, one event, and one reaction at a time.

"Open eyes are no match for an open mind" - Dave Echols

The *Passed* Generation

1 Homecoming

Molly Hurley had just completed the process of transferring dough for sweet rolls onto a baking pan when, through the open kitchen window, she heard a car approaching. She knew it wasn't her own car. She'd heard it often enough from the window when her daughter Sue drove it to easily recognize its sound.

Once the car stopped in front of the house rather than in the back where household cars normally parked, Molly paused and listened intently. As she expected, she heard the car door slam and the car drive off. Those sounds told her young Tom Purlmen had come home.

As half of the live-in housekeeping staff for Thomas and Elizabeth Purlmen, Molly was acutely aware of the goings-on at the residence. Molly and Sue had been there for 9 months now, just one week shorter than the period of time the Purlmens' son Tom had been away at private school. Neither Molly nor Sue had ever met Tom because the Purlmens had purposely waited until Tom left for his final high school year to hire not one, but two persons to help around the house. They'd done this because Thomas was gravely ill, and they didn't wish to have Tom know just how ill his father was before they were ready to tell him. For this reason, Thomas and Elizabeth would not allow Tom to return home at all during the school year. Instead they traveled to visit him during school holidays and vacation breaks.

Molly wiped her hands on her apron and made her way through the kitchen and dining room to the closed den door. She knocked and called out, "Mrs. Purlmen, I think your son is coming to the front door. He must have taken a cab from the airport."

Elizabeth replied, "That means he took an earlier flight. I told him we'd have a limousine there to pick him up at 4." She glanced at her watch. "It's only 3. You go to the door and let him in while I call and cancel the limousine. He might not have his key."

The order surprised Molly. She'd expected one or both of the Purlmen parents, Thomas' illness notwithstanding, to go to the door to greet their son on his homecoming from high school graduation and his trip abroad. It was also Saturday, May 13, 1967, the day after she thought she'd overheard them talking about their son turning 18.

Molly mused over those facts as she made her way to the front door where, about 5 steps from the door, she heard the distinct click of a key in the lock. She hesitated as the door opened, then took 2 more steps and stopped. Before her stood a young man, looking no older than his 18 years, but very much like a much younger version of what Thomas Purlmen had looked like months earlier. He had a suitcase in one hand, another one behind him, and what looked like a stuffed laundry bag next to it.

Like Molly, Tom had expected either his father or mother to be the first person he saw when he entered the home. He'd purposely taken an earlier flight to show them how independent and mature he'd become by making the trip from school to England and home without help from his parents. Instead, he saw a woman he'd never seen before. She was taller and younger than his mother. She had fair skin, an attractive face, and a ready smile. Her light complexion and slightly curly black hair prevented Tom from easily guessing her heritage, but his curiosity about the issue faded when she smiled. The pause he'd felt at first glance dissipated as Molly's smile put him fully at ease. He spoke first as he set his suitcase down.

"Hi. I'm Tom. You must be the new maid."

Molly replied, "I'm Molly. My daughter Sue and I are the maids, cooks, and housekeepers for the next couple of months before we move out to be with my Aunt Bernice. Your parents are in the den. Do you need any help with your things?"

"No, thank you, Molly. I'll take care of them."

Turning away, Molly said, "Good. I've got work to do." With that, she turned and began to walk back toward the kitchen. As she did, she wished she had reminded Sue to hurry to the grocery store and back without stopping to do any window shopping, daydreaming, or wasting time wondering how she could get rich. The early arrival of the Purlmens' son meant this homecoming dinner would have to be ready sooner than originally expected.

Tom set his suitcases down just inside the door, then retrieved his laundry bag and placed it next to them. He felt warm inside as he entered the home he'd grown up in after more than 9 months of absence. This was the first time he'd ever been away from home for so long a period. He strode to the den door and, avoiding all protocol, entered without knocking.

Thomas spoke first.

"Happy birthday, son. How was England? Wasn't going there better than having us go to your graduation?"

Thomas had greeted and then asked both questions of his son without getting up from the overstuffed office chair behind his desk.

Tom went straight to his mother, who was standing in front of the desk near the room's sofa. He gave her an unemotional hug as he replied. "Going to England was great. I saw a lot and I wouldn't mind handling real estate and construction over there."

"You'll do nothing of the sort," said Elizabeth as she barely returned the hug while easing away from Tom to look him up and down. "We need you here with us," she added as she sat on the sofa.

"Your mother's right," Thomas chimed in. "We sent you on that trip immediately after graduation so you could get more of a feel for being grown-up than you ever could have by just being away as a student at school. We planned on you returning on your 18th birthday ready to become the man of the house." He paused before adding, "You need to work with us as much as possible as soon as possible because you never know when you might get drafted for the war."

Elizabeth didn't appreciate the Vietnam reference. "We won't discuss the war anymore. We'll concentrate on doing what's best for us, and if the war gets in the way, we'll deal with it at that time."

Thomas recognized the firmness of Elizabeth's demand and quickly agreed. "Right. We'll not worry about it. Chances are you won't get drafted anyway. In the meantime, I've got some things I need to show you Tom, man-to-man. Pull that chair over to the coffee table."

As Tom turned to retrieve the chair from the other side of the room, the joy he'd initially felt when he first saw his parents that day subsided, mainly because he could see his father again had aged dramatically since he'd last seen him. Tom thought he had noticed his father's accelerated aging before leaving home for his last year at school, but months of separation between both times they visited him at school made the change unmistakable. His father had continued to lose weight and his thinning hair looked far more like salt than pepper.

Even more noticeable was that his father was now sporting a mustache and short beard that seemed to be there solely to mask his gaunt face. His mother and father were both in their mid-40s, but his father now looked at least 20 years older than his mother. The difference was not only in looks. His father had always had the last word in the house, but the brief conversations they'd had so far gave Tom the feeling his mother was going to be the one in charge from now on.

In the meantime, Thomas, with some effort, pushed himself up from his chair and walked slowly around the desk to the sofa where he sat down next to Elizabeth. In front of them on the coffee table was a 12-inch square cushion upon which sat a small cast iron combination bank and a gold cigarette lighter.

Tom slid the easy chair to the opposite side of the coffee table and sat down. He hadn't previously paid much attention to the items, but as he viewed them now as the centerpiece between him and his parents, they piqued his interest.

Thomas spoke. "The bank is unlocked. Open it and gently dump everything in it onto the cushion."

Tom did as his father asked. Amid cotton balls and a small handkerchief that had been used to eliminate any rattling, 3 items emerged. They were a pocket watch, a gold coin, and a ring.

Thomas said, "These are our family heirlooms. You don't know how much I've been looking forward to the day I could pass them on to you."

Thomas tried to speak in a solemn and dignified manner but couldn't hide the pride and joy in his voice as he picked up the watch, coin, and ring. He handed each one to Tom.

Tom was wide-eyed as he studied the items he saw. He wasn't sure if he should thank his father now or if he should wait for the remainder of the speech he knew was coming. He hesitated and sure enough, his father continued.

"I got the watch from my father – your grandfather – when I was 18. It was just before I got drafted and went off to war. That was a few years before I met your mother."

Thomas turned, smiled, and gazed at his wife.

Elizabeth smiled slightly at the reference as she looked into Thomas' eyes. He then wrapped his left arm around her shoulder as she allowed him to pull her a little closer. The two silently relived cherished memories of their life and love together, with neither sure of exactly which memory the other was entertaining, but each confident the others' thought was well worth the brief interlude.

Tom kept staring at the items, fully aware of his parents' tender moment, but he felt somewhat out of place as they exchanged that special look. It's not that he was embarrassed or ashamed – it was just that he'd noticed the tender moments had been increasing both times they'd visited him during his school year. What was also apparent to him was that his mother's slight smiles somehow seemed to wane to a sadness he could sense more than see. This particular episode was no different as they held the same position longer than any time he'd previously witnessed.

Just as Tom's awkward feeling was morphing to impatience, Elizabeth abruptly broke the mood and began reminiscing about her own family heirloom.

"Your father's family has those heirlooms, but my side of the family has only passed down this ring I wear from mother to daughter when the mother dies. We wear it rather than keep it locked up."

Then, after taking a moment to admire the ring on her right ring finger, Elizabeth added, "Since you don't have a sister, one day your wife will wear it."

Rather than allowing Elizabeth to expand on the sidebar about her ring, Thomas continued his conversation.

"It hasn't been easy keeping quiet about the coin, watch and ring for all these years. One reason I never showed them to you before now is that I didn't want you to get too curious before I thought you were man enough to handle true valuables."

Thomas paused and nodded his head toward the safe. It was black with 3 silver gray dials. The inscription "Tiny Mite Bank-Safe" could be seen above the dials.

"That little safe used to be a toy," he said. "Those 3 combination dials with 6 numbers each worked okay for a toy, but what we did – well actually what my father did – was to alter it so it's now almost impossible to open without knowing the combination and how to use it. It's made of cast iron and we..." Thomas corrected himself again. "I mean *he* blocked the slot for coins."

Thomas looked at Elizabeth and said, "I guess it's time to give Tom the combinations."

Elizabeth nodded her agreement.

Thomas picked up the safe and closed it. He then adjusted all dials to the zero position before setting the safe down and saying, "3 – 6 – 4 – 5. Top to bottom, then up again to the middle dial. There's an easy way to remember the combination, but we'll get to that. Put those heirlooms down so you can try it."

Tom tried the combination and the safe opened.

"Normally the watch, coin, and ring are kept in the safe, but I have this old cigarette lighter here today because I was thinking about adding it to the heirloom collection." Looking at Elizabeth he added, "But your mother doesn't want that to happen."

"The Surgeon General says smoking is no good," Elizabeth interjected. "It's not appropriate to relish or worship something like that. You gave up smoking before we were married. You probably should get rid of that lighter."

Elizabeth had spoken firmly, giving the impression to both men that she'd had the final word on the subject.

Thomas had previously believed he and Tom might be able to overrule Elizabeth, but her tone erased that premise. He suggested a compromise.

"Enough said. Maybe we can just keep the lighter with the other heirlooms and not call it an heirloom."

"That would make more sense," Elizabeth responded. "But I still don't want it included with everything else."

Thomas didn't reply to Elizabeth's last remark. Instead, he turned his attention back to Tom and spoke.

"The little safe is important, but this ceremony is about those heirlooms. Before I continue, look in the bottom right-hand desk drawer of my desk and get my Instamatic camera."

As Tom got the camera, Thomas arranged the watch, coin, and ring on the cushion. Then, when he'd been given the camera, Thomas took a picture of just those 3 items. The camera used instant film that took about a minute to develop. Thomas waited for the required minute for the picture to develop and was pleased with the result. He then nodded in the direction of the heirlooms.

"I want to give you the full rundown on how important they are to me and your mother, and how important the original one was to my father, my grandfather, my great-grandfather and how meaningful and important the oldest one and the newer ones should be to you."

By now all feelings Tom had of awkwardness and impatience dissipated and became a singular intense feeling of anticipation. His father had always spoken to him frequently, but having this special man-to-man conversation about things important to his father to the point where having a woman involved – albeit his mother – was acceptable, meant that whatever the message was, he needed to listen intently.

Thomas stared at Tom, leaned forward, rested his forearms on his thighs, interlaced his fingers, and began the conversational journey.

"My father – your grandfather – I wish you could have met him," Thomas started. "I know I've told you this before, but let me tell you again. He went out of his way to look out for me. Not only by how he held onto the family money and didn't squander it when other folks were losing money during the depression, but also by the way he raised me after my mother died. It was just him and me. We had a housekeeper and a cook, but they didn't live here with us like Molly and Sue. Instead, he let them live in one of the apartment buildings rent-free."

"Dad taught me the value of a dollar, negotiating skills, and how important it is to keep on top of your work. From the time I was 16, I was the one responsible for collecting the rent. Not the past due rents. I collected rent from people who always paid on time."

For a moment Tom began to wonder why this information was being rehashed, but then he remembered the heirlooms and relaxed as his father continued.

Thomas sensed Tom's puzzlement so he quickly addressed it. "As I said, I'm going over all this so you have a better idea of why those heirlooms are so important to us."

He picked up the watch and looked at it a moment before continuing.

"This watch has been with the family the longest. It had originally been a gift from my great-grandfather to my grandfather. My great-grandfather bought it on the day my grandfather was born. His idea was to create a family heirloom in honor of my grandfather's birth that was to be passed down from son to son at some appropriate time in each son's life – at 21 or getting married or something like that."

As soon as he said, "21," Thomas realized he'd said the main thing he'd wanted to eliminate from the ceremony – that particular age. Not wanting to draw any additional attention to the number by correcting himself, he hoped Tom hadn't noticed the reference.

Thomas continued with, "It's an expensive watch, but he was able to afford it because he owned most of the property we own today, including this estate. Anyway, he wound that watch only one time, the day when my grandfather was born. My father said that became the tradition. Only wind the watch when you receive it, and then put it away for safekeeping until the time comes to pass it on."

It was now that the reference to the age of 21 would mean something, but Thomas continued as if he'd never mentioned it.

"My grandfather officially gave it to my father when he turned 18, which was the day he and other 18-year-old men were supposed to report to register for the World War I draft. The watch got wound for only the second time that day and then it was put away for safekeeping. Dad said they held a little ceremony with the watch while hoping for the best outcome of the war in Europe. Fortunately for my father, the war ended 2 months later and he didn't get called to go off to war. That made Dad a little superstitious. From then on, he treated the watch as if it was a good luck charm or something like that."

"Dad talked to me often about the watch and how lucky he'd been to not have to go to war. He probably talked about it too much, which is the main reason I haven't tried to impress you with the watch or any of the newer heirlooms while you've been growing up. They're important to us, but they're not magical or anything. They're important because they're ours and they're being passed down through our family."

Thomas handed the watch back to Tom. He then leaned back so he and Elizabeth again sat shoulder to shoulder.

"Anyway, the day he found out the armistice had ended the war, he went out and bought a wall safe for the watch. He took it home and convinced his father that they should keep the watch locked up. Once they installed the safe and locked the watch in it, they kept it there. As I said, Dad believed more in luck than the importance of the watch being a family treasure and he kept his good luck charm locked away in the safe untouched for many years. They didn't even open the safe when I was born."

Tom was surprised to hear about a wall safe having been installed in the house. This was the first time he'd ever heard it mentioned. With renewed interest, he listened as his father continued to speak.

"Years later, in 1942 when I turned 18," Thomas was saying, "I was still too young to have to register for the draft, but later that year they lowered the age requirement. On the day I was to register, my father presented me with the watch. I guess he thought it would end the war or at least shorten it so I wouldn't get drafted. Things didn't happen that way. I took the watch, gave it the traditional wind, and then we locked it in the safe. I got drafted into the army 6 months

26

after registering. If there was magic in that watch, it didn't have anything to do with me entering the second World War."

Thomas paused before saying to Tom, "Now go ahead, wind the watch and set the time."

Tom then set the watch and slowly wound it as his father resumed the conversation.

"That watch used to be the only heirloom, but me being in the war changed that. After about a year, I was stationed in England in a place called Weymouth - you know the place where your great-great-grandfather was born. It was one of the ports soldiers shipped out of on their way to the D-Day invasion. I had only been there a few weeks when I was notified my father had died. They wouldn't let me go home, but they gave me 24 hours off. I took the time to go into town and at a little shop I saw this British coin."

Thomas picked up the coin and handed it to Tom.

"It's a King George Sovereign gold coin and now it's worth a lot of money – way more than its face value. The value will probably continue to increase for as long as people continue to buy and sell coins. I could afford it because my father had made sure I left home with plenty of money. Anyway, I got the coin because the portrait on the face of the coin reminds me of Dad."

Tom didn't fully appreciate the resemblance to photos he'd seen of his grandfather until Thomas added, "without the full mustache."

Thomas then picked up the ring and said, "Now put the coin down so you can try on this ring."

Tom placed the coin on the cushion as Thomas handed him the ring.

"It's a man's ring with a ruby stone. I bought it soon after the D-Day invasion started. The main reason I got it was because I wanted it as a remembrance of all the men who died during the D-day battles and as a memento of how precious life is. I'd lost my father a few weeks earlier and had gotten the coin for him. Since my job kept me in Weymouth and I didn't have to deploy to France, I wanted something to remember all the guys who had given me their money and other valuables they couldn't take or be able to use when they left for D-Day."

Thomas paused for a moment of reflection and added, "Like this cigarette lighter I got from one of the guys who never came back."

Turning to Elizabeth, he renewed the discussion regarding the lighter saying, "Which is why we should at least keep it as a memento heirloom."

That statement swayed Elizabeth so she acquiesced with, "Alright, go ahead and keep it with the other heirlooms. I believe I'd rather have it stored away than to have it in your drawer to remind you that you used to smoke."

"Good," answered Thomas. He turned back to Tom and continued. "Now wrap the heirlooms in the handkerchief and put them back in the little safe. Make sure everything is snug so it won't rattle. Use extra cotton balls if you need to. Then close the door and turn the dials. Make sure it locks."

Tom did as he was told, but an underlying concern had him baffled. He'd caught his father's reference to 21 and noticed that heirloom presentations were never at the predesignated age, so he wanted to ask his father why he'd been given the heirlooms now rather than at 21. Was it because he'd graduated? Because he'd turned 18? Because of the potential of being drafted? He had a sense that something was going on, but he didn't feel comfortable asking about it. The heirloom stories were interesting, but why were they being handled now?

Thomas interrupted Tom's thoughts as he continued speaking.

"We have a painting of Weymouth port that your great-grandfather cherished. Having it is almost like having another heirloom. It doesn't fit with the decor of the house, so we found a much better place for it in the wine cellar. It's hidden behind the wine cellar door if you keep the door open as you normally would while you're in there. That means you have to close the door behind you once you get inside if you want to see it."

With extreme effort he tried to mask, Thomas stood and reached out to help Elizabeth to her feet. Elizabeth recognized Thomas was struggling, so she preserved the ruse by standing more on her own than with his assistance. Without a discussion, both had decided the time to let Tom know the extent of Thomas' illness had not yet arrived.

Nodding toward the den door, Thomas spoke to Tom.

"Lead the way to the wine cellar. Let's put those heirlooms back where they belong."

The command caught Tom off guard. Though not locked, the wine cellar had been off-limits to everyone except his father for as long as Tom could remember. He'd been at the door when his father had gone in to retrieve or replenish stock, but he'd never before ventured inside. His mother had given him stern warnings about entering long ago and she was one whose warnings should not be ignored. This had to be a special occasion if not only he, but also his mother would be joining his father there.

As they walked toward the basement door, they passed the kitchen, whereupon Thomas saw Molly and called out to her, "Molly, when will dinner be ready?"

"In a little over an hour, Mr. Purlmen," Molly responded.

"Thanks, Molly," said Thomas. "You and Tom have already met, right?"

"Oh yes. I met him at the front door."

"Good. Is Sue around?"

"No sir. She's at the market getting a few things we need."

"Fine, we'll be ready for dinner whenever it's ready."

"Alright. I'll let you know."

As the Purlmen clan continued walking toward the basement, Molly hoped she'd been accurate with her timing. "Sue should have been back by now," she thought to herself. Molly had given the time she thought it would take to cook the meal along with another 20 minutes for however long Sue might take to return with things missing from the preparation ingredients.

There was no valid reason for Sue to be wasting time anywhere with anyone Molly was aware of. Both of those boys, Wayne and Frank, that Sue used to be interested in, had been drafted into the army. That made it unlikely a rendezvous had been planned.

Molly had been worried about Wayne, who was Sue's first fling with infatuation. She was glad he had been drafted only about a week after the relationship began. Sue and Wayne exchanged letters frequently for a couple of months after that, but then Wayne's letters abruptly stopped. Sue was disappointed, but Molly was able to convince Sue that someone's first love is usually not their last love and, more importantly, not always their best love.

Apparently, with Molly's advice in mind, Sue met and had another love interest in a boy named Frank. This latest fling was more worrisome to Molly as Sue began to find excuses to be away from the house far more often than normal. Molly suspected but could never prove that things between Sue and Frank had gone beyond a friendly relationship. She tried to get Sue to open up about whatever future plans she and Frank had, but Sue's responses were always evasive.

Needless to say, Molly was elated when that relationship ended the same way as the one with Wayne. Military service and a final letter from Frank did the trick. Molly's elation was only tempered by the fact that previous to these two young men, Sue had never dated anyone. She'd grown into an attractive woman who unfortunately did not appreciate herself. Her right leg was about an inch shorter than her left, which gave her a slight limp. While she could hide the limp if she wore her orthopedic shoes or consciously altered her method of walking, her right leg became a focal point as to how she judged herself rather than herself as a whole.

As if on cue, Molly heard her car being driven and then stopping in the back of the house. Sue would then be coming through the basement and upstairs with groceries within a few minutes. Molly barely heard Sue close the car door and didn't hear the basement door being unlocked, opened, or closed at all. This didn't surprise Molly. Sue's self-consciousness about her shorter right leg caused her to habitually move quietly to avoid drawing attention to herself.

Once inside, Sue quietly set the bag of groceries down and changed from street shoes to the maid shoes she wore while inside the house. While doing so she noticed light illuminating the bottom of the wine cellar door down the hall. She didn't give it much attention. It had to be Mr. Purlmen getting some dinner wine. What she didn't understand was why Mr. Purlmen would be drinking at all, given the fact his worsening health condition had been divulged to her and her mother and he hadn't had any wine with dinner for months.

Meanwhile, from within the wine cellar, Thomas continued his conversation with Tom.

"When did your great-great-grandfather come to this country?" Thomas asked Tom.

Having had the answer drummed into his head for as long as he could remember, Tom immediately replied, "1839 when he was 4."

Thomas continued, "We chose that combination for the wall safe because it's something the painting should always remind you of. Also, it reinforces the fact that these heirlooms are symbolic of our family's heritage from generation to generation. Everything about them means something to us, but remember, the heirlooms are not only symbolic - they're really valuable too."

Thomas paused for a moment and then in a hushed tone he said, "That's the combination to the wall safe, except you have to transpose the 18 and the 39, making the combination 39-18-4, left, right, left. It's also the combination to the little safe, in a code we came up with, using just the last two numbers of the year and how old he was. That gives you 3, 9, and 4. Since the numbers on each of the dials only go up to 6, we use this formula. The first dial is 3. For the second number, you subtract 3 from 9 leaving 6. The third number is 4. For the last number, you subtract 4 from 9 leaving 5. Easy to remember.

Top dial 3, middle 6, bottom 4, back to the middle, and turn to 5. Now let me see you open and close the little safe again and then open the wall safe and put the little safe in it."

By now, Sue had retrieved the groceries and had silently walked to a point just outside the wine cellar door where she paused and listened. The only part of the conversation she overheard was that of Thomas saying, "We chose that combination for the safe because it's something the painting should always remind you of. Also, it reinforces the fact that these heirlooms are symbolic of our family's heritage from generation to generation. Everything about them means something to us, but remember, the heirlooms are not only symbolic. They're really valuable too."

Sue realized if she was discovered lingering at the door she'd be accused of eavesdropping, so she left the spot and went upstairs to join Molly in the kitchen.

"What's going on down there? Who's down there? Did their son come home? What heirlooms?" Sue asked all of her questions without pausing for individual answers.

"Slow down Child," Molly admonished in a hushed voice while using her pet name for Sue. "You don't need to be slinking around here worrying about what they're doing. They took their son down there. I don't know why."

Molly gestured impatiently for Sue to come closer.

"Come on, give me the things I need," she said, taking the bag of groceries from Sue.

After a moment, Molly asked, "What do you mean heirlooms?"

"I heard Mr. Purlmen talking about them."

"They must have some in their family. I never heard them mention any. Rich folks usually have expensive ones, but folks like us usually have something like a Bible or family pictures. The only thing we could call an heirloom is the wedding picture. You know, the one with Mama, Daddy, my grandparents, and Aunt Bernice."

Sue answered, "Yes, I know. I haven't paid any attention to it for years but I know it's one of the pictures you keep on the dresser." Then she quickly added, "That's one of the reasons why the top of the dresser always stays so cluttered."

Molly ignored the last remark and instead replied, "You should appreciate your relatives, especially the ones you never met, like your father."

Molly spent a moment lamenting the fact that Sue's father Roberto had been listed as MIA during WWII and they'd never been married. She didn't even have a picture of him. She brushed the thought aside and refocused on the wedding picture saying, "Aunt Bernice looked so young in the picture. I'm looking forward to moving in with her when we leave here. Now let's get finished with dinner. I told them it would be ready in about an hour and that was 10 minutes ago."

The two women worked in silence for a few minutes before Sue broke the silence. "I wonder what kind of heirlooms they have," she said, completely ignoring her own family's heirloom.

Molly recognized the snub immediately. "Don't worry about other folks' heirlooms. Our heirloom is important to me and it should be important to you. I don't have anything else that's been passed down from Mama, Daddy or Aunt Bernice. And don't forget that Aunt Bernice doesn't have any pictures of her parents at all."

Sue had been quietly listening to Molly's conversation as if interested, but her curiosity from hearing Mr. Purlmen describe the heirlooms as being "really valuable" had her mind racing. She wanted to ponder how she might at least take a look at the expensive heirlooms, so she baited Molly into continuing her one-sided oration about their own Hurley photo heirloom.

"Tell me again about everyone in the picture, Mama."

Knowing her daughter, Molly sensed that Sue was being less than sincere, but Molly's emotional attachment to the photo overcame her suspicion. She relished any opportunity to speak about family to Sue, even one tainted with feigned interest.

"Mama and Daddy had a small wedding," Molly began. "The only people there were Mama and Daddy, their parents, Aunt Bernice, and the preacher and his wife. Mama's mother came from Ireland and her father came from Wales. They met somewhere in or around Freetown, Maryland."

Sue was only half listening to her mother's oration about their family. Thoughts of valuable heirlooms in the house were heavy on her mind, but she had the wherewithal to nod her head affirmatively from time to time as Molly continued to speak.

Molly was saying, "Mama told me Daddy's parents came from Virginia. His great-grandfather's family had been slaves in Georgia before they moved to Virginia. He never knew them or his grandfather or grandmother. He told Mama that his father met his mother when they both were around 22. She was from an Indian tribe. Each one of them had very light skin. In fact, they were almost light enough to pass for white."

Molly shook her head and continued. "I don't think they ever tried though. From what I heard, they decided to move North because racism around where they lived was pretty bad. They got married in Maryland and settled near Freetown, over on the eastern shore. Then they had Daddy. He met Mama in high school. They were both pretty young when they got married, but it didn't last too long."

Molly paused to sigh and state, "It lasted long enough for them to have me, their only child."

With that, she shook her head and shortly continued speaking. "That Indian part of our family I heard about always fascinated me. I used to ask Mama about it and she said that Daddy's mother had been a member of one of the tribes in the Sioux Nation. She didn't know which one. Daddy had told her about it before they split up. I was only 2 when he left and I don't remember him at all. After they divorced, Mama said he got remarried to a woman who already had a little girl and they lived a few hours away. Mama didn't like talking about him and never tried to let me see him or to get him to come and see me."

Molly now became reflective. "I've told you many times that the only thing I got from my father was the fact that my grandmother was from one of the Sioux tribes. That's why I named you Sue and not Susan. The only picture I have of him is the wedding picture. It's a copy of the original because Mama said Daddy took the original when he left."

The women had made quick work of the meal preparation and had things fully under control. As they cleaned the utensils they no longer needed, Molly added her own take on their heritage. She spoke in a voice so low it was as if she was talking to herself, "Daddy's colored father and his mother were so fair-skinned that no one knows what we are."

Sue heard the remark and it caused her to break away from wondering about Purlmen heirlooms to reply defensively, "Mama, you shouldn't say colored. You're supposed to say black. Anyway, it's not like it was when you were growing up. People don't care so much anymore."

"Well, it's still pretty important to a lot of people, so just be glad you can go anywhere and do anything you want if you set your mind to it."

Sue said nothing as she braced herself for what experience told her would likely follow her mother's previous statement.

Molly said the exact thing Sue dreaded hearing.

"You just need to stop worrying about that leg."

Sue had heard about allowing her leg to hinder her advancement many times before and as always, it caused her to retreat from the conversation. Neither spoke for a while as they continued to prepare dinner, however, their dialogue caused Molly to reminisce more about Sue's father Roberto. While she didn't know too much about him firsthand, a friend of a friend had spoken about him many years ago. From those stories she'd heard, and from what little she did know, Molly was able to piece together a brief profile of the man.

Roberto and his brother Eduardo had been orphaned while both were young, Roberto 13 and Eduardo 17. Eduardo had taken charge and reared Roberto, but rather than accept any assistance from anyone, they resorted to lying and stealing. They lived a life of freedom from school and had no permanent home. Abandoned buildings became their refuge.

That style of life lasted for several years but eventually landed Eduardo in jail and Roberto on his own. By that time Roberto was 19 and that's when he met Molly. The 14-year-old Molly was easily smitten by Roberto, who seduced her that first night. Roberto made plans the next day to settle down and have a wife and family, but he was without a job. Foolishly he decided he'd manufacture some cash by stealing a few hundred dollars' worth of merchandise. The plan backfired. He was caught and sent before a judge, who decided to go against the norm and offer induction into military service in lieu of prison. Without Molly as a mate, Roberto would have accepted jail, but he chose the army. He felt that jail might ruin the relationship.

Roberto was made to enlist immediately and was medically examined and inducted into the army the very next day. He didn't remember Molly's last name or address, so he was forced to list his brother as the person who would always know his whereabouts. Within a week he found himself in basic training. A few months after that he was in the Pacific war.

Meanwhile, Molly had few clues as to what was going on. She'd heard Roberto had been arrested and then quickly joined the army, but she didn't know how to get in touch with him. The loneliness she felt at first was terrible, but weeks later that loneliness seemed miniscule compared to the anguish she felt when she realized she was pregnant. On top of that, she had to endure her mother's disapproval of the situation. After all, Molly was going to have a child at a young age by someone her mother had never met. However, as is usually the case, it didn't take long for the friction to blow over. The two soon set their sights on the necessary tasks to bring a child into the world and to do what would be best for the infant.

When Sue was a few weeks old, a friend of a friend told Molly that Eduardo had received information that Roberto had been listed as missing in action during the war. By then Eduardo had been released from prison and returned to his life of crime. However, before Molly got a chance to speak directly to Eduardo, he'd been shot and killed during a robbery.

Molly then became a prisoner to the hope and prayer that one day Roberto would return, but in the meantime, she was a young mother living at home with her mother as her sole support. This lasted for a while, but as soon as she could, she began working as a housekeeper and cook. As luck would have it, she was hired by a family as a live-in housekeeper, and even better, the employers welcomed Sue. That job lasted for 23 years, which gave Molly and Sue a stable residence through all of Sue's school years and beyond the passing of Molly's mother. It only ended when the employers retired and moved to Florida.

Molly and Sue then toyed with the idea of moving in immediately with their sole relative, Aunt Bernice, but decided to work for maybe another year or so before making that move. They applied to an agency and there was a match. The great references Molly and Sue had received from their former employers meshed perfectly with the Purlmen family's query at the agency to hire excellent live-in domestic help for about a year.

While Molly and Sue had been lost in their own thoughts, the Purlmen family had been continuing their heirloom ceremonial tasks. After hearing his father's statements regarding the heirlooms being really valuable and the combination details, Tom placed the little safe on the floor and attempted to remove the painting from the wall. There was a little slack in whatever had it fastened to the wall, but he could not easily pull it free.

Thomas had been waiting for this moment. "You have to tilt the painting about a third of the way counter-clockwise before you pull it. There are two nails behind it that are offset to keep the painting from being easily removed. Of course, you have to replace it the opposite way. You should be okay from here."

This time Tom gave the painting a slight twist and pull. He then removed the painting to expose the safe built neatly into the wall. Silently he spun the dial clockwise as he had been taught to do with combination locks, until he got to 39 where he stopped, spun the dial back to 18, stopped, then spun the dial directly to 4. He tried the handle and opened the safe, which had ample room for the tiny safe. He completed the tasks of inserting the tiny safe, closing the wall safe, spinning the dial, and rehanging the painting without further instruction.

"That's it," Thomas said. "It'll be years before the safe is to be opened again. It could be decades. You want to wait until you have a son and he turns 21 or he gets married or he has a son. The decision as to when the heirlooms get passed along will be up to you in accordance with the wishes of your great-great-grandfather's original plan that we've all followed. Only 3 people now know of the heirlooms and this safe - let's keep it that way."

Thomas paused to allow himself the luxury of reviewing the day's events and how he'd been handling what was somewhat of a rite of passage for Tom. He at first had not wanted the heirloom ceremony to be marred by the 18 vs. 21 age reference and hoped it hadn't registered with Tom, but now he was hoping it had. That's the main reason he mentioned it again. Having done so should make it easier to segue into the subject of his illness later, but right now he wanted to talk about something else.

He decided his next move should be to delve into the main contents of the wine cellar – the wine and other spirits. Up to now, Tom hadn't been allowed to consume alcohol and had never shown the desire to do so. Thomas and Elizabeth had discussed how and when to formally teach Tom to respect alcohol, but they hadn't set the date until earlier that day when Elizabeth agreed it would be alright for Thomas to do so in conjunction with the heirloom ceremony.

"We need to choose a nice wine to go with dinner," Thomas began. "Take a look around, Tom. You know your mother and I used to like to have a little each day." Thomas had again made a veiled reference into why the heirloom ceremony happened sooner than what had been planned by stating the words 'used to'.

Continuing, Thomas said, "You know, Tom, I'm glad you've never asked for any alcohol and you've never given me the impression you would try to sneak any."

"Or cigarettes," Elizabeth interjected.

Thomas nodded in agreement with the statement and echoed, "Yes, or cigarettes."

He then paused to weigh Tom's reaction. All Tom did was slowly and silently shake his head from side to side, indicating, "No," but the wine cellar had always intrigued him. Fear and respect had always been the buffer that hindered any inclination he might have had to indulge in alcohol or cigarettes.

"Good, that's perfect," Thomas said. "We'll choose something light to go along with our meal. We never overindulge." He glanced at his watch. "We have time to look things over. I want you to get used to being the one who chooses the wine from now on."

Elizabeth wasn't happy Thomas was obviously planning to have some wine, but she reasoned it would be alright as long as it was no more than a sip. Rather than complaining, she reminded them of her presence by stating, "Dinner should be ready in another half hour."

"Alright," Thomas said. "Let's use this time wisely. Tom, you're 18 now. Remember, it's still illegal for you to drink anywhere except right here at home and then only when supervised by your mother or me. Now look around and ask any questions about whatever you're not sure of."

Tom felt as if he'd been on a magical ride all day. He'd been absorbing a lot of information and now the one thing he was most curious about in the house – his parent's wine cellar – would now be under his charge. Not that he envisioned himself as someone who would overindulge, but rather as someone who was considered grown enough to become educated about alcohol. He felt as if he had the world at his fingertips.

The downfall of fully thinking that way is the tendency to overlook the idiom that literally describes gravity and often metaphorically describes life – what must go up must come down.

It took about 10 minutes for Tom to select – with Thomas' assistance – the dinner wine. They departed the wine cellar and went upstairs where Molly greeted them.

"Dinner is just about ready. The sweet rolls will be coming out of the oven in about 5 minutes."

"Good, we'll be ready by then," Elizabeth said. She then took care of formal introductions. "This is our son, the other Mr. Purlmen."

The way Elizabeth presented the name and her tone of voice gave Molly and Sue strict forewarning that the formal title was to be used.

To her son, Elizabeth said, "Tom, this is Molly and that's her daughter Sue."

Tom sheepishly said, "I already met Molly. Nice to meet you, Sue."

"Hello," was Sue's curt response. Inwardly, she felt it was demeaning to have to address this young man barely out of high school as Mr. Purlmen, while he would be referring to her by her own first name.

"Hello again, Mr. Purlmen," Molly said in her most pleasant voice. She instantly recognized Sue's displeasure at the class distinction the naming convention represented. In order to deflect some of Sue's tension, she added, "I hope you like what we fixed. Your mother had us make it especially for you."

"It smells really good," Tom replied.

Before anyone else, namely Elizabeth, had an opportunity to put two and two together and recognize or analyze Sue's tension, Thomas had an inspiration.

"Tom," he said, "Go to the den and get my camera. I believe I left it on the sofa. We need to take some pictures."

Once Tom returned with the camera, Thomas decided to have Elizabeth and himself seated side by side with Tom standing behind them. "Give Molly the camera," he directed.

Molly took the camera, aimed, and then snapped the shutter. After waiting a minute, Thomas checked the picture.

"Good," he said. "Now take a couple more."

Molly tried, but the camera was empty and Thomas had no more film. Molly offered a solution.

"I have a camera that uses regular film, the kind you have to take somewhere to get it developed. I'm sure there are at least 10 unused pictures left. I'll be right back."

Molly hurriedly left and minutes later returned with her camera. She took two pictures of the Purlmens.

"I'll get these developed soon," Molly told them.

"Hold on. We should take a couple more pictures." Thomas was in the mood for picture taking. "Tom, why don't you take some pictures of your mother and me and then some of us with Molly and Sue? I'll get some more film for both cameras tomorrow and drop the film off to be developed at the same time."

As Tom reached for the camera, Thomas said, "It's too bad we can't include everyone in the picture."

"We can, Mr. Purlmen," offered Molly. "There's a timer on the side of the camera so you can take a picture a few seconds after you set it up. I'll show you."

Elizabeth had been quiet during the photography session, but she now wanted to speak up to object to Thomas' suggestion to include Molly and Sue in a family picture. Only the fact that it was Molly's camera kept her from voicing her opinion. Thomas, on the other hand, enjoyed the back and forth process of Molly setting, aiming and then moving back into position to be in the picture so much that he had her take 3 pictures that way.

There was still some unused film in the camera, but Molly refocused everyone's attention on something that was far more important than the photo shoot.

"You all need to have your dinner now before it starts to get cold," Molly told them. "I'll make sure I get the film developed before we move."

With that, the Purlmens settled into their respective seats at the table.

The dinner meal progressed the way Tom remembered with two notable exceptions. The first, under what seemed to be the watchful eyes of Elizabeth, Thomas had small, almost petite portions. Secondly, and most telling, Thomas poured himself an almost non-existent portion of wine. Tom was thinking, but more so hoping, that his father was on a health kick. However, deep within his psyche, he feared trouble was brewing.

Like many children, Tom felt his parents would be there for him throughout the years without growing old and feeble, however the changes he'd seen suggested otherwise. He couldn't help but reason to himself that his father and mother had been setting the stage with his trip to England and the heirloom ceremony as a prelude to some bad news. Especially the part of the ceremony where 21 was the set age for the presentation until some extenuating circumstance got in the way. The fact that past extenuating circumstances were never good was troubling.

Following the meal, Elizabeth went about the business of again taking over and reacclimating Tom to being obedient to the matriarch of the home.

"Tom, take your suitcases and laundry up to your room so I can sort through things. Then you can come right back downstairs so you and your father can finish talking. I'll join you later on."

Thomas agreed. "Go ahead. By the time you get back downstairs, I'll be in the office."

While Tom and Elizabeth were away, Thomas took his glass and the almost-full liter of wine into the den. He hurriedly poured himself a full glass and, rather than sipping, drank it down without pausing to catch his breath. He then poured himself another full glass to sip and enjoy. He knew he shouldn't, but for this occasion, he felt he needed it.

When Tom entered the den, the first thing Thomas asked was, "Have they started cleaning the kitchen?" He was referring to Molly and Sue. When Tom hesitated Thomas added, "Check and make sure or your mother will have a fit."

While Tom went to the kitchen, Thomas downed the glass of wine in his hand and poured himself another. He could feel the effect of the wine and thoroughly enjoyed it. He didn't stop there. He again emptied the glass by dumping the contents down his throat. He then refilled his glass and waited for Tom to return.

In short order, Tom returned with the answer Thomas had expected.

"Yes, they're busy cleaning things up."

"Then come in, shut the door, have a seat, and let's talk."

As Tom did as he was told, Thomas took a sip of wine.

Almost instinctively, Thomas then asked, "Where's your glass? Do you want a little more?"

Tom didn't, but feeling his father's question was more of a directive hinging on an order, he replied in the affirmative. "Okay," he said. Not seeing a glass for himself on the desk, he left to retrieve one from the kitchen.

Thomas drank the remainder of the wine in his glass quickly, so when Tom returned, he had to pour some in each glass. He knew he'd had more than he should have and way more than Elizabeth would have allowed, but he felt he needed to be in a mellow mood to begin this discussion with Tom. He took another sip of wine and got right to the point.

"I'm sick. I have the same issues that killed my father. I'm

43

supposed to watch what I eat and what I drink."

To emphasize he was not following drinking part of the doctor's orders, he took a long sip of wine and refilled his glass with the remainder of the wine in the bottle.

"I need new kidneys, my liver is shot, and I hate dialysis."

Thomas paused to take a deep breath before explaining.

"That's why the heirloom ceremony happened now, on your 18th birthday."

The admission confirmed Tom's earlier premonition that the ceremony was a prelude to bad news. A day that had started so wonderfully had turned into the worst day of his life. Now it was his turn to want to do something. He thought he should maybe take a sip of wine, but he couldn't move. He was transfixed and unable to do anything except sit and wait for his father to continue to speak.

Thomas paused only long enough to take a deep breath, drain the remainder of the wine in his glass, and take another deep breath before changing the tone of the conversation from his own issues to Tom's status in the family and relationship with his mother.

"Tom, you're now the man of the house. I want you to always take care of your mother and do what she tells you to the best of your ability. She knows what's best."

Tom was only able to shake his head in the affirmative as he fought back tears. Thomas noticed and made the right move to prevent an outburst.

"Why don't you go and see how your mother made out with your things," he asked. "I'm tired. I'll be up in a few minutes."

Just as he finished his statement, he reached out and held onto Tom's glass of wine.

Tom knew he shouldn't leave now. Through his sorrowful state, he could see his father urgently needed help, but he couldn't force himself to do what should have been done. Instead, he turned and left the room, deciding not to face things head-on.

Thomas, on the other hand, had an epiphany. He thought,

"Wouldn't it be best for me to bow out of Elizabeth's and Tom's life now? My Elizabeth knows the business and I've turned over the heirlooms to Tom. I'm done."

He then guzzled the remainder of the wine, and with one final thought of, "I'm tired of lingering on," he died.

2 The Encounter

The next few days seemed to pass like a blur. Elizabeth had immediately gotten busy stoically and steadily handling matters. She had Thomas privately laid to rest 3 days after his death. She made sure Tom was present as often as possible while she completed tasks, but he was of little help. He felt overwhelmed by things that were happening and carried a twinge of guilt from not being able to help his father that fateful night.

For Molly, it was business as usual as it should have been for Sue, except for the fact that Sue had the added pressure of feeling the need to solve the heirloom puzzle. She knew she needed information she could only get from Tom Purlmen – correction Mr. Purlmen, but she hadn't yet had an opportunity to talk to him alone.

Chances go 'round, and for Sue, it finally came the day after the funeral. Tom came to the kitchen to get a banana while Sue was there mopping the floor. Tom didn't want to step on the floor, so he asked Sue to get one for him.

"Sue, could you get me a banana, please? I might need a snack while I'm out with my mother," he said.

Tom had never previously spoken to Sue one-on-one. Normally, there was no need to. Molly and Sue did their work and otherwise kept to themselves. However, the question he posed while no one else was around created the opportunity for Sue to test Tom's resolve to maintain the class distinction Elizabeth's naming convention had previously set.

"Sure Mr....uh." Sue purposely hesitated to give Tom a chance to react. If he said nothing Sue would go ahead and add 'Purlmen', but she certainly hoped he would instead ask her to refer to him as 'Tom'.

He took the bait and in a hushed voice said, "Please call me Tom unless my mother is around."

Sue's reply was almost a whisper. "Okay, Tom." She suppressed the huge grin she felt like making and instead smiled sweetly as she retrieved a banana. "Here you are Tom," she said as she handed it off to him.

"Thank you, Sue," Tom replied. That short exchange was the best thing he'd experienced in the past few days. He would have continued the conversation except he feared his mother, or Molly for that matter, could soon be within earshot.

As Tom retreated to the den, Sue rejoiced in her triumph of getting rid of that Mr. Purlmen title. It was the first step to breaking down barriers to being able to manipulate him to give her the information she craved. She wasn't sure what the next step should be, but knowing she had only 3 more weeks to work it out kept the task on her mind.

Sue continued to clandestinely include Tom's name when speaking to him whenever she felt she could get away with it unseen and unheard, however giving him the greeting of the day was all she could do for more than a week. That limitation changed on the tenth day following Thomas' death when she finally had multiple opportunities to discover more about the heirlooms.

Molly had chosen that particular day for in-depth cleaning of the entire house because Tom and Elizabeth were scheduled to be gone until late in the afternoon. Molly's cleaning strategy was for one person to begin on the top floor and the other in the basement, dusting, sweeping, vacuuming, and mopping as necessary. At some point, they'd meet on the first floor to complete the task. Sue eagerly volunteered for the basement duty. She figured that this would be her first opportunity to explore the off-limits wine cellar uninhibited.

She quietly entered the wine cellar, closed the door, looked around, and then around again. She saw no safe, but, remembering that she'd also heard 'painting' being mentioned, she focused her attention on the only painting in the room. By lifting the bottom of the painting, she could see the dial of the safe. Her hands trembled slightly as she hurriedly straightened the painting and left the wine cellar. Now that she knew where the safe was, the next step was to get the combination.

Remembering the painting should somehow remind the Purlmen family of the safe's combination, Sue continued her cleaning duties while racking her brain to discover a strategy to get the information from Tom. The best thing she could come up with was to tell Tom that she needed to find a way to remember certain amounts in recipes without having to look them up. As luck would have it, that same day also provided the opportunity.

Tom and Elizabeth returned late that evening after having dinner at a restaurant. Neither had informed Molly or Sue that they would be eating out. Elizabeth's explanation was she'd thought she'd mentioned it, although she knew she hadn't. Unwilling to accept the responsibility and feeling slightly guilty because of it, she remarked that she was tired and immediately went off to bed.

Tom had a briefcase full of papers and announced he was also tired. "I'm going to bed myself after I file some of this paperwork," he said. He knew the truth and actually felt bad for Molly and Sue, but he knew he couldn't openly disagree with his mother.

Tom went into the den while Molly and Sue began the process of cleaning the kitchen. After about 10 minutes he returned to the kitchen and quietly apologized.

"I'm sorry about the mix-up. Mother forgot to tell you we'd be dining out."

Molly accepted the explanation immediately. "Oh, that's alright. I know how busy it's been for her. Don't you worry about it."

Sue said nothing. Instead, she picked up 2 of the 3 containers of food that would need to be stored in the downstairs refrigerator. As she hoped, the apologetic Tom offered to help.

"Let me help you," he said.

Molly didn't object and Sue wasn't about to.

"Thanks," Sue said. "That last container is kind of heavy."

Sue and Tom said nothing to one another until they'd gone downstairs and stored the containers. Sue broke the silence.

"Thanks, Tom," she said softly as she leaned against the refrigerator as a suggestion to Tom that he should mirror her nonverbal decision to linger downstairs.

Tom understood and made no move to leave. There was something about the relaxed way Sue was leaning that put Tom fully at ease.

Sue continued the conversation. "You know, it's hard for me to remember how much of each ingredient goes into some recipes we use a lot. I don't know how Mama does it."

"Some people just have good memories," Tom said. Sue's question made him feel important, so he added, "And some people use word association."

Hoping to get Tom to open up even more than he'd already done, Sue acted as if she didn't know what he was talking about.

"What's that?" she asked.

"That's when you take something you know and will probably never forget and use something about it to remember something else."

"Like how? I'm not sure how that would work."

Now Tom opened up way more than he should have. "It's like what my family does. A special thing that we will never forget is that my great-great-grandfather came to this country in 1839 when he was 4 years old. No one would ever be able to guess that, especially if you mix up the numbers."

As soon as he'd said it, he knew he shouldn't have, but scheming Sue strategically removed the potential of Tom having a guilt complex by personalizing her reply.

"I see. I'll think about some things that are important to my family. Thanks, Tom."

Sue pretended she was pondering her own family's special dates as she left the side of the refrigerator and started toward the stairs, but she was actually burning the information she'd heard into her memory.

"1839 when he was 4 – 1839 when he was 4," she kept silently repeating to herself.

She also felt Tom's statement 'if you mix up the numbers' was potentially important.

Sue knew she would never forget what had been divulged to her. She vowed to herself that she would try to open the safe that very night.

It was around midnight when Sue felt comfortable enough that Molly was in a deep sleep to slowly and silently get out of her bed and ease out of their bedroom. She left the door slightly ajar and made her way down the hall, beyond the refrigerator, and finally to the wine cellar door.

Although she'd previously only opened it once, she remembered the door didn't squeak. She opened it, stepped inside, and closed it just shy of all the way to avoid the sound of the door closing. Turning on the light was a potential problem, but Sue reasoned that no one would be wandering around and, since she'd made no noise, it was alright to chance it.

The light switch seemed louder and the illumination brighter than earlier that day, but that didn't slow Sue down. She attempted to lift the painting, but couldn't. Thinking quickly, she twisted it side to side and was able to pull it from the wall. There she saw the safe. After placing the painting on the floor, Sue went to work on her safecracking skills. Her first attempt was to spin to 18 right, 39 left, 4 right. Sue tried the handle, but the door did not open. Her second attempt was 39 right 18 left, 4 right. Sue again tried the handle and this time the door swung open to reveal the tiny safe. She picked it up and examined it. Seeing 3 dials, she at first thought to try the same combinations, but on closer examination found the dials only read from 1 to 6. Not wanting to linger in the wine cellar any longer than necessary, she decided to close the wall safe, replace the painting and take the tiny safe with her to examine it closer when she had more time.

As slowly and silently as she'd gone into the wine cellar, she slipped out of it, closed the door, and walked slowly down the hall. She opened the bedroom door and slipped back into her bed along with the little safe, which she stashed beneath her pillow. The initial phase of her quest to check out the heirlooms was now complete.

The following morning, she waited until Molly left the bedroom to decide on a better hiding place. She settled on a shoebox she kept her extra bedroom slippers in. The flat shoes that had come in the shoebox had long since been discarded and she'd kept the shoebox mainly because she liked the way it looked. It was of a pale lime color that reminded her of the limeade her mother sometimes made. Sue smiled at the memory, mainly because she knew her mother always added enough food coloring to distinguish the beverage from lemonade.

As it turned out, the shoebox was an excellent choice. The flexibility of the slippers allowed the safe to fit snugly and prevented any movement. With that, she rearranged shoeboxes in her closet to hide the lime shoebox behind and under other boxes of shoes so it could not be seen without moving other boxes.

Satisfied now with her progress so far, Sue turned her thoughts to what her next step should be. She reasoned that if given the right opportunity, she might be able to get enough information from Tom to find out if valuables were indeed inside the tiny safe. If the contents were truly worthwhile, she would keep them. If not, she'd merely return the tiny safe to the wall safe. The trouble was, she had no clue about how to go about making a move toward that next step.

An unexpected opportunity for Sue to interface closely with Tom began the following evening. Elizabeth and Tom had spent the entire day away from the home, and apparently whatever Tom had eaten earlier that day did not agree with him. He stayed in bed all the next day while Elizabeth anxiously took care of him. At least Elizabeth was the one to go in and out of his room with meals. Molly and Sue still did the cooking. By dinner time Tom felt fine, but he didn't let on. He told his mother he wanted something light for dinner and again ate in his room. When he awoke the next morning, he was hungry and refreshed. That had been the first time he'd been able to lay in bed all day since he'd come home and it felt so good that he wanted one more day of relaxation.

Tom was so engrossed in feeling comfortable that he almost missed the movement of his bedroom door as Elizabeth opened it to peek in. With his decision to avoid doing much of anything that day, he slowly shut his half-opened eyes and hoped his mother didn't notice he wasn't asleep. To his relief, she gave no indication she knew he was awake.

Elizabeth spoke in almost a whisper, "Tom, are you feeling better?"

Tom didn't answer or move, so Elizabeth spoke a little louder. "Tom, we need to get ready to go see the attorney."

Tom decided he should answer this time, so he disguised his voice to sound as if he'd just been awakened.

"What time is it?" he asked.

"It's 9 and we need to leave here by 10."

Tom had forgotten they'd made the appointment, but he made up his mind he didn't wish to go.

"That's too early," he said. "I couldn't be sure I'd feel up to it until sometime this afternoon. I think we should reschedule the meeting for next week."

Tom raised one hand to his forehead and massaged it by moving his hand back and forth for effect. The strategy worked as Elizabeth relented.

"I'll call and let Rodney know."

Elizabeth went straight to the kitchen where Molly was doing some light cleaning.

"Fix something for Tom right away so I can take it up to him," Elizabeth told Molly. She then left to make her call.

Molly was surprised at the request. She'd been under the impression the Purlmens would have breakfast at home before leaving and would not return until late. For that reason, Molly had Sue take their car to the garage for some repair work. Her plan was to have the Purlmens give her a lift to the library where Sue would meet her later. Now it seemed that she and Sue would have to be available at the home all day.

Meanwhile, Elizabeth tried to make her call but found that the attorney was not yet in. She returned to the kitchen, retrieved the breakfast for Tom, and took it up to him. She followed her normal routine of easing into Tom's room and called out to him, "Tom, here eat this breakfast now, and then you can go back to sleep."

Tom was famished and wasted no time in sitting up in bed to start to dig into the breakfast.

Elizabeth watched Tom as he began eating and then left to again try to call the attorney.

"I'll be back in a couple of minutes," she told him.

Elizabeth tried phoning the attorney again with no luck. After about 20 minutes she returned to Tom's room to find the tray on the floor and Tom rolled over as if already asleep. He looked so peaceful that Elizabeth said nothing. Instead, she walked over to the tray and lifted it as silently as she could before leaving the room and gently closing the door behind her. She returned the tray to the kitchen before going into the den to again attempt to contact the attorney. This time she was successful.

"Rodney Stoner's office, attorney at law. This is Kim. How may I help you?" The female voice was loud, distinct, and clear through the receiver at Elizabeth's ear.

"This is Mrs. Purlmen. I need to change my appointment with Rodney."

"Yes, Mrs. Purlmen. Change it to when?"

"Next week."

"He'll not be available at all next week."

"Is he in?"

"Yes."

"Let me speak to him."

"Sure, hold on please."

The next voice Elizabeth heard was that of the attorney. "Hello Elizabeth, how are you today?"

"I'm fine Rodney, but Tom isn't. We won't be able to meet with you today."

"Elizabeth, it's important that we get things settled as soon as possible. There are some items that can wait for a while, but other things should be handled right away. I delayed leaving for vacation until today instead of yesterday for the sole purpose of meeting with you. I'll be gone for 10 days. Are you sure you can't make it today?"

"I can, but Tom is not able."

"Tom doesn't need to be here. I only need you."

"I wanted Tom to become more involved in family business matters."

"There's plenty of time for that, but certain legal matters come first. If you can come in today, I'll have you out of here in about 20 minutes. We can all get together after I return to get Tom more involved."

"Well, if it's that important..."

"It is. Can you be here in an hour?"

"Yes."

"Thanks, Elizabeth. I'll be expecting you then around 11:30."

"I'll be there Rodney. Goodbye."

"Goodbye Elizabeth."

Elizabeth went about the business of hurriedly readying herself by having breakfast, showering, and changing into a comfortable outfit. Then she began to plan her day for what she needed to do after the meeting. Fully mindful of the fact that she'd fouled up 2 days ago when she forgot to tell Molly they would not be home for dinner, Elizabeth wanted to make sure she got things right today. She'd already told Molly they'd be out until late, so by continuing to give Molly and Sue the rest of the day off, she would be making up for the other day. She'd get some deli sandwiches for lunch and worry about dinner arrangements later. She found Molly and discussed her plans.

"I'll give you a lift to the library now. Mr. Purlmen will be here all day, but you don't have to worry about lunch or dinner. You keep your plans. I'll be back here in time to see about Mr. Purlmen. We'll probably go have dinner at a restaurant."

Molly was relieved. Today had been the first day in weeks that she and Sue planned to go to the library as early as possible and not return until closing time. There were no chores to do at home, so they could spend hours away from the monotony of caring for the home. The library was her favorite escape and Sue also enjoyed going there.

Molly happily responded, "I'm ready now Mrs. Purlmen if you are."

"Alright, let's go so I can get back here before Tom wakes up."

Elizabeth and Molly left and had been gone for about 90 minutes when Sue reached the cross street where she needed to decide whether to continue to the library as planned or to check to make sure Molly had already left. Since the mechanic had greatly over-estimated the expected duration of the repair, Sue decided to first check at home to see if Molly was still there.

Once home, the first thing Sue noticed was that Elizabeth's car was gone. That meant if all things had gone as planned, no one would be home. This would mark the very first time she'd ever had the house all to herself. She figured she might be able to do some searching and discover the secret to the combination of the little safe without having to glean the information from Tom.

With larceny on her mind and greed in her heart, Sue entered the house and stopped at her and Molly's quarters. It was vacant. Then she looked and listened for signs of anyone else in the basement or first floor. As she hoped, there were no signs of anyone being there. She climbed the stairs and went straight to Tom's bedroom door. She listened for a moment as she heard a radio playing. For that to happen with no one home was extremely unusual. Could it be that Tom was home? Maybe he didn't have to spend the day with his mother.

Sue was so intent on the potential of confronting Tom or discovering information, she used no alibi or excuse to continue her quest. She calmly and boldly opened his bedroom door and peered in. There she saw Tom lying on his side, eyes fully opened.

Tom had been expecting his mother to come back to the room to give him an update as to how the attorney visit would be handled but was pleasantly surprised to see Sue. He spoke first.

"Hi, Sue."

"Hi Tom," Sue replied as she began walking towards Tom. "Are you feeling better?"

"I feel fine. I'm just relaxing. Where's everybody?"

"They're all supposed to be gone all day," Sue replied.

"No, my mother was supposed to go to a meeting, but that got changed."

"No..." Sue cooed. "If she didn't go to the meeting, my mother would still be here. They're both gone. We're here alone."

Tom thought a moment and decided Sue was correct. "I guess you're right. She must have gone to her meeting without me. She won't be back for hours. We were supposed to be gone until late this evening."

Sue figured it was now or never to make her move. She had continued slowly moving closer to Tom's bed and was now close enough to lean forward and nudge the mattress with her upper thigh. She asked, "Do you mind if I sit here so we can talk?"

Any inhibitions Tom had toward Sue dissipated at that instant and the only obstacle to Tom becoming outwardly amorous toward her was his lack of knowledge as to how to begin. Sue sensed this and knew she was in control but was unsure about how to go about getting what she wanted without giving Tom all *he* wanted. Making a snap decision, she chose to get him in a compromising position and see if he would become more openly talkative about family secrets. Sitting on the bed, she leaned so the side of the small of her back rested against his left side. She relaxed her torso and enveloped him with her right arm. She then rested her right elbow on the bed beside him.

Leaning close to his face, she smiled and whispered, "Your bed feels really nice."

This caused Tom to blurt out, "You want to try it?"

Sue hadn't expected this quick invitation, so she hesitated before making her next move.

"Maybe. I thought we would just talk."

It was now Tom's turn to hesitate. "Okay, we can just talk."

Sue felt back in control now, so she resumed her objective. She lied saying, "I tried using that strategy you told me about with the recipes."

Tom's amorous mood had hit an obstacle, but it wasn't to be denied. His desire to make love to Sue was a yearning he meant to fulfill that day. "Don't I get a reward?" he replied.

Sue knew it was a make or break question where she needed to forge ahead or abandon the cause. "Sure," she said leaning forward to plant a kiss on his lips.

The magnetism was mutual as she suddenly enjoyed the act, although her enjoyment was enhanced by her ulterior motive. Tom enjoyed it because the encounter was his first chance to have sex. At that instant, Sue made up her mind to give Tom one final chance to back out of the situation. Simultaneously, she wanted to make sure he knew he could take the opportunity if he so desired.

"Actually, I wouldn't mind trying out your bed right now," she said.

For Tom, things couldn't happen fast enough. He wasn't sure about what to say or do next, so he just went with the flow. In an excited voice, he simply said, "Come on!"

Without missing a beat, Sue stood and walked around to the other side of the bed. There was a lounge chair next to the bed and as she began disrobing, she deliberately placed each item of clothing on the chair. She hesitated when she got to her bra and panties and glanced at Tom. He was still on his side, obviously still in his pajamas, facing away from her. With avarice for riches and her own desires edging her on, she removed her undergarments and eased into the bed with Tom.

Sue felt that if she couldn't get the combination this time from Tom, sex could be the catalyst to cause him to give it and maybe more to her at some point. After all, she'd found that Wayne and Frank both seemed to have one-track minds about wanting to be alone with her in order to steer her into bed. Neither got many opportunities, but they both had the same rule of always using protection, which she was in favor of. Sue also was in favor of them loosening their otherwise tight hold on some of whatever money they had whenever she asked about 'spare change' for things she wanted.

Tom had never before been with a nude woman, but his manhood needed relief from the confines of his pajama pants. He pulled at his pajama's waistband. All snaps parted and he was ready for action. He nearly cried out in delight when Sue reached over and turned him around. She continued to pull him until he finally got the idea and slid on top of her. Sue reached down and guided him inside. They made love awkwardly, but passionately. It was quick and Tom found himself out of energy and breathing deeply. He now just wanted to lay back and relax, but his first-time-with-a-woman shyness triggered the strength he needed to refasten his pajamas.

Sue, on the other hand, maintained her composure and immediately eased out of the bed to begin dressing. She first put on her panties, pantyhose, skirt, and shoes. Then, to preserve some of the togetherness of the moment, Sue slipped on her bra but left it unhooked in the back.

"Here, come fasten this for me," she instructed Tom.

Obediently, Tom sat up and eased over to where Sue was standing. Once there, he found it rather difficult to align the individual hooks and eyes. He then sat up all the way so his legs dangled off the side of the bed. He wanted to give the task his full head-on attention.

"Weird invention," he muttered, fumbling with the hooks.

Sue let Tom continue to fumble and did not hurry him along or try to assist him. She wanted to let him savor the moment without any pressure. The only thing she had any concern with was the fact that they hadn't used any protection. That was a first for her, but she'd heard rumors that a thorough internal cleansing immediately after sex would likely prevent pregnancy. She made herself a mental note, not realizing the rumored contraceptive method was virtually useless.

Meanwhile, after dropping Molly off, meeting with the attorney, and picking up turkey sandwiches from the deli, Elizabeth returned home and was surprised to see Molly's car in the driveway. Her curiosity was aroused. She felt she should do everything possible to use this opportunity to ascertain whether her housekeepers were totally honest or not. She'd been told they would be away until the evening, so for them to return this early was unacceptable. After all, they would be leaving in only 2 more weeks.

Elizabeth stealthily entered the house and first checked the basement and downstairs areas. No one was about. She now grew suspicious of multiple facts. Sue was supposed to be at the repair shop or the library, but she was in the home. That would not have been a huge problem had she been in the basement or the first floor, but she was in neither. Molly was not at home. Tom was supposed to be resting in bed. Her own original schedule had been for her to be away from the house until late. The convergence of time and opportunity for hanky-panky was obvious. With all that in mind, Elizabeth very quietly climbed the stairs and went directly to Tom's door and listened. She believed she heard Sue's voice saying something like, "Here, fasten this for me," but she wanted to be sure.

As anger within Elizabeth began to boil, she could scarcely keep from flinging the door wide open. Somehow, she kept her composure as she wanted to catch them in the act. She pushed the door open just wide enough to see Tom mumbling something while fumbling with Sue's bra hooks. In that same instant, she was relieved to see Tom wearing his pajamas and Sue fully dressed, except for a semi-hooked bra and no blouse. Elizabeth immediately let what she saw and her overwhelming wish for Tom to maintain his innocence to influence her mind. She believed that she'd gotten home just in time to interrupt what looked to be the prelude to sex. However, lost in the shuffle of Elizabeth's emotions was that 'fasten' and not 'unfasten' had been said, which meant playtime was likely over, not just beginning. Nevertheless, every bit of Elizabeth's raw instinct to protect her son from the woman in his bedroom now burst into play.

"Just what do you think you're doing? Get out of my son's room! Get out of my house! You and your mother are fired! I want you out of my house now!" Elizabeth screamed as she pushed the door wide open.

Sue immediately grabbed her blouse and put it on without fully fastening her bra. Elizabeth moved away from the door to allow enough passage for Sue to leave without feeling threatened by a physical confrontation. As Sue hurriedly left the room and ran down the stairs, Elizabeth followed well behind while shouting insults and instructions.

"I knew I shouldn't have trusted you! What kind of people are you? I never should have hired you! I don't want you back in my house! Get out of here and don't ever come back!"

Sue put her blouse on while running toward the front door. Fortunately, the lone hook Tom had finally gotten fastened held the bra in place. She left the house straight through the front door instead of through the basement. Now she found herself outside with no purse and no keys for the house or the car. Not that she'd have re-entered the house – not after seeing the fire in Elizabeth's eyes. The immediate problem was that she didn't have access to the car. She'd have to walk the few miles to the library and deal with having to explain the situation to Molly. As she walked, she began to formulate an explanation that Molly would find acceptable. At least she hoped she could conjure up a passible sham of a tale.

Reaching the library, Sue found Molly in her usual place, which was a table behind encyclopedic reference books where very few people ever gathered. She was relieved to see no one else was around as she gave Molly her version of the incident's sordid details.

"That Purlmen boy tried to take advantage of me," she blurted out in a hushed and excited tone.

"What happened?" Molly was immediately wide-eyed and fully attentive.

"He said he spilled something on his floor and that I should get it up right away. Then he tried to undress me when I went into his bedroom."

"What did you do?"

"Mrs. Purlmen came home and caught him. She blamed me and threw me out of the house. She fired us both. I ran out of there with no keys. I had to walk here."

"Well, I've got my keys. We'll go right back there and get our things. I'm glad we're almost packed and ready to leave. We should call the police and have him arrested."

"No Mama, he only tried to undress me," Sue said innocently before compounding the lie by adding, "Nothing else happened."

Sue had no desire to get the police involved. To tell the truth, she wanted no more discussion of the incident. Her goal was for her and Molly to get their things and get out of town as quickly as possible.

Molly thought about it for a moment and agreed. "I'll go to the phone booth and reserve a room at one of the hotels. Then we'll take a taxi to the Purlmens' and get our things out of their house. Everything we own should fit into the car. I'm sure the taxi driver will help us load things."

Molly appeared even-tempered, but she was inwardly seething at the thought of young Mr. Purlmen molesting Sue. Not only from what he'd attempted to do but also for the audacity of his mother to treat her son as some innocent little boy who never did a bad thing in his life.

"Young men like that can't ever be trusted," Molly muttered to herself but loud enough for Sue to hear. "If they go unpunished when they're young, they get bolder and meaner as they get older."

Sue did not respond. Instead, she did her best to appear sad but unhurt. She didn't want Molly to entertain any more thoughts of trying to do anything more than retrieving their belongings and putting unpleasant memories behind them.

Molly became business-like as she completed calls to reserve a hotel room and request a taxi. As they waited for the taxi to arrive, Sue did her best to get Molly thinking in future terms. "Do you think that maybe we can go to Aunt Bernice's tomorrow? I hope so," she asked.

Molly hadn't planned to barge in on Aunt Bernice 2 weeks earlier than expected and had no idea if her aunt was home or not, but the idea was intriguing. She decided to find out.

"I'll call her now and tell her we can be there tomorrow. Broad Creek is only a couple of hours away, so if we leave by around 10 in the morning, we can be there by early afternoon."

Molly had the desk clerk change 3 dollars for coins and left to make the long-distance call. A couple of minutes later, Molly came back with the answer.

"Aunt Bernice is expecting us tomorrow. She's thrilled we'll be there earlier than we planned and I am too. She said she had been under the weather lately and that she wanted to get in touch with us about a month ago to see if we could come sooner than expected."

Sue smiled at the news. "That's good, Mama. I wish we could just go tonight."

"No, Child," Molly answered. "We still have to get the car and our things. By the time we're done with all that it will be pretty late. We'll get a good night's sleep and leave tomorrow morning."

"Yes, Mama."

Sue had momentarily put their belongings out of her mind, so being reminded of them now was disheartening. She thought to herself, "I hope we can get away from that house with no more trouble..."

* * *

Earlier, Elizabeth had followed Sue after she'd left Tom's room, though not too closely, to make sure Sue left the house. She was glad that Sue had left in the most expeditious way, which was through the front door. This meant Sue knew she had been ousted like a stranger who had absolutely no intimate knowledge about the house or any legitimate business within the house. Beyond that, since Sue had not said or done anything to the contrary, Elizabeth believed Sue was totally in the wrong and Tom was completely innocent of any wrongdoing. She returned to Tom's room to discuss the situation.

"You can't trust people like that," she began.

Tom was quick to answer. "She was trying to get money from me," he lied.

"That's the worst kind of woman to get involved with. Was this the first time she tried?"

"Yes. I didn't expect anything like that to ever happen."

"It was probably the first time she had a chance." Elizabeth then surreptitiously doubled down on her assumption that she had arrived home before things had gone further than she feared.

"I'm glad I got home before anything happened, Tom. Don't you know you could have gotten into a lot of trouble if she had gotten into bed with you?"

Tom didn't perceive "trouble" within the pleasurable experience he'd enjoyed with Sue, but his mother's reaction had created an overwhelming sense of guilt. That guilt was so strong that it buried all of his good feelings toward sex. His mother's disapproval of the incident shook him to the core and soured the memory of the affection he and Sue had shared. Lovemaking had quickly gone from magnificent to grotesque.

Although each was unaware at the time, this mother-son post-incident review had planted the seeds of impotence within Tom's mind. Accordingly, he made a solemn vow to himself that he would never again succumb so easily to romance. With that mindset, he now gave his mother an answer that he meant to apply not only to the current situation but also to potential sexual encounters in the future.

"Yes mother, I understand. Something like that will never happen again."

"Good. Now get dressed so we can get their things out of this house. I don't ever want either of them back in here."

Elizabeth left and went to the basement room Molly and Sue shared. Once there, she immediately began to get rid of everything they owned as completely and quickly as possible by bundling hanging garments in the sheets and pillowcases off the twin beds. Thankfully for Elizabeth, there weren't many things to bundle as there were 6 medium-sized boxes apparently packed and ready to go. Relatively few things remained in the dresser drawers, so it was easy to add those things to the bundles with the hanging garments.

Now it was time to deal with things that couldn't easily be bundled. There were a few things on top of one dresser while the other was cluttered with various items. There were also many boxes of shoes. Elizabeth's solution was to retrieve 3 rather large boxes. She filled 2 with boxes of shoes and planned to use the last for items on top of the dressers.

By now Tom had arrived to help remove things from the room.

"Where should we leave this stuff?" he asked

"Out in the back on the ground. Don't put any of this junk on the front porch."

Tom took a few of the pre-packed boxes outside and was surprised to see Molly's car parked in its usual spot outside the basement door.

"Their car's still here," he reported when he returned.

"That hussy probably left her keys somewhere. Go find those keys, Tom. We'll pile everything next to their car. I don't want them back in this house," she repeated before adding, "When you find the keys, open the car and let down the driver's window. Don't forget to take any of our house keys off the keyring. Leave the keys on the driver's seat. I don't even want them to have a reason to ring the bell."

After searching for and locating Sue's purse and keys, Tom continued to shuttle boxes outside.

Meanwhile, Elizabeth began to pack things from the top of the dressers. Along with other items were pictures. Without paying full attention, Elizabeth dropped the last photo she handled onto the wooden ornament at the foot of one of the beds. The glass shattered. Elizabeth picked up the picture and saw that it was ruined. The glass shards had cut it in such a way as to make it useless as a worthy keepsake. Examining it closer, Elizabeth did not recognize anyone in the photo. She reasoned that the picture must be of some importance to Molly, but inwardly felt some justification and happiness at having this small tragedy happen as a result of what she considered to be Sue's action.

However, those pleasant feelings quickly faded as Elizabeth had a sudden bout with her conscience. Even though she was still loaded with a tremendous feeling of anger, she respected property ownership. She realized the old picture must have belonged to Molly, and Molly was not the culprit. Elizabeth's wrath was toward Sue. Molly was guilty only by association. The thought of the picture having belonged to Molly caused a twinge of remorse to creep into Elizabeth's mind. Now she wanted to dispose of the broken photo as if it was evidence of a crime.

To avoid having Tom involved in a cover-up of the photo's destruction, Elizabeth hurriedly cleared all traces of the incident. Rather than depositing the glass and photo in the trash, she dropped them into one of the pillowcases. She heard Tom returning, so she hid the pillowcase beside the bed so he wouldn't see it.

Needing time to dispose of the broken photo, she asked, "Did you arrange those boxes so you could put the sheets full of clothing on the boxes? Don't just leave them strewn around haphazardly on the ground."

Tom hadn't, so he sheepishly replied, "No," and turned to take care of the task.

Elizabeth interrupted his movement. "Take the last bundle of clothes to the door, arrange the boxes, and then put it on top of the boxes. Why make two trips when one will suffice?" she reasoned.

Tom left, allowing Elizabeth to retrieve the pillowcase with the ruined photo and find a better hiding place. She didn't want to go too far or take too long, so she chose a place they rarely visited, which was the utility room. She opened the door, found the light, and was able to locate a clear space behind what she figured was the heater. She then hurriedly went back to Molly and Sue's room and found Tom had not yet returned. Of the several items left to be removed, Elizabeth was able to carry all except two toward the basement door where she met Tom.

"Here, take these and come back and get the last two," she said.

Still inwardly seething at the thought of Sue trying to seduce her son, in her most evil tone she continued, "I'm going to call a junk dealer and have them take everything else in that room out of this house. We can decide what to use the room for later. I want every trace of every memory of them out of here."

Tom said nothing. He knew from his mother's tone she meant what she said and he didn't want to take the chance of saying anything that might cause her to blame him for what had occurred. He vowed to himself that he would forever listen to and abide by her rules to the best of his ability. With that in mind, once he placed the last of the items outside, he immediately went to his mother with a suggestion.

He boldly said, "Mother, I think we should go out to dinner tonight so we can discuss what you did with the lawyer today."

Though still peeved with all that had transpired, Elizabeth felt Tom was acting more mature, so she agreed.

"Yes, let's get away from here. I don't want to be here when they get their belongings."

Pausing to think again about the ordeal, Elizabeth had more to say.

"If they don't get everything away from here tonight, I'll have someone haul the rest of the junk away tomorrow."

Tom felt his mother's anger had been reignited, so he quickly moved to mitigate the damage.

"I'm sure they understand they need to get their things tonight. We can go to dinner and go see a movie. It'll take our minds off today."

Tom's suggestions had the calming effect he'd hoped for. They left for dinner and the planned movie with Tom fervently hoping Molly's car and all the things strewn about would be gone when they returned.

As it turned out, there was no confrontation. By the time Molly and Sue arrived at the house by taxi, the Purlmens had already left for the restaurant. Molly had the taxi driver take them to the back door and was astonished to see their things piled around their car. They'd been unceremoniously tossed out like so much trash. Seeing sheets and pillowcases they'd slept on being used as clothing bags and tarpaulins added insult to injury. Not wanting to give the taxi driver any additional information than what he immediately saw, Molly paid him and sent him on his way.

"The nerve of that woman throwing our things out here like we're nobodies," Molly muttered.

As Molly walked to the car, she saw that the driver's window was down. Sue's keys and handbag were on the front seat. That was a relief because she didn't want to ever reenter the house. Then Molly noticed the house keys were off of Sue's keyring. She wasn't surprised and almost expected it, but she still felt annoyed. Those missing keys reaffirmed the fact that they'd been expelled.

Defiantly, Molly took the house keys from her own keyring, opened the back door, and tossed the keys to the floor. The act was not like her, but her ire at what Sue told her about the incident, coupled with the decision to not report the crime, made Molly want to do *something* to the Purlmens. Then, as she closed the door, she realized the deadbolt could not be set, but that inability made her feel just a little bit better. Who cared if the house was not as secure as possible? Also, if the Purlmens felt they were justified in tossing clothing into bedding and then putting everything on top of boxes that sat on the ground, she could leave their precious keys on the floor. This way they would have to bend down and pick them up.

Sue had been watching her mother without speaking until Molly closed the door, whereupon she asked, "Mama, did you unlock the car doors? We need to load everything and get out of here."

Sue wanted no part of any conversation regarding how or why they were leaving. She just wanted to get away from that place.

Molly unlocked all the doors and the trunk as Sue began to deliberately place items in the car. She was trying to see if she could locate the lime shoebox containing the little safe. It was nowhere in sight. The only thing that gave her hope was seeing 3 rather large boxes she didn't recognize. Hopefully, the lime shoebox was in one of them. She kept the thought in mind as they completed the loading and drove off to get dinner before going to the hotel where they planned to spend the night.

There was one important thing left to do that should have screamed for Sue's attention, but her preoccupation with the whereabouts of the safe, along with the abundance of drama they'd experienced that day, pushed it to the far reaches of her mind. That thing was the unreliable rumor about giving oneself a thorough internal cleansing following a sexual escapade.

Elizabeth and Tom returned from the dinner and movie hours after Molly and Sue had left. They were both pleased at not seeing the car or any of the other items they'd left outside. The only thing that negatively affected Elizabeth's mood was when she saw that the house keys had been thrown on the floor. Tom saw the daggers in her eyes and quickly retrieved the keys. He knew the best thing to do was to say or do something to ease the tension. He came up with a workable solution.

"I'll get in touch with a salvage or donation company first thing in the morning to clean out that room," he offered.

The thought appeased Elizabeth. "Good idea. As I said, we need to decide what to do with it once every trace of them is gone."

Then, after a moment's pause, she added, "And I hope I don't ever have that girl's name in my mind, coming out of my mouth, or coming out of someone else's mouth again for as long as I live."

Elizabeth's last statement closed the book on what happened that day and marked the beginning of a mother and son business relationship that would run like a well-oiled machine. That is, for many years until the awkward mixture of too much business and not enough pleasure combined to lead to an eventual demise.

3 Topsy-Turvy

A calm had increasingly come over Molly as the miles remaining to Aunt Bernice's dwindled to fewer than one. Sue had fallen asleep, but Molly now implored her to wake up.

"We're just about to Aunt Bernice's now, Child. Time to wake up."

Sue woke up from her nap still anxious about the circumstances that got them there weeks sooner than planned. She was glad the ugliness of their departure from the Purlmens' house was physically behind them, but the mental anxiety lingered on. She hoped being with Aunt Bernice would quickly erase every thought of the previous day from her mind. To her relief, her mother's next statement indicated she felt the same way.

"Don't you say a word to Aunt Bernice about why we came early. I don't want to upset her. As a matter of fact, we don't need to discuss it anymore. The subject doesn't ever need to come up again."

That was music to Sue's ear. "Yes Mama," she replied.

There was a car parked in front of Aunt Bernice's house, but Molly knew her aunt hadn't owned one for at least 10 years.

"I wonder who's visiting Aunt Bernice?" Molly pondered aloud.

Ordinarily, Sue would have jokingly said something about Aunt Bernice having a male suitor, but her own circumstance thwarted that idea.

Molly saw right through Sue's hesitation, so she made the kind of inference Sue normally would have.

"Maybe she's got a boyfriend." Molly's attempt at humor lacked the punch that Sue's would have delivered, but the point was well taken. This was Molly's way of telling Sue to be herself.

The women gathered only the belongings they needed for overnight and proceeded to the front door. They heard brisk footsteps shortly after ringing the doorbell. Surely that wasn't Aunt Bernice.

The door swung open to reveal a woman about 40 who greeted them with, "Hi, I'm Carla, Miss Bernice's caregiver."

"Hello. I'm Molly and this is Sue. We're Aunt Bernice's nieces."

"I know. She told me you'd be here today. I was supposed to work with her until the end of the month. I found out only yesterday that today would be my last day with her. She's in her bedroom."

Molly and Sue left their belongings near the front door and walked to Aunt Bernice's room.

Carla followed and said, "I just want to tell her goodbye. She knows I planned to leave as soon as you got here."

Aunt Bernice was in bed reading when the women came into her room. She laid the book down and motioned for Molly and Sue to come to her. They exchanged hugs and Aunt Bernice excitedly exclaimed, "I'm so glad you came early. I didn't want to tell you over the phone that the doctor said I need someone with me 24 hours a day. I was afraid I was going to have to go to a nursing home."

"That won't happen," Molly assured her. "At least one of us will be with you at all times."

Carla bade each of them goodbye. "You take care, Miss Bernice. Molly and Sue, I'm glad to have met you," she said while handing a folder to Molly. "You'll find information about diet and medication here. Miss Bernice has my number if you ever need me. Goodbye."

After Carla left, Aunt Bernice's room became filled with catch-up conversation as the women continued talking almost nonstop for hours. Molly and Sue assured Aunt Bernice that they would provide her with all the care she needed and only find jobs if they could work on shifts where one of them could be at home when the other wasn't. In reality, they didn't need to take jobs. Aunt Bernice was financially well off enough to easily maintain the home, but neither Molly nor Sue wished to simply live off of their aunt.

It was Molly who finally looked at the clock and decided they should think about having dinner. Molly took on the chore. She fixed dinner within the dietetic standards outlined in the instructions she got from Carla. After dinner, they had what seemed like an endless stream of additional things to discuss. Again, Molly was the one who became cognizant of the time.

"It's after 9:30. Aunt Bernice, you know you should be asleep by now. We've had a long day so we need to get some rest too."

Aunt Bernice smiled, "Don't you worry about me. I sleep whenever I feel like it." Referring to the guest rooms she added, "The front bedroom is the biggest, but the other one has the bathroom."

Sue quickly made the decision. "I'll take the biggest one so Mama can have the one with the bathroom."

Molly and Sue spent a peaceful night and awoke the next morning ready to face the challenge of tending to Aunt Bernice's dietary and medicinal needs. Thankfully, Carla had the home well stocked with all things necessary. Shortly after breakfast, Molly suggested to Sue that the car should be unloaded.

Though she hadn't mentioned it, Sue had been waiting anxiously for this moment. She'd wanted to suggest the unload, but feared Molly would recognize it as an out of character statement and grow suspicious. Instead, with the best matter-of-fact voice she could muster, she simply replied, "Okay."

They unloaded the car and placed everything onto the living room floor and then began to sort items. Finally, there were only 3 boxes left. Those were the larger boxes that neither Molly nor Sue had packed. Molly was the first to open one.

"This box of shoes must be yours because I know I don't have a shoebox that looks like this one."

Sue forced herself to remain calm as she immediately recognized the lime shoebox that contained the safe. "I'll take that box of shoes up to my room," she said. Then she asked, "What's in the other boxes?"

Molly checked the next one. "Things from the dressers are here." She opened the last box. "These are my shoes."

Sue volunteered to help Molly. "Let's take yours up first and then I'll come back and get mine."

"Alright," Molly answered, somewhat surprised that Sue had made the offer. It wasn't that Sue was lazy, but she'd always been the type of person who worked as if she was adamantly opposed to doing an ounce more work than the next person.

Sue didn't recognize that her positive attitude switch would arouse her mother's curiosity, but since Molly said nothing, the point of conjecture passed by unexplored.

When Sue took her box of shoes to her room, the first thing she did was open the lime shoebox to make sure the safe was still there. It was. Seeing it again lifted her spirits. Had someone else mentioned it to her she would have been in denial, but she was becoming obsessed with the safe and the idea it contained riches. She pondered for a moment about possibly going to a locksmith but quickly abandoned the idea. No, she'd simply hold onto it for now and in time she would deal with it. She was still deep in her thoughts when Molly came into her room.

Molly asked excitedly, "Is the picture of Mama and Daddy's

wedding in that box? I want to show it to Aunt Bernice."

"No Mama. Only my shoes are here."

"Did you see it among anything else?" It was a rhetorical question. She'd seen everything Sue had seen except for the box of shoes Sue had taken. "Do you think we could have left it on the ground or in the car?"

"No Mama. I know we got everything."

Molly was hurt and angry. She then showed a side of her personality Sue had never before seen. Instead of the angry calm she'd displayed when Sue told her of the seduction attempt, she displayed her wrath.

"That means that woman must have done something with it. I'm going to call her right now and let her know she can keep our last week's pay, but I want my picture."

Sue said nothing as Molly stormed out of her room to make the call. She just wanted to be free of the Purlmen conflict.

As Molly went downstairs to the phone, she began to think of some hostile things she might say regarding how she and Sue were thrown out of the house, especially if the photo was never returned. Her anger was fueled not only by how they'd been evicted but also by the reason they'd been evicted in the first place. It still rankled her to think that a woman who was attacked could easily be in a situation where the best course of action seemed to be to allow the culprit to go uncharged and therefore unpunished.

It wasn't until she reached the phone that Molly realized she had no idea what the Purlmens' phone number was. She had never bothered to commit it to memory, and she didn't wish to ask Sue if she knew it. Since Aunt Bernice only had a local phone book, Molly dialed 411 for the long-distance number. Having to do so calmed her down. She dialed and the operator answered.

"Directory assistance, may I help you?" The voice through the receiver was soft and friendly.

Molly then asked for the number. "Hi, I need the telephone

number for the Purlmen residence in Glenville, Maryland."

"I'm sorry, ma'am. You need a long-distance operator for that location. That number is area code 301-555-1212. I'll connect it for you."

"Thank you," Molly answered.

While waiting for the long-distance operator, Molly could feel the anger and tension she'd felt only minutes ago begin to subside.

"It's probably best to be civil and not start an argument," she thought to herself.

Before she could formulate in her mind what to say, another operator spoke.

"Long-distance," stated an operator in an extremely pleasant tone.

"Operator, I need the telephone number for the Purlmen residence in Glenville, Maryland."

"Thank you." There was a short pause. "That number is 301..."

Molly interrupted her. "Oh operator, I don't have anything to write the number down. Could you connect it for me?"

"Certainly," came the reply.

"Thank you."

"You're welcome."

Molly then heard the sound of the ring current being sent to the Purlmens' phone. She took a deep breath and almost hoped no one would answer. Her dialogues with the operators had caused her anger to dissipate to the point where she simply wanted her photo and nothing else.

"Hello?" It was Mrs. Purlmen

Molly took another deep breath before answering. "This is Molly. One of my pictures is missing." She purposely didn't say anything negative about the termination or how their belongings were left outside.

Elizabeth had hoped she'd never have to speak to Molly again, but she knew she would have absolutely refused to speak to Sue. As it was, it was only because she knew the true disposition of the picture that she decided not to hang up on Molly. She'd speak to her, just this once, to spin a tale that Molly should accept as a final act to eliminate the need for any future contact.

"I'm sorry Molly, but all your belongings were put outside. Anything that remained in that room was cleaned out by a disposal company this morning. And to be quite frank with you, the room is being painted later today."

Elizabeth had spoken in her most authoritative voice, hoping the promptness of the room makeover she described would be a total turnoff to Molly. She let the information sink in and waited to see if Molly had anything else to say or if she would simply accept the explanation and hang up.

Molly sensed that it would be hopeless to attempt to get additional information, but since she wasn't satisfied, she tried anyway.

Molly asked, "Did we leave anything outside?"

Elizabeth was now sure she had the upper hand, so she made her move to end the discussion once and for all.

"Look, I told you that all your belongings were outside. A disposal company came and took everything else out of that room. I mean everything. The bed, the dressers, the carpeting – everything. Nothing of yours is here."

To pile additional emphasis on ending the conversation and the relationship, she added, "There is no reason for you to ever call here again."

Molly's quest for retrieving her lost picture now became a secondary issue as she understood that Elizabeth's statements were aimed to figuratively treat Molly and Sue's existence in the Purlmen home as garbage to be thrown out. Whereas she'd initially toyed with the idea of having the pay they were owed forfeited as a kind of inducement to get the picture back, the treatment she was receiving caused her to simply want to end the discussion.

There was another pause as Elizabeth waited for Molly to reply and Molly pondered whether to simply hang up or to say 'Thank you' before hanging up.

Elizabeth interpreted the pause as a great opportunity to get in one last dig.

"If your daughter had not done what she did then none of this would have happened," she firmly hissed.

That loosened Molly's tongue.

"What you heard and what I heard about what happened are apparently two different things. In my experience, when two stories are at far ends of the spectrum, the truth usually winds up being somewhere in the middle."

After saying that, Molly decided it was time to end the conversation.

"Goodbye," she said, but did not hang up the phone. She waited for Elizabeth to respond.

In Elizabeth's mind, Molly's last statement was misplaced and out of kilter. She normally would have wanted to pursue the implication, but decided not to. She was just glad Molly and Sue no longer had any reason to contact her. Instead of prolonging the conversation, she took the initiative and simply hung up without saying a word.

While she said nothing, Elizabeth had one final act to perform before removing any trace of the Hurleys from her home. She went into the utility room and retrieved the pillowcase with the ruined picture. Without opening the pillowcase, she simply bundled it and placed it into a small plastic bag. She tied that bag and then tossed it into a trash can for disposal like the garbage she felt it was. To her, that last act seemed appropriate, fitting, and proper. She felt that, as of this day, the Hurleys were truly gone from her life.

Meanwhile, Molly suppressed her disappointment by promising herself that one day she might try to get in touch with her stepmother, stepsister, or possibly some other relative within her father's other family to have a new copy of the wedding photo made. Her biggest issue was that she didn't have much knowledge as to how to go about contacting one of those relatives.

Molly knew her father had died over 30 years ago, which was a few years before Sue was born. As she understood it, her father's wife had not informed anyone from the Hurley family about his death, not even Aunt Bernice, who, other than Molly and Sue, was his only surviving relative.

Molly could only hope that the picture was kept somewhere and enough time had passed to soften old hardline attitudes her father's new family had established. That hope helped to mitigate the distasteful feeling she had toward the Purlmens in general and Elizabeth in particular. Molly decided to discuss the possibility of getting a copy of the missing photo with Aunt Bernice. She opened the subject when she took breakfast to her aunt.

"You'll like this breakfast," Molly told her. "It's one of the ones circled on the instructions as a favorite."

"I'll bet it's a poached egg," Aunt Bernice guessed.

"You're so right. I hope you like the way I fixed it."

After a quick taste Aunt Bernice replied, "It's perfect."

"I hope you like every meal Sue and I fix for you."

Molly waited a few minutes while Aunt Bernice enjoyed her breakfast before mentioning the photo. "Do you remember the picture of you, Mama, Daddy, and their parents when Mama and Daddy got married?"

Aunt Bernice stopped eating, wiped her mouth, and broke into a wide grin. "Oh yes, you know I do. I never had a copy, but I remember you had one."

"I used to have one, but I can't seem to find it."

"Oh," said Aunt Bernice, visibly disappointed.

"Mama told me that Daddy took the original. Maybe someone in his new family has it."

"Well, you'll never get a copy from that lady he married if she's still alive."

Aunt Bernice's facial expression suddenly went from looking sad to looking thoroughly disgusted. That disgusted look was the prelude to a verbal rampage.

"I only met her once when I visited them in Branchport, and she's a mean one. I wouldn't have met her then but your daddy called me and told me he had gotten married again. He said his new wife had made sure no one from our side of the family even knew they were getting married. He didn't tell me why. He just wanted me to come and visit them and meet her. Once was enough. That was the longest weekend I've ever had. I looked forward to Sunday afternoon so I could get away and not have to look at that woman's face anymore."

Aunt Bernice paused so she could try to remember additional negative things to say.

"I think she was using your daddy. I don't think she worked a day in her life. She had a daughter before they met. I believe that little girl was about 10 years older than you."

After thinking for a few more moments, Aunt Bernice resumed her character assassination. "I think she was too old for your daddy. Too old and too set in her rotten ways. Her nasty attitude is probably what killed him. There's no way he could have died a happy man. She didn't even have the decency to let us know that he had passed. He'd been gone over a year before I found out."

Aunt Bernice had one final shot to fire before completing her onslaught.

"Forgive me, but my brother was a fool for rummaging around in a trash can looking for a prize."

Hearing Aunt Bernice's overly candid and scathing opinion was a huge disappointment for Molly, but she did her best to hide it. If her father's sister had such a lousy view of her in-laws, chances were slim that they would honor an inquiry from anyone else in the family, especially since so many years had passed since her father's passing. She told herself that she would just have to cherish the memory of her relatives in the picture and accept its loss.

Moving on from that setback, Molly now focused on what needed to be done to care for Aunt Bernice. It took her and Sue only a few days to get accustomed to the necessary routine, enabling them to begin their quest to find employment by the end of the first week. Good fortune smiled on each as both found jobs within 2 weeks. Their hours were such that they were able to provide the constant care they'd promised to Aunt Bernice.

Providing constant care and working kept Molly and Sue busy. Molly took it in stride and it became routine for her. For Sue, it was becoming a strain. She felt as if she was locked into a world of monotony and boredom with no time to do what she wanted to do. She was so wrapped up in feeling down about her situation, it took her about 6 weeks to give more than a passing thought to the safe.

Beyond that, and what should have been the first thought on Sue's mind, she'd missed her period by 3 weeks. Also, she'd been feeling nauseous. Instead of accepting these symptoms of pregnancy, she tried her best to ignore them. Actually, she did more than just ignore – she was in denial to the point of not wanting to face anyone else about her condition.

Nature was on Sue's side to help hide her changing body. It took almost a full 4 months for her to truly have to alter what and how she dressed to hide her bulge. She likely would have been able to make it to 6 months or beyond except that 5 months to the day after they'd arrived, Aunt Bernice was hospitalized.

The hospitalization was the beginning of the end for Aunt Bernice. She was hospitalized for only 3 days before passing. The house and all Aunt Bernice's worldly goods were passed on to Molly. Although she now could easily cease working, Molly had no desire to do so. She changed her hours to coincide with Sue's, giving them more time to be together.

Sue had now been pregnant for just under 6 months and Molly finally took notice. Although it was the first time Molly had been around a pregnant woman on a daily basis other than herself during her own pregnancy, she approached the situation like a seasoned pro.

She asked firmly and directly, "Sue, are you pregnant?"

There was no mention of 'Child' as she often affectionately called her daughter.

Molly's tone and directness obliterated any thoughts Sue may have initially had to conceal the truth. She quickly answered, "Yes."

"How long have you known? Who's the father."

Sue ignored the first question and settled on the second. "It's from that..."

Sue now hesitated for a moment. She knew she had to admit she'd lied when she said nothing happened with Tom, but to tell the whole truth was out of the question. With that in mind, she forged ahead.

"...that time with Tom Purlmen. I didn't want to tell you everything then. I thought the one time he forced me was the end of everything."

"Oh Child," Molly began, falling back into her affectionate motherly state. "You should have let me know the truth from the beginning."

Sue knew she now had the opportunity to reestablish her version of the truth. Uppermost in her mind was the possibility of being able to force Tom Purlmen into accepting some of the responsibilities of being a father. She posed the question to Molly in a veiled statement.

"We should let them know that Tom is going to be a father," she offered.

Molly immediately rejected the idea.

"No, Child. They would fight it. It wouldn't be worth the trouble. They'd turn all the facts topsy-turvy and drag us through the mud."

Molly paused to take a deep breath before continuing.

"There's no way she would concede that her son was anything but a saint. And anyway, you told me she blamed you for what happened."

Molly paused again as she thought back to her phone conversation with Elizabeth before adding more to herself than to

Sue, "I don't ever want to speak to that lady again."

It hadn't been lost on Molly that Sue had called the young Mr. Purlmen 'Tom'. It bothered her that Sue seemed so comfortable doing so. Her every instinct told her there was likely more to the story than she'd heard so far. Maybe much more.

Sue got the drift that it was probably useless to get the Purlmens involved immediately, so she abandoned the idea for now. She began to reason with herself to accept her situation. "Yes," she thought, "I'm pregnant. The father is a well-to-do young man. At some point, she could probably contact him and have *him* acknowledge his responsibilities."

Sue's thoughts then drifted to the little safe that held the Purlmen family heirlooms. She brightened by thinking, "My child will be the rightful owner of the heirlooms at some point. Having them could help reaffirm the bond to Tom."

Surprisingly, Sue wasn't thinking about Tom with marriage as a goal. Instead, she was thinking along the lines of having access to more for herself and her baby than what Molly had to offer. The home she and Molly shared now belonged to Molly as did the remainder of Aunt Bernice's wealth. Her strategy was to have more than whatever Molly allowed her by being patient and giving birth to a healthy baby. After that, she and Molly could enjoy raising the baby together until the right time and opportunity arose to challenge the Purlmens.

Sue finally spoke in a way that gave the impression she'd fully acquiesced to the motherly advice she'd been given.

"Right, Mama. We can take care of the baby ourselves."

Although Sue's stated position on the matter was what Molly ultimately wanted, she detected insincerity on Sue's part. That, coupled with the fresh story of how Sue got pregnant and her over-familiarity with 'Tom', indicated to Molly that there was *way* more to the story than she'd been told. However, rather than immediately probe for additional information, she decided to keep her suspicions to herself. She figured the truth would come out at some point, but she couldn't worry about that now.

Molly began to concentrate on the current situation. Sue would be giving birth in a few months, so forward planning should commence immediately. Since they were financially stable without either having to work, they would both give notice that they'd be leaving their respective jobs. They'd convert Aunt Bernice's bedroom into a nursery. Sue would begin to have regular doctor visits. Beyond that, Molly knew there were many additional things she hadn't yet thought of that would need to be done before and after the baby arrived.

Digressing again to thoughts that included the Purlmens, Molly hoped at some point there would be a meeting of the minds and the two families would reach a consensus over how to raise the child. Then, just about as quickly as that hope came to mind, Molly rejected it. Why worry about what the Purlmens would or wouldn't do? No matter what their relationship had been, it didn't matter now. It was up to her and Sue to step up and do whatever they could to do the right thing for this new life. Besides, Molly found herself rapidly growing fond of the idea of having a grandchild to help nurture. Surely Sue's maternal instincts would become enhanced to help her mature to become the kind of woman Molly had always hoped she would become. Given that outlook, she began to feel as if she didn't need to hear any more of the hidden information regarding Sue and Tom. Now she began to dread the thought that one day she'd learn more about them than she wanted to know.

Molly was correct in assuming she would learn more about Sue and Tom. The first bit of knowledge came 3 months later on a memorable day in the form of a couple of tiny items.

It happened on the morning of Thursday, February 29, 1968, with Sue's expected delivery date still 3 weeks away. When Molly awoke and looked in on Sue, she found Sue gently rocking her head back and forth while humming to herself. Molly had never seen Sue act this way before so she questioned it.

"Are you alright, Child?"

Sue stopped rocking and humming to answer.

"I'm fine – just bored."

Sue was lying. She'd felt changes within her body over the last two hours that were different from any she'd felt before. At first the changes were mild, somewhat indescribable and intermittent, but the intensity had been steadily increasing. However, since it was 3 weeks before her expected due date, she decided to dismiss what she was feeling to avoid being dragged into the doctor's office. She was uncomfortable, but the discomfort was not overbearing. Right now, she just wanted to be left alone, so she gave Molly an errand to run.

"Mama, I feel like having a grapefruit this morning. Are there any left?" Sue asked, but she knew full well there were none left. She'd eaten the last one the previous night.

Since she didn't know, Molly admitted as much. "I don't know. Let me check."

Molly left, returned, and then reported her findings to Sue.

"No, no grapefruit. I was thinking we should go to the market later this morning anyway. Why don't you get ready so we can go somewhere for breakfast and then stop off at the market on the way back home?"

Sue had no desire to get up. "I'm not that hungry. I'd rather have you run to the market so you can get the shopping done while I relax and wait for you. I'll be ready for some grapefruit in about an hour and you should be back by then."

Molly had no argument for Sue's reasoning. After all, the earlier she got to the market the less crowded it would be. She agreed and said, "I'll add grapefruit to the shopping list. Anything else?"

"No, that's all I can think of," Sue answered, speaking in the most pleasant and confident voice she could muster to suppress showing a reaction to the sudden pressure she felt in her lower back. For some reason, she was truly in denial of the probability of being in labor.

Molly was completely taken in by Sue's act. She took the bait and said, "I'll be back in a bit. You just relax."

Sue did the best she could to do just that, but the 5 minutes it took for Molly to leave felt like an eternity. It wasn't until Molly left that an important task Sue had in the back of her mind became an obsession. As soon as she heard Molly close the front door, Sue got up and went to her closet. With some difficulty, she bent down and moved shoeboxes until she got to the one containing the little safe. Holding the lime shoebox was uplifting for her. It was as if she needed it with her before she could fully acknowledge the fact that she was about to have the baby.

Sue's contractions intensified just as she climbed back on the bed. For the first time since she started feeling changes in her body, she was unable to suppress a groan. She knew for sure the birthing process had begun. Focusing on the shoebox, she opened it and unpacked the little safe before tossing the shoebox back toward the closet. She examined the safe for just a moment before she felt a contraction so strong that she dropped the safe on the bed beside her and laid down on her back. Fear overcame her. She wanted to get to the telephone and call for help, but couldn't do anything beyond laying there hoping no more pains would come. That was not to be. Over the next 45 minutes, the pain got increasingly worse until she started feeling like her hips were being thrust apart. Instinctively she began to push. It hurt, but she could feel the pressure in her abdomen moving. Suddenly she heard the front door open and close.

"Mama," she cried out. "I'm having the baby!"

Molly got to her in a flash and saw that the baby had almost fully emerged. "I'll call for an ambulance," she shouted.

"No, don't leave me," Sue implored her.

"Alright. The baby's almost out. Push."

Sue gave a push and delivered a baby boy. Molly began drying him with the blanket first before rushing off to call for an ambulance. She returned in about a minute with an armload of towels. It was then that she took stock of the amount of blood still oozing from Sue. She first covered the baby with a towel before attempting to mop up the blood in the bed.

By now the infant had begun crying on his own, so Molly felt he would be fine. Sue was a different matter. Molly spoke to her. "Sue, are you alright?"

Sue was breathing heavily and had closed her eyes, but she opened them as she replied to Molly. "Yes, I'm fine. Where's the baby?" she asked.

"He's right here."

"Let me see him."

Molly didn't want to alarm Sue by pointing out how much blood she'd lost. She figured the ambulance would be there shortly and the medical professionals would take the necessary steps to curtail the bleeding. She obliged Sue's request and picked up the baby so Sue could view him. The umbilical cord was still attached, so she laid him beside Sue as close to her eyes as she could manage without pulling the cord unnecessarily. The spot she placed him happened to be where his head was just beneath the little safe. That's when Molly noticed it.

"What's this?" Molly asked as she picked up the safe.

Sue was busy looking at the baby and didn't acknowledge the question. It was as if she was in a mental fog. Instead, she absently stated, "I want to name him Norman. Norman Hurley. I like it."

Hearing the name caught Molly completely off guard and took her mind off the safe. She laid it back where she'd found it.

"I like it too. It sounds good." Molly repeated the name herself. "Norman Hurley." She wondered why Sue had opted to not use the surname Purlmen, but she let it pass. This was her grandson and if the Purlmens wanted to mount any kind of challenge in the future, so be it. She wouldn't stand in their way, but she wouldn't go out of her way to assist them.

Molly then asked, "No middle name?"

"Thomas, of course," Sue responded.

Even Sue didn't know where that declaration had come from. She'd just blurted it out as more of a reflex action than a planned decision. In her weakened state, she decided that the name Norman Thomas Hurley did more than just sound good. It was also the most sensible middle name she could come up with as a means toward an end. She hadn't previously discussed names with Molly because she'd let it be known she wanted to do it on her own. She had made up her mind that a boy would be Norman and a girl it would be Norma. She never gave the middle name even a passing thought before that moment. Having Thomas as the middle name suddenly seemed like a great way to keep the Purlmens involved. At some point in time, they would surely acknowledge the baby.

Then Sue remembered the safe that was still near Norman's head. In a continuation of the same determination she had just summoned to cut through her mental fog, she added, "That safe holds the family's heirlooms. It belongs to Norman because he's a Purlmen."

Molly immediately asked, "What are you talking about?"

Before Sue could answer, the doorbell rang.

"The ambulance!" Molly exclaimed. I'll be right back."

Molly hurried downstairs to answer the door. While her mind was primarily focused on getting the 4 emergency workers inside and up to Sue and Norman as quickly as possible, the mystery within Sue's last statements had her confused. She was beginning to get the feeling that it was quite likely Sue and Tom Purlmen had both been up to far more mischief than either she or Elizabeth Purlmen could possibly have fathomed.

Molly's thoughts of what may have transpired during the Sue and Tom escapade vanished when she heard one of the emergency workers say, "She's not breathing," and a moment later say, "She's lost a lot of blood."

Molly had been standing back to allow the medical personnel to work unimpeded, but now she moved forward to see what was happening. Norman seemed to be fine and had only one person tending to him. Sue's condition was another matter. Molly couldn't suppress a gasp when she saw what Sue looked like. She appeared lifeless. It was then that one of the attendants ushered Molly out of the room.

The remainder of that evening became one long heartache for Molly. Sue was rushed to the hospital in the first ambulance and Molly and Norman were transported there in the other. Upon their arrival, Molly was informed that Sue had not survived. On the other hand, Norman was fine, but he was kept overnight for observation. Molly could have also remained there, but she instead decided to go home.

Molly took a taxi home to spend the night in an empty house for the first time in years. She was sad, but instead of allowing heartache to overwhelm her, she resolved to put the time to good use. The first step was to force herself to go into Sue's room to survey what cleaning needed to be done. She found that the emergency personnel had done a good job of bundling sheets and towels so no blood or birth remnants were visible. She had to either unwrap the bundle and individually clean items or to dispose of everything intact. For Molly, the correct choice was obvious. She took the entire bundle downstairs to be discarded.

Once Molly returned to the bedroom, she surveyed what else might have to be done. The only thing out of place was a lime-colored shoebox near Sue's closet. Molly picked it up and put it in the closet. It was then she thought about Sue's clothing. She decided she would donate every item. She couldn't fit into anything Sue had worn. Anything else she didn't want could also be donated or disposed of.

Molly paused for a moment to think about how life would be for her and her newborn grandson but instead found herself caught up in thinking about what life could have been for Sue. That leg, that slight imperfection of having one leg shorter than the other, had always carried too much of Sue's focus. She was an intelligent girl and had good grades in school, but she'd allowed what she considered to be a physical shortcoming to hold her back. Had she pursued all of her good traits and, of course, not dreamed of an easy path to wealth, she could have been successful at virtually any chosen career. The thought of Sue's could have, would have, should have been life path not only saddened Molly, but it also triggered a segue to a long-dormant urge to reminisce about Sue's father, Roberto. It had been a quarter-century since she last saw or heard anything about MIA Roberto, and if there ever was an appropriate time to free herself of any leftover hope for a miracle reunion, this was it. The direct link to Roberto was now gone.

Molly's mind snapped back to focus on what she'd wanted to think about in the first place. She immediately promised herself then and there that she'd give her all to provide Norman with the best upbringing and opportunities within her powers. She realized that, just like Roberto and Sue, Norman would ultimately have to decide between right and wrong, but he would never be able to point a finger at her and whine about not being given the proper foundation to use as a springboard to success.

In another sense, although Molly naturally had some misgivings about not having had a male companion in all these years, she had her priorities set as straight as an arrow. For her, children should always come first until they were either fully grown or hopelessly lost in some misery of their own making. She'd done the best she could for 25 years with Sue, and she was now poised to devote another 20 years or so with Norman.

Just as she was about to leave Sue's room and go to her own bedroom, Molly again noticed the tiny safe. It was now on Sue's dresser. For the first time since Sue had mentioned it earlier that evening, she remembered Sue had said it contained what was now the family's heirlooms. She'd also said that it belonged to Norman because he's a Purlmen. Just what had Sue meant by that? The family's only heirloom had been the now-missing wedding picture. Questions swirled in Molly's mind. Where did the safe come from?

Could it be that Sue and Tom had collaborated to get married or just to get together for the fun of it? Did the safe represent some sort of pact between the two? Was it a payment? What would a then 24-year-old woman want with an 18-year-old young man?

These and other questions in Molly's mind led to an uneasy feeling that the safe could have been the cause, and now the result of those heirloom questions Sue had asked during their employment at the Purlmens'. The safe could very well hold the Purlmens' heirlooms. If so, the fact that one day one of the Purlmens would come to claim it was a strong possibility. But, how could they? They didn't know where Molly now lived. At least she didn't recall giving specific information to the Purlmens about the exact location of Aunt Bernice's home. Sure, they knew she and Sue would be leaving and going to live with their aunt, but that information had been given in passing. Molly remembered she'd listed her aunt as next of kin at the employment agency, but no one from the Purlmens' household had ever given the impression they cared to know anything in-depth about Molly's family.

There was another possibility. Maybe Sue had given Tom their new address. That would have been the only way they'd know and the thought bothered Molly. She wanted to be free from the Purlmens for now, and she didn't want them to come around looking for their heirlooms, at least not right away. It wasn't that she cared about the Purlmens' heirlooms for monetary value or anything else. Her concern was that someone – probably Mrs. Purlmen – would open a nasty conversation with her about the safe. Once the conversation was opened, she would feel obligated to let the Purlmens know about Norman, and she had no desire to share Norman with the Purlmens any time soon. He was to be her responsibility to raise.

Molly now displayed a bit of the same kind of deceit Sue sometimes embraced. Rather than call to inform the Purlmens of the safe or mail it back to them, she decided to hold on to it. She felt somewhat justified. After all, her heirloom was missing on account of something the Purlmens had done. Now they could suffer, at least for a time, the pain of losing something dear to them. Not that she planned to keep the safe from them if they ever asked for it. She simply wouldn't volunteer to inform them she had it just yet.

Storing the safe was now in order, and Molly had no problem finding the perfect place to secure it. That odd-looking lime shoebox she'd just put in Sue's closet would be perfect. Molly retrieved the shoebox, wrapped the safe in a hand towel, and placed it into the lime shoebox. She then took it to her bedroom to store in her closet.

Before Molly reached her closet, she had an afterthought. While unpacking, she'd retrieved and store her camera in one of her dresser drawers. She knew it still contained unused film along with pictures that had been taken with the Purlmens. If she was to have the film developed now, she feared she might throw away any pictures of the Purlmens. No, she decided, that wouldn't be right. It could be that one day she might decide to show the photos to Norman. It would be best to store the camera along with the safe and deal with both items sometime in the future. Through a perplexing set of circumstances, the camera and safe had become a couple of strange bedfellows.

As a token of burying the past, Molly now took the time to remove all the shoeboxes from her closet. She then placed the lime shoebox into the corner and stacked the other shoeboxes on and around it. The tangible links to the past were now out of sight, and the plan for the future was to get them out of mind.

The next few days were filled with many adjustments to Molly's normal routine, but she settled easily into her role as the keeper of her and Norman's castle. Using love, discipline, and ongoing attention to detail, she taught and nurtured him to become a well-rounded and obedient child. By the time he entered kindergarten, Norman was reading and writing well enough to handle second-grade work. School officials suggested that Molly allow him to skip grades, but she declined the offer. She preferred to have Norman stay with children his age and learn to work with others to help them succeed.

One thing Molly feared was that Norman might one day feel inferior or neglected with neither his mother nor his father around to help raise him. She'd made sure he knew from the start that she was his "Nana" and that she was his only guardian, but she knew at some point in time she would have to explain more about his parents. She wanted to give him sufficient information to satisfy his curiosity, but she didn't want to go overboard with details that wouldn't do anyone any good. Discussing Sue's death would be sad but not too difficult, since she could limit that discussion to the day Norman was born. His father's status would be a different matter. Though Molly had thought about what she might say, when the day came that Norman wanted more information, she still wasn't quite ready.

It was during his second week of kindergarten that he came home and asked, "Nana, what happened to my mother and father?"

"Well Norman, your mother was sick around the time you were being born and she got weak and died." After saying that, Molly had to do a tap dance around the truth.

"Your mother wanted to surprise all of us with who your father is so she kept it a secret. She didn't even tell him. She was going to tell us all after you were born. Maybe one day we'll find out and we can all meet him."

"Oh," Norman thought for a moment then asked, "How will we know it's him?"

"There are ways to tell, but we don't have to worry about that until the time comes, right?"

"Right."

It was surprising to Molly that her explanation satisfied Norman as well as it did. He didn't dwell on the subject and seldom spoke about his parents through the years.

What Norman did do was concentrate on being the type of child Molly encouraged him to be. That being the case, he worked hard to excel in school and was quite successful in all subjects. His scholarly acumen was so acute that school officials continued to encourage

Molly to allow Norman to skip a grade each year, but Molly decided to delay it until Norman reached senior high school. It was then that he and his classmates would undergo their biggest transformation from being a unit to being individuals within the system. A change at that time would not have much of an impact until Norman graduated a year ahead of his former peers, but they'd cross that bridge when they came to it.

The most important thing for Molly was to raise Norman to the best of her abilities. Just as she'd done with Sue, Molly's world consisted of mainly home life with frequent visits to the library. Social life was non-existent. Her goal was to have Norman become successful at whatever he chose to do with his life. In so doing, she prepared him for good things to come.

4 Wedding Bells

Elizabeth Purlmen controlled the Purlmen family business and life with the ever-obedient Tom supporting her every suggestion. While that arrangement resulted in quick decisions, Elizabeth didn't know for sure whether Tom was gaining the necessary self-assurance to run the business or to take charge of his life. She didn't seem to realize the biggest problem was that she lacked enough confidence in Tom to back off and let him take charge of things.

Their business and lives ran like that for many years. Now it's possible that if Tom had not had the escapade with Sue, his mother would have slowly loosened her reins on him. That, or maybe at some point Tom would have had the courage to rebel against the dominance and demanded greater freedom. However, his mother's reaction to that incident had instilled a fear within his mind he simply couldn't shake.

Tom maintained an all business and no pleasure lifestyle for the sake of not giving his mother any reason to disapprove of him. He spent every waking moment seeking to gain her approval. That meant no social life at all unless they were together. He did not date. His was a bland existence his mother did not complain about, and the style of life he was living was good enough for him. However now, a full 21 years after his high school graduation, it was his mother who decided on this, his 39th birthday, the time had come for a change.

Having dinner at a restaurant that night was no surprise. They often ate out. What was surprising was the restaurant and its location. It was an exclusive restaurant and it took them over an hour to drive there. Tom got the impression his mother was going to treat his 39th birthday extra special. As it turned out, he found he was a hundred percent right, but certainly not in any kind of way he would have dared to imagine.

Once inside the restaurant Elizabeth took charge after the hostess greeted them with, "Good evening, Madam, Sir. Do you have a reservation?"

"Yes," Elizabeth replied. "Elizabeth Purlmen."

The hostess scanned her reservation list and said, "Oh yes, here it is, a table for two."

Elizabeth then asked, "Do you see where I requested a table in a secluded area?"

"Oh yes, and the maître d' will take care of that," replied the hostess as she motioned for the maître d'.

Once the maître d' arrived, the hostess directed him with, "Two for section E. Seat them near the back wall."

The maître d' bowed toward them and said, "This way Madam, Sir."

He led them to a room within the restaurant where small private parties were held.

While Tom was used to dining out with his mother, they'd never been to a restaurant as formal as this. He wasn't used to having multiple waiters tend to their every need. This much fanfare gave him the impression that he was going to have one heck of a great birthday celebration for the first time in his life. He was far more accustomed to a simple acknowledgement of the day and some small gift.

Following the wine, appetizers, meals, and desserts, Elizabeth asked for coffee and the check. She took a glanced at the check when it came, pulled enough money from her purse to cover the check along with an ample tip, and motioned for the maître d'.

She told him, "Here you are, I don't need any change."

"Will there be anything else?"

"We'll have more coffee and that's it." This signaled to maître d' that Elizabeth wished for them to be left alone.

Tom now knew small talk would no longer dominate the conversation. Whatever was on his mother's mind would be forthcoming immediately, and he needed to give her his full attention.

Surprisingly, she came at him from a direction that took him totally by surprise.

"Tom, we're the last ones in the Purlmen family." Elizabeth chose her words carefully. "We need to start thinking about the future."

Then, shockingly, she hit Tom with a rhetorical question to use as a springboard to the actual discussion she wanted. She asked it directly and almost accusingly.

"Tom, when are you going to think about getting married?"

Elizabeth knew full well Tom had not been dating, that is, unless he was the slyest and sneakiest person the world has ever known. This just happened to be the most tactful way she could think of to open the subject. Tom knew that she knew why he didn't date and that she knew he knew she knew why he didn't date. Well, at least she knew he never displayed any kind of enthusiasm toward making a move toward dating. The bottom line was that his attitude spoke volumes. He really didn't want to date, but as always, he played her game.

"We've been too busy, Mother," he responded, rather than facing up to his shortcomings. "I haven't had a chance to meet a lot of women."

The reference to a lot of women implied he was

meeting *some* women, so he quickly covered his tracks with, "I mean any women outside of the business."

"Mm-hmm," was Elizabeth's response, which signaled to Tom that he needed to expand on his shallow answer.

Tom weakly took the cue with his response, "Well, I guess I should start dating."

Elizabeth was dissatisfied with Tom's tone so she gave him a push.

"You're 39 now, Tom and by that age, most men are married with children. I'm getting older and I have no grandchildren. You need to start dating. You've been letting yourself go. You're not in the same shape you used to be. I think you should go to a gym and lose about 15 to 20 pounds." She paused to let Tom get a word in edgewise if he chose to.

Tom felt he needed to say something, but what he said was a total cop-out as he tried to reword and reuse the same excuse he'd used earlier. "It's just that we've been so busy, Mother and..."

"Hogwash!" Elizabeth immediately cut him off and then blasted him with a tirade she knew would hurt him to the core. "Your father and I always told you since you were a little boy that we would not put up with poor excuses and I'm not going to do it now. If you have a good reason something can't be done, then you need to work at overcoming that reason. Right now, you don't have a reason and I don't want to hear that lame excuse about being so busy again. You're not getting any younger and women around your age are finished having children or should be. You need to spruce up and find a younger woman who doesn't have children and is ready for marriage and a family."

Tom was crushed by his mother's words. He interpreted what she had said as being worse than a threat – it was an ultimatum. Simply put, he had to work on getting married.

However, there were problems with that directive. First, he didn't know how to approach a woman for a date. His only encounter with a woman had been that disaster with the housekeeper Sue, which in and of itself led to the creation of the second problem. He was impotent, and he knew it. He'd lost all interest in making love. Those two problems combined to make a third problem. He didn't have the confidence to try to build a relationship, which made him genuinely afraid to try. It was a point of fact that if his mother never made the request, he'd happily spend the rest of his life a bachelor. Unfortunately, he couldn't bring himself to give an honest reply, not with his mother's ultimatum hanging over his head. He felt he had to lie.

The best Tom could muster as a decent answer was to say, "Right mother. I'll start tomorrow. There's that gym here in town near the college. I'll join and start working out so I can get back in shape."

To the surprise of both of them, Elizabeth accepted his answer by saying, "Good idea."

Elizabeth's normal initial reaction to most anything involving Tom's decision making was to poke and prod for finite details and then interject her suggestions in the form of demands. However, this time, she deferred her judgment. Her maternal instinct told her to allow him to make things happen.

Tom had given his answer with the expectation that he'd be getting additional advice, but when none came, he knew he was on his own to get the job done. That meant by any and all means necessary, he had to succeed. Failure was not an option. At 39 and many years beyond his last attempt to maintain his physical fitness, Tom was fearful of even the thought of rigorous training. He'd shunned it as much as possible during his high school years and avoided it at all costs ever since. He wouldn't undertake the task now except he reasoned there was no way he could ever find a woman young enough to bear children without making himself over as a younger-looking eligible bachelor. That thought, along with the pressure his mother had applied, gave him the courage to visit a gym the very next day.

Tom arrived at the gym at 8 a.m. sharp, thinking that he would get there as soon as it opened, but to his surprise saw from the sign on the door that it opens daily at 5:00. This meant to Tom that he could easily fit an exercise regimen into his work schedule. All that was left for him to do was to sign up, which was easily done. Registration was a breeze. He was given a tour, a sales pitch, a credit signature card, and was then assigned a personal trainer for his initial indoctrination period. To his surprise, they expected him to begin working out that very day. He almost cringed when a tall extremely fit young man approached with hand extended.

"Hi, I'm Freddy and I'll be your personal trainer," the man said.

Tom stood and meekly took Freddy's hand. He was uncomfortable with the firmness in Freddy's grip, but the feel of the grip awakened a resolve that told him he must do whatever it takes to become fit like Freddy. Whereas he normally would have introduced himself as 'Mr. Purlmen', he dropped all formality and, wanting to be 'one of the boys', he replied, "Hi, I'm Tom."

"Let's get started, where's your gear?"

"I thought today was just to sign up."

"No problem, we can start the next time you're here. But don't forget you only have 2 weeks of free personal training, and if you don't start today, you'll lose a day," Freddy told him before adding, "You could come back later today if you like."

Tom was thinking about what Freddy said. He hadn't given a thought about what he needed to work out in before. Freddy sensed that this was an opportunity to give a sales pitch.

"Of course, you can always buy new stuff here," Freddy offered. "We've got a nice little shop and we have everything. We could outfit you from head to toe. We don't carry any cheap stuff. You'll look better and feel better wearing what we have to offer."

"Okay," was Tom's reply.

Freddy would have pointed to where the store was and allowed Tom to make the purchases on his own, but he said to himself, "This guy knows from nothing." Instead, he said to Tom, "It's right over here, let's go," and led Tom to the store.

Freddy had Tom purchase two of all necessary items except sneakers. He explained to Tom that it was easier to have an outfit ready to go daily instead of having to clean and use the same outfit every time he trained. As an afterthought, he reminded Tom to get a lock and a gym bag.

Once the purchases were complete, Freddy gave pre-workout instructions to Tom.

"Take your gear to the locker room - remember it's upstairs - and then after you change, meet me in the weight room. That's the room downstairs toward the back of the gym on the right. I'll be in there."

The men parted ways, allowing Tom to assess how far he'd gone into getting out of shape, and how far he would need to go to get back in shape. He would love to have a physique like Freddy's but was sure that would be out of the question. As he continued to dress, he reminded himself that he had to get this done and it was best to start that very day. There was no way he wanted to face his mother without being able to report daily progress to her, at least not during the first days of his venture into physical fitness. Thinking further about her, he reasoned it would make him look good to go home after the first day with a workout behind him rather than having to say he'd joined the gym but wouldn't begin working out until the following day.

Tom's 2 weeks with Freddy went from excruciating to satisfying. Unused muscles screamed back at him at first, but after the first week, Tom began to feel and notice the positive changes his body was undergoing. He also surpassed Freddy's instructions and expectations by working out every day without giving his body a rest.

Freddy had news for Tom on the final day of the initial 2 weeks of personal training. His smile gave it away as soon as they saw one another.

"You look happy," Tom said to Freddy as they shook hands before the training session.

"I am," Freddy replied. "This is the last day of your indoctrination training. If you want to continue to work out with a personal trainer, it will cost you extra."

Tom was about to answer, but Freddy didn't give him a chance to speak. In a somewhat hushed voice, he continued.

"If you do want to continue with a personal trainer, it will have to be with someone else. This is my last day here. I didn't tell the boss that the job I really wanted has given me a start date for next Monday. I'll be taking the 2 weeks of vacation time this job owes me beginning tomorrow and I'm resigning from here at the end of next week. I won't have any reason to come back here again because I already belong to a gym much closer to home."

Freddy saw the disappointment on Tom's face, so he reassured him.

"You'll be alright. All you have to do is continue to come in and work out like you've been doing. Remember, you've been coming every day when you don't need to come in more than 5 times a week. Plus, you told me you felt comfortable those couple of days when you worked out on your own. You'll be alright," Freddy repeated.

Tom reasoned that if Freddy had confidence in him, he was supposed to at least pretend to have enough confidence in himself to accept the challenge.

"Sure," Tom answered. "You helped me get started and I can take it from here."

Though he wasn't sure about what he was doing, Tom knew he had to keep up appearances for the sake of all involved, especially his mother. That thought got him through the day's session and geared him up for continuing without a personal trainer. He could opt to pay for a new person, but somehow, he felt it would be akin to being a traitor to Freddy. No, he'd continue on his own and use the knowledge Freddy had given him to become the man he felt he needed to be.

Month's passed and Tom's physique did improve. He bought new clothes, dyed what little gray he'd seen in his hair, and did his best to emulate younger men. Had he continued to use an honest strategy to get in shape, he probably would not have slipped into an abyss. Or if he had used more patience. Or if he had not met that guy Larry at the gym. The bottom line was that a lack of sufficient willpower caused a terrible domino effect that eventually took control of his life.

Larry was a man who emitted an outwardly snarly presence. He had big muscles in his arms, chest, and neck. Curiously, he also had a huge gut that was balanced over a pair of knock-kneed spindly legs. He'd never previously spoken to Tom, but on this particular day, only Larry and Tom happened to be in the weight room. Tom was surprised as Larry ventured over and began a conversation.

"Hey, my name's Larry," he said, extending a hand.

Tom was somewhat flattered by the greeting by this muscled man and took Larry's hand enthusiastically. "I'm Tom."

"You been coming here long?"

"About 6 months."

"Yeah, I've seen you here before. You look like you're getting in shape, but I think you've hit a plateau."

Tom thought a moment about the accusation. The phrase 'hitting a plateau' had never before been mentioned to him.

Larry could tell Tom was confused by the remark, so he explained what he meant.

"You know, when you get to a point where no matter how much you work out, you don't seem to make any more progress."

Tom now understood. "Right," he said. "I seem to be in the same shape now as I was a few weeks ago."

Larry saw his opening. "What you need to do is what I decided to do – get a little help."

Tom was both curious and apprehensive. "What kind of help?" he asked.

"They got this stuff called steroids – we call it juice. It helps you get where you want to be." Larry flexed his biceps. "Check out these big guns. Juice got them for me. The only problem is getting it. You need to know how to get it and how to use it. Plus, you have to have the money and be able to deal with the needles."

Larry had added 2 of the 3 turnoffs for prospective clients at the end of his pitch. If money and needles didn't turn Tom off, he more than likely was genuinely interested. The unmentioned third potential turnoff was that Larry was offering illegal steroids.

Tom was more than interested, he was wholeheartedly intrigued. In an attempt to show his manliness and financial stability, he chose to do some minor boasting. "I can afford it if I think it's worth it, and I can handle needles."

Larry immediately scheduled their first session. "Okay, we can meet at your place or mine. You gotta have 50 bucks each time. I just inject the juice into the muscles you want to work out."

Tom was quick with the answer to the question as to whose place they would meet. It would certainly not be anywhere around his mother. "Your place will be fine," he said.

"Okay. Now, how often we do it depends on what kind of juice I have and how much we use. The stuff's not available except by prescription, so you can't let anyone know you're using it without one. Don't worry, I'm an expert."

Larry had mentioned illegality in a roundabout way, but by now Tom was hooked on the idea. For him, there was no turning back.

The final details of their agreement needed to be settled, namely the address, the date, and the time. Larry made the arrangements to seal the deal.

"Come see me when you're about to go to the locker room and I'll meet you up there and give you my address and phone number," he said. "We can decide on the day and time then."

Tom made the commitment and lived up to all parts of the bargain that would become his date with the devil. Over the next several months, he was transformed into a virtual poster boy for the positive and negative outcomes of illegal steroid usage. Yes, he did get muscular results, but Larry the expert was anything but that. As time wore on, he seemed more and more like someone Tom never would have dealt with on any level. The problem here, however, was that Tom had no idea as to whom else he could turn to for the juice.

Toward the end of a year since he began his quest to find a mate, Tom began to learn about some of the negatives of his decision to use anabolic steroids. His knowledge, however, did not come by the way he was feeling, but rather by what he happened to read in an article. That article discussed the potential for heart, liver, kidney problems, and infertility from steroid use. What he learned made him think about those consequences. What if his heart, liver, or kidneys were in bad shape? What if he was sterile? Maybe he needed to curtail his association with Larry, who had by now stopped showing up at the gym and was only available by phone whenever he decided to answer it. Tom immediately made an appointment with a doctor to have his overall health condition checked.

The initial doctor's office visit was bad, but the second one was a disaster. It included test results from the first visit and the news was horrible. Tom was diagnosed as having a heart murmur along with liver and kidney issues. Sadly, on top of that, the doctor told him he was sterile and therefore would not be able to father a child.

Tom was shaken from hearing the news, but he hid his feelings from the doctor. He especially knew he could not allow his mother to find out. He decided to keep up appearances and finally begin to make an effort to find a wife. So far, he had only concentrated on getting in shape as if finding a mate would somehow just happen. He now had to make a move. Since the only place he spent time socializing was in the gym, he guessed he should start there. The first place he decided to look was in the gym's aerobics class sessions, which he'd shunned up until now. There were always attractive young women there. Maybe one there would be interested in him.

Aerobic exercise classes can be a daunting adventure for anyone, but for those who aren't dancers or aren't used to coordinated movements, it can be a nightmare. For Tom, there was additional pressure in the form of his memory of how his only venture to a dance floor turned out badly when he was a freshman in high school. He'd tried to imitate the way he saw the other boys moving, but it only took about 5 seconds before snickering, hooting, and outright laughing about his lack of ability began. A crowd of his schoolmates, both black and white, had made him the brunt of cruel jokes about his lack of rhythm and coordination. The one joke aimed at him that hurt the most was the statement, "He's about as white as they come." What perplexed him was that it was a white student who said it. That teasing had always stuck with him, and it made him feel as if he didn't socially belong to anything or anyone anywhere. Fortunately, he now had months of muscle toning behind him and, with the added support of the supplements he'd been consuming, he also had courage enough to sign up for a class.

Tom began as the quintessential class klutz and relegated himself to the back of the class and as far from the entrance as possible. To his credit, he worked hard to keep up with others, and in the wake of a few sessions, his perseverance began to pay off. After about a month he thought about moving closer to the instructor to show off his abilities to perhaps get noticed by some young lady in the class, but he couldn't bring himself to make that move. Instead, he continued to go to the same place in the room for each class he attended as though that spot was his and his alone to occupy.

Tom's reluctance to move was finally rewarded when a young lady began attending that same class. She had the same tendency to want to be in the back of the class and as far from the door as possible, thereby winding up right next to Tom. The one big difference is that the young lady came into the class as an expert at every move the instructor made. Tom couldn't understand why someone with that much ability wouldn't want to be near the front of the class where she could be seen. He dared not think that she stood next to him for the sake of being near him. He didn't know if he should try to open a conversation with her or just continue to show up and hope that maybe something positive would 'just happen'.

Instead of making any kind of move, Tom began studying and fantasizing about the young woman. He admired the way she carried herself. She displayed an all-business type of attitude, not paying particular attention to anyone. She had a lovely face, a shapely figure, black hair, and a light honey-toned complexion that looked as if she had a permanently perfect tan. Tom was smitten, though his only involvement with the young lady had thus far been as someone he exercised next to during aerobics class. She'd given no outward indication she even knew he was alive.

Surprisingly, Tom's lack of experience and timidity was what finally engineered a decent conversation, even though the catalyst was a thunderstorm that interrupted power during the class. With no music and only dim emergency lights illuminating the room, there was nothing to do except either immediately give up on the class and leave, or wait for a while to see if the power was restored. It so happened that the young lady chose to wait and Tom, ever hopeful, did the same. The young lady was the first to speak.

"I was just getting warmed up. I hope they begin the whole class from the start and don't just pick up from where we left off."

Tom looked directly at the young lady through the dim lighting to make sure she was speaking to him and not to someone else or no one in particular. To his delight, she was looking directly into his eyes.

As matter-of-factly as he could, he responded, "Yes, me too. I like coming to this class."

Now Tom hoped the lights would not come on for quite a while and the conversation would continue. As it happened, he didn't need the power outage for the young lady to continue speaking as she extended her hand and spoke.

"My name is Marlena. Mar-LAY-nuh." She spoke her name slowly and distinctly, emphasizing each syllable so there would be no mistake about the pronunciation.

Tom happily took her hand and his apprehensiveness about talking suddenly vanished.

"I'm Tom. You know, Marlena, the way you can do all the aerobic dances, you should be the instructor."

"Oh no," Marlena answered with a chuckle. "I just like staying fit. I used to just dance at home, but I can't play music loud enough there."

Tom had never previously given working out at home a thought, but he could imagine what his mother might say if he ever tried it there. He quickly dismissed the notion and continued to speak to Marlena.

"I like your name, Marlena. How do you spell it?"

"You're about the first person who's ever asked without trying to spell it themselves or change it to Marlene. It's M-A-R-L-E-N-A. You say it using the Spanish pronunciation with the accent on the second syllable and the Spanish vowel sounds. You know, where the 'E' sounds like a long 'A' and the 'A' sounds like 'AH'." Marlena paused for a moment then added, "I can't stand for anyone to call me Marlene. When they do, it's like they don't respect me."

Tom was quick to reply, "I think the name Marlena is perfect. I wouldn't try to change a thing."

His last remark was spoken just as the lights came back on. Even though his eyes weren't fully adjusted to the sudden full illumination, Tom noticed a smile on Marlena's face at what he'd said. He continued speaking.

"Now all we need to do is have them start the music."

"Right – from the beginning."

As they both had hoped, the instructor announced she would conduct the full session.

"We got our wish," Tom said as the music started.

"Perfect," Marlena replied.

After the aerobics session ended, Tom made the first move to continue their conversation.

"That was good," he offered. "Long sessions should be the standard."

"I agree."

As Marlena seemed to have ended her wish to talk, Tom felt he should also back off. He said nothing more as the room began to empty. The instructor seemed to always be in a hurry and was one of the first out the door, while Tom always lingered so that he was the last to leave. This day was no exception. What was different this time was that Marlena also lingered, rather than casually leaving as others left. Once the two were alone, Marlena spoke.

"I'm not always comfortable when guys are in aerobics class. A lot of them just seem to want to look at the women rather than try to seriously work out. You're different."

Tom wasn't sure how to answer but felt he needed to say something in a gentlemanly way to let Marlena know he was interested. For someone with no experience, his episode with Sue notwithstanding, he did quite well.

"You're an extremely attractive woman so it's no wonder men want to look at you."

The innocent and sincere way in which Tom stated his viewpoint was perfect. Marlena fully accepted the compliment without any hesitation.

"Thank you. Wow. That's so nice of you to say." It was now Marlena's turn to not know how to keep the conversation going.

Surprisingly for a man romantically inexperienced, Tom recognized he was in control. He correctly interpreted Marlena's susceptibility and surreptitiously pressed on to elicit additional information.

Glancing at the clock he noted, "Look at the time. I'd like to talk with you some more, but I need to get out of here and get to work. How about you?"

"Oh, me too," answered Marlena who added, "Will I see you tomorrow morning?"

"Definitely. I'll be here bright and early." Tom wanted to delve into personal information, but he figured everything he needed to know would come out in due time.

As they were about to leave the room, Tom put on the charm.

"After you," he said, bowing slightly and offering the door to Marlena.

Marlena smiled and accepted the offer. Instead of simply walking quickly towards the women's locker room, she strolled as an obvious offer for Tom to walk alongside her. Tom accepted the offer and they walked together silently. Though the walk was short, only about 10 steps, they both felt a new chapter in their lives could be unfolding. Each looked forward to what the following days would bring into their budding friendship by way of discovering what issues, answers, and information they would be willing to share.

The next day, after the aerobic session, Tom began the question and answer period as innocently as possible.

"Do you work around here?" he asked.

"Yes, in the college," Marlena replied. "Where do you work?"

Tom had anticipated the question and was ready with an answer that wouldn't sound too boastful. "I manage real estate along with a construction company."

The only word that stuck in Marlena's mind was 'manage', giving her the impression that this man was someone important. Yes, she was interested in developing a relationship with a man, but she didn't want someone her family would not have approved of had they still been alive. She decided to get to know Tom better on her own terms.

"What time do you get off?" she asked.

"I'm usually finished by 5:30 or 6:00."

"Me too. If you want to get together around 7 for dinner, we can meet at the café right next door. It's never crowded on Thursdays and the food is good."

"I've seen it. I'll be there." Tom immediately began to mentally prepare for the rest of his day. He didn't have anything pressing to do that would make him late, and he knew his mother wouldn't object to him going out on his first date and leaving her alone. Beyond that, he had to make sure he said and did all the right things over dinner.

Marlena also began her mental preparations. She wanted to find out everything she possibly could about this man this first time they were out together and make sure to not let her guard down. After all, she knew absolutely nothing about him other than he worked out a lot and was a manager. She was also sure he was more than 10 years her senior, and at not quite 21, she could not legally drink. If he liked to drink, that could be a problem. Plus, he was a nice-looking guy, so what about other women? That could *really* be a problem. She needed to watch out for any potential pitfalls and evaluate Tom with an open mind.

That last admonishment to herself gave her pause. It reminded her of what her adoptive father had once said.

"Open eyes are no match for an open mind," he'd told her.

Marlena had responded with, "I know it means to *think* beyond what you see on the surface. Don't worry, Dad. I'll always remember the message and do the best I can."

Marlena felt she'd do fine. Tom seemed to be a really nice guy, so all she needed to do was to gather as much information about him as she could and then take time to evaluate what he said. After all, there was no timetable and she had no need to rush into a relationship.

The evening's dinner began with small talk, mainly about the gym and working out in general. Later, Tom began to turn the conversation toward more personal revelations.

"This is the first time since before I graduated from high school that I've been to a place like this," he said, attempting to figuratively narrow the obvious age gap by referring to younger days. "I eat out but usually at a deli or restaurant."

Marlena wasted no time trying to get additional information. "Do you usually eat out by yourself?" she asked.

"By myself or with my mother." Tom had wanted to get his mother into the conversation as soon as possible and this was the perfect opportunity. He then stretched the truth to a degree.

"My father died just after I graduated high school so I've been making sure Mother is alright."

He didn't want to let on that his mother was perfectly alright to the point where she was the head of the household. She was also the true manager and the owner of the business he'd alluded to as the one he managed.

Furthering the coverup, he added, "I've been so busy with work that I haven't had much time for socializing. Until I decided to start going to the gym, my daily routine has always been working, eating, and sleeping. That's it."

Marlena could scarcely believe what she was hearing. She thought to herself, "How could this guy possibly be an eligible bachelor at his age? Wait – I don't know his age." She then decided to use a roundabout method to discover Tom's approximate age before giving him access to hers.

"When did you graduate?" she asked.

Tom knew this was the first big hurdle he couldn't fudge, so he simply let it fly. "I graduated from Chattle High School in 1967. It's a private school a few hours away from here." He watched for a negative reaction from Marlena, but all she did was respond.

"I graduated in 1986." Like Tom, she watched for a negative reaction but saw none from him.

Both were now confident that age would not be a factor as to whether the relationship would grow or not. They pressed on, with Marlena throwing caution to the wind and giving more information to this stranger than she normally would.

"Let me tell you about my past," she began. "I was adopted. I don't remember my birth parents. I was orphaned on May 31, 1970, as a result of an earthquake in Peru. I was a toddler at the time and I have no recollection of being with my parents, being orphaned, coming to the United States, or being adopted. It may not have been a legal adoption, because my parents never went into details about it. I don't know how they were able to get it done, but they must have known what they were doing because I've never had any kind of identification problem."

Tom knew of the catastrophe and said, "Yes, I remember reading about that earthquake."

Marlena continued her story. "Anyway, they arbitrarily chose February 29th, 1968 as my birth date because everyone thought I looked about two and a half by the time they adopted me on the first of September in 1970. Two and a half years earlier than September 1st is March 1st, but because it was a leap year, they backed it up to leap day, 1968. They thought it would be a great way to celebrate me."

Marlena paused for reflection then continued.

"The only thing I kept from Peru is my name. They said the only language I knew was some Spanish and I told everyone 'mi Nombre es Marlena' when they asked me my name in Spanish. Mom and Dad thought using that name would be a perfect way to celebrate my heritage. That's why I don't let anyone change the pronunciation or the spelling."

Marlena paused again before adding wistfully, "I would love to go back there one day."

For Tom, this information potentially gave him room to maneuver his wants to intermingle with hers. He blurted out, "Other than when I was away at school, the only place I've ever traveled to is England. I wouldn't mind visiting South America myself."

Thinking that he'd perhaps been too forward, Tom retreated somewhat. "Maybe one day I'll decide to travel again. You just never know."

Instead of being upset at the travel reference, Marlena was intrigued. "You shouldn't get stuck on someday doing things. If you can afford to go you should take the time and go."

Tom felt Marlena was opening the door wide enough for him to make a direct pass, but he was reluctant to do so on such a large scale. He chose to see if he could give her enough room to see if she would try to encourage him to make an offer.

"I can afford to go pretty much anytime," he said evenly in an attempt to make his statement sound matter-of-fact rather than boastful. "Maybe I should start thinking about it. The first thing I need to do is to renew my passport. I know the one I used for England expired years ago."

Marlena was now trapped in the cat and mouse game. She wanted to get more involved with Tom, but her lack of experience with men had her groping for the correct way to go about it. Unbeknownst to her, she was relying on the fox to protect the henhouse. Her next statements showed just how much she had succumbed to attraction without paying sufficient attention to realities. Her eyes were wide open but her mind had closed the door on anything resembling caution. She made the decision to open up even more to Tom.

"I've done some traveling, but only because my Dad's job kept moving him from place to place. Mom and I had to tag along wherever he wound up. They both kept after me to watch out for getting involved with the wrong people, so I made up my mind a long time ago that I would always watch my step. So far, I've been like you. Not dating, I mean. I've been on my own since just after high school when both my parents died and all I've done is complete two years of college. I'm working now to save enough to continue toward a bachelor's degree in maybe a year or two."

Marlena paused to decide whether she'd said enough or too much, but Tom made the decision for her by not responding. She continued.

"The best possible thing that could happen for me is to get into a situation where I'm dealing with someone who wants the same kind of life I dream of. I want to have a nice family and that's going to take meeting the right kind of man."

Tom was amazed. Here before him was a young attractive woman

114

openly laying everything he wanted right on the line. He lost all sense of strategy and fell in line with the mood of the conversation.

"I'd say we're both looking for the same things," he told her before boldly adding, "I've been seriously thinking about settling down and having a family. You seem like you'd be the perfect woman for any man."

A more experienced woman would have held up a huge stop sign, but Marlena had been swept off her feet. She'd decided to follow Tom wherever he wanted to lead her. She stopped just short of saying something like, "All you have to do is ask".

Instead, she replied, "That sounds nice. I'm glad we're looking for the same things."

Missing from the equation were in-depth background checks and any kind of amorous actions by either one of them. Their entire relationship was based on each admitting they wanted the same kind of things. Foolishly, they both decided to go for broke and each began to mentally inch toward marriage during their first date. Tom, whose main wish for a relationship was to please his mother, still had to overcome the problem of having to produce a child without the benefit of sexual relations. He figured he'd be able to get around that by giving Marlena the kind of life she wanted and convincing her to be artificially inseminated. Of course, his mother could never be told about it – she would never stand for that kind of descendant. Plus, he needed to avoid letting his mother know Marlena had been adopted, which would also be a huge issue for her. He figured that any other potential loose ends could be taken care of as long as he convinced Marlena to accept his way of handling his mother.

Tom wasn't aware that Marlena also had hang-ups, but he would have been delighted to know her attitude would fit quite well into his situation. Her mother and father had shielded her from boys all her life. She was still a virgin and had programmed herself to take no action on the desires that her feminine hormones elicited from within her body.

Given their individual feelings and experiences, it was no surprise that at the end of the meal when they parted ways, they shook hands and, with their free left hands, gave each other a lukewarm but friendly hug. It was as if their right arms represented a barrier that shielded each from physically getting to know one another. Neither even gave a thought to exchanging a kiss.

The non-existence of romance became their norm. Tom had only been kissed in an amorous way by Sue and that episode had turned out badly once his mother got involved. Marlena, on the other hand, had never been kissed. Beyond that, their attitudes regarding sexual relations were non-issues as neither felt any kind of inclination to make a move in that direction.

Tom put his master plan into motion during their second date. He began to display - not flaunt – the fact that he was financially well off. He also began to feed information to Marlena about his mother and said it was best to wait before introducing them to one another. He mentioned that his mother could be pushy and always wanted things done her way. He made it plain that he had everything under control and all it would take to make things right was for both of them was to be patient.

What made waiting easy for Marlena was the day Tom took her to his home when he knew for certain his mother would not be there. Seeing the house is what truly sealed the deal for Marlena. She'd never been in such a lovely home before and was ready to say yes to marriage even before Tom worked up the nerve to officially pop the question. Finally, taking what he knew about Marlena into consideration, he clumsily asked for her hand in marriage after little more than a month.

He told her, "If you say yes to marrying me, I would love for us to get married in Peru. We could fly there and get married and stay for about a week."

Marlena was all for it. "Oh yes," she said. "I already applied for a passport. I was hoping you would ask me and I knew you wanted to travel too, so I started getting prepared."

"I applied to get mine updated the day after we first spoke," Tom answered. "I received the new one last week."

Things were working out perfectly for Tom, so he kept pushing. He wanted any potential delays to be identified and overcome as soon as possible.

"I'll start making all the arrangements," he said. "You'll be able to quit that job and give up that apartment. Of course, as I told you, we have to be married first."

Realizing he had proposed without a ring he added, "Actually, we need to go ring shopping first."

After 2 weeks, their to-do list was almost complete. Rings had been purchased, Marlena had received her passport, airline tickets had been purchased, hotel reservations made and wardrobes had been readied. Tom convinced his mother that he should go on vacation after not having one for over 20 years. Finally, only two of the most important tasks remained to get done.

First, Tom had gotten engaged to someone his mother didn't know, and secondly, he had no idea about how to go about getting married in a foreign country.

As for the first problem, Tom decided to continue the ruse about taking a vacation and keeping his mother in the dark until the deed was done. He reasoned that she would simply have to accept whomever he introduced as his wife.

The second problem was more of an issue. Tom was vaguely aware of marriage legalities in the United States. He'd heard of marriage licenses, blood tests, registration and marriage officials, but was clueless about how marriages were arranged and performed in Peru. He visited the library and started researching on his own instead of consulting an official source.

It didn't take him long to find a section in an encyclopedia about Peruvian marriages that piqued his interest and showed just how insincere his proposal to Marlena actually was. It read in part that church marriages in Peru are not legal without a civil ceremony. That would put Tom firmly in control if he arranged for a church marriage only and didn't let Marlena know about the need for a civil ceremony. He would have that to fall back on in case the relationship went sour. Later on, if everything worked to perfection, having a private ceremony in the United States to make it legal would be little more than a formality.

Tom realized then he had a latent desire to be in control, much the same as his mother liked to be in control. It made him feel powerful and that felt good. Armed with this new-found power, he figured he only needed to find a clergyman in Peru who would perform a church marriage ceremony without questioning whether a civil ceremony had been performed. Realizing that money would likely be enough to take care of whatever convincing was necessary, he planned to carry enough cash to satisfy all his needs.

Tom's plotting and planning worked to perfection. He took care of all the arrangements and spared no expense. Their round-trip tickets were in first class. Their room was in a lavish hotel with double beds. Most importantly for him, he had a fortuitous meeting with the right person who was able to schedule the primary purpose of the trip – a sham of a marriage.

The marriage service was performed in a little church near Lima, Peru where the clergyman spoke a little English and officiated the service for a lot of money. Even had Tom not been aware of the difference between religious and civil marriage laws in Peru, he would have questioned the validity of the marriage. He thought it was too quick and haphazard to have anyone believe it would be deemed legal in the United States.

Marlena had no qualms with any of the goings-on. She happily went along with everything that Tom planned as if she was on a never-ending magic carpet ride. In fact, she was so happy that, while she felt she was ready for it, she wasn't consumed by the expectation of traditional marriage consummation that evening. Since they'd already been cohabiting the same room, albeit in separate beds, she didn't feel any pressure to become more amorous than they'd previously been. She relaxed and waited for Tom to make the first move.

Tom had been apprehensive that Marlena would expect him to make love this night, but his philosophy about sex had not changed. While he now had the right to make love, he still didn't have the will to encourage it.

When Marlena went about her normal routine and got into her own bed, Tom felt as if his power over her had increased tenfold. He figured he'd be able to discuss his impotence and infertility with her at some point fairly soon. After all, she wasn't taking care of her wifely duties by choosing to sleep in a separate bed, so she couldn't blame him if he insisted on artificial insemination. In doing so, she could give him the child he needed without doing the one thing normally necessary, which was to have sex with him. This would make their marriage purely one of convenience and material things with no romance whatsoever. That kind of setup seemed fine to Tom. Unfortunately, he didn't realize his reasoning was warped and that his way of thinking was setting the stage for Marlena to feel used.

Tom decided he would wait until they were settled under the same roof with his mother before discussing children with Marlena. He felt like he was in charge but not so much in charge that he was confident he could simply dictate his strategy immediately to Marlena and have her accept it.

As for his mother, he had to soothe any objections she might have for his choice of a wife by producing a grandchild for her quickly. He knew that the bottom line for what was most important to her at this point in her life was for her to see the beginning of a new Purlmen generation. That thought remained in his mind as they completed their stay in Peru and traveled back home.

Home. Tom hadn't thought about how best to introduce his mother and his wife to each other. He was fearful, no doubt about it. Not at how his mother would feel in the long run, but just that initial shock. He could beat around the bush and attempt to ease Marlena into the household, but on second thought, that would reduce the feelings of power and control he had gained. No, he would call his mother out of courtesy once back in town and tell her he'd gotten happily married to an attractive young lady named Marlena and that they'd be home soon. Buoyed up by this thought, Tom began to prep Marlena after the jet had landed and they'd taxied to the gate. He felt he had the perfect plan.

"I'm going to call Mother as soon as I can get to a phone booth. She'll be shocked, but it will be a good shock. She knows we've been dating, but I never told her how serious we'd gotten. I wanted our marriage to be a total surprise."

Marlena timidly asked, "Do you think she'll like me?"

Tom cautioned, "She won't act like it at first, but it will be my fault because I kept it from her. Don't worry, as sweet as you are, it won't take long for the two of you to get along just fine."

Tom's assurance alleviated Marlena's fears and she relaxed. She felt she should just be herself, trust Tom, and all would be well. After they'd retrieved their luggage, they went directly to a pay phone so Tom could make the call. Marlena was at his side.

He deliberately dialed an incorrect number and quickly hung up the phone before reporting to Marlena, "The number's busy, she must be on the phone."

Knowing he didn't want Marlena around during this first conversation, he asked her to go get fountain drinks, hoping he could reach his mother out of Marlena's earshot. As soon as Marlena left, he redialed using the correct number. The phone rang and his mother answered almost immediately as if she anticipated a call.

"Hello?"

The sound of his mother's voice caused Tom to take a deep breath as he hoped he could quickly give her the right amount of information in just the right way to make Marlena's assimilation into the family as smooth as possible.

"Mother, I'm back and I've got a big surprise for you." Tom waited for a response from his mother before he continued.

"I was waiting for a call from a plumber. He was supposed to give me a quote to replace the outside faucet." Elizabeth now addressed Tom's statement. "What kind of surprise?"

In a measured tone and as if from script Tom stated, "Our future is now. I have a great looking young wife who is sure to make both of us happy."

Tom expected a verbal response from his mother, but there was nothing but silence. He was forced to continue to speak.

"We'll be home in about a half-hour. Do you want me to pick up anything or is there something there for us to eat? We didn't eat during the flight, so we're both hungry."

Still no response from his mother so Tom made another attempt to elicit conversation.

"We could all go to dinner," he offered.

Elizabeth finally spoke. "Why did you tell me you were going on vacation if you were going away on a honeymoon?" she challenged. Before Tom could answer, she quickly added, "Did you get married before or after you left?"

Tom backtracked to fill in a few blanks. "It's the lady I told you I was dating. Mother. We got married when we went away. I wanted it to be a big surprise. Her name is Marlena. She's young and quite attractive. When you see her, you won't believe how perfect she is for me."

Marlena returned with their fountain drinks just in time to hear Tom's last remarks. She smiled. Tom returned the smile as he heard Elizabeth's reply.

"I'll decide *that* on my own when I meet her, Tom."

"Sure, Mother. Now do you want me to bring something or are we going out for dinner?"

"You can stop at the deli and get whatever you want. I want a pastrami sandwich. I'll see you when you get here."

"Okay, it will be in about an hour or so."

Elizabeth tried to maintain her feelings at an even keel, but she was vacillating between a delicate balance of disappointment and anger at not having been a part of the marriage ceremony versus exuberance that the marriage had finally happened. However, it didn't take long for that see-saw to tilt to the side of leaning heavily toward being excited to meet her daughter-in-law. Rather than being able to focus on things to say to admonish Tom for his elopement, she began to concentrate on Marlena.

"Mar-LAY-nuh," Elizabeth spoke the name aloud slowly and phonetically to herself to get a feel for it. The name sounded like it was Spanish to Elizabeth, but she quickly assured herself that Tom would not just marry someone without knowing the person's family history and heritage, given the importance she'd always put in the Purlmen family history. She reasoned that the given name was just a name and that the most important thing was the person and family it represented.

Elizabeth interrupted her thoughts about what her daughter-in-law might be like by forcing herself to focus on things she needed to do. She showered, changed clothes, set the table, brewed coffee, and busied herself by doing some light dusting. She did her best to avoid thinking about questions she wanted to ask Tom and Marlena about marrying the way they did because she knew she'd try to answer every question she had in her mind on her own.

"I never even met the woman," she thought to herself.

Elizabeth felt a flush of anger at not only the thought but also in the knowledge that she'd already slipped and let herself get caught up in anxiety over the situation. She didn't want to work herself into a frenzy and not be able to give the woman a chance, whoever she happened to be.

Just as she heard Tom's car pull into the driveway, she gathered enough strength to reassure herself by thinking, "Tom's married. He's got a wife. One day I'll be a grandmother." She managed a smile. Her smile was still evident when Tom opened the door and greeted her.

"Hello Mother, meet Marlena," Tom said.

Elizabeth said nothing to Tom but rather looked behind him at Marlena with disbelief. That this attractive young - that is, *very* young woman was Tom's wife was shocking. Hiding her astonishment as best she could, she greeted Marlena warmly.

"I'm so glad to meet you, Marlena."

Marlena replied, "Oh Mrs. Purlmen, I'm glad to finally meet you too."

Elizabeth had long ago decided how her daughter-in-law should address her.

"Please call me Mother," she said. "We're a family now."

"All right Mother," Marlena replied.

The two women instantly bonded and conversed as if they'd known each other for years, which amazed Tom and made him unsure of how he should respond to the situation. He began to feel somewhat awkward and out of place standing there with them. But for the fact he had the bag of sandwiches in his hand, he would have made up some excuse to leave immediately. The food gave him the crutch he needed to add something worthwhile to the conversation.

"Well, let's eat," he said, hoping he wasn't going to get caught up in what he felt would become a for-females-only meeting of the minds.

Resuming her take-charge attitude, Elizabeth thwarted Tom's effort.

"What threshold did you carry Marlena over, Tom?" she asked in a threatening way.

Tom had forgotten about the threshold carry and hadn't completed the tradition. He didn't want to lie and say he'd already done it because it would have been one more thing his mother would not have been a part of. He knew he was cornered. He hesitated while contemplating a decent answer.

Marlena came to the rescue. "Oh mother, he has food to carry and no one has a camera handy to take a picture. We can do it later or tomorrow. Right now, we're starved."

Elizabeth would never have accepted such an answer from Tom, but her wish to bond with her new daughter-in-law allowed her to treat Marlena's statement as a sufficient answer. So sufficient in fact that not only was the threshold carry not accomplished that day, it was never again even mentioned. This was the first of many things Elizabeth accepted from Marlena that she never would have accepted from Tom, but at first, only he recognized that fact.

Tom had gone from being his mother's son to becoming his mother's daughter-in-law's husband within a few minutes of introducing his wife to his mother. He felt a twinge of jealousy over their budding relationship. He'd never felt that way about his mother's dealings with anyone before, but he did everything he could to suppress any outward show of this new emotion. Accordingly, he witnessed examples of this brand-new mother and daughter-in-law bond practically every day. They seemed to never run out of topics for discussion or to get tired of being together.

Tom believed the only thing with the potential to elevate his importance would be for Marlena to become pregnant. Even though a pregnant Marlena would command a lot of attention, he would be the 'Lord and Master' of the household, and if he had that status, the bonding of Mother and Marlena wouldn't matter so much. A pregnant woman naturally gets special attention, and the expectant father can easily accept the fact without being jealous. For all intents and purposes, he is content to be proud and can bask in the glory associated with being a father-to-be. That fact weighed heavily on Tom's mind every day. It caused him to think more and more about how he would have to become a father-to-be without the ability to perform any of the requisite duties.

Tom figured it wouldn't be long before his mother would begin to drop subtle and, knowing her, not so subtle hints about wanting an heir. So far, the only move Tom made toward that end was to revisit his doctor for a full physical exam. The results were similar to the previous ones, only they were becoming progressively worse.

Tom fully accepted the prognosis and faced up to his predicament. He was not in good physical condition anymore and he would never be able to father a child. His only hope was to at least *appear* to become a father by convincing Marlena to undergo artificial insemination. That knowledge made Tom know he was at the base of a steep uphill climb, but climb the hill he must.

5 Marital Miss

Over the next 2 months, the Purlmens' household became one of outward routine with an undercurrent of unanswered questions brewing beneath a seemingly peaceful surface. Tom had maintained his own bedroom, which was quite full of his belongings. Marlena settled into the spare bedroom adjacent to Tom's. Elizabeth silently accepted what she felt was a curiosity by assuring herself the two likely shared the same bed during the wee hours of the night, but it certainly did seem like a strange arrangement to her. Strange behavior or not, at this point in her life she longed for a grandchild so much that she didn't care how they went about their love life. Elizabeth simply wanted to hear that a baby was on the way. Accordingly, she dropped the subtle and not so subtle hints that Tom had predicted she would, while watching and listening for signs of pregnancy. Sadly, she detected no positive clues at all.

For Tom, those 2 months represented a period of uneasiness. He almost worried himself sick pondering his best course of action to satisfy his mother's need, which he knew was centered on Marlena having his child. That is, *appearing* to have his child. With his inability to biologically father a child and his deteriorating health issues in general, he needed to approach Marlena at the right time and in the right way to get things moving in the right direction.

Marlena's 2 months had her in a world where she continually felt more and more like a daughter to her mother-in-law, which was great, but far too much like a little sister to her husband, which was a curiosity, to say the least. The ongoing absence of affection, public or private, became more of an expected norm than an overlooked function with each passing day.

It hadn't been lost on Marlena that Elizabeth wanted grandchildren – at least one grandchild – and the hints to that effect were made quite often. However, Marlena's inexperience with just how to go about getting Tom to become more amorous had her stymied. She'd always felt lovemaking would 'just happen' with married people, but when it was not forthcoming, she reasoned that it could be that some well-to-do folks operated under their own set of whims and rules.

The realization that all persons and their attitudes about all things are as varied as each is an individual is often difficult to grasp, but the plain truth is that all men and women are unique unto themselves. Each person operates from within their own mind to react to, for, and about the world around them. For Marlena, this was made apparent to her when her well-to-do theory was destroyed on the two-month anniversary of their marriage. As a ruse, Tom suggested they go out to dinner alone that evening in celebration of the day, but in reality, he needed to be well out of his mother's presence to discuss things with his wife.

He started with small talk over dinner, then plied her with the possibility of maybe taking a cruise or overseas vacation the next year for their first marriage celebration. In general, he did all he could think of to put her in a cheerful mood. Then, to keep the conversation as secretive as possible, he moved to a seat closer to Marlena, made sure he had his subtle lies in order, and then lowered the boom.

"I guess you're wondering why our marriage hasn't been consummated," he began.

"Yes."

Marlena's one-word answer wasn't what Tom had hoped for. He'd wanted to get more of a feel for Marlena's state of mind about the subject, but her silence forced him to supply all the input. He continued.

"I found out I had some health issues just after we got back from Peru," he lied. Then, to validate his lie, he offered the truth. "I'm looking and feeling older by the day. I don't have the strength I used to have. I don't have the urge to work out anymore to stay fit."

Marlena still said nothing, but Tom knew she was intently listening to his every word.

Tom continued his argument. "My bad health has made me impotent, and the doctor said I wouldn't be able to have children on my own. He then told me that a good alternative is for you to be artificially inseminated. No one would ever know except us."

Tom paused for a moment and then added, "Especially not Mother. She would never stand for it."

Tom had a flashback to when his mother had angrily banished Molly and Sue from the house and quickly warned, "She would throw us both out of the house."

Marlena was shocked by Tom's statements in general, but she was appalled by the suggestion of artificial insemination. Not being able to remember or have any knowledge of her biological parents had always been a sore spot for her. On top of that, she'd lost her adoptive parents. At this juncture, she wanted no part of becoming pregnant by an unknown individual to produce what she'd heard others call a test tube baby. Plus, she didn't like the nerve of Tom worrying so much about Mother's reaction being that she would never stand for it. Why would he think that *she* herself would stand for it? Marlena was flabbergasted and immediately rejected the suggestion.

"I'm not doing that, Tom. If your doctor says you have a problem, then the first thing we need to do is get a second opinion. Maybe a specialist can help."

Marlena thought for a moment and added, "People don't get married and then, without ever sleeping together, decide on artificial insemination in just 2 months. That doesn't make any sense to me."

Marlena's last remark provided a segue for her to slightly alter the gist of the conversation. "By the way," she asked, "When *are* we going to at least sleep together and give things a try?"

Tom had now been pushed into a defensive position and he knew he had to get out of the corner he'd been painted into. Instead of answering the question directly, he went out on his own tangent.

"We have a good relationship, a beautiful home, money, and Mother loves you. Why wouldn't you do everything possible to keep things the way they are?"

Marlena knew her question had been ignored but she also realized what Tom said was true. Her circumstances were great financially, but the marriage lacked affection and now what she felt should be the correct way to start a family. While inwardly she didn't think there was any way she would ever change her mind about childbearing, she nevertheless allowed Tom to continue by not answering.

He did just that. "You know Mother wants you to have a baby. She's been tossing hints for weeks. Something has got to happen soon and the quickest way is for you to agree to artificial insemination."

"You're right about Mother wanting me to get pregnant, I know that," Marlena answered. "What I don't know is how you think you can keep something like artificial insemination hidden forever. You say you know she wouldn't stand for it, right? Well, I don't think you know her as well as you think you do. Anyway, I still think we should go to another doctor first to get that second opinion. If the second doctor says the same thing, then it's time to bring Mother into the conversation. If she knows there's a problem, she'll be understanding, but if we go through with artificial insemination without telling her, we'll just be living a big fat ugly lie."

Tom quickly restated his feelings about probable reactions from his mother regarding her descendants. "There is no way we could ever tell her about artificial insemination. There'd be some serious ramifications if she ever found out. I know she would throw both of us out. Not only that, I believe she would probably disown us."

"I don't think she would. Not if she knows the truth from the start."

"I guarantee she would," Tom hastily responded.

The need to convince Marlena of the urgency of her becoming pregnant was foremost in Tom's mind. He argued further.

"Marlena, I don't think this can go on for much longer without Mother asking direct questions."

"Maybe it's time she did."

"Listen, Marlena," he answered. "I'm talking about what's best for us and the family. Having a baby is important to us, but it's way more important to Mother.

After making that statement, Tom felt emboldened enough to raise the ante of his arguments by bringing more ugliness into the discussion.

Leaning closer to Marlena's ear he whispered, "If we don't have a child, you know she'll blame you."

Marlena pulled away from Tom so she could turn her head and stare into his eyes. The statement hurt her not only for the implication that Mother would not be reasonable enough to accept Tom's shortcomings, but also because Tom was hinting that he could put a spin on the situation that would point to her, rather than him, as the problem. Not wishing to escalate what was becoming a volatile situation, she decided it was time to try to calm things down.

"Tom, I think the best thing to do right now is to give each other some space so we can evaluate how things stand between us. Let's just go home and try to relax."

Marlena had spoken slowly and deliberately, but her mind was racing. She thought to herself, "How could something so perfect get so wrong so quickly?"

She began to think about what she could do to maintain a comfort zone away from Tom to avoid the potential of being nagged by him on an ongoing basis. Her first idea was to get a job away from the family business. By doing so, she would not have to depend on her new family's wealth. She decided to check the want ads the first chance she got. Then, even if this "need to have a baby" issue was never resolved, she would still have something to fall back on, just in case.

Tom interrupted Marlena's thoughts with, "Sure, let's go home. We can get through this okay. We just need to go about it the right way."

Now that Tom had broken the ice on his need to have Marlena get artificially inseminated, he wanted to include it in every conversation he and Marlena had outside of Elizabeth's presence. As a matter of fact, he was determined to the point of developing a strategy that included understanding just how to use some of Marlena's own words to his advantage. He began during their drive home that night.

"You know," he began, "I think you're right about seeing another doctor or a specialist. Maybe there is something the first doctor overlooked. Tomorrow's Monday. I'll do some checking around, probably in Calbert. They've got a big medical center there, so I'm sure they've got some of every kind of doctor in the area."

Marlena felt better after hearing what Tom said and told him so.

"Good idea. Start with that so we can get through this thing together."

Tom heard and felt the relief in Marlena's voice, so he added, "And if all else fails, we can discuss alternatives. We just need to make sure Mother doesn't know what's going on."

Although Tom didn't mention artificial insemination as an alternative, Marlena recognized the reference. Her thoughts once again focused on trying to find a job so she could be prepared for a worst-case scenario. She decided she would go job hunting, beginning the very next day.

Tom and Marlena each left the house early Monday morning after delivering vague excuses to Elizabeth. They went their separate ways and both found success fairly rapidly. Tom located a fertility specialist by the name of Dr. Brandon. He anticipated this new doctor would confirm the previous doctor's findings and would then want to meet with them both. Tom figured that the follow-up meeting would be a perfect opportunity to have the doctor assist him in convincing Marlena that artificial insemination was their best course of action.

Marlena was selected on the spot at the third company she visited that morning. It was the branch office of a large new firm called VECTICOM. She was given a start date of Wednesday of the following week. The initial requirement was for her to travel to the main office and complete a 3-day course. Marlena was elated. The main office was in Branchport, about 400 miles away. She'd certainly be able to relax and feel better by taking a flight there, attending class and learning new things, without having to listen to Tom's incessantly trying to persuade her to undergo artificial insemination.

That evening was one of all smiles in the household, with Elizabeth dropping various baby hints and Tom and Marlena holding onto their separate secrets for discussion when they were alone. Tom and Marlena were upbeat because each felt they'd had a successful day. Elizabeth's cheerfulness was the result of the good vibrations generated by the others' attitudes. She had a feeling that this might be the day she'd hear that Marlena was pregnant, but time wore on with no such announcement.

Finally, Elizabeth gave up waiting to hear good news about a baby, at least for the evening. She was still curious about why they had both been so happy but figured they were still getting used to each other and they wanted to be alone. Then again, it could be they *thought* Marlena was pregnant but wanted to be sure before making an announcement. That would be perfect!

Elizabeth began to think they may have already noticed early signs of pregnancy. Now she was ready to leave them so they could talk. She chose to go to bed early that night, making it easy for the others to go into the den to begin their discussion of the day's events.

Once they were alone in the den, Tom spoke first. "I saw a fertility specialist in Calbert," he reported. "His name is Dr. Brandon. He's going to be the perfect doctor for us to work with. I had a thorough examination and I'll be going back to see him Thursday for test results. I also made a follow-up appointment for both of us to see him the following Wednesday. He'll probably want to examine you too."

Marlena was happy about Tom's news, but she knew what she had to tell him would surely temper his good mood.

"That's great, Tom, but next Wednesday is no good," she began. "I was hired for a job that starts next Wednesday. The appointment will have to be on a Saturday, if they have Saturday hours."

Tom was crestfallen but bravely continued to display an outwardly cheerful demeanor.

"I don't know why you felt you needed to do that," he said. "We don't need the money and what are you going to do if you do get pregnant? Work for a few months and leave the job? You know we're set for life. You only need to continue to learn the business and be a part of the family."

Marlena countered with, "Women like to have their own jobs. It doesn't matter about pregnancy. Jobs nowadays accept women having babies, and they have programs and processes in place to handle the situation."

She didn't want to appear she was backing out of the prospect of becoming pregnant, so she added, "They probably have Saturday hours at the doctor's office. Check for the first opportunity to go so we can listen to what they have to say."

Tom had no suitable argument for Marlena's position so he accepted it as sufficient. He assumed he only needed to get her into the specialist's office to have the doctor help convince her to undergo artificial insemination. He felt his more immediate problem was having to explain Marlena's job to his mother.

"I don't think it would be a good idea to let Mother know you've got a job just yet," he told her. "Let's keep it to ourselves."

Marlena wasn't pleased with Tom's suggestion to keep her job a secret, so she asked, "Why shouldn't we tell Mother? What's she going to say? Why wouldn't she want me to get a job?"

"I'm not sure, but I don't think her reaction will be good."

"Frankly, I don't think she'll have a problem with it. The work I'll be doing deals with communication and customer service, which fits right in with things I can do for the family business. It will be fine."

"I think you should hold off on getting a job until we deal with the specialist, Marlena. Miracles do happen. Maybe you'll be pregnant within the next couple of weeks."

"Yes, and maybe not. By the way, I'll be working at that new place, VECTICOM. The branch office is here in town, but the main office is in Branchport. I have to go there to formally sign up and train for 3 days."

"I don't know how Mother is going to react to that," said Tom.

"I told you that what I will be doing will benefit the family business, Tom. Oh, and before I forget, when will all the documents come back that show we're married? If I don't have things like my new social security card, I'll have to use my maiden name when I complete the paperwork."

"I guess that stuff takes a while to come back," lied Tom, knowing full well he'd never lifted a finger to get anything whatsoever done to try to register the sham of a marriage he'd orchestrated.

Tom had forgotten all about the fake marriage so he had to quickly fabricate a cover story.

"The first time I mailed the documents," Tom said, "I forgot the stamps. Once I got the returned mail, I sent it all out again. Anyway, it's no big deal if you sign up using your maiden name. They'll have no problem updating the records later."

"Right, I know. It doesn't matter when it gets done."

"Uh-huh, now back to this job. Maybe we should just keep quiet about the job and say you're going to Branchport to visit some girlfriends for a few days. That should do it. No one would expect me to go along to help you visit with a lot of women."

"I hope you don't expect me to get in the middle of what you tell Mother if it's not the truth," Marlena warned. "My job starts a week from Wednesday and that's 10 days from now. I'll call tomorrow to book a flight. I'm certainly not going to drive for 8 or 9 hours each way."

"Okay," Tom said. "I'll think of something to tell Mother."

Marlena was frustrated by Tom's constant worry about his mother. She stood to leave the den and stated, "I'm going to go get some sleep."

Reaffirming the need for secrecy, Tom said, "Remember, we need to keep Mother out of what's going on. The only thing she wants to hear from us is that you're pregnant."

Marlena felt like shaking her head in disgust, but she instead settled on leaving the room without acknowledging Tom's statement.

Elizabeth woke the next morning earlier than she normally did. She was still in high spirits from the joy in the air the previous evening. She felt the only thing that would have created such an atmosphere was a pregnancy announcement, so she was on pins and needles as she waited for the others to get up and go downstairs for breakfast.

To wake early is great if there is something to do, but not so if one wakes early with nothing to do except sit around and get bored. That's what happened to Elizabeth. After a half-hour she could stand it no more, so she went downstairs to brew coffee.

Marlena had been listening for the sound of someone going

downstairs, and when she heard footsteps she recognized as Elizabeth's, she listened to make sure Tom didn't follow his mother downstairs. She'd already advised Tom that she was not going to back him up on that 'girlfriends in Branchport' tale, so she planned to intercept him if he tried to join his mother downstairs for a private conversation.

Tom had also been waiting to hear footsteps but his target was Marlena. He wanted to remind her to remain mum on things they'd discussed.

The stalemate ended after about 10 minutes, with Marlena making the first move. As soon as she left her room, Tom exited his room and walked with Marlena to the stairs.

"Remember, we need to keep things quiet," he said.

"I've got it all under control," answered Marlena.

"Okay then, let's look happy. Mother will have questions if we don't look like we're happy."

Marlena rolled her eyes as they descended the stairs, and found herself involuntarily smiling as she did so. She'd remembered how rolling her eyes had gotten her into trouble a few times in elementary school, and catching herself doing it now caused her to smile at what was a private joke.

When Elizabeth saw them entering the kitchen seemingly happy together, she burst into a big smile. "You both look happy and hungry," she said. "Who wants pancakes?"

"Oh, I'll make them, Mother, if that's what you both want," said Marlena.

"Sure, I do," Tom replied.

"Well..." Elizabeth said.

"You know it's no problem," Marlena told her. "I'll do it. You did most of the work already because mixing the batter is harder than anything else. Does anyone want eggs too?"

Neither answered so Marlena started working on the pancakes.

As she did, she began the discussion about her job to make sure

Tom didn't tell his tale about a girlfriend reunion.

"Mother, I only had a couple of years of college, but I've got an opportunity to work professionally in the communications field. It's at that new company in town, VECTICOM. They say I'll get plenty of training and my proficiency will increase much faster by working than by taking college courses. Their timetable is that new hires right off the street should become experts in a few months. The knowledge I gain will help with the business. The work is not supposed to be physical or stressful. I'll know for sure, beginning Wednesday of next week."

Elizabeth wanted to speak, but she felt it wasn't her place, even though the statement had been directed at her. She expected Tom to say something, but he sat with what looked to be a half-smile pasted on his face.

Marlena bailed him out with a further explanation that included the magic word.

"Tom and I talked about it. I can work even if I get pregnant, up to around 8 months. I wouldn't want to just sit around bored for 9 months anyway. I believe getting the job is the right thing to do."

Elizabeth had wanted to hear Marlena *was* pregnant without the 'if', but just hearing the word was enough to allay a negative reaction.

"Do you really want to do that?" Elizabeth asked. "Do you think it will be worth the time and trouble?"

"Yes, I do. That's why Tom and I talked about it."

Bringing Tom into the discussion made sense, as long as Tom stepped up and did the right thing. He didn't. Instead of siding with and supporting his wife, he tried to outguess what his mother was thinking. He added his thoughts on the matter to support what he believed to be his mother's true feelings.

"I don't think it's the best way to learn about our business," he said.

Tom's statement irritated Elizabeth. She'd already accepted Marlena's answer, although it took the pregnancy reference to thoroughly convince her. She mainly asked the questions she did to confirm that Marlena truly wanted to go to work. She firmly addressed her son.

"Tom, Marlena said she is going to work so she can help with the business. If she thinks it's a wise move, then I do too. She says the work isn't hard."

Elizabeth was borderline angry with Tom and let it be known with her added statement. "You should know by now that sometimes you have to do things for a business outside of the business, which is fine as long as whatever you're doing will help the business." For emphasis, Elizabeth then slowed her speech rate and added, "In other words, Tom, you're supposed to make business decisions that make sense."

Tom felt like a fool and said nothing.

By now Marlena had served everyone, and as they began eating, she and Elizabeth exchanged small talk as Tom wolfed his food down. Once all had eaten their fill, Marlena decided she'd better discuss her upcoming trip to Branchport now rather than later. She didn't want to take a chance that Tom would stumble on it too.

"Before I forget, I need to make flight reservations this morning for next week. The first few days of the job will be in the main office in Branchport. I'll get 3 days of training before coming back and working in the branch office."

This time Tom had enough sense to speak up. "Right," he said. "I'd go along, but if I did, I'd be bored for 3 days, and work here would get backed up."

"I can handle the business, Tom, if you want to go," Elizabeth said.

That was the absolute last thing Marlena wanted to have happen.

"Tom's probably right, Mother," Marlena said. "I know I'll probably have to do a lot of studying when I'm not in class. They told me during the interview that the training is intense and there are test standards I have to meet. I'll be fine traveling alone."

Breakfast ended with each one's feelings somewhat in disarray. Elizabeth wasn't pleased that Marlena was going to take the job, but after she'd heard Marlena mention pregnancy, most of her negative feelings had been neutralized.

Marlena was thankful that she'd spoken up to eliminate the tale Tom wanted to tell. Now that her job and trip were common knowledge, she only had to deal with Tom's push for artificial insemination.

Tom didn't know if he was coming or going. He wished he could handle his mother as easily as Marlena seemed to be able to. His only hope was that Marlena would soon get pregnant so he could feel elevated in status. He wanted to feel like he was more than just his mother's son.

Tom's Thursday follow-up visit with Dr. Brandon went as Tom had expected. The main point was that Tom was reconfirmed as being sterile. Dr. Brandon also repeated what Tom knew about his failing health, but Tom wouldn't allow the conversation to dwell on his state of well-being.

"I know all about my health problems," Tom said. "Let's discuss artificial insemination. I already made an appointment for this coming Wednesday so I could bring my wife in, but we need to change that to a Saturday. Are you open on Saturdays?"

"Yes, but they're usually booked up pretty far in advance," Dr. Brandon replied. "You may have to wait a few weeks."

"I don't want to wait too long to get started," Tom said.

"Hmm. Hold on. You know, now that I think about it, you may not have to wait too long," Dr. Brandon told him. "I'm pretty sure there was a cancellation for early this coming Saturday unless the receptionist found someone to fill it. Let me check."

Dr. Brandon left the office and returned a few minutes later with good news.

"You and your wife are now scheduled for this Saturday morning at 9:30," he said while handing Tom a reminder appointment card.

"That's perfect," Tom replied. He felt like he was floating on a cloud, but he kept his wits about him and used good sense to make a special request.

"Please don't mention anything about my health condition to my wife other than my being unable to be a father. This is all about artificial insemination and nothing else."

"Sure, Mr. Purlmen. I understand," Dr. Brandon assured him.

The Saturday appointment went according to Tom's plan. As per his agreement with Dr. Brandon, Tom's overall health was not reviewed, but there was a quick mention of his infertility. In accordance with Tom's wishes, artificial insemination rapidly became the preferred point of the consultation, and Dr. Brandon did a thorough job of discussing the procedure.

Marlena knew she was being pressured, but because she didn't want to fan the seeds of hostility, she listened. She did not want to flatly tell them she wasn't going to go through with it, so she used a logical approach to appease Tom.

"I'll get thoroughly tested myself on the first available Saturday," she told them and then asked the doctor, "Do you know when that will be?"

"I'll check," the doctor replied.

As soon as Dr. Brandon left the office, Tom gave Marlena a pep talk.

"This is going to work out perfectly," he said. "I believe we found the right doctor to get this done."

"He does seem to be a good doctor," Marlena agreed without elaborating. She just wanted to leave the office.

Dr. Brandon returned and spoke to Marlena as he handed her a reminder card. "I'll be seeing you 4 weeks from today at 10 a.m. Okay?"

"That will be fine," answered Marlena.

Tom rose and shook the doctor's hand.

"Thanks, doctor," he said.

"Thank you. Both of you," Dr. Brandon replied.

As they left the doctor's office, Marlena was uneasy about what her best course of action should be. Things were moving rapidly in a direction she was sure she would ultimately reject, but the pressure she was under made it difficult to make an intelligent decision. She wished her class in Branchport was to start on Monday so she could have some free time right away from Tom, but she'd already been scheduled for Wednesday.

Because Marlena had inquired about flights so close to her travel dates, she was stuck with the limited flights that were available. Her reservations had her leaving Tuesday afternoon, and the return flight wasn't until Saturday afternoon. This would cause her to spend Friday night in Branchport rather than at home.

When Tom continued the artificial insemination discussion on the way home, Marlena was glad her return flight from Branchport would force her to stay there an additional night. Tom was incessantly talking about every good point he could think of and played up the importance of producing a grandchild for his mother.

"No matter what else happens," he was saying, "Whether you have a job or not, Mother will be so proud once you are pregnant. Do you think she likes you now? She'll go out of her way to make sure you get taken care of forever once it happens."

Tom had tried to make a convincing statement, but his move backfired. Marlena was becoming overwhelmed by the feeling of being used and fought back.

"Marriage is about more than just making Mother happy by me getting pregnant," she said. "I mean, I want to start a family, but it's supposed to be about us – all of us. I got married for marital bliss, but if getting pregnant just to appease Mother is the only goal then this is more of a marital miss."

She glared at Tom as he parked the car outside their home and firmly stated, "Let's do this the right way."

Tom knew he'd hit a nerve, but he also kept his eye on the prize.

He resolved to not mention anything about pregnancy for the remainder of the day, but he decided to continue to hammer the idea home from Sunday until the Tuesday flight time. Oh, he'd be the perfect husband and do everything he could to keep Marlena happy before she left for Branchport. Still, he needed to make her think about all the good her pregnancy would produce. He figured enough of Mother's hints and his insistence would cause Marlena to finally acquiesce to his demands. After all, what else could she do? What woman in her right mind would leave the situation she was in?

Tom woke the next morning demonstrably upbeat for a couple of reasons. The first was the knowledge that Marlena was scheduled to see Dr. Brandon for what Tom expected to be the beginning of her pregnancy. The second and more important thing was to give the illusion that all was well in his and Marlena's relationship. If there was even a trace of discord before Marlena left to go to Branchport unaccompanied for a few days, there would be some raised eyebrows.

Marlena woke the next morning looking forward to her trip, but that was only a slight diversion from pregnancy concerns. She dreaded the thought of having to listen to Tom preach to her up until flight time. She realized the best way to prevent it was to not be stuck anywhere alone with him. She did a good job Sunday. She even managed to joke about it to herself. She'd heard of the idiom 'dialogue of the deaf' in school but thought that its theme was a little farfetched. How could people have ideas so diametrically opposed that they simply refuse to even consider the other's opinion? That is, people other than politicians? Well, here she was, thoroughly immersed in that quagmire. She smiled and shook her head at the thought.

The smile about her private joke waned late Sunday morning when she found out that Monday was a going to be a different matter. Unfortunately, Tom convinced her to plan to spend the full day with him. Now all Marlena could do was to use what was left of her 1 day of Sunday freedom to prepare herself for the onslaught she knew

Monday would bring.

Tom had told Marlena he wanted a full day with her on Monday mainly because he knew his mother expected it, but also because he wanted to hammer his pregnancy message home. He wanted to discuss it Sunday too, but he could tell Marlena was avoiding him. As he continued to explore his mind for additional ammunition, he thought about his ace in the hole, namely his health. If he died, Marlena would wind up as Mother's sole heir, but he figured his mother would have an issue with that. He felt there was no way she'd want to view Marlena as having married into being the very last of the Purlmens.

Tom took his reasoning one step further. He remembered that, since his mother was the last remaining descendant of her own family, Marlena would also represent that side of the family's last descendant. It stood to reason then that the most intelligent path for Marlena to follow would be to allow for a smooth transition by becoming the parent of Mother's grandchild through artificial insemination. Tom truly believed Marlena's pathway to happiness forever was for her to see and do things his way.

Tom's flawed logic had become the catalyst for many things that were not right in the home, but as is usually the case, some of those things would wind up as positives and some as negatives. There were going to be some huge ripples in the river of life for the Purlmens as the passage of time opened doors for them that no one could ever have predicted.

6 Rainbow's End

When Norman reached high school, Molly finally relented and allowed for the skipped grade. He graduated from high school with honors. In college, he chose business management with a minor in real estate and attended the local college full time year-round. In so doing, he was able to graduate early, summa cum laude, at the age of 21. He was offered the job he sought with the firm he wanted after his first interview.

He arrived home bursting with pride. "Nana, I got accepted for the job!" he exclaimed to Molly. "I could start with them in a week if I wanted to move nearer to the main office. If not, I'll be on the waiting list behind a few other people for a position in town. I told them I would probably wait for something local."

"That's great," Molly told him, ignoring the reference to moving. She teased, "Could it be they just like the way you look in that suit?"

"Come on, Nana. They liked my resume and I was able to give them good answers to everything they threw at me. I just don't like the thought of moving. I should have told them that from the start."

"Well, I still like the suit. Hold on while I get my camera."

Molly had a sudden inspiration. It had been 21 years now since she'd stored the safe and camera. While she still wasn't comfortable at the thought of doing anything with the safe, she felt the time had come to get the film developed. She only hoped the film wasn't ruined because she had waited so long.

When she got to her closet and opened the box, she was relieved to find the camera on top of the hand towel she'd wrapped the safe in. She was glad she didn't have to look at the safe. She quickly removed the camera, closed the box, and again stored the lime shoebox in her closet.

Checking the number of remaining pictures to take, Molly saw that there were 5. She resolved to take all 5 that day and take the film herself the next day to have it developed. No way did she want Norman to see the pictures before she got a chance to sort through them. She returned to the living room and began having Norman pose.

"Alright, we need to take 5 pictures so we can use up all this film," she said.

Norman noticed the camera. He knew immediately it wasn't the one he owned or the one he'd seen Molly use.

"Hey, Nana. Is that a new camera?" he asked.

Molly hadn't anticipated the question but took it in stride.

"No, it's an old one I haven't used in years. I need to finish up the film. You just stand there. Now smile. Turn left. Now turn right. Smile. Give me a better smile..."

When all the film was used, Molly turned to take the camera back to her room. Norman was surprised she hadn't asked him to take it to be developed, so he volunteered.

"Do you want me to take the film to be developed?" he called after her.

"No, I'll do it tomorrow. Right now, I want to talk to you about something. I'll be right back."

Molly was glad she had thought about how to decline Norman's offer to get the film developed. While she'd told him about her own mother and father, she'd never before shared any information regarding her missing heirloom picture with him. Thinking about the safe, the camera, and the pictures it held, coupled with Norman's excitement over his dream job, inspired her to speak about what she had long ago discussed with Aunt Bernice. She wanted to see if she could get Norman interested enough in the heirloom picture to at least travel to Branchport to see if someone from her father's family had a copy.

When Molly returned, she opened the special subject that was near and dear to her heart. "I used to have a picture of my mother and father at their wedding. It only had them, their parents, and Aunt Bernice in it. I just can't find it now."

Norman asked, "What happened to it?"

"I'm not sure. The thing of it is, mine was just a copy that my mother had. My father took the original with him when he left."

Molly paused to give Norman a chance to comment, but he remained silent.

"Aunt Bernice told me they lived in Branchport, but the last she'd heard from any of them had to be more than 40 years ago. I wanted to try to see if they kept the picture, but Aunt Bernice told me it was probably of no use, so I left it alone."

This time Norman did speak. "We can try to find out. I don't need to go to work tomorrow. I already told Duane at the construction site that I needed to go for a job interview and he might not see me until Monday. Maybe never again if I get the job. Do you want me to take you to Branchport so we can start searching?"

"Well, I don't know," Molly replied. "It's almost a 5-hour drive to get there and that's a long time for me. Plus, we might have to stay overnight for a couple of days."

Molly hadn't been turned off by the drive or overnight stay. She just didn't want to be an integral part of the photo search that could become a fruitless effort. She preferred to have Norman make the trip and do the best he could do. She would rather stay home and wait for the news, good or bad, but she didn't want to just come out and say it. While she was not superstitious, she was conscious of the level of excitement and heightened expectations a physical search would create if she played an active part. That being the case, she made her pitch to Norman.

"I was hoping you'd like to go there and try to find it by yourself."

Norman jumped at the chance without a moment's hesitation. "Sure, Nana. Give me all the information you have and I'll leave tomorrow."

"You probably already know just about as much as I do, Norman."

Norman recited information as he remembered it. "I know your father's name – Henry Hurley, and you said he lived in Branchport."

"Right," answered Molly. "You know, I don't believe I ever told you his middle name. It's Horace." She thought for a moment. "There are a few other things I knew that I don't remember right now. After dinner, I'll write down everything I can think of. I'll also look through some of Aunt Bernice's things. Now that I think about it, I do believe I saw some reference to names and addresses somewhere."

"Okay, Nana. I'll leave tomorrow morning." Norman changed the subject. "Is dinner ready?"

"I'll have it ready in a half-hour. Why don't you change out of that nice suit and get into something comfortable? You have a long trip ahead of you tomorrow."

After dinner, Molly got busy with pad and pen to jot down all the information she knew and could find in Aunt Bernice's things. There wasn't much she could write down and she wasn't very confident what little she had would be enough. She thought for a moment that maybe she should tell Norman to forget about making the trip. That moment passed as she knew she'd always have a lingering doubt about whether she was making the correct decision if she canceled. In order to get some closure, she knew an attempt to connect to her past would have to be made. With that in mind, she slept peacefully that night.

The next morning after breakfast, she handed the list of facts to Norman. He looked it over and then read everything aloud.

"Henry Horace Hurley born July 31, 1907, died December 23, 1947.

Got married to Alice Marbury. Married name Alice Hurley, who was about 10 years older than Henry.

She had a daughter, Elaine Marbury who was born November 24, 1921.

They lived on 320 Dupont Street in Branchport."

"Right, that's all the information I have," said Molly.

"I think this will be easy if any of them or their relatives still live there," Norman reasoned.

Molly tried to temper some of Norman's confidence with what she figured might be a problem. "Well, I have to tell you this - Aunt Bernice didn't like Alice Marbury's attitude."

"Aw, Nana. People change. Usually, when people grow older, they also grow some sense. You told me that before."

Molly couldn't deny what she'd told Norman about people changing, but the memory of Aunt Bernice's outburst aimed at Alice Marbury years ago lingered on. But maybe, just maybe, the woman's attitude had finally changed for the better. With that possibility in mind, Molly agreed with what she'd previously told Norman.

"Yes, that's right, Norman. Most people grow older and grow some sense," she repeated. "You have a safe trip. Stay as long as you have to. When are you supposed to report to work?"

"Monday, at the old job. Remember, I said I'm not going to take the job out of town. I'll just stay on the waiting list for the local company and work construction until they call. I'll stop in to let them know my decision before I leave. I'll only be gone a couple of days at the most. I'll see you no later than sometime Sunday."

They exchanged hugs.

"Do you want me to pack a lunch? It'll be better than something you grab along the way."

"I'll be fine Nana. I'm ready to get started. This should be fun."

"Alright. I'll see you Sunday."

"See you Sunday."

Molly watched as he drove off, hoping with all her heart that Norman would find someone from the family who had the picture. She had long ago suppressed how much it meant to her, but now that an attempt was being made to retrieve it, the emptiness she felt without it returned. The perfect outcome would be for Norman to return with the photo in hand. The thought of that happening buoyed her spirits and made her smile.

Molly felt so good now that she didn't hesitate to retrieve the camera and remove the film. She took it to a retail store that advertised one-hour film processing. When she returned hours later and picked up the packet of pictures, she immediately stuffed it into her handbag. She wanted to wait until she was home before viewing them.

Once home, Molly first saw and admired the photos of Norman. After setting those aside, she leafed through the rest of the photos and paused to look at any that didn't include anyone from the Purlmen family. She then added each one to the pile that had Norman's photos. Now down to the last 5 pictures, she studied each one.

What she saw was like being transported back more than 20 years. Two of the pictures were of only the Purlmen family and they looked just as she remembered them, except Tom was obviously camera-shy. Although he'd held his head down in both pictures, she could see Norman's resemblance to the image.

The final 3 photos included herself and Sue along with the Purlmens. The first 2 were not very good because the picture was snapped while everyone was doing something that was not photogenic. The last one, however, would have done the best of photographers proud. The pose, expression, and clarity of everyone in that one was excellent. Everyone, even Tom, was looking straight at the camera.

Initially, Molly zeroed on Sue, who looked as if she'd been forced to take a mug shot under duress. Then her eyes widened as she focused on Tom. While Norman resembled Tom in the other pictures, she was unprepared for how much he looked like the image of Tom Purlmen in this last one.

Molly closed her eyes and thought about Norman posing the same way Tom had and then looked again at the photo. If ever the idiom "spitting image" needed an example, Norman, when compared to Tom's likeness in the photo, was just about the perfect fit.

Molly knew then that if the time ever came for any of the Purlmens to see Norman, no matter how cloudy their memory of the way Tom looked when he was Norman's age, the picture would provide the visual proof of heredity. Molly knew it was a good thing, but in a way, it was also sad. She felt that no man in his right mind would refuse to claim a paternal relationship with his son, especially one who looks as much like his father as Norman does. That would mean Tom Purlmen would immediately snatch Norman away.

Not that Molly would fight it. No, she couldn't and wouldn't. Norman was a Purlmen, and Sue had spoken of aspirations to get Tom Purlmen involved in Norman's life in some manner or fashion. It was just that so many years had passed and both she and Norman had been together as a family since his birth. That would make it difficult to let go.

Molly had another thought. What if Tom Purlmen has gotten married and had other children? How would Norman be accepted after all these years? He could have multiple half-brothers and half-sisters by now, with each trying to be more important in their father's eyes than the others.

Molly forced herself to stop wondering about the unknown. She picked up the 5 photos that included the Purlmens and put them in the lime shoebox with the little safe. She then let her thoughts drift to something more pleasant, namely Norman's trip and her hope that he would find the photo she longed for.

For Norman, the road trip meant he was going to attempt to do something important for his Nana, and that always made him feel great. He resolved to do all he could do to find that picture and make his grandmother happy.

Arriving in Branchport in the early afternoon, Norman first got some lunch, then went to a phone booth to see if anyone with the last name Marbury was listed in the phone book. Finding none, he tried Hurley. Sure enough, he saw Alice Hurley, 320 Dupont Street. That's just what he hoped to see.

That was so easy it could have been done from home. Dialing the number, he got his first disappointment. The number was no longer in service. Rather than being discouraged, he bought a map of the city and found his way to 320 Dupont Street. A large truck was parked outside and workers were hauling things from the house and depositing those items in the truck. He spoke to one of the workmen.

"Hey, how are you doing? Are the people who live there moving out?"

"No," one of the men replied. "We're cleaning everything out of the house. The lady died a few weeks ago and no one from her family wanted anything saved. They live out west and they told the lawyer to get rid of everything." The man shook his head. "I don't think any of them even came to the funeral. Sad."

"That *is* sad. I traveled over 200 miles to see if there was a picture of my grandmother's parents and grandparents anywhere. Did you see any pictures in the house?"

"Yeah, there are pictures. You'd better run in there and check because they're about to get tossed. There are two boxes of them right behind the front door."

Norman rushed inside and found the boxes filled with pictures, with some in albums and a few of them framed. He moved the boxes outside and out of the workmen's way. He then checked each one for the photo he'd come for. It didn't take long for him to find one that fit the description Molly had given him. It included 7 people. There were two seated in the front, one standing behind and between, and two older couples to the left and the right. This had to be it! He felt a rush of pride and happiness at the good fortune of getting there when he did. The way the men were clearing things from the house, another hour may have been too late.

Norman spoke again to the same workman.

"I found what I was looking for, but I don't think you should throw away these other pictures. How can I get in touch with the relatives?"

"You're probably wasting your time," the man answered. "If those relatives wouldn't come to the funeral, I doubt they care about pictures, but if you like you can check with the lawyer."

The man handed Norman a card and said, "This is the lawyer's card, and when you talk to him, let him know you took the pictures. Ordinarily, stuff like that gets thrown out because no one will buy it. This other stuff gets sold or donated so he won't mind. He's a good guy."

Norman took the card and drove to a phone booth to make the call. As the workman had stated, there was no issue with Norman taking the pictures, but the lawyer wouldn't divulge information about the relatives. He told Norman he needed to clear it with his clients first.

That posed no problem for Norman. Although he could make the drive home that night and arrive quite late, he decided to stay at a hotel so he could get an early start in the morning. That way he could phone home to report the good news, maybe find a gym for a workout, have a good meal, and hopefully be able to box and ship the pictures to that neglectful family, whomever they happened to be. Thinking about it, he mused to himself, "They might be some of my relatives and if they are, I need to let them know that you don't treat family the way they treated that lady."

Rather than blindly looking for a place to spend the night, Norman returned to the home and again spoke to the workman.

"Hey, where are the hotels in the area?" he asked.

"Just go down to the corner, make a right, and go about a half-mile. There are two hotels on the right and one across the street. The best one is the first one you get to. They have a good restaurant and live music on Friday evenings. Did you call the lawyer?" he asked.

"Yes, and he said it's okay for me to take the pictures. Thanks for the directions. Take care."

"You too."

It was 4 p.m. when Norman arrived at the hotel and booked a room. He took his bag to the room and then shuttled the two boxes there. Once settled in, he contacted the lawyer again for an update. The lawyer gave him the name and number of the departed lady's relatives and Norman wasted no time making the call.

"Hello," came a female voice through the receiver.

"Hello, I'm Norman Hurley calling from Branchport. I have some pictures that belonged to Alice Hurley. I was wondering if you're one of her relatives and if you'd like for me to send them to you."

"No, I'm not a blood relative. I don't think any of her blood relatives are still alive. Her daughter passed away about 10 years ago. I was married to her daughter's only son and he passed away about 5 years ago. I only met her once and I probably already have copies of all the pictures."

After a pause, the voice continued. "I'm Louise Allen now. I got remarried. You said you're a Hurley. Are you related to her second husband?"

"Yes, I'm the great-grandson of Henry Hurley. I was raised by his daughter Molly Hurley. She wanted the photo of her parents' wedding that included her aunt and grandparents. I found it in one of the boxes of photos."

"Boxes?" Louise seemed surprised. "About how many pictures are you talking about? I had seen one album and I think 4 or 5 framed pictures. Maybe there are some I never knew about."

It dawned on Norman that many of the pictures could have belonged to his great-grandfather and those were likely not displayed after Henry Hurley had died.

"The ones you never saw could have been from my side of the family. I'll take all the pictures home with me tomorrow. I should be there by early afternoon. I'll have my grandmother check them out. Once she's finished sorting through them, if there are any from your side of the family, I'll let you know, okay?"

Louise liked the idea. "That sounds great. I'll be here all day tomorrow. You can call any time before 9 tomorrow night."

Norman was about to answer when Louise interrupted him.

"Just remember we're 3 hours behind you. I know you said you'll be in sometime tomorrow afternoon, but I wouldn't like the call before 11 in the morning, my time. That would be 2 in the afternoon for you."

"Sure," Norman replied. "Take care."

"You too. Goodbye."

"Goodbye."

Norman felt upbeat after his conversation with Louise. Rather than being stuffy and standoffish, she left the impression that she cared and likely just couldn't make the cross-country journey to the funeral. He also remembered his grandmother had said she'd heard Alice Hurley was hard to get along with, so that could have been the reason for it. Anyway, it wasn't his problem. He now took care of the next task, which was to call home and report his findings.

Molly answered on the first ring as if waiting impatiently right by the phone.

"Hello?"

"Hello, Nana, guess what? I got the picture you wanted and a couple of boxes of pictures we need to sort through when I get back. The lady – Alice Hurley – had died and her ex granddaughter-in-law Louise had told the lawyer taking care of things to get rid of everything in the house. I got there just in time to save both boxes of pictures. I'll be home with them tomorrow. Any of them that don't belong to our side of the family, I'll ship to Louise."

"Hold on, don't go so fast. You found the picture? That's like finding a pot of gold at the end of the rainbow. You said two boxes of pictures? That's good because you never know what you might find at the rainbow's end."

Molly was impatient so she tried to get Norman to come home sooner than he'd planned.

"It's early yet, Norman. Why don't you come home tonight so I can go through the pictures before I go to bed?"

"I already booked a hotel room, Nana. Don't worry, I should be home in time for lunch tomorrow. We can't call Louise before two o'clock anyway. She lives in California, so I guess that's why she didn't make the trip to the funeral."

"Oh." The disappointment was apparent in Molly's voice, but she understood. "Alright. I'll have something ready for you when you get here. Just let me know when you are about an hour away."

"Sure, Nana. I'll see you tomorrow."

"Alright, drive safely."

"Okay, goodbye."

"Goodbye."

Norman now had some time on his hands before he'd be ready to have dinner, so he went to the hotel clerk for advice on how to spend the next few hours. The clerk's first suggestion was perfect.

"There's a good gym about a mile from here. There's another one that has a pool You get a free daily pass for the one without a pool every night you stay here."

"Cool. I'll take a pass for the one without the pool. What about a good place to eat?"

"Our restaurant. It's really a club. They don't allow children. There's live entertainment Friday and Saturday evenings. Sometimes Sunday afternoons too."

"Oh yeah, someone told me about that. I'll go work out and then come back and have a good meal. Thanks."

"You're quite welcome, Sir."

Norman was glad he'd packed his workout clothes. He got directions, gathered his things, and drove to the gym. Once there he began his normal routine of light aerobics before doing some weight lifting. He planned to stay at the gym until around 7 p.m. before going back to the hotel restaurant for dinner. Then he'd get a good night's sleep and depart early the next day with the pictures for his grandmother.

This day had been one of great fascination for Norman. Little did he know that things of even greater fascination were still to come.

7 Doppelganger

At just about the same time Norman found the picture Molly wanted, Marlena's class had ended about a mile away. As it turned out, unlike all the other students in her class, Marlena had no travel plans scheduled for that evening. That meant she'd have the rest of the day and the next morning to think about Tom's pregnancy demands unencumbered by anything or anyone associated with the class. Up until now, the need to focus on classwork took precedence over her problem at home. Now she would be able to give her domestic issue a lot of thought.

She remembered how Tom had begun to put added pressure on her beginning that past Monday. He'd taken her to breakfast, an early movie, a late lunch, and dinner. During and between each stop, he used every argument awkwardly disguised as a reason to persuade her to succumb to his wishes. He figured he was making some headway, as Marlena didn't argue his position, but he was wrong. Marlena had told him she needed to think about things and get herself tested before continuing the conversation. This nagging was causing her to retreat into a shell. Particularly disturbing was what Tom had suggested Tuesday on the way to the airport.

"I was thinking," he'd said, "that with all the land we have on our property, we could easily subdivide and build another home or two right next to the main house. That way our children would have a big head start on life. No mortgage or anything, and they would also be right here near us. They'd be here for Mother and us. At some point in time, we'll all need some help. None of us are getting any younger. Of course, we can wait until they get older, you know, around 16 or 17 before we build, so they can choose things they want in the house."

That argument turned Marlena off. She could tell that Tom was giving a dissertation about what he wished his early adulthood had been like. The mother-and-son bond he was accustomed to and relied on was actually a burden. Marlena knew Tom didn't want to live with his mother forever like he was her little boy, but he didn't have the wherewithal to stand up and man up.

Try as she might to not be judgmental, Marlena found herself beginning to resent Tom's nagging to the point she began weighing the value of having material things. The price for keeping those things seemed too high if it meant she had to jeopardize her convictions about artificial insemination. Why couldn't he just allow her to work things out on her own? His arguments were adding unnecessary fuel to the fire burning inside her against doing what he wanted.

As they were parting, just before Marlena was to board the plane, Tom launched a final underhanded attempt to elicit full support for his argument by tossing a deceptive pledge into the mix.

He said, "I promise I'll do any and everything Dr. Brandon recommends for us to have a child, okay?"

Marlena was hesitant to go along with Tom's okay. She felt doing so would be the equivalent of both of them saying they would go along with whatever the specialist said, and that wasn't the case. She wasn't about to give a blanket okay with artificial insemination hovering over her head, so she said nothing.

Tom didn't want to let her off the hook. He repeated, "Okay?"

Marlena sidestepped having a direct argument with Tom over his proclamation. Her reply put things back into the perspective she wanted. "We'll both listen to what he has to say and go from there."

They'd parted company with Tom hoping he'd gotten enough of an agreement from Marlena to go along with the specialist's recommendations. On the other hand, Marlena hoped Tom understood that anything the specialist had to say would be taken as a suggestion only, and by no means was it to be considered the final word. Though she vowed to herself to at least listen to professional advice, her current feeling was that artificial insemination was, is, and will always be out of the question.

Marlena pushed those thoughts from earlier in the week out of her mind now as she eased her rented car into a parking space at her hotel. She gathered her belongings and started to go straight to her room when she decided she didn't want to remain cooped up again this night. She'd studied the other nights and used room service for meals. Getting out of that room for something other than class just might provide her a good opportunity to figure out the direction she would follow once she returned home. She approached the front desk where a female clerk greeted her.

The clerk asked, "May I help you?"

"I hope so," Marlena replied. "This is my third day here and all I've done is go to class, study, eat, and sleep. What do you recommend?"

"Well, it depends on what you like to do. There's shopping, a museum, a library, clubs, two nice gyms – you name it and we probably have it."

"I wouldn't mind going to a gym," Marlena said. "I always feel relaxed when I go to one. Does either one offer daily rates?"

"They both do, but you don't have to pay to go to the one that doesn't have a pool. We give complimentary passes for that one."

"I don't need to swim so I'll take the complimentary pass."

The clerk reached into a drawer and gave a form and pen to Marlena. "Just fill this card out. I'll stamp it as valid for today and then all you need to do is remember to take a photo ID with you when you go."

"Okay, that sounds good. After I work out, I'll probably come back to the hotel, call room service for dinner, and relax for the rest of the night."

"Well, if you want to do more than just come back to have room service bring you dinner, the big hotel across the street has a nice restaurant with live music on Friday and Saturday night."

The clerk noticed that Marlena looked at her quizzically for the suggestion to go across the street to the competition, so she explained.

"They don't care if we tell people about the restaurant and music. To tell you the truth, they want us to let people know. After all, children aren't allowed in the club, so we get our share of business here."

The clerk stamped Marlena's pass and while handing it to her said, "I think you'll have a great night."

Marlena went to her room to gather her gym equipment. She removed all her jewelry before leaving for the gym and stored them in her suitcase. She'd always been wary of going to a gym, particularly one she was unfamiliar with, decked out in expensive rings and bracelets.

So now, in one of those unbelievable coincidental twists of fate that countless individuals have experienced, Norman and Marlena were heading to the same gym at around the same time.

Norman arrived first and, when he checked in, the gym's front desk person gave him the same dinner and music advice he'd heard from the hotel clerk. He then changed quickly and went into the weight room. He figured a good hour or so of pumping iron would be the perfect way to work up a good appetite for the meal and music he'd promised himself he would enjoy later that evening.

Marlena arrived at the gym almost an hour later than Norman and asked the front desk clerk about the start time for the advanced aerobics class.

"About a half hour ago," came the reply. "There's a class tomorrow afternoon."

"That won't work for me," said Marlena. "I'll be on a plane heading home tomorrow afternoon. I thought I might work out tonight to relax my mind after 3 days of classes."

"Sorry about that. But if listening to good music and having a nice dinner would relax you, there's a club at the big hotel on East Vernon Road. I don't know the exact address, but you can't miss it. It's the hotel across the street from 2 hotels on the left."

"I drove past that hotel. I know where it is," Marlena replied. Then she had a thought. "Would it be alright for me to take a look at the aerobics class for a few minutes? she asked. "I might be able to learn a couple of new moves by watching."

"Sure," the clerk responded. "The class is in the room right past the weight room, down the hall on the right."

"Thanks, and thanks for the tip about the music and dinner," said Marlena as she began to walk toward the aerobics class. "I was told about the club earlier today, so it must really be nice."

"It is. I'll probably go there tonight when I get off," the clerk said.

As Marlena walked down the hall, she noticed the weight room wall was made of glass. If she had known, she would not have chosen to take a look at the aerobics class. She had no desire to walk past men who were working out while she was in street clothes. For whatever reason, it seemed to her that men reacted differently in a gym when a woman in street clothes was heading anywhere except the locker room or the exit. She felt out of place and made sure she kept her head and eyes facing forward. The last thing she needed was to have some guy think she was making eyes at him.

As Marlena passed the weight room, Norman noticed her but she didn't see him. Norman immediately stopped his workout. He very much liked what he saw, and rather than resume his workout, he kept staring.

Marlena only watched the aerobics class for a few moments because what they were doing was not as advanced as she'd hoped. She turned to leave, but on her way out, she dropped her guard and glanced into the weight room. That's when she saw Norman sitting on the work bench. They locked eyes. Marlena was dumbstruck because she knew it wasn't Tom she was looking at, but it *was* Tom. It seemed as if the older-by-the-day man that she knew had suddenly been reincarnated as the younger man she was now staring at.

They both recognized there was mutual interest, with Norman's interest being one of wanting to meet this attractive woman. Not only did she look good, she also seemed to have perked up as she looked at him. He knew he'd never seen her before. There was no way he could ever forget the attractive face and figure he was looking at. Beyond that, the way she was getting an eyeful of him overcame any desire he had to resume his workout. He continued to stare.

Marlena's interest was one of wonderment, awe, and an indescribable wistful yearning that this younger image of Tom was actually Tom. She wanted to get closer to observe this man to find things about him that didn't seem like a younger Tom. At the same time, she wanted to find things about him that *did* seem like a younger Tom. But she knew she couldn't continue to look at him. As it was, the long look they'd already exchanged was more than enough to make her feel she'd given him one of the biggest eye-contact come-ons a man could ever want.

"You working out or girl watching?" asked a man who wanted to use the bench Norman was parked on.

"Girl watching right now," Norman replied.

He stood to allow access to the bench while continuing to watch Marlena for as long as she was in view. He spoke again, more to himself than the man who now occupied the workout bench.

"Seeing that pretty lady has interrupted my workout in the best way," Norman mumbled. "I think I should go take a shower and get out of here right now. Then I can go back to the hotel, change clothes, and get something to eat. I've got a long drive tomorrow."

Norman spoke again to the man with what he considered an extremely important question. "Hey, by the way, do you know her?"

"No, but I'd like to," came the logical but uninspired reply from the man who apparently wanted to work out now and worry about women later.

"Yeah, I'd like to know her too. Take care," said Norman as he started to walk away.

"You too," grunted the man as he continued his workout.

While Marlena walked toward the exit, she wanted to turn her head and eyes back toward the Tom look-alike, but she forced herself not to. She correctly felt, from the way he'd looked at her, he was watching her every step as she left the gym.

Outside, feeling it was a little early to go eat, Marlena did some quick window shopping to hopefully erase the vision of the man she'd seen from her mind. She figured she'd go to the club she'd been referred to so she could eat, enjoy the band and do some thinking about the problem she would face when she arrived home.

Back at the hotel, she stopped at the front desk and asked for the shuttle, even though it was only a 5-minute walk to the restaurant. Informed the shuttle was on a run and wouldn't get back for about 10 minutes, she decided to wait. She took her gym clothes to her room and returned to the lobby. It was then she remembered she'd left her jewelry in her room, but she opted to leave it there rather than go back to retrieve it. She reasoned she was only going to get a meal and maybe listen to music for a while, so she didn't need jewelry.

She also didn't need the few minutes of idle time while waiting for the shuttle. There was nothing to do in the lobby except think about the man she'd seen. She'd been touched by not only his likeness to Tom, but also the genuine warmth she thought she saw in his eyes.

Marlena quickly tried to dash the thought. She figured she must be imagining things. That warmth must have been wishful thinking.

Her mind had to be playing tricks on her to keep her from thinking about the problems at home. That, or fate was teasing her with the image of what her husband should look like and how she should perceive him reacting to her.

The few additional minutes Marlena spent in the lobby felt like an eternity. She tried thinking of the 3 days of training she'd just completed to avoid fantasizing about that man. The strategy didn't work. It wasn't until she got into the shuttle and told the driver where she wanted to go that she finally had something different to concentrate on. In short order, she'd be having dinner and listening to good music. She could think about home problems later that evening with a clear head. Then she'd have all night and a flight home before facing Tom with whatever decision she came up with. She began to relax and felt better about her ability to handle things, although the vision of that man still lingered on.

When Marlena arrived at the club, Norman had just come down from his room and was also on his way to the club. He saw Marlena walking from the shuttle toward the club entrance and hurriedly left the hotel entrance so he could arrive at the club entrance in time to open the door for her.

"Thank you," Marlena said without taking notice as to who was opening the door. Her mind was still digesting the vision of the younger Tom she'd seen earlier at the gym.

Norman followed Marlena to the bouncer, who asked to see an ID. While Marlena fumbled for hers, Norman quipped from behind her, "I'm only 5," referring to his standard leap day joke of having a birthday only once every 4 years.

Marlena simultaneously found her ID and glanced around to see Norman. She muffled a gasp and, to maintain her composure, she stated, "I'm only 5 too."

They all shared a laugh as the bouncer double-checked the IDs in disbelief.

The bouncer then remarked, "Man, I was born on February 12th during a leap year and I always wished my birthday had been 17 days later. I would have been a leap-day baby just like both of you. I never met anyone born on February 29th before, and now I've gotten two in a row."

"Sorry you missed your opportunity," quipped Norman. "You only get a single chance out of every 1,461 days."

While handing the IDs back to them, the bouncer said, "Yeah, I know. I missed out. Ya'll have a great evening."

As they walked toward the club's hostess, Norman asked of Marlena, "Did you get the same dinner advice from the clerk at the gym that I did?"

Marlena answered in almost a whisper.

"Yes, he told me I'd get a good dinner and hear some great music here."

Before either could say another word, the hostess asked, "Two?"

Norman glanced at Marlena. She was looking at him as if she wanted him to answer, so he did.

"Sure," Norman said.

The hostess escorted them to a booth where both could easily view the band with a comfortable sideward glance.

"The music sounds good and it's not too loud. I like that," Norman said.

Marlena had been mostly silent since the leap year conversation. She was still overwhelmed by being face to face with this man who had the same features, mannerisms, and voice of a younger Tom. She knew from conversations she'd had with Elizabeth and Tom that for two generations, there had been no additional relatives on either side of the family. Both of Tom's parents had been their parents' only child. Marlena had heard it said that everyone has a twin somewhere, but the resemblance to Tom she saw in the man she was with was uncanny. Her mind was mired in disbelief.

Norman interrupted Marlena's thoughts and held out his hand, "We never introduced ourselves. My name is Norman."

Quickly and surprisingly as she took his hand she answered, "I'm Marlene."

Marlena didn't admit to herself at first why she felt the need to disguise her name. She'd never done this before, but in her heart of hearts, she knew the ownership and pride she'd always had in her name had become secondary. Her initial rationale was that she simply wanted to have an innocent and unencumbered evening with a stranger. By remaining anonymous, she would be able to relax and feel free from the issues and pressures of her home life before returning home the following day. However, it wasn't long before the seemingly innocent act of going incognito became part of a master plan.

After they ordered dinner and wine, Marlena began to open up. She asked, "Do you go to that gym a lot?"

"No, that was my first time there," Norman answered. "I've never been to Branchport before. I only came here to try to get an old photo of my grandmother's parents. I was lucky to get it. A salvage company was about to throw it away. My grandmother's stepmother had died and they were at her house throwing out all the things they felt had no value."

"Who gave them permission to just throw things away?" asked Marlena. "What about the lady's relatives?"

"She had no blood relatives. Her daughter and grandson both died years ago. The closest one to her was her grandson's wife, but she had gotten remarried. She's the one who wanted everything thrown out," he said. "If I had gotten there a couple of hours later, the picture would have been gone."

Norman shook his head and said, "I'm glad I stopped them from just throwing away the other old pictures that were there. I was able to get in touch with the grandson's wife and I'll be sending them any pictures my grandmother doesn't recognize."

"That's good," Marlena said. "I think calling them and asking if they wanted the pictures was the right thing to do,"

"Yes," Norman continued. "The lady lives in California and I guess that's why she didn't come to the funeral. I'm just surprised the lawyer hired a salvage company to come in and clean everything out without any discussion about pictures. It's like some people don't care too much about the history of their family. It doesn't make sense to me."

They exchanged friendly conversation over their meal while the band played in the background. Later, when the waitress came and asked about dessert, they both refused so she left the check. Marlena reached for her purse, but Norman stopped her.

"I got this," he said, leaving enough money to cover the bill along with a tip.

Just then the band announced their last song before they would take a break. It happened to be a ballad. As the first strain played, Marlena recognized the tune.

"Oh, I love that song," she said.

"Then let's dance," said Norman as he rose and held his hand out to Marlena to lead her to the dance floor.

Marlena eagerly accepted Norman's hand. As they danced, thoughts swirled in her head about wanting a child, not wanting artificial insemination, and the potential of having found the perfect man to satisfy those needs. Beyond that, for both of them, the closeness of their bodies, along with the gently rhythmic sway of the music, induced a greater level of excitement than either expected. Norman pulled Marlena closer as an almost involuntary show of affection, and Marlena silently answered the move by clinging tighter to Norman. As far as each was concerned, their dance of love could have gone on forever.

Then, as the final stanzas of the music played, it was Marlena who took the initiative.

"It's still pretty early. Maybe we should go somewhere and watch TV or something," she offered. Immediately fearing she may have been a little too forward, she added, "We could go see a movie if you'd like."

Norman wasn't going to let this opportunity slip by untested.

"We could go to my room," he boldly stated. "I'm staying overnight right here in this hotel."

That was perfect for Marlena. "Okay," she answered.

They left the restaurant as a happy couple looking forward to a romantic evening. Both were in awe of their good fortune. Within a couple of hours after they'd first locked eyes, they were in the midst of a relationship that could best be described as love at first sight.

Norman remained as cool and calm as he could, but he was enthralled by the possibility of having found the right woman to build his life around. Every fiber in his being was attuned to doing all the right things in all the right ways to make this relationship grow and last.

Marlena's infatuation was different. While she had the same type of feelings as Norman, her desires were tempered by her need to remain focused. She couldn't allow loving emotions to cloud the vision of what she was trying to do, so she forced herself to remain goal oriented. Her first thought was that it was a good thing she'd removed her rings before going to the gym. And not going back to her room to retrieve them was perfect. This was better than good karma, this was providence. She was going to get this artificial insemination done by Tom's alter ego - his clone - his – his what? Marlena tried to remember the synonym for clone she'd learned years ago and never believed she'd have the need to use. Doppelganger. That was it, doppelganger. She would have a baby by Tom's doppelganger. At least she was going to try.

As they walked toward the elevator, Marlena tried to formulate a workable course of action. This was a one-shot deal, so everything had to go just right. From all she'd read, she knew she was in the midst of the most fertile time of her cycle. She had to make sure she didn't let on to Norman her actual identity or give him any clue as to how to contact her after that night. Most importantly, he had to make love to her without using any protection.

By now they'd reached the elevator. Although Marlena was anxious for this night to happen so it could fulfill her wishes, she was also apprehensive. She was still a virgin. What if it was a problem? What if Norman didn't like her? What if he backed off and didn't want to make love their first night? What if, what if, what if...

For Norman, this day and now this evening had been a dream come true. His infatuation with Marlena had escalated the allure of the day to greater heights. That infatuation had Norman ready and willing to take things as far romantically as Marlena would allow.

Norman was more accustomed to girls he and his friends had known. Those interactions had been 'hide and seek games' where the main objective was to gain physical satisfaction for self. This was different. Norman wanted to please Marlena. He wanted this budding relationship to blossom to a permanent union of two leap day persons who just happened to meet while both were away from their respective homes.

There was no hesitation from either one as Norman unlocked and then opened the door. Marlena entered and immediately sat on the sofa. Norman was glad he'd chosen this upscale suite rather than some dive with little more than a bed and a bath. They gazed into each other's eyes and any latent hesitancy Norman felt vanished as he sat beside Marlena. The look they shared got the ball rolling. They enjoyed warm, enduring, and loving kisses with both wanting to escalate to more intimate things, but with each initially too timid to take the next step.

Norman's manhood finally broke the stalemate. His desire for Marlena had grown physically unbearable, so he suggested a solution.

"We should get more comfortable," he offered.

Norman immediately felt Marlena go from sweet and loving to melting into his arms as if they were one.

"Okay," she whispered, unable to muster more of a response.

Norman stood and helped Marlena to her feet. They walked into the bedroom where they began to disrobe slowly and deliberately. It was as if they'd undressed together many times before. There was no awkwardness. Instead, there was only the same feeling of oneness that had been escalating since their first meeting. They made love twice. Norman knew he'd found his soulmate. He was totally in love. Exhausted and sweaty he figured he should shower to cool off.

"I'll be right back," he said in a low voice, "I need to take a quick shower."

Meanwhile, Marlena had been fighting with herself as to whether she should give in to the tremendous feelings she had toward Norman or return to Tom. She reasoned she had to go back. After all, she was a married woman, but what she felt for Norman had her in a stranglehold. Had Norman not stated he would get up to take a shower, Marlena would not have moved a muscle. She would have spent the night and made plans to work on how best to leave Tom. As it was, this was the only type of break that would give her the strength to go back to her own room and she knew it.

"Okay," she answered.

As soon as Norman went into the bathroom and turned on the water, Marlena sprang out of bed and hurriedly dressed. She wanted to leave a note but decided the best thing to do was to simply disappear. She needed to get as far away from Norman as possible and pray their paths would never cross again. Every fiber in her body told her that Norman was the right one for her, and she knew she would never be able to walk away from him again. It made her sad. She wiped tears from her eyes as she left the room.

When Norman returned to the bedroom and saw that Marlene had left, he felt sorry for himself. It was as if none of the uplifting things he'd experienced over the past few days mattered much anymore. For the first time in his life, he felt alone. Defensively, he tried to reason things out. Maybe Marlene was just a woman out for a one-night stand. She hadn't said very much about herself. She might have something to hide. Maybe she was in some kind of trouble. If so, then the way she ran out on him was all for the best. They didn't know each other at all, so it wasn't a good idea for them to have made love the very first night they met.

The negative things Norman was imagining weren't enough to ease the growing pain that was gnawing at him. Surprisingly, it wasn't painful because of how quickly they'd gotten intimate. It was painful because of how perfect their intimacy had been to him, but it couldn't have been that way for her. Otherwise, how could she possibly have made such a sneaky exit?

Norman felt terrible that he'd let his emotions and imagination run away as they did, but he chalked it up to a lesson learned. He'd be more careful in the future. Now that he had found and lost what he thought had been the perfect partner on the very same night, he was unsure he ever would or ever could feel that same way about a woman again.

It took a long while for Norman to stop feeling sorry for himself. The one thing that eased his mind was that the reason for his trip to Branchport had been satisfied. He'd been able to retrieve the photo his grandmother craved. By focusing on what would be a joyous homecoming, he was finally able to relax enough to get to sleep.

Marlena's trip back to her hotel room had her on pins and needles that someone might see her disheveled appearance and begin asking questions at this late hour. However, once she arrived safely in her hotel room, her wariness ended and guilt began to overtake her. Not about cheating on Tom. That didn't cross her mind at all. She felt guilt from not having said anything to Norman when she left. She found herself wanting to call Norman but that would be impossible. If she spoke to him, she would go back to him. Writing to him in the future was out of the question since she had no clue about how to get in touch with him. No, she would have to let him go - that is most of him. If all had gone as she'd planned, she and Norman would be the parents of the child who would solve the problems she was having at home. The thought gave Marlena the solace she needed to get a good night's sleep.

When Norman awoke early the next morning, he still felt the nagging pain from having found and lost the love of his life in the space of a few hours the previous night. He was only able to find solace by forcing himself to remember what the picture represented to his grandmother. Once he returned home and handed the treasured picture over to his grandmother, the joy in the home would mask any leftover remnants of his sorrow.

"Here they are, Nana." Norman burst through the door with both boxes of pictures and set them down in front of Molly.

"Good morning to you too," Molly replied. "You should have called me and let me know you'd be home so early. You must have left there at 6 in the morning. It's not even eleven o'clock now. I was worried about you."

"Good morning, Nana. I'm sorry. I didn't sleep too well and I wanted to get the pictures to you as soon as I could. The one I know you want to see is in this top box. Here, you open it so you can see it."

Molly was smiling broadly as she opened the box and picked up the photo to examine it. She saw the images were sharper and the frame far better than the copy she'd owned.

"Norman, you will never know how much this means to me. This is the oldest thing our family owns." She was still beaming as she said, "Now we have our heirloom back."

Molly gave a fleeting thought to the hurt she'd felt when her picture was lost more than 20 years earlier. Having an even better one in her hand now erased much of the lingering ill will she felt toward Mrs. Purlmen. So much so it crossed her mind that she still had the Purlmen heirlooms safely tucked away in the tiny safe and maybe she should get it back to them.

That last thought passed quickly. She didn't know the full story about what had happened between Tom and Sue. If the Purlmen heirlooms were important to them, they should reach out for them.

As it was, Molly was still hesitant to tell Norman what she knew about his father. No, she'd continue to wait for Tom Purlmen to make the move and at that time she would inform both Tom and Norman about their relationship. This way Tom could deal with his mother. Molly certainly wasn't looking forward to another dose of Mrs. Elizabeth Purlmen's attitude at its worst.

Molly refocused on her own heirloom and Norman. "I'm going to put this picture on my dresser where it belongs," she said. "Then I'll put together whatever you want for lunch. You made my day with this picture. We can go through the ones in the boxes after lunch."

"I might be kind of sleepy after lunch," Norman admitted, "But I'll help you with them."

"And what do you want for lunch?" Molly asked as she walked away with the picture.

"You know it doesn't matter what you make because it's always good. I'm just glad you're happy."

As he watched Molly leave, Norman was struck by how happy she looked. He knew he couldn't let any of yesterday's disappointment detract from her joy. He resolved to share and bask in her happiness and continue to be the best grandson he could be for her. He doubted he would ever forget the previous day, but he was certain that one day, someday, he would regain that feeling of perfection with someone.

8 Cover-up

The following morning marked the beginning of Marlena's plan to stage the cover-up she fervently hoped she would need. She figured her best course of action would be to silently proceed as if she was definitely pregnant. She'd tell Tom she would go to the doctor alone and then tell him she decided to proceed with the artificial insemination as a one-shot attempt to become pregnant. She would tell him she had made a spur of the moment decision and she would never do it again. Doing so should appease Tom whether she was pregnant now or not. If she was, all problems would be solved. If not, she reasoned she could always go to Mother and have an open and honest discussion with her.

Rather than calling Tom to pick her up when she landed, Marlena took a taxi home. Happily, no one else was there. Since only Tom's car was gone, Marlena figured they would only be away from the house a for short time. Maybe they were out for a late lunch. Seizing the opportunity to ease her way back into the home, she left her bags inside and got into her car and drove off. This way they'd know she was home and had likely gone for a meal herself.

The truth was that Marlena took the opportunity to go straight to the library to read about pregnancy. She wanted to reinforce what she already knew with as much additional information she could find as quickly as possible. An hour later, bolstered by the knowledge she'd gained, she drove home ready to tell Tom she would try artificial insemination once and only once. There would be no second attempt if the first was unsuccessful.

When she returned home, Marlena found the others there. After greetings and small talk, Marlena began to launch her plan.

"I'm still hungry. I'd like some of that good chocolate cake we get from the bakery," she stated. She hadn't eaten, so she was famished, but she couldn't think of another way to satisfy her hunger and quickly be alone with Tom to launch her pregnancy plan.

Not surprisingly, Tom was also looking for an opportunity to further his version of the pregnancy plan, so he jumped at the chance to be alone with Marlena.

"Sure, I'd like some dessert too," he replied. "Mother, we'll bring back some for you if you'd like us to."

Sensing the two wanted to be alone, Elizabeth declined. "No, I've had quite enough to eat and I don't believe I'll want anything sweet after dinner. But if they have any fresh cheese or blueberry Danish or croissants, you can get some for breakfast."

The stage was now set for Tom and Marlena to have another clandestine meeting to continue their separate plots to become parents.

"We'll be back in an hour or so," Tom said.

"Take your time," Elizabeth told them. "I have things to do anyway."

Almost as soon as Tom and Marlena got into Tom's car, Marlena broke the news she was bursting to tell.

"I decided to give that artificial insemination thing just one try,".

Tom's excitement over the positive aspect of Marlena's proclamation caused him to completely overlook the limiting factor. He enthusiastically responded, "Great! I'll call and make the appointment as soon as we get home."

Marlena had anticipated that part of Tom's response so she had her answer ready.

"No, I'll take care of it. I promise to get it done very soon. Probably before the end of the month." She paused before adding, "I want to do it my way so when it happens, it will be a big surprise for you and Mother."

Tom couldn't argue with the logic. It would likely be better for him to not know the details until Marlena made the announcement. "Good idea," he said. "This is great!"

Marlena thought to herself, "This is way better than great. This is perfect."

Aloud she stated, "I want this to work out just right. I'll do everything I need to do to make it happen."

And happen it did, although actually, the seed had already been planted to make it happen. Marlena was delighted when her normally-like-clockwork period didn't come on the expected day and ecstatic when another day passed with no sign of it. That gave her 2 more weeks before the scheduled follow-up meeting with Doctor Brandon. She immediately called his office and told the receptionist she would not be able to keep the appointment. When asked about making a new date, Marlena said she would let them know, but she never gave that office another thought. She didn't want to have anything more to do with the fertility clinic or the fertility specialist Dr. Brandon. She wanted everything about her pregnancy to be, in her way of thinking, normal.

Afraid of the possibility of a false alarm, Marlena decided to wait another week before visiting her own doctor for professional confirmation. As expected, Marlena received the joyous confirmation that she was pregnant. Now all that was left to do was to decide when and how to let the others know. Since Tom was privy to more information - albeit incorrect information - than Mother, it would probably be better to tell them at the same time to put them on equal footing. Marlena waited until they'd sat down to dinner that evening as a trio to deliver the gift of a rhetorical riddle.

"Does anyone want to guess how many people will be here at the dinner table about 9 months from now?" she asked.

Elizabeth's huge smile at the news seemed to brighten the room and was only surpassed by her exclamation, "You're pregnant!"

Tom was more subdued, but he did show his elation. "That's great. I hope it's a boy."

"I'll let you know as soon as I find out," Marlena said before adding the obvious statement, "I'm really excited."

Elizabeth, still beaming from the news, began making grandmotherly statements and plans. "I'm going to begin to start window-shopping right away for all the things we'll need no matter if it's a boy or girl."

Tom and Marlena stayed silent for the moment, both hiding behind their pregnancy secrets. Elizabeth would have dominated the conversation anyway.

"I'm so glad the bedrooms are all large enough to hold a crib. And we can start getting the spare bedroom ready for when the baby gets older. We've got so much to do," she said.

As Elizabeth continued her preparations, the other two felt the weight they'd been under had been lifted. The house became more of a home as days and weeks turned into months. Joy all around was evident as they shared the experience of the gradual changes in Marlena's body.

The joyous atmosphere in the home lasted until about 6 months into the pregnancy. That was the day when Tom happened to see and recognize Dr. Brandon at a service station.

"Hey, Dr. Brandon," Tom held out his right hand to shake Dr. Brandon's hand. "Thanks."

Dr. Brandon shook Tom's hand somewhat quizzically and asked, "Thanks for...?"

"For doing a great job." Tom reasoned that while surely the doctor remembered him, he wouldn't necessarily associate him with Marlena. He gave a hint.

"Marlena, my wife. We only came in the one time together, but the artificial insemination did the trick."

Dr. Brandon was puzzled. "I think you need to thank yourself. I remember your wife. She didn't want the procedure." He then added, "Your ability to overcome obstacles must have taken a turn for the good of things."

The look on Tom's face made the doctor want to run and hide. He needed to end the conversation immediately.

"I've got an appointment and I don't want to be late," said the doctor as he quickly got into his car and drove off.

For Tom, the wheels had just fallen off his happy wagon. He had never before even considered the possibility that Marlena had been unfaithful. Marlena had never given any indication of being a playgirl or someone who would ever go for a one-night stand. She also always seemed to be in the best of spirits about things, but something certainly seemed to be wrong. He needed to find out why Dr. Brandon had acted the way he did.

As soon as he could, Tom stealthily began to do some backtracking of financial transactions. It didn't take long for him to find out the last payment to the fertility clinic was for the day both he and Marlena had visited there together. Further, the only medical transactions Marlena made since then were for visits to the same facility she normally used, and that firm did not offer artificial insemination. It was obvious that Marlena had gotten pregnant from direct physical contact. Tom was incensed, but his reaction to his anger became the worst thing he could do. He began to use alcohol excessively to find an answer in the bottle instead of at least confronting Marlena for an explanation.

Tom went on a binge for the next 2 months. He remained practically homebound and was damaging his weakened kidneys further by overtaxing them with alcohol. Actually, he wanted to kill himself before the baby was born. It was difficult enough for him to have to think about Marlena and see her changing condition, but he was afraid that having someone else's baby around might put him over the edge.

As Tom's condition worsened, Marlena decided to give up her job rather than take maternity leave when she reached the end of her 8th month. She planned to use the skills she'd acquired to help with the family business anyway. For her, aside from the way Tom was acting, things could not have been more perfect.

The baby boy arrived right on schedule and Marlena named him Toby. Tom had made it plain to her that the name 'Tom' was out of the question. That was the only thing Tom did towards helping with Toby. He withdrew from Marlena completely and made sure there was always an excuse to not be around Toby.

Those first few months of having an infant in the house became more strained each day until Elizabeth could take it no more. She knew something was going on, and she finally broke from her previous decision to not interfere by making what seemed to be a great suggestion. On the surface, the suggestion seemed innocent enough, but it would eventually change every aspect of the Purlmen hierarchy.

"Tom," she began one morning, "why don't you prepare an heirloom presentation so we can have a ceremony when Toby is 6 months old. After all, those things have been locked away for over 20 years. We should get them out of the safe anyway so we can clean and polish them."

Elizabeth let her words sink in before adding, "I'm getting older and I don't want to wait another 20 years for Toby's ceremony."

Tom hadn't thought about the heirlooms at all since that day so many years ago when he placed them in the wall safe. It was not only because that particular day had turned out so badly, but also because he'd never again closed the door to view the painting that covered the safe. It was truly a case of out of sight out of mind. Hearing the heirlooms mentioned now gave him a good feeling. He was well beyond the hurt he'd felt when his father had died. He was instead able to zero in on how intelligent an idea it had been for his family to hide the safe that way. It made him want to see the heirlooms again and caused him to let nostalgic feelings guide his answer.

"That's a good idea about getting out the heirlooms. I'll work on something," he said, but he didn't like the reference about doing it for Toby. He'd be getting the heirlooms out for his own sake.

Tom dismissed the thought of writing a ceremony and focused on going to the wine cellar to look at the heirlooms and feel closer to his family. He envisioned the way it had been when it was only his mother, father, and himself in the home. The thought gave him sufficient resolve to not take another drink that day. He was now on a quest to be as alert as possible and stay awake late into the evening so he could get into the wine cellar after everyone else was asleep. Time seemed to crawl that evening for Tom, but finally, he was confident he would not be disturbed.

It wasn't until he got up from the desk and began to leave the den that he realized he would need a couple of combinations.

"Let's see," he mumbled to himself as he remembered the wall safe combination was the year and age his great-great-great-grandfather left England. "1839 when he was 4 with the 18 and 39 transposed."

He reminisced at how clever his father and grandfather had been to have associated the combinations with their family's past. That thought buoyed his spirits as he made his way to the basement and opened the wine cellar door. Switching on the light, he did the one thing he hadn't done in years. He turned around and closed the door to reveal the painting of the Weymouth port.

For the first time in his life, he paused to look at the painting for a few seconds to appreciate it as art. Then, as if transported back to the only time he'd previously removed the painting from the wall, he remembered to give it a twist while pulling gently. He accomplished the task effortlessly. He then gently placed the painting on the floor and leaned it against the wall.

Opening the wall safe was no problem either. He managed it without a hitch. It wasn't until he swung the door open that he encountered a problem. The safe was completely empty! He stared for a moment in disbelief before his mind began racing in an attempt to solve this mystery. He knew his mother hadn't removed the little safe. She certainly would have mentioned it had she done so. As a matter of fact, she would have made *him* open and remove the little safe. There were no signs of a break-in either. Someone with knowledge of the safe and the combination had to be the culprit.

Suddenly another vague memory came to Tom's mind. Sue, the maid from long ago, had been the only one to whom Tom had ever confided any potentially useable information about the safe's combination. She had to be the one who got into the wall safe. That meant the heirlooms had been gone for over 20 years. What was he to do now?

Tom dreaded the thought of telling his mother the heirlooms were gone because at some point the possibility that Sue or Molly had stolen them would likely come up. He knew any mention of Sue would surely reawaken the now-suppressed angry explosion his mother had previously displayed, and he never wanted to relive that experience. No, he'd have to use a different strategy to get around the loss of the heirlooms.

Another possibility came to mind. Maybe he could delay dealing with the heirlooms by admitting he and Marlena were not legally married. On the surface, that solution would be better for him, but he tossed the idea aside almost as soon as he thought of it. His mother's eruption during the Sue escapade would be miniscule compared to how she'd react to the news that Marlena wasn't his wife.

He didn't dare to even stop for a moment to consider using the fact that Toby was not actually a Purlmen as a reason to not have the heirloom ceremony. Doing so would be a prime example of how to cut one's own throat.

Then it came to him. Maybe he *could* use Toby's conception as a way to avoid the heirloom ceremony. Not directly, of course, but there must be some kind of roundabout path he could follow that would eliminate any additional mention of those heirlooms. He was still extremely resentful about the entire pregnancy episode, and he wanted no part of furthering any kind of action to help perpetuate the myth that Marlena and her son were Purlmens. Even though logically speaking, he had been the one to push Marlena to have a child and would have accepted one conceived through artificial insemination as being his own, he reasoned that he shouldn't be expected to accept a child who had been born as a result of Marlena's affair. He would use Marlena's unfaithfulness to somehow get her out of the house.

That reasoning led to Tom feeling exuberant. He was happy he'd never truly married Marlena and had never been intimate with her. He was delighted they'd never even shared a kiss. He was glad they slept in separate rooms. Every negative thing he could think of about their relationship became a crutch he used to bolster his self-esteem. In short order, however, his exuberance and self-esteem combined to become an anger that was fueled by everything he hated about his predicament. The main thing he hated was having Marlena and Toby living under the same roof with him. He wanted them out.

"That's right," he thought. "I don't want to have Marlena or Toby in this house. They're not Purlmens and they don't deserve anything they've been getting from us. I just need to figure out how to get Marlena to leave and take her son along with her."

9 Rejection

The more Tom thought about Marlena's escapade, the angrier he became, and that anger fueled a ruthlessness that compelled him to want a drink. He closed the safe, replaced the painting, and chose a bottle of brandy to help him plan his next move. Foremost in his mind was how best to plot a course to get Marlena and her son out of his life.

Anticipating the need for additional comfort and courage in the bottle, he chose 2 more bottles before retreating to his room. Once there, he stored two of the bottles in his nightstand before breaking the seal and opening the third. He then tried to morph into what he felt the manner of an outlaw or hoodlum would be. He was about to take a swig when he paused. He needed to focus on being as rough, tough, and stern as possible to confront Marlena and get her banished right away. Thinking back again to the dismissal of Sue and her mother Molly, he began to weigh his options to do the same with Marlena and her son. He didn't need a drink. He needed a plan.

He certainly couldn't easily arrange to evict Marlena while she was physically in the home. Unlike with the housekeepers, Marlena and her son were living there as family members and not hired help. No, the confrontation to split up had to be done in some other place, and the biggest hurdle would be to get their belongings out of the house. He wouldn't be able to get away with tossing things out in the yard. He wanted them out of his life, not out on the street. He could get a place and they could all move there as a family before leaving and returning home, but the plan had issues. Not only would his mother know where they were, but he'd also have to live there with Marlena and Toby for a while.

Tom felt as if he'd hit an impassible snag, but while he screwed the cap back on the bottle and expanded his thoughts, he put things into a better perspective. He could rent a furnished apartment at least an hour away for a few months. That would be easier. He could then lure Marlena to the apartment and have the confrontation to get Marlena and Toby out of his life as soon as they went to the new home. He'd give her some cash and maybe enough in checks to live on until she got a job or reconnected with her son's father.

Her son's father. That thought caused Tom's anger to boil up again when he thought about Marlena's deceit. It hardened his resolve to get her out of the house even more and he immediately began to make the plan a reality.

The following morning, he found a place via telephone with no problem. Furnished townhouses were available at a place called Lakeview Villa in Lakeview, a town a couple of hours away. They advertised rentals by the day, week, or month. Tom made arrangements to rent a place that was immediately available and gave a verbal commitment for 6 months of residency. Still fueled by burning anger, he had enough energy to drive to the bank for cash, to Lakeview to pay for the rental agreement, secure the garage door opener remote and house key, and finally back home.

Once home, Tom called a limousine rental firm in Lakeview and arranged to have a limousine waiting for him at the Lakeview townhouse Saturday morning.

Tom continued to develop his plan. He had to get his mother out of the house and away from Marlena early the following day and have her return home too late to see her. In short, he didn't want them to ever see each other again. He checked entertainment listings and purchased two tickets for a play the next evening, which happened to be a Friday. He woke the next morning before anyone else and was waiting for his mother in the kitchen.

"I'm glad I woke up before you did," he told her. "I'm going to the office with you today so we can enjoy breakfast, lunch, dinner, and theater together. Let's make a full day of it."

Elizabeth gave him a 'what's gotten into you look', but was pleased with how it sounded.

"You must be feeling better, Tom. All the rest you've been getting must have been what you needed."

Tom didn't offer an explanation. He instead tried to hurry her along. "Let's get going, I've been away from the office way too long."

Elizabeth complied and was ready in a flash. It seemed to her that Tom had suddenly become a new person. She relished the idea of him becoming more of a doer with ideas and plans rather than just a yes-man whom she felt was constantly leaning on her as if she was his permanent crutch. Something had lit a fire under him and Elizabeth felt it was a good thing, even though the current evidence was only in the form of meals, a day's work, and a theater event.

Tom was elated his plan was moving along so well, and with him doing the driving he was in total control. He made his mother feel like a queen. The entire day was filled with joy for both of them.

Strategically, Tom waited until they were on their way home to further his eviction plot.

"Oh," he began, "Marlena said she is going to visit a college friend very soon for about a week."

Elizabeth didn't like the idea and said so. "With a newborn baby? That doesn't make sense."

Tom was ready for something like that. "Her friend is the oldest of 8 siblings and has had a lot of experience with babies. It'll be fun for her and good for Marlena."

Elizabeth wanted to argue the point, but she didn't want to ruin a pleasant day by adding negativisms. They drove the rest of the way in silence. It was well after 11 when they arrived home and, as Tom had hoped, Marlena and Toby were likely asleep.

Tom pressed on with his strategy. "It's almost midnight so I know you'll probably sleep in late tomorrow morning. I'll be up early with Marlena and the baby. We won't see you until late in the day. We've got errands to run in the morning and afternoon, so good night."

Elizabeth was still miffed about Marlena's upcoming trip and offered no objection to Tom's quick good night. "Alright, good night," was her terse response.

Although Tom didn't like the way his mother had bid him goodnight, he was elated when she closed her door. He could now turn his attention to phase two of what had to happen that evening. He needed to advise Marlena to be ready with Toby so they could leave home early in the morning. The problem was he'd never before knocked on her door. Fortunately for Tom, he was rescued by Toby, who began to whimper. Tom listened intently as the whimpering stopped and moments later, he heard Marlena leave her room. She had apparently given Toby a pacifier and was now going to get a bottle.

This was Tom's chance. He went downstairs to the kitchen on the pretense of getting a snack. Once there, he met and spoke to Marlena.

"If you're not busy tomorrow, we need to go sign some papers."

To avoid obvious questions, he quickly added, "Insurance papers and such."

Marlena was surprised to see Tom at that hour but shocked he had something to say. She answered, "I can be available all day."

The confirmation was all Tom needed to proceed to the next phase of his plan.

"Good. Be ready around 8 a.m." He then thought quickly and came up with a way to avoid a potential pitfall.

"If you happen to see Mother, don't say anything to her. She doesn't like to discuss certain things and insurance is one of them."

Tom knew it wasn't true, but better safe than sorry, just in case the two women happened to see one another in the morning.

When Tom awoke the next morning just after 6 AM, he hurriedly dressed without taking a shower. He pulled his chair close to his bedroom door and sat down, silently listening for any sound that would let him know Marlena was up and about. At around 6:30 he heard her leave her room and go downstairs to likely to fix a bottle for Toby. He followed her but didn't speak until they'd reached the kitchen.

"Make sure you bring along enough things for all day," he said in a hushed voice. "I don't plan to return until this evening."

"All day?" Marlena repeated. Then she stated, "I wish you would have told me yesterday, but all right."

Tom didn't try to hurry Marlena along verbally, but he did linger in the kitchen and glanced at his watch a couple of times before telling her, "Let me know what you need for me to put in your car."

"In my car?"

"Yes, we'll be taking your car. Where's the stroller?"

Marlena gave Tom the commonsense answer his rhetorical question deserved.

"It's downstairs in the room next to the outside door where it always is."

"I'll go put it in the car. Will you need help carrying anything else?"

"Yes, you can take the baby bag and I'll get Toby. He's asleep, but he'll probably wake up and want a bottle."

Tom answered, "That's alright, you can sit in the back and feed him while I do the driving."

Marlena sensed some underlying scheme was brewing and

questioned Tom's actions. "What's going on? Why are we leaving so early to see an insurance guy?"

"It's a surprise," said Tom, "Just bear with me."

Marlena had to admit to herself that Tom had been acting better toward her since the day before, so she deduced the underlying scheme must be a pleasant one. She began to look forward to whatever Tom had planned.

Two hours later they arrived at Lakeview Villa and Tom eased into the parking space in front of the garage for townhouse number 62. Reaching into his pocket, he pulled out the garage door opener remote. He then aimed it toward the garage door and depressed the button marked OPEN.

As the door slowly lifted, Tom simply said, "This is your new home."

He drove into the garage and unlocked all the car doors. He then exited the vehicle.

Tom hoped his statement had somehow made Marlena realize she should simply accept the fact that she was no longer welcome in his home without him having to talk about it, but he knew better. He knew a storm was brewing, but he didn't want it to begin with a bang. He tried a matter-of-fact approach to ease into the conversation.

Opening the trunk, he removed the stroller and said rather loudly, "Where do you want me to leave it?"

Marlena, still sitting in the back seat, heard his voice, but was shocked by his previous statement of 'this your new home'.

She asked herself, "Just what did he mean by that statement?"

Not wanting to ask questions while sitting in the back seat, she waited for Tom to open the door so she and Toby could exit the vehicle and Tom could tell her what was going on.

Tom began to sense he was bungling his well-laid plans. He needed to stop talking in riddles and get straight to the point. Marlena had not answered his question about the stroller, and the closed car door was a huge stumbling block that hindered having a face to face confrontation.

However, instead of opening the door to confront Marlena, cowardly Tom took the stroller to the door leading into the townhome kitchen. After unlocking the door, he entered and took the stroller in and rolled it to a place near the table. He then waited for Marlena to get out of the car and come into the kitchen. He'd taken the easy way out. The garage was hot and stuffy so he knew Marlena would soon have to come inside.

Tom left the kitchen door open and waited. He was right, Marlena did get out of the car with Toby, but she was fuming. She wanted answers and she wanted them now. She held Toby in her arms as she marched through the door.

"Exactly what is going on?" she asked

"This is your new home," Tom answered. "Look around. This place is completely furnished with everything you need."

"What's this all about?" asked Marlena angrily.

"It's simple, *we* don't want you in our home anymore." He had emphasized the word "we" to infer to Marlena that he and his mother were in synch with what he was saying.

Tom now blasted her with everything he could. "Your baby is not a Purlmen. You probably don't know whose baby he is. I mean, it would have been okay if he was conceived through artificial insemination, but it isn't okay that he was conceived from you running around. Here are your keys, and the garage door opener. Here's your lease agreement for 6 months plus a few thousand dollars cash in this envelope. You can keep the car since it's in your name anyway. I'll ship the title tomorrow along with anything else I think you need. Mother and I want everything of yours out of our house as quickly as possible. In case I've forgotten anything, call me Monday morning at 10. After that, I don't ever want to see or hear from you again."

Marlena was stunned. She'd thought there was no way Tom could have known she hadn't gotten pregnant by artificial insemination, but his tone and mannerisms said otherwise. She wanted to tell him the truth about how she'd gotten pregnant, and that Toby's father actually *was* an anonymous donor. The only real difference was that the insemination wasn't artificial. It had also been, as she'd insisted, something she had given just one try. She wanted to argue that it was the only way she'd have ever gotten pregnant, but would it be worth the effort? Tom had mentioned Mother, and if Mother approved of what Tom was doing, the final word on the subject had already been spoken. Marlena began to push back against the tidal wave Tom had unleashed. She first directed the conversation toward her mother-in-law.

"Mother fully accepts Toby," Marlena shot back. "She loves him."

"My mother doesn't want either of you," Tom lied. "We discussed things all day yesterday. Why do you think we were out so late? She told me she didn't want to see either of you again."

Tom was on a roll now, lying through his teeth.

"She told me she'd be throwing away every photograph of you and your son as soon as we left this morning."

Marlena's anger had by now changed to sadness. She was crestfallen and felt betrayed. She wanted to hear no more of anything Tom had to say, but she did want to reach out to Mother to at least offer an explanation.

"I'd like to speak to Mother," she said, softly and evenly.

Tom crushed the suggestion because he knew he couldn't allow it to happen.

"That's my mother and the last thing my mother told me last night was that I should tell you she never wants to see you again. She also said that if you do happen to meet, do not call her Mother. She doesn't want you. Get it through your head. You cheated on me and you're a liar. She even called you some names I don't want to repeat. And don't think you can ever come back in case I'm not around. I hid a letter telling her you cheated on me and Toby is not my son. You know she wouldn't stand for that. Neither one of us want you.

194

Have a good life, but leave my mother and me out of everything you and your man friend, whoever he is, decide to do."

Tearfully grasping at straws, Marlena responded with, "But I'm your wife."

Tom fired back with the marriage secret he'd never previously divulged to her. "You're not my wife. We're not married. Maybe I should add *that* to the letter I hid for my mother. What we did in Peru was not a legal ceremony. Religious ceremonies in Peru are for show and mean nothing without a civil ceremony. You can check it out for yourself. Why do you think I told you I took care of all the legal necessities? Nothing was ever done to give the marriage any validity. I didn't trust you from the start so I left myself some wiggle room in case you turned out to be a tramp. You and I are nothing to each other and my mother agrees. We've never even slept together. Face the facts. We're through."

With that said, Tom went to the front door, opened it, and peered outside. "My limousine is here," he announced as he shut the door behind him.

Marlena was devastated but she held herself together. She felt the best thing she could do was to accept what Tom had said at face value. Since he knew there had been no artificial insemination, he had the upper hand. He could use that fact, along with his marriage revelation and medical issues, against her to override any attempt she made to discuss the situation with Mother.

Immediately, Marlena decided she needed to get away from this new home Tom dumped her in. Sure, it looked like a nice place, and financially it made sense to stay there, but Marlena felt trapped. There was no way she wanted to live in a place where she could potentially be contacted by Tom to be harassed or used like a pawn. In a little over a week, she moved to an apartment in town. Not satisfied, she soon moved again, this time to another town hours away. She left no forwarding address. She put as much physical and mental distance between her and the ugly episode as she could.

After closing the door behind him, Tom eased into the limousine feeling good about how he'd handled himself during the confrontation with Marlena. Now, during the ride back home, he focused on how he could now make Marlena's departure ugly enough so Mother would never search for her. He couldn't admit to Mother that the baby wasn't his. To do so would make him look like the victim of the worst kind of rejection imaginable. His mother would likely tell him he'd chosen a woman who had no morals and use words like hideous, vile, and despicable to describe her. That would be way too far over the top. No, he'd simply say Marlena decided to move back to where she'd grown up so she could be with her friends and start a new life. He was sure he could work it out as long as he had a believable statement, rationale, or rebuttal for every question or argument Mother might pose.

About an hour into the drive, Tom realized he was famished, so he had the driver stop to get something to eat. While there, the bravado Tom had felt during the confrontation with Marlena began to wane, mainly because he would now be tangling with his mother. The one thing that bolstered him was that his cruel deed had already been done. There was no turning back. He had to deal with his mother the best way he could.

In accordance with his gutless way of dealing with his mother, he decided he'd better ease into the confrontation with his mother by phoning her before he got home. After he finished his meal, he made the call. He broke the news as soon as Elizabeth answered.

"Marlena's gone. We were supposed to be having breakfast. I went to the men's room and came back to the table and she wasn't there. She left a note saying she's leaving and doesn't ever want to see us again. She wants me to put all her belongings in storage."

"What? What are you talking about? Where's Toby?"

"She took him along with the car and I don't know where she went. She warned me something like this was going to happen and that she didn't want to live with us."

"She never gave me that impression. What was going on between you two?"

"Nothing, Mother. I gave her everything she ever wanted. She knows I've been sick, so what more could I do?"

"You could call the police and get them involved. It's against the law for one parent to take a child from the other parent."

"What she's done is not illegal, it's unethical, but not illegal unless we get a court order."

"Well, we have to do something, Tom. I should call Rodney."

"No, let's keep it in the family for now. Let's give her some time to think about what's she's done. She has no money and we don't know where she's going or where she's planning to stay. I think we should let her get established somewhere before we even think about going to court."

"I don't want to go to court, Tom, but I don't think it's right to let things go without doing something about it."

"Doing nothing might be the best thing we can do, Mother. She'll need us before we'll need her."

"Unless she already has a plan. Do you think she might have a man helping her?"

Tom didn't want to get caught up in that accusation. "No, she never told me she wanted to be with someone else. She only said she doesn't want to be with us."

"Tom, you said she wants all her belongings put in storage? That doesn't make any sense. I don't like any of this." His mother was getting exasperated and began grasping straws.

Elizabeth asked, "What about that friend she was going to visit? Why don't you call her?"

Tom had forgotten the lie about Marlena's friend he'd previously fed his mother.

"Uh, she never gave me that information. I don't even know the lady's name."

Tom needed a break because he felt like he was going to get

caught up awkwardly in the twists and turns of the scenario he was offering. He had to end the conversation.

"Listen, Mother. I need to call for a limousine, don't do anything until I get home."

"Where's the car?"

"I told you she took the car. It's in her name anyway. Please let me call for a ride home now and we'll talk when I get there."

Tom breathed a sigh of relief when he hung up the phone. He felt the most difficult part of his planned exit from life with Marlena was over. He kept that thought in mind as the limo took him home and he confronted his mother. He was weak in the knees but he answered every question and argument she had with lies, deceit and in an insidiously cunning fashion he never before realized he possessed. To his surprise, she seemed to accept his stated wisdom that Marlena would either come to her senses and return or at some point in time, they should do their best to find her and demand visitation rights with Toby. Of course, Tom didn't want either outcome to happen. He figured he would be able to put his mother off indefinitely. Maybe he could wait a few weeks and claim Marlena had found someone new. He could also say that she refused to divulge where she was living and had refused to allow visitation rights.

Yes, he would think of something. The dream of life as it used to be seemed to be within Tom's grasp. He was sure he'd be able to convince his mother that he was all she needed in her life. All he had to do now was to play his cards right.

10 Repentance

Tom's dream of having life with his mother return to the best of what he remembered while growing up deteriorated rapidly in just a few weeks. That was as long as he could fool himself into believing such a thing was possible. His mother's distress over the loss of Marlena and Toby was apparent, and Tom knew his weak explanation had been a disaster. In a knee-jerk reaction to tolerate the guilt he felt, he tried to camouflage the ugliness by torturing his body.

Tom began using pills in addition to booze and the combination was devastating. In short, the time quickly came when he realized he wouldn't be able to handle the environment he'd created. Substance abuse was making him feel worse physically and mentally than the mental anguish he'd been trying to appease. He seldom left his room. He relied on his mother to bring him meals. He'd reached the point in time where he had to face the facts. He was making himself sick to a point where he felt like he was near death. In short, Tom was on a collision course with rock bottom. There was no question that he would hit it. The only unknown was where he would land.

Had it not been for his mother, Tom would likely have faded into an oblivion that would have ended with him killing himself without reaching out for help. However, motherly love, or more accurately, his drive to live his life for his mother, hit him like a tidal wave. He felt he had to do whatever he could to appease her.

Through the foggy haze that enshrouded his mind, he came to grips with what he had done. He'd made his mother sad. Because of him, the heirlooms were gone. He'd committed a terrible wrong to Marlena and Toby. He needed to make amends and get them back home. The current situation was terrible and he could blame no one but himself.

Tom gathered all the mental strength he could muster, and with the same calculated determination he'd used to lure Marlena into and then out of the Purlmens' household, he began to devise a plan. He had to make things right. It would be symbolic of his repentance to his mother for all the major wrongs he'd committed. Knowing the key to making things right and likely the most difficult piece of the puzzle to fix was Marlena, he wrote her a letter. He could only hope that she would read it and accept it as enough of a reason to forgive him and return home.

He rambled but was able to piece together a narrative he felt Marlena might respond favorably to. He wrote:

Marlena - I'm sorry. I did you so wrong in so many ways but please try to forgive me and come home. Not to me. I'm deathly sick and I don't believe I'll last another week. Come home to Mother. You know this is where you belong. You and Toby. I want you and my son to be here. Yes, my son. I should have accepted him from the start. I lied to you when I told you I'd hidden a letter to Mother telling her Toby was not my son. I would never do that and you must never do that either. She would not stand for it. She would not have accepted artificial insemination either, so we will keep that suggestion between us and no one else. Please don't ever tell Toby either. Let

200

him grow up as a Purlmen. I also deceived Mother about why you left. I told her that you left for your own personal reasons and gave no clues about why you wanted to leave or where you were going. Mother is devastated. She needs you here. I haven't told her about the illegal marriage ceremony in Peru. Please don't you tell her that either. She would have problems with you if she believed we had a child and we weren't married. I'm going to tell her that I sent you and Toby away because I couldn't handle the responsibilities of being a husband and father and I couldn't step up and be the man I was supposed to be. Just feeling that you will allow me to persuade you to come home is all I need to feel that I have finally become the man Mother always hoped I would be. Please destroy this letter after you read it. Only you and I should ever know the facts it contains. Remember, there is no hidden letter for my mother. Please trust me and please come home to her. Tom

Tom didn't bother to proofread the letter. He placed it into a small envelope and sealed it. On the outside of the envelope, he wrote 'To Marlena – Personal and Confidential.' He inserted the small envelope into a larger envelope and addressed that envelope with the Lakeview address. Then he stopped to think about how he'd left her. He'd been pretty nasty and evil to Marlena when he dumped her in Lakeview. What if she'd moved so she could not be easily found? What name was she using? He decided to make sure she was still residing in the same place.

A quick call to the rental office confirmed his worst fears. Marlena had moved out after about 10 days and had left no forwarding address. None of Marlena's mail had been coming to the Purlmen home, and the rental office made no mention of undelivered mail. That meant Marlena had dealt directly with the post office to have mail forwarded somewhere else. He then contacted VECTICOM in the hope that Marlena had gone back there to work, but they let him know she hadn't returned. Tom had hit a dead end.

After hiding the letter under one of his dresser drawers, Tom faced the reality of the situation. It was time to call in the big gun. He knew his mother would be able to help, so he opened the subject that morning when she brought him breakfast.

"Mother, we need to talk about Marlena," he blurted out. "Every single thing that has gone wrong is all my fault. We need to do everything we can to find her and bring her and Toby home. I called her old job at VECTICOM, but they said she never went back there to work."

Elizabeth was surprised at this sudden admission from Tom. For him to go so far out on a limb was totally unlike him. She looked deeply into his eyes in an attempt to discover a clue as to his confession, but she saw only calmness, clarity, and a determination she never knew he had. It was as if the lid over a pot full of coverups had been removed and the façade of normalcy both of them had been trying hard to maintain was now exposed. She answered his statement feeling confident that, for whatever the reason, he had matured into the type of man she'd always wanted him to be.

"Tom, I'm glad you said that," she replied evenly. "I knew Marlena would not have snuck out of here the way you told me she did. Now, let me hear all the facts so we can find her."

Tom had to get his story straight and it had to be plausible. The most logical thing he could think of was to throw another fact into the mix – the missing heirlooms. He knew his mother felt they were priceless valuables, so bringing them up in the right way would surely shift blame to Sue. Since Sue wasn't around, it wouldn't matter if she took most of the heat in her absence. After all, it had been over 20 years since they had last seen her or even mentioned her name.

"Well," his story began rather truthfully, "things began to get bad when you wanted me to get a ceremony together for the heirlooms. I went to look at them to get a good feeling about them. After all, we haven't done anything with them for over 20 years."

Elizabeth looked at him quizzically as he'd gone from talking about Marlena to talking about heirlooms. Tom half expected his mother to question what the heirlooms had to do with Marlena since the ceremony she'd requested hadn't happened. When she said nothing, Tom averted his eyes from hers and took a deep breath to steady his nerves. He could only hope his mother hadn't previously removed the heirlooms at some point in time, but logic ruled that out. He knew for sure she would have informed him if she had. He continued with the explanation he knew would make her emotions boil.

Tom said slowly and calmly, "The heirlooms aren't in the safe."

Came the explosion. "What do you mean they're not there? Did you take them out? Who would have taken them? I've never opened that safe. Who has been down there?"

"No one, Mother. No one I know of. Nobody who did go down there would think to look behind a painting on a wall that's hidden behind an open door unless they knew something was there."

Tom was apprehensive about mentioning Sue so soon, but he felt it was better to get it done right away while the heat was already on.

He blurted out, "The only person I can think of is Sue."

As expected, since Elizabeth was already fuming, there was no further explosion. However, hearing the hated name 'Sue' dredged up bitter memories. That meant that fuel had been poured on an angry fire and guaranteed the flame would not be easily extinguished.

Elizabeth asked her next question through gritted teeth. "And just why do you say that, Tom?"

"She asked me some questions about things that use numbers and I tried to help her."

"Help her how, Tom?"

"I told her our family remembers numbers by using dates we'll never forget."

Tom knew his next statement had to be made, but he truly dreaded making it. This was what would implicate him as an accomplice. His only comfort was in knowing he wouldn't have anything worse to say about it.

"As an example, I gave her the combination we use for the wall safe," then quickly added, "I never gave her the combination for the little safe."

Elizabeth wanted to rant and rave, but she held her anger in check. She'd finally realized her rage did nothing to help the cause. Her focus began to shift toward wanting a satisfactory resolution instead of continuing to wallow in her wrath.

With a surprisingly calm voice loaded with a putdown dripping with disgust, Elizabeth stated, "I'm sure that once that thieving girl had the safe in her hands, she was able to get inside of it."

As an afterthought, she added, "But just maybe she kept it intact and is holding on to it. And if she did open the safe and she sold something, we might be able to track it down."

Tom felt he'd better turn the conversation back to Marlena.

"I was devastated when the heirlooms were gone, Mother. You know, being sick I didn't need the added pressure of dealing with the missing heirlooms. I just got mad with everything and everybody."

Things were now set up so Tom could fully blame himself under false pretenses for Marlena's departure. If he played his cards right, the wrath might not be too great. He realized if things didn't go as planned, his mother would never forgive him, but he needed to give it the best effort he could.

"I told Marlena to leave. I wasn't taking care of myself and once I knew the heirlooms were gone, I felt like I had nothing of myself to give to Marlena and Toby. I was a failure. I lied to Marlena and told her you and I had discussed some personal things and you wanted her out of our lives."

"You did what?" Elizabeth's spat out angrily, making it clear a further explanation had to be given. She knew she'd never said anything bad to or about Marlena.

Tom was now going to expose one of the things he'd put in the letter for Marlena's eyes only. He originally had not wanted to tell his mother, but it seemed to him he had to. He just hoped he was up to the task.

"Let me explain." Tom could feel Elizabeth's rekindled rage brewing, so he did his best to cover himself by stretching the truth.

"I never knew in Peru a religious ceremony is not enough to get legally married. You have to have a civil ceremony for it to be legal. I don't know, maybe the priest who married us was not even truly a priest, because he never mentioned it. I didn't find out about it until after we got back here. It was all my fault. That means Marlena and I were never married."

"But why didn't you just get married here when you found out, Tom? How could you just leave something like that unresolved? What's wrong with you?"

Tom had his flimsy excuse ready. "I'd gotten pretty sick by the time I found out. As I said, this is all my fault."

Elizabeth felt as if she'd been kicked in the stomach as she listened to Tom spin his web of twisted logic. The more he talked, the less sense he was making. His last statement and subsequent excuse for not getting married almost put her over the edge. She wanted to lash out at him as she finally conceded to herself that her son was the type of man who would take advantage of a sweet young woman and treat her badly. On top of that, he now had a son who didn't legally have the Purlmen name. Swirling in her mind was the thought that her only son was a villain who himself was not worthy of being a Purlmen.

Many questions raced through Elizabeth's mind, but the urge to utter them was overcome by a calm determination to do everything possible to begin to look for solutions rather than to continue to place blame.

In a low and as calm a voice as she could muster, Elizabeth made her feelings about the lack of a valid marriage as clear as she could.

"Tom, I'm truly ashamed of you for having done Marlena so wrong. I cannot imagine anyone being so evil as to marry someone, find out they're not legally married, have a child, and then not do the right thing by getting married as soon as possible. You have a son to consider. You'd better hope Marlena never finds out. If you think she wanted no part of us before, after that nonsense you pulled, she'll never want to set foot in this house again. And I don't blame her. I know I wouldn't have put up with it. My mother and my grandmother wouldn't have either. No man in our family would have ever done something like that to a woman. At least no one until you tried to get away with it."

Elizabeth shook her head and repeated, "I'm ashamed of you."

Tom finally opened his mouth to speak, but Elizabeth cut him off.

"Don't say a word. There's nothing for you to say, and you had better not ever bring up the fact that you're not married again unless it's to get married and get rid of that stigma," Elizabeth warned. "Listen, I'm going to contact Rodney Stoner. He should have some idea about what can be done."

As Elizabeth left the room to get the lawyer on the phone, Tom was finally able to breathe a sigh of relief and wipe away the sweat that was beginning to pool on his forehead. He'd weathered the storm a little easier than he'd ever imagined he would, except for the disclosure about not being married. He'd miscalculated that part of his plan. He knew his mother would be angry at the revelation, but he was shocked when she boiled over to make it a veritable inferno. Outside of Marlena and Toby not being there, not being married had been the focal point of her displeasure. The heirloom discussion had become insignificant by comparison.

In the den, Elizabeth found and dialed the lawyer's number.

"Rodney Stoner's office, attorney at law. This is Kim. How may I help you?"

"This is Mrs. Purlmen. I need to speak to Rodney."

"Let me see if he's free."

The next voice Elizabeth heard belonged to the lawyer.

"Hello, Elizabeth. How are you?"

"I'm fine, but Tom and I need some help."

"Sure. What can I do?"

"Rodney, I need is to have someone – maybe a private detective – do some checking on some very personal issues. I'm talking about things that cannot be divulged to anyone under any circumstances. As I said, these things are very personal."

"As long as whatever you are concerned with is not criminal, a private detective may be your best bet."

"I thought so. Can you recommend someone?"

"I know a few who are good, but the one I would put at the very top of the list of those who can be fully trusted to not divulge any information, is one by the name of Harvey Stevens. He is the most tightlipped one I've ever dealt with when it comes to discussing clients' business. I know he's ex-military and he's proud that he, his father, and his grandfather are all college graduates, even though his great-grandfather was a slave."

When Elizabeth hesitated rather than answer, Rodney gave her all the reassurance she needed.

"In this day and age, we all need to gauge an individual's ability based on what they've shown they're capable of doing. Of course, that's the way it should have always been, but we can't chase water that's already gone past the bridge. You said you wanted a particular type of detective and Harvey is absolutely the best one I know. As a matter of fact, I can pretty much guarantee you'll feel the same way once you meet him."

"It's just that this is so important and private, Rodney."

"Elizabeth, listen to me. I've been handling things for your family for over 30 years. When you and Thomas hired me, you said it was because the other 3 legal firms you had didn't meet your expectations. Now, I don't think I've ever heard a complaint from you, have I?"

"Well, no..."

"I've always given you personalized service and I've always done things promptly for you, right?"

"Rodney, I've always thought you should be a politician."

Rodney laughed. "I'd never make it. I vote person, not party, and right over wrong. I believe in action along with fair and informed compromise. Also, I'm honest. One of my strongest dislikes is how way too many powerful people search for problems with how other powerful people handle an issue rather than working together to clean up a mess. You know what I mean? I believe some people are just finger pointers."

"Get off your perch, Rodney. I was just letting you know that I really need the right type of person."

"Listen, the private part of your problem is why I'm recommending Harvey. He's like me, 100% honest. If I had a personal issue that I needed help with, I'd choose him above all others. Pretty much every detective I know can likely help, but most engage in shop talk – you know, war stories about cases they've had. Harvey never does, and he'll give your case his full attention. Incidentally, he's semi-retired now and he only accepts clients on a case by case basis."

Elizabeth was convinced. "Good. Give me his number and I'll arrange a meeting."

"It would be better if I call him and have him contact you. I may have to convince him to take your case."

Rather than argue the point, Elizabeth allowed her long-standing trust in Rodney to be her guide.

"That will be fine."

Rodney gave Elizabeth one more bit of assurance. "I'll call Harvey right away and find out if he will take the case. I'll give you a call back as soon as I know."

"Thank you so much, Rodney." As an afterthought, she added, "And please, don't ever let anyone know that I asked you about a private detective."

"You know I wouldn't do that, Elizabeth. I'll be in touch."

Rodney hung up the phone knowing he'd only persuaded one

half of the prospective new client and detective relationship that the connection would be the right one. Harvey had notified Rodney about his semi-retired status months ago. Rodney had been reluctant to take on assignments to the point of closing his downtown office and changing his home number to an unlisted one. Harvey had also sold his house and moved into a condominium.

Rodney could only hope he'd be able to convince Harvey to take on the case, especially since he had very little up-front information to give him. All he could do was give it a shot and hope for the best. He found and dialed Harvey's number. It took 5 rings, but he finally got an answer.

"Hello." came through the receiver.

"Hey, Harvey. It's Rodney. I've got a family in need for you to help out." Rodney had decided to avoid beating around the bush because he figured Harvey would have seen right through any attempt to sneak up on the request to take on a case.

"Rodney, how have you been?" Harvey had already made the decision to avoid the work proposition being offered.

"I've been busy, how about you?"

"I'm mostly retired and happy doing whatever I want whenever I want. To tell you the truth, I plan to go to the golf course this afternoon and hit some drives or maybe play a round."

Rodney took the response to mean there was less than a slim chance Harvey would take the case, so he laid out the proposition as convincingly as he could.

"Listen, Harvey, this lady and her son need you pretty desperately. They've got money so that's no problem." Rodney quickly added, "They need the best detective work money can buy."

Mentioning money produced a negative reaction.

Harvey replied, "Man, I'm set for life. I'm good to go if I never take another case."

Realizing his mistake, Rodney backtracked to explain.

"No, what I meant to say is that these people have some extremely

209

private things to discuss that are way more important than money. They need someone who knows what he's doing and is trustworthy with private matters. Someone like you. I told them that you are the best."

Since respect for privacy had always been high on Harvey's list of priorities, he decided to gain whatever information he could before making his decision.

"Give me what you know," Harvey said.

Rodney had very little to provide. "They didn't give me too much. I've been the family's attorney for over 30 years and I only know them professionally. The husband died more than 20 years ago and his widow and son live in Glenville. This is the first time they ever approached me with anything more than something legal, but the way the lady spoke, there must be something important going on."

Harvey's curiosity had been piqued. "Okay, I'll give them a call. You know, it's a good thing I didn't reserve a tee time with anyone or I'd be golfing in an hour. Give me the name and number."

"Good. Elizabeth Purlmen, that's P-U-R-L-M-E-N. Hold on while I get the number."

As Harvey took down the information, he thought about how easy he'd been talked into taking a case he didn't need. He wanted to change his mind, but he was the type of person who, once he gave his word, would not go back on it.

"When will be the best time to give her a call?" Harvey asked.

"Right away," Rodney replied. "She's really anxious."

"Okay, but the next time you need a favor, you need to put my name on the bottom of your list."

"Sure."

"Better yet, tell the client to call my office."

They both laughed at the reference to a non-existent location.

Rodney added, "Seriously though, they need help badly."

"I'll give it my best shot. Take care."

"You too. Enjoy your retirement."

"Thanks, and when will I see you on the golf course?"

"The next time I get a break from work so I can work on my game."

"All you have to do is retire."

"Hey, I do what I gotta do. Right now, I've got another client to contact. Let me go to work."

"Okay. I'll see you around."

"Yep. See you." In a quick afterthought, Rodney added, "Wait, Harvey. Give me 5 minutes to call the Purlmens and let them know you'll be calling."

"Sure thing. I'll be calling them in 5 minutes."

Harvey began to feel better at the prospect of taking the case. He didn't need the work and was practically retired, but it felt good to have been chosen over other firms and individuals because of his skills.

Once Rodney contacted Elizabeth and let her know Harvey would be calling in a few minutes, Elizabeth sat anxiously at the desk and anticipated how the conversation with Harvey would go. She hoped this stranger she was going to share family secrets with was going to be as up to the task as Rodney had stated. She was so engrossed with what she should say that the ringing phone gave her a start.

"Hello."

"Hello," came the reply from the telephone receiver. "I'm Harvey Stevens and I'm calling for Mrs. Elizabeth Purlmen."

"I'm Mrs. Purlmen."

"Rodney Stoner gave me your number and said you had some extremely personal and sensitive issues you needed help with."

"Yes, I do."

"Alright, first off, it would be best that we meet face to face. I want you to be comfortable with me and I want to get comfortable with you."

"That's fine."

"Good. When can we get together?"

"What are your office hours?"

"I'm semi-retired and I work on an as-necessary basis. Would you prefer to come to me or would you rather I come to you?"

"Oh, would it be possible for you to come to my home? My son is rather sickly and he has some of the information."

"Sure, I'll come by. When is best for you?"

"The sooner the better. How quickly can you come?"

"Where do you live?"

Elizabeth gave Harvey address information and he pondered for a moment before answering.

"Give me one hour and I can be at your front door."

"We'll be expecting you."

As soon as they hung up their respective phones, Elizabeth returned to Tom's room with the good news.

"You need to get up Tom. A private detective will be here in an hour."

"I don't feel up to it, Mother. I'd rather meet him right here in my room."

While Elizabeth didn't approve of what Tom had said, she decided she would accept it. After all, he was sick.

"Alright Tom, but just be ready with as much information as possible."

After glancing around the room, Elizabeth decided it would work out fine as a meeting place. There was the tv tray that Harvey could write on and she retrieved a folding chair in addition to the lounge chair already in the room so both she and Harvey could sit. Once the room was set, she retreated to the kitchen where she brewed coffee and prepared some snacks.

The doorbell rang in just under the hour Harvey had predicted by 5 minutes. Elizabeth appreciated his promptness as it supported the confidence Rodney had bestowed on Harvey. She hurried to the door and opened it to reveal a tall well-dressed brown-skinned man who greeted her with a friendly smile and the same courtesy and respect she would have expected had she visited him in his office.

"Good evening, Mrs. Purlmen. I'm Harvey Stevens. We spoke about an hour ago."

"Yes, please come in Mr. Stevens."

"Thank you. You can call me Harvey, and how would you prefer to be addressed?"

The question caught Elizabeth completely off guard. She couldn't recall ever being asked about name preferences before. She quickly weighed her answer by a simple deduction. Her lawyer, whom she addressed and was addressed by on a first name basis, gave this detective his highest regard. If he was comfortable with first names, she decided she would give him that same respect. Besides, she needed his full cooperation and expertise to solve her problems. Now was not the time to worry about any kind of class distinction.

"Please call me Elizabeth, Harvey. My son Tom is upstairs in bed, so we're going to meet in his room."

In a rapid continuation of the thought and likely to subconsciously garner sympathy, she added softly, "He's not well. He has some internal issues that will likely prove fatal."

"I'm sorry to hear that," said Harvey. "I'll be at your service to do whatever I can do to help you with whatever issues you have."

"Thank you. Tom's room is upstairs, second room on the left. I'll be right up with some fresh coffee and a few snacks."

"Do you need help with anything?"

"Oh no. I want you to go meet Tom."

"Okay, upstairs, second room on the left. I'll go up and meet Tom."

Harvey strode through Tom's open bedroom door and was astonished to see someone who looked to be at least as old as Elizabeth. The man's hair was littered with gray, and he had a mustache and beard that looked long overdue for a trip to the barbershop.

Harvey didn't dwell on what Tom looked like. Instead, he continued toward Tom with his right hand outstretched.

"Tom?" He asked and immediately continued with, "I'm Harvey Stevens. Your mother told me to come up and introduce myself."

Tom was at first taken aback that someone would just walk into his room unaccompanied, but he was shocked that the man standing before him was black. Under normal conditions, neither one of those things would have been expected. However, the lack of formality the man portrayed convinced Tom to take both things in stride. As quickly as his anxiety had been raised, it dissipated and he began to feel comfortable.

"Yes, I'm Tom," he said as he took Harvey's hand. "Sorry I'm not up, but I'm a bit under the weather."

"No problem, I understand. Please call me Harvey. Is it okay to call you Tom?"

"Sure. Have a seat."

"Thanks, Tom."

Elizabeth came through the door with the coffee and snacks and placed them on the tv tray. She wasn't satisfied and stated as much.

"I need to get a larger table."

"Would you like for me to help you?" Harvey asked.

"Oh no, I'll be right back."

After a few more minutes the room was set and the feeling out process began over coffee. Harvey began the task.

"I don't know how much Rodney told you about me," he began. "I've worked on cases for him over the last 20 something years."

"Well, he said you were one of the best," Elizabeth replied. She then added mainly for Tom's sake, "Especially at maintaining the utmost confidentiality about your clients."

Harvey smiled. "I always do that to the utmost. Let me tell you why. I was in the military years ago and went through training for doing things similar to what I do now. Confidentiality was hammered into us then and I took it to heart. Most of the other guys did the same thing in varying degrees, but some were real blabbermouths. I was about the only one of their peers who told them they needed to be cool, but I've found that once someone is a storyteller, they will always be a storyteller. Some of the other guys never seemed to fully appreciate the importance of someone else's privacy, but they probably never got burned by being over-talkative."

Harvey paused to take a sip of coffee before continuing.

"I may have been the only one who got a real-life lesson, though, even though I didn't need it. Something occurred that had nothing to do with any kind of case I was on. I mean, something happened over the course of many years that solidified my belief in respecting everyone's privacy. I like to use it as a story I can give as an example as to why I can be trusted with every other person's business."

"A year or so after my military training was complete, I happened to be in the mess hall having lunch when a sergeant with a tray full of food came in and sat at the same table as I. It was no big thing. We both had barely made it into the mess hall before it closed and we were two of a very few soldiers there. Anyway, he struck up a conversation. You know, like how long before you get out, where are you from, where have you been – that kind of thing. Well, this particular fort we were in was thousands of miles from where I grew up, and he'd grown up thousands of miles from my home. The one thing he mentioned that I connected with was this. At one time, he'd been stationed at a different fort about 10 miles from where I was born and raised."

Harvey paused to take another sip of coffee and glance at Elizabeth and Tom. He had their full attention.

"The sergeant told me he'd had a girlfriend in my home town on a street a couple of blocks from where I lived. He started reminiscing about the lady, her home, her children, and other things, so I got curious. That's when I asked for her name. He got kind of indignant and hushed up. He told me he would never start spreading information around like that. I didn't say anything more about it and

215

I never saw him again after that day."

After another sip of coffee, Harvey continued.

"A good 12 or more years later, I was in a bar and grill in my home town. The place was packed that day, so I had no choice but to order a meal at the bar because I didn't want to wait who knows how long for a table seat. I hadn't been there for 5 minutes before a lady came in fuming. She sat down next to me and ordered something to eat and a 6 pack of beer to go. While waiting for her meal, she struck up a conversation. She told me she had been ordered by her boyfriend to go buy some beer, and she didn't appreciate it. Seems he'd just gotten home and conventional logic dictated that he should have stopped for beer on his way in."

Harvey paused for coffee before continuing.

"Anyway, she went from complaining about her current boyfriend to reminiscing about her 'soldier friend from about 12 years ago'. The more she spoke about that soldier friend, the more I got the other side of the exact same story I'd heard from that soldier 12 years and over a thousand miles from where we were seated. An eavesdropper seated on her other side asked for the soldier's name, but she clammed up and told him she would never put the man's business in the street."

"That incident really struck home to me about how important it is to maintain total secrecy. I believe if you want a secret to remain a secret, keep it totally secret from everyone else. It's like the six degrees of separation theory where any person can be connected to any other person on the planet through a chain of acquaintances with no more than five intermediaries. There have been studies that bear this out. That's why in my business, I take absolutely no chances with confidentiality. I don't retell any stories about any of my cases in any way, shape, or form."

Harvey paused to let his words fully sink in before adding what he felt should close the story and allow them to deal with the present case.

216

"Believe it or not, I left some pertinent information out of that true story I told you about the soldier and the lady, even though it wasn't a case of mine. That's how much I respect everyone's privacy. They didn't want their personal information made public so I don't offer any more clues about that situation."

Harvey took another sip of coffee and leaned back in the chair. This signaled he'd finished the true story he felt should convince Elizabeth and Tom he was a perfect choice for the sake of privacy. He couldn't have known the fact that Elizabeth had not only invited him into the house sight unseen but upstairs into Tom's room meant he had already been fully accepted as the right man for the job.

Tom had no qualms whatsoever. His mother's okay was all that was necessary for him to feel confident about Harvey's ability. What remained now was for Elizabeth or Tom to begin to speak about the case. Normally Elizabeth would delve right into the facts, but she held back. She rightly decided to let Tom take the lead. The silence was almost deafening as she and Harvey waited for Tom to speak. After a few moments, he finally took the hint and began.

"Well, I'm pretty sick," he said. "And being physically sick can lead to mental issues if you let it. I let my problems get in the way of my marriage and I forced my wife to leave."

Tom hadn't remembered to add Toby into the discussion right away, but he caught his omission quickly enough to add, "She left and took our son with her."

"Any ideas about where they might be?" asked Harvey.

Tom knew he had to lie, at least in front of Elizabeth.

"No. I have no idea," he said. "She's originally from California, but she doesn't have family there."

"Okay. What's her name and what's her maiden name?"

"Marlena Bell-Purlmen. That's spelled M-A-R-L-E-N-A. Her maiden name is Bell. She added the hyphen to Purlmen when we were married."

"Her age?"

"She's 23," Tom said and then thought about the car. "She has a 1990 Cadillac Seville. It's gold with a tan interior. I don't remember the plate number."

The back and forth questions and answers regarding Marlena and Toby continued like this for a while until the exchange finally ended with a couple of photos of the pair being handed to Harvey.

"I believe this should be enough information to start," he said. "I'll begin researching today and I'll give you a status tomorrow."

Harvey stood to leave, but Elizabeth, who had remained mostly silent, now spoke.

"Wait, there's more. We have another matter for you to consider."

Harvey sat down again and waited for this additional case to unfold.

Elizabeth forced herself to remain calm and unemotional as she began to discuss the heirlooms.

"We've had certain heirlooms in our family for generations and we believe they were stolen a little over 20 years ago."

When Elizabeth hesitated after making her statement, Harvey asked, "The police had no luck?"

"I never got the police involved and I don't ever want them involved," Elizabeth sternly replied. She then explained the situation.

"We never do anything with the heirlooms until they are handed down. Other than at that time, they're always locked in a safe. When my husband and I handed the heirlooms down to Tom back in 1967, we locked them in the safe and none of us thought about opening it until a few months ago. We were planning to have a little heirloom ceremony to honor the birth of my grandson. That's when Tom found out the heirlooms were missing. That safe is hidden in a place that absolutely no one would look for it and of course no one knew the combination except for us."

Tom decided he should now divulge how he believed the combination was shared. He knew if he left the explanation up to his mother, she would likely spit the information out through clenched teeth.

"I made the mistake of giving the combination to one of the housekeepers we had," he confessed, deftly dancing around the need to utter the name 'Sue'. "It was all my fault."

Elizabeth winced at Tom's statement but buried the urge to say something immediately. Anything she might have said right away would not have been pleasant.

"Do you think they'd still have those heirlooms?" Harvey asked. "Were they valuable?"

Hearing the word "valuable" relaxed Elizabeth's tension, and she was able to focus more on the heirlooms than Tom and Sue. She proceeded to put the same spin on the heirlooms' value as she had always done.

"They'd be valuable to anyone, but they're priceless to us. We stored them in a small cast-iron safe that was inside a wall safe. Maybe the thief just kept the safe or maybe she sold what was in it – who knows? I would just like for you to attempt to find out the truth about it."

"I understand," said Harvey. "Most folks don't realize that many things are a lot more valuable than what they're worth in dollars and cents."

"That's right," Elizabeth answered. "And just like the other problem, we do not want the heirlooms discussed. We absolutely do not want the police involved."

"Sure. Give me as much information about the housekeeper as you can."

Elizabeth spoke openly now to give Harvey the best possible chance to successfully find the heirlooms. She rightly assumed Tom would do his best to sugarcoat or avoid certain details in anything he had to say.

"Well," Elizabeth began, "there were two of them, a mother and daughter team. The mother's name was Molly and the daughter was

Sue. I never was too fond of Sue, but Molly had been perfect for the job. Sue is the only one I suspect would have been the thief. I don't believe for a second that Molly would have been involved. I know we don't have any pictures of them, but I'll give you all the information I can. Their last name is Hurley and I remember that they were supposed to move in with their Aunt, uh, Bernice, I think."

Elizabeth pondered for a moment and added, "I don't remember what town it was right offhand, though. Tom, do you know anything else about them?"

Tom didn't believe he had anything more to add, but he knew better than to even give a hint that he had any additional knowledge about the Hurley family in front of his mother. "No, Mother," is all he said.

Harvey was still taking notes, so there was a pause in the conversation.

When finished he asked, "Just what exactly were the heirlooms?"

Elizabeth was quick to answer. "A pocket watch, a gold coin, and a ring."

Remembering the lighter, she added, "There is also a gold lighter. You know, I do have a picture of the watch, coin and ring somewhere. It'll take a little time for me to find it for you because it's in amongst many other old pictures."

Hearing his mother mention the picture was music to Tom's ears. He sorely needed a reason for his mother to leave the room so he could have a private discussion with Harvey. He'd previously been at a loss as to how to make it happen.

Tom eagerly chimed in, "Yes, I remember that picture. It's in one of those boxes of pictures in the basement. I'd help you look, Mother, but I don't feel up to it."

"I can get it myself," she said to Tom. To Harvey, she said, "I don't think it will take more than 15 or 20 minutes to find it."

"That'll be fine," replied Harvey.

As soon as Elizabeth left the room, Tom whispered to Harvey, "I need to talk to you in private. Please close the bedroom door."

Harvey complied and returned to take a seat, this time moving his chair as close to the bed and Tom's head as he could.

"I need to give you more information about things. This is stuff you can never repeat to my mother."

"I understand, I won't say a word," Harvey assured him.

Still speaking in a hushed voice, Tom explained, "It will be impossible to get Marlena to come back unless you give her the truth about certain things, but you can only do that if she also promises to never give the information to my mother or anyone else."

Tom paused to give Harvey a chance to agree with this condition.

"Sure, and that's the way I'll present it to Marlena."

"Okay," began Tom. "Mother doesn't know, but I rented a place in Lakeview so I could take Marlena and my son there and leave them. Once we were there, I made up a bunch of lies. I told Marlena my mother had agreed to dump her there. I told her she was not welcome back in the house. When I got back home, I told my mother Marlena had left because I'd become sick and she just wanted to get away from us. Marlena would not have left because of that. The truth is she only left because I said and did some really ugly things."

Tom stopped to collect his thoughts before continuing. It was then he remembered the letter he'd hidden.

"There's a letter I wrote that I wanted to send to Marlena, but I never got the chance. When I checked to make sure she still lived in the same place, I found out she had moved and I didn't know how to find her new address. Pull the top left drawer of my dresser all the way out. You'll find it there. It has the address I moved her to."

Harvey followed Tom's directions and retrieved the letter.

Tom continued. "What the letter contains is only for Marlena's eyes. If you can't find her, please hide it or destroy it, but never let anyone else see it under any circumstances."

Harvey folded the letter and placed it in his pocket.

"Is there anything else you can tell me about Marlena?"

"Well, you can tell her I admit I was deceitful."

Tom didn't want to give the full rationale for the statement, but he realized he needed to completely explain what he was talking about.

"Don't ever tell my mother that I told you, but the truth is I planned to have a fake marriage ceremony all along. I wasn't looking for a wife. I was only looking for an heir for my mother's sake. My mother knows that Marlena and I weren't legally married. I told her about it this morning and she was livid. It's the kind of thing my mother doesn't want anyone to know about, so you can't tell her you know. The thing of it is, even though I told her the marriage wasn't valid, I said that it wasn't done on purpose. The truth is, I meant for it to be that way."

Tom paused to collect his thoughts. He teetered on the idea of admitting to Harvey that he'd also told Marlena about the fake marriage, but his mother's reaction to the revelation gave him pause. If the marriage situation was so terrible in his mother's eyes, he couldn't bring himself to admit to Harvey that he had already told Marlena. If he did, he'd have to also admit that he'd lied to Marlena about having told Mother about it and that he'd lied about Mother agreeing to put Marlena out. He found it too much to take. He lacked the courage to put all his cards on the table. He was a coward, and he knew it. He'd let Mother and Harvey deal with the problem of Marlena already knowing about the fake marriage. Maybe Marlena was as livid about it as his mother had been. If so, it could be the one thing that would make getting her to come home an impossible dream.

Tom dropped his head in misery at the possibility. He closed his eyes and took a deep breath before raising his head, opening his eyes, and continuing.

"Anyway, after we had the fake marriage, I had told Marlena I would be taking care of all the necessary paperwork, but in reality, I did nothing. But hey, listen. I've only told you in case you need it to help persuade Marlena to come back. If you don't need to mention it, please don't."

Tom sadly shook his head before continuing.

"Let me tell you, Marlena and Toby were perfect additions to the family. In fact, they were so perfect, I became jealous of how much they meant to my mother. I've been the villain. That's why you need to find them."

With this admission, Tom had lifted a monumental load off his chest. He was now able to articulate final instructions to Harvey.

"Remember, do whatever you have to do to get Marlena to return, but none of these things I explained to you can ever be repeated to my mother.

As an afterthought, Tom added, "Now if you think you need more information, give me a call. Also, give me a number so I can reach you if I think of anything else. But right now, move your chair back where it was and open the door so my mother doesn't suspect anything."

As Harvey stood to replace the chair, he recalled something his father had said to him about choices in life.

"You know Tom, what you've told me reminds of something my father said to me a couple of times. He said, 'Son, every decision you make while crossing the river of life is either a stepping stone or a crumbling bridge. Always do your best to choose wisely'. It sounds to me like you're doing all the right things now to pick up the pieces from a crumbling bridge."

Tom said nothing as he pensively mulled over what Harvey had said.

When Tom remained silent, Harvey felt he'd either overstepped Tom's comfort zone or what he'd said was too much of a riddle. However, rather than retreat and let the moment go, he took things to another level.

"There's something else my father told me that has always stuck with me," Harvey began. "He said, 'It doesn't matter if someone was born in a back-alley flophouse or got raised in a gutter. Everyone's job is to do the right thing and make the right choices in life. That philosophy also applies to someone born with a silver spoon.'"

Tom still said nothing, so Harvey replaced the chair and took out a business card. He felt he must have misjudged Tom, so he wanted to change the subject. He spoke again as he handed the card to Tom.

"Listen, Tom, you can call me anytime. If I don't answer, just leave your name, number and the best time to return the call. Never leave any personal information on the recorder."

Tom smiled. He hadn't been turned off. He'd been lost in pensive thoughts. Now he was again ready to speak.

"After what you told us about the soldier and the lady, you don't have to worry about that."

Then, reflectively, Tom had more to say. "I'm glad I feel like I can trust you and I'm glad you told me what your dad said about how to cross a river. It's hard to believe I've been speaking to you about things I would never tell anyone else, but I do need to tell you one more thing. I know I'm not long for this life. I doubt I'll last another week. My kidneys are shot, my liver's not good and some other stuff is going on. The most important thing I want to do from now until the end is to have faith that you will find Marlena and Toby. You need to get them to return to comfort my mother. To tell you the truth, I hope I'm gone before you find them. That's how ugly I was. I don't deserve to ever see them again."

Harvey started to interject, but Tom stopped him.

"Please, there's nothing to say. Just use my words and your interpretation of my state of mind to bring them back home. That's the best thing you can do."

Harvey responded with the assurance Tom craved.

"I'll do the best I can to make it happen. You can be sure of that."

The two men exchanged a warm handshake just as Elizabeth returned to the room with the picture.

"I found it," she said, handing the photo to Harvey.

"Thank you," he replied, looking it over. "I don't think I'll need it at this time unless you don't mind my holding onto it. I can always make a copy and give it back to you."

Harvey thought for a moment and then said, "Here's what I'll do. I'll take everything I have so far and do a little research tonight and tomorrow morning. Then I'll come here to return the original picture. We'll discuss the fee for my service at that time."

He looked from Tom to Elizabeth and then back and forth again.

"Is there anything else?" he asked.

Neither had anything to add, so Harvey shook Tom's hand and bade him goodnight. He and Elizabeth left Tom's room and descended the stairs and made their way to the front door. It was there that Elizabeth reminded him to maintain privacy.

"Harvey, I'm so glad we can trust you to keep this whole business confidential. There's nothing worse than to feel like family secrets have been exposed to neighbors or strangers."

"My sentiments exactly," Harvey told her. "I couldn't have put it any better."

Elizabeth extended her hand and Harvey shook it firmly.

"Goodnight, Elizabeth. I'll be in touch."

"Goodnight, Harvey."

Harvey's trip home allowed him to organize the data he'd received that day. He felt he had enough clues to begin his search along with a subcategory of what he could openly reveal to Tom, Elizabeth, and Marlena. The truths, half-truths, and downright lies that had been revealed to him would help his search, but now, more than ever before, he had to be certain that whatever should be hidden would remain hidden. He reasoned that it would be best to treat Tom and Marlena more or less as one entity. Elizabeth, however, had to be treated as the person having the *least* privilege to be aware of everything that was going on. It would seem strange. After all, she had hired him, but she would be the one most kept in the dark.

Harvey waited until late morning the next day to call the Purlmen residence to let them know he could be at their home within an hour or whatever time thereafter they'd like. Elizabeth answered and they settled on 1 p.m. sharp. Once there, Harvey delivered the original photo he had copied along with a payment plan.

"For this case, I think the best thing to do is for you to purchase my services with a retainer fee. Since I'll likely have to be on the road and spending time away from home, let's go with an even thousand dollars. I keep good books and I'll save all receipts. Does that sound alright?"

Elizabeth didn't bat an eye. "That will be fine," she said. "I'll get you a check."

As Elizabeth walked toward the den, Harvey called out to her, "Would it be alright for me to go up and say hi and goodbye to Tom?"

"Yes, you know where his room is. I'll be up in a few minutes."

Harvey quickly made his way to Tom's room where he found Tom sitting up in bed and apparently waiting for him.

"Harvey, I'm glad to see you."

"How are you feeling, Tom?"

"As well as I can, under the circumstances. Anything to report?"

"No, too early yet."

"Okay. You have all my faith and confidence that you'll get things done the right way."

"You can count on me to do my best."

"That's all I need to hear to make me feel like I'm standing solid on one of those stepping stones you told me about."

Tom took a deep breath before slowly and evenly continuing with, "Just knowing you'll take care of things gives me the peace of mind I need."

Tom didn't elaborate on what he needed peace of mind for, but Harvey figured it had a lot to do with Tom's diminished physical condition. His thought was confirmed when Tom held out his hand to Harvey and said, "Goodbye, my friend. Tell Marlena I'm sorry and they need to come home."

"I'll bring her back one way or the other," Harvey assured him.

"Perfect. I'm sure you will."

When they broke their handshake, Tom closed his eyes and turned away, indicating he wanted some quiet time. Harvey turned to leave the room just as Elizabeth was entering.

"He wants to rest," Harvey told her.

Elizabeth decided to double-check for herself and asked, "Tom, are you feeling alright?"

"Fine, Mother. I just want to take a nap."

"Alright."

Elizabeth and Harvey went downstairs and to the front door where Elizabeth handed Harvey the check.

"Here you are, Harvey. Keep us informed."

Taking the check, Harvey asked, "Do you want a daily update or one only when I have important progress to report?"

"I'd be happy with a call every few days at a minimum or right away if you have something major to report."

"Then Elizabeth, I will call you no later than Wednesday. With luck, you'll get a call sooner before then."

"That's fine. Thanks, Harvey, and good luck."

"You're welcome, Elizabeth. I'll do my best."

As soon as Harvey left, Elizabeth returned to Tom's room and was surprised to see him sitting up and writing a note. He spoke when he saw her.

"Hi, Mother. I'm just jotting down a few notes. Why don't you come back in a few hours so we can decide on dinner?"

"Alright, I'll be back later."

Tom had actually been writing instructions to Elizabeth.

Mother, please make sure Marlena and Toby get back home safely. Let them know I'm sorry for all the confusion I caused. And thank you for standing by me. Please make sure the doctor doesn't keep me alive as a vegetable. My time has come. You, Marlena, and

Toby need to make things work as a family. Goodbye.
Tom

Satisfied with his note, Tom first swallowed twice the ordinary dosage of the prescription sleeping pills he had been hoarding for months. He opened 8 additional capsules and dumped the contents into a glass of brandy. For the briefest of moments, he paused to ponder the path he'd taken to his planned fate. He'd openly admitted the mess they were in was all his fault, but his inner conscious told him his mother's overbearing presence also played a huge part in decisions he'd made. That realization triggered a guilt complex for blaming his mother for any of his actions because he knew he could have been a stronger person.

With his mind now spinning in a vicious circle of cause and effect for his shortcomings, he decided the best thing he could do for the sake of everyone was to continue with his plan to end it all. He downed the potion he'd prepared and relaxed. As he had predicted, he didn't last a week. For that matter, life was over for him that same day.

Elizabeth first noticed the bottle of brandy and empty glass when she went back to Tom's room to discuss dinner. She wasn't very surprised to find his body lifeless. She almost felt like she was reliving Thomas' death years ago, with one distinct difference. Tom had left a suicide note. Elizabeth read and destroyed it immediately. She then removed the glass, pill bottles, and brandy from the room. She wanted to reduce the chance of having Tom's death ruled a suicide.

Almost without emotion, Elizabeth then called Dr. Gregory to advise him of the situation and impressed upon him the need to have the cause of death be due to the natural causes Tom was being treated for. She wanted to have the body released quickly for burial. The doctor obliged her wishes and the same funeral home she'd used for Thomas was able to prepare the body for burial Wednesday morning. Elizabeth accomplished every task necessary to get the body in the ground with a stoic determination primarily fueled by the belief

Marlena and Toby would soon be home.

Harvey called Elizabeth Wednesday evening with his first update, and it was apparent that Elizabeth had been near the phone. She answered before the end of the first ring.

"Hello."

"Hello, Elizabeth. This is Harvey. I wanted to give you an update."

Elizabeth was disappointed Harvey hadn't said he'd found Marlena, but she did want to know what had been done thus far.

"Yes?" was all she said.

"I found where she had been living for a short time prior to moving."

"Where was that?" Elizabeth asked.

Harvey had anticipated the response and was ready with an answer.

"Now you know I don't like to give anyone more information than is necessary to accomplish the mission I've been hired for. Once I find Marlena and get you back together, the two of you can exchange all the information you want."

Elizabeth was at first surprised at Harvey's statement, but she quickly realized what he'd said made sense. Instead of arguing she used the opportunity to segue into the news about Tom.

"Yes, I understand that it's the right thing to do." Collecting herself, she continued with, "Tom died the same day you were here just a few hours after you left."

"Oh, wow, I'm sorry," was all Harvey could immediately think of to say.

"We knew he was sick and he wasn't going to live long."

Elizabeth made sure she used the correct strategy to expand on Tom's demise. There was no way she wanted even the slightest hint of suicide to be mentioned as she continued.

"The doctor and funeral director did what they needed to do to get him ready for burial this morning. I've only been back home for a couple of hours."

Harvey thought back to the last time he'd seen Tom and realized the somewhat morbid discussion they'd had then was Tom's way of saying he knew for a fact he would not be alive when Marlena was found. He suspected suicide but followed Elizabeth's lead to treat it as death from natural causes. Empathetically, he moved the main thrust of the conversation back to what would be important to get Marlena and Toby home.

"Do you want me to let Marlena know about Tom when I see her?"

Elizabeth didn't hesitate or mince words.

"Harvey, I want you to do and say whatever you think you need to do or say, just so they come back home."

"Then that's what I'll do. I don't think I need anything else right now Do you need anything else from me?"

"No. Just find them soon and get them to come back home, and by the way," Elizabeth slowed her speech rate to make a point. "I'm going to tell you something that might help to convince her to come home, but only mention it if all else fails."

"Sure, but there are many things that shouldn't be discussed over the phone," Harvey replied. "What kind of information is it? Is it something really personal that should only be discussed privately in person?"

"No," Elizabeth quickly answered. "It's personal and it really hurt me when I heard about it from Tom. But I do think you need to know in case Marlena somehow found out about it and she believes I don't want her to come back because of it. Please don't mention it to her unless she brings it up or you need to. It's that ugly."

"Alright," Harvey said. "What is it?"

Elizabeth blurted out, "Tom never married Marlena. They got married in Peru and the rules there are different from what they are here. Tom found out they weren't married once they got back home, but he never lifted a finger to straighten it out. He just fed Marlena lies. He never told her the marriage in Peru was nothing but a sham. I'm embarrassed and hurt about it. Nothing like that has ever happened in my family before. Now, because of Tom, my daughter-in-law and grandson are not here with me."

Elizabeth had to fight back tears for a moment before continuing.

"That's why you need to get them back home. I need to have them with me so I can take care of them the way Tom should have. Just remember, Harvey, don't embarrass Marlena by saying anything about how she and Tom were never married unless you need to do it as a last resort."

"I'll do my best and you know how I feel about giving out information," Harvey reassuringly told her.

"Yes, I know," Elizabeth replied.

The statement of trust Elizabeth displayed with her answer motivated Harvey to raise both his and her expectations with, "I plan to find them before the end of the weekend."

Hearing Harvey's proclamation lifted Elizabeth's spirits.

"Wonderful. That would be wonderful," she said.

"Yes, you can depend on me, Elizabeth. You rest easy and take care. I'll be in touch soon. Goodbye now."

"Goodbye."

11 Discovery

By promising quick action, Harvey had set himself up to be a hero if he found Marlena soon or an absolute failure if he didn't. However, he was now confident he would succeed. He'd finally gotten some good information about her location.

Marlena had been living in the Lakeview apartment, just as Tom said, but she'd quietly moved out days later to an apartment on the other side of town. She didn't stay there long either. She had immediately begun to make arrangements to move again. That second move would have slowed Harvey's search down considerably except for one thing - Marlena didn't have a telephone. She'd borrowed a friendly neighbor's phone to inquire about Piney Orchards in Millburn. That neighbor overheard Marlena's conversation and, while Marlena didn't directly give the neighbor details about where she was moving, the neighbor considered Piney Orchards to be a forgone conclusion. When the friendly ex-neighbor saw Harvey at the door of Marlena's vacant apartment, she couldn't help herself. She told Harvey she heard Marlena say she was moving to Piney Orchards in Millburn, a few hours away.

Now that he'd found out where Marlena was likely now residing, Harvey had lunch and began the trip to Millburn. An overriding theme was apparent. Marlena was doing her best to get away and stay away. Bouncing from one place to another was a good way to disappear if no forwarding information is revealed, and so far, Marlena had covered her tracks well. She'd not left formal notice of her whereabouts at all. If not for the casual mention of her probable newest location by her ex-neighbor, Harvey would still be spinning his wheels.

"Man, she really wants to be completely out of Tom's life and leave no easy way for him to trace her movements," he muttered to himself.

Harvey was glad he had the additional information regarding the marital split Tom had provided to help him encourage Marlena to return. The fact that she had forfeited prepaid months of rent to hide meant convincing her to return wouldn't be easy. Imagining what Marlena's mental state might be and the way he'd have to juggle the truth between what Tom had told him and Elizabeth told him, Harvey began to get the feeling that Tom's death might wind up being the most convincing argument he could use.

At 6 p.m. that day, Harvey arrived at the Piney Orchards townhouse complex where he had been told Marlena was residing. He toyed with the idea of getting Marlena's address from the realtor, but caution told him it would be best to initially search for the car and then hopefully find the name on a mailbox. He'd taken enough of a chance surreptitiously getting what information he could from Marlena's former neighbor. He certainly didn't want to arouse suspicion that he was a stalker or some other unsavory character so close to her home. Doing so would surely make the task he came there for even more difficult.

Harvey went into his undercover mode. He drove through the

entire complex and did not see the car. It was getting late, so he found a motel room and had a meal, figuring Marlena's car would be back later that evening. He just hoped there was only one gold Cadillac in the complex and it belonged to Marlena.

When he returned an hour and a half later, he found a gold Cadillac parked in space number 105. He knew the numbered space where the car was parked did not necessarily coincide with the apartment number of the owner. Some places use that method to prevent potential burglars from simply deducing that no car in a particular space meant there was a strong possibility no one was in the home with that same number. A name on the mailbox would enlighten him, but it was a little too dark to attempt to read the names on the mailbox cluster that served the nearby homes. Using a flashlight to read each name would look suspicious, so he decided to wait until the next morning to look again.

The evening dragged by for Harvey. He'd found Marlena and he was anxious to talk to her, but at the same time, he knew he had to be on top of his game so as not to overstep the boundaries of any of the secrets within the secrets he would be discussing with her. Then he remembered he could use any or all of the family secrets to get Marlena to return home. Only Elizabeth would be left in the dark about certain items. The overriding factor here was to make sure Marlena fully understood she could not ever divulge family secrets.

Harvey waited until after lunch the next day to return to the complex and located the name M. Bell on the mailbox numbered 103. He was glad he had waited to confirm the address rather than simply going to the 105 address the night before. Because Marlena hadn't returned until sometime after 7 the previous day, Harvey decided to come back around that time. He didn't want to be observed loitering around the complex for hours on end.

Harvey returned at 6:55 and only had to wait for a half-hour before he saw the gold Cadillac pull up and park. He'd already determined the best way to introduce himself was to first let her get inside her home for about 15 minutes before attempting to contact her. He watched as she took Toby out of the car and made her way home. Precisely 15 minutes later, with Tom's letter in hand, he rang her bell. Then heard the sound of footsteps approaching the door and finally a soft female voice.

"Yes, who is it?"

"My name is Harvey Stevens. I'm a private detective and I need to discuss some things with you."

"A private detective? What do you want?"

"I was hired by Mrs. Elizabeth Purlmen to find you and let you know she wants you and Toby to come home," replied Harvey, purposely leaving Tom's name out of the statement.

Marlena thought for a moment before asking, "What about Tom? He told me they didn't want me around."

Harvey felt Marlena was already contemplating the possibility of a reunion so he upped the ante.

"Mrs. Purlmen hired me, but both she and Tom stated they wanted you home." He paused to let that sink in and was glad Marlena was silent because he added, "Tom passed away last Saturday. He was buried on Wednesday. I only met them both a week ago."

"Tom died?" Marlena asked.

"Yes, his mother gave me the news on Wednesday."

Hoping to have Marlena allow him to come in or at the very least open the door, he added, "Tom gave me this letter he said was for your eyes only. He didn't even want his mother to know the contents. Why don't you take a look at it?"

Marlena then cracked the door open, and with the security chain still intact, accepted the envelope. Harvey allowed Marlena all the time she needed to read and digest the contents of the letter.

After reading the letter, as a last vestige of needing reassurance Harvey was on the up and up, Marlena asked for proof that Harvey was who he said he was.

She asked, "Do you have a badge?"

"No, I only carry my license because I don't ever want someone to confuse me with the police."

Harvey retrieved and gave his detective license to Marlena for her perusal.

After looking it over, Marlena opened the door and, once inside, Harvey gave his standard line to further introduce both parties to one another.

"As I said, I'm Harvey Stevens. "You can call me Harvey, and how would you prefer to be addressed?"

"Marlena is fine."

"Alright, Marlena. I hope what we've spoken about so far has you ready and willing to go back home as soon as possible."

"Not so fast." Motioning to a chair she continued, "Please, have a seat."

Harvey sat down and immediately began probing for whatever reasons Marlena had to not go home.

"Mrs. Purlmen wants you to come home. What's keeping you from going back?"

"Tom told me she didn't want me there."

"I don't know what the letter from Tom said, but he told me he told you many lies, mainly because of his physical condition. One of the things he confessed to me is that your mother-in-law never wanted you to leave. He gave me the information about how he tricked you into the place in Lakeview. He said he never told his mother about that. Probably the most important thing he told me is that you and Toby were everything to and for his mother and that he was jealous."

Marlena didn't know how to respond. Combined with what she'd read in the letter, what Harvey was saying sounded perfectly logical, but she didn't know how she could be sure.

Harvey had an inspiration. "Why don't we call Mrs. Purlmen? You have two phones, don't you?"

Marlena nodded affirmatively and added, "Yes."

"Fine. I can be on one phone and you can dial her number. Let me do the talking at first and then you can take over if you feel comfortable. Would that work for you?"

Marlena was enthused. "That sounds good. You can use the phone next to you and I'll use the one in the kitchen."

Marlena dialed Elizabeth's number and called out to Harvey, "It's ringing."

Harvey picked up the receiver.

Both heard Elizabeth pick up her phone and answer, "Hello."

Harvey spoke. "Elizabeth, this is Harvey. I found Marlena."

"You did?" Elizabeth's joyful voice exploded out of the phone. "How is she? How's Toby? Where are they?"

Hearing the excitement in Elizabeth's voice, Marlena needed no prompting to speak.

"We're fine, Mother. We missed you so much."

Harvey held his receiver out toward Marlena so she could hang hers up and take a seat and talk, but she ignored him while the women continued their discussion.

Elizabeth's excitement was apparent as she spoke. "I was so afraid I would never see you again. Tom told me he had been mean to you and lied to you about me, but you should have known I would never turn against you or Toby."

Marlena was ready to cry but fought back the tears. What helped calm her was the next logical thing for her to say. "I'm sorry about Tom. He was a good person but being sick changed him."

Marlena was surprised by Elizabeth's reply as she didn't dwell on Tom.

"Well, he did the right thing in the end," Elizabeth said and quickly added, "Now when are you coming home?"

"I just leased this place..." Marlena began.

"Break the lease. I'll pay for whatever is needed to get you home."

"I also have a job."

"Give them notice you'll be leaving to come home."

"I'm off until Monday. I can give them notice as soon as I go in."

"Marlena, that's 3 days from now. I want you to come home *now.*"

"Well Mother, I could drive there tomorrow and back here on Sunday, but that's a lot of driving."

Harvey had been listening to just one side of the dialogue with the phone away from his ear, but he'd gotten the gist of what they were saying and reentered the conversation.

"Elizabeth, we're about 4 hours away. It's pretty late for Marlena to make the trip alone, but I can drive them there tonight. I'll get them there before midnight and I'll drive them back tomorrow. Then on Monday, Marlena can begin the process of leaving here and going home permanently."

"I'm not going to want them to leave again so soon, Harvey," Elizabeth said. As an afterthought, she added, "Maybe I'll go back with you tomorrow. Yes, that would be good. Do you have a place for me to stay, Marlena?"

"Oh yes, Mother. It would be a great minivacation for you."

"Then it's settled. Harvey, you don't mind being the chauffer, do you? If you can't do it, I can order limousine service."

"I don't mind at all," said Harvey. He was actually glad to do it, especially the 4-hour drive to Elizabeth's home. That would give him plenty of time to reinforce the importance of maintaining family secrets.

During their trip, they engaged in small talk, and only once did Marlena begin to discuss the letter. Harvey stopped her immediately and told her the story about the soldier and the lady and how important it was to not divulge anything to anyone. That seemed to do the trick and the subject didn't come up again.

When they reached the Purlmen home, Harvey gave Marlena a final word of caution.

"No matter what, make sure you stick to the same version of why you left home that Tom told Elizabeth, but only mention it if she wants to talk about it. Somehow, I get the feeling she wants to sweep all those negative things under the rug, but you never know. Above all, don't mention anything that will stain her memories of her son."

"Don't worry. I understand. I won't do anything to hurt her."

Harvey added, "And that letter, I hope you destroyed it. When Tom and I were alone, he told me some things I thought were bombshells, but whatever is in that letter must be pure dynamite."

"It is and don't worry, I'll keep it to myself."

"Good. Let's go see Elizabeth."

Much love was shared that evening as the women celebrated their reunion. Harvey had to wait patiently for them to get beyond their initial excitement before he could get Elizabeth's attention. He needed to ask her some questions. He was ready to focus on the other task he'd been hired for, which was the heirloom search.

"Elizabeth, can I ask you a couple of questions?"

"Yes, what do you need, Harvey?"

"I need to know if there is anything more you can tell me about the other situation."

That tempered Elizabeth's excitement only slightly. "Like what?" was her response.

"Do you have any more information on them. So far all I have are first and last names and an aunt named Bernice."

"Well, that's all I know, except..." Elizabeth let her last statement trail off as she gave the subject additional thought. She then continued with, "You know, I do believe Molly mentioned a relative who lived in Branchport. I'm pretty sure that's it. Branchport."

Hearing the name 'Branchport' being uttered gave Marlena a start, but she was sure no one noticed. She had done her best to keep memories of Branchport and Norman off of her mind and usually did a good job of it. She took a deep breath and forced herself to focus on what the others were saying.

"Thanks," Harvey said. He felt he was now armed with enough information to begin to search for the heirlooms, so he was ready to leave. "What time will you folks be ready to leave tomorrow morning?

"We should leave right after lunch, so make it 1 p.m. sharp," Elizabeth said. As an afterthought, she added, "You know you're welcome here for lunch if you'd like."

"Thanks. I'll call around 10 to let you know one way or another."

Harvey did return the following day for lunch and had the family at Marlena's home right on schedule. He was glad to have been around Elizabeth and Marlena for a long enough period to get a feel for the back and forth conversations they had. Happily, there was not even a hint of Marlena overstepping the boundaries of what she should divulge to Elizabeth and no attempt by Elizabeth to probe for additional details. Once he'd dropped them off, he felt comfortable enough to turn his full attention to heirloom recovery with the town of Branchport as the starting point.

Branchport was 6 hours from Millburn, so Harvey reserved a hotel room and waited until the next day to begin the journey. Since it was Sunday, he drove leisurely and promised himself he would relax for the remainder of the day. He arrived in Branchport around dinner time. Once there, he found a hotel and reserved a room for 3 nights.

This would be like a minivacation for Harvey, even though he would be spending his time working. He figured he could begin the search the next day after a good night's sleep. He was full of confidence he'd track down at least remnants of the family there since he had been given a few Hurley names to chase. Surely there would be a trace of at least one of them in that town.

It was not to be. Harvey had no luck finding anyone fitting the description of any of the Hurleys he was looking for. That meant the search had to be expanded and time spent on the case would increase. He added an extra night to his hotel stay and woke late on Thursday morning feeling discouraged by his lack of progress. He'd searched for 3 full days without finding a trace of the family. His confidence about finding them quickly waned considerably. He wanted to give

Elizabeth a quick update, but Marlena's number was unlisted. He called Elizabeth's number to at least leave her a message, but to his surprise, Elizabeth answered the phone.

"Hello."

"Hello, Elizabeth. What are you doing there? I thought you were on vacation at Marlena's."

Elizabeth laughed. "No, we came home yesterday. Marlena's job let her leave and the rent has been settled. I wanted to get them back here as soon as possible."

"That's great." Harvey now had to hand over the bad news. "No luck in Branchport. I haven't found anyone who knows of any Hurleys that fit the descriptions you gave me."

"You're not giving up, are you?"

"That's entirely up to you, Elizabeth, but I don't want to just continue to spend time searching without some kind of lead to help point me in the right direction."

"Let me think. I know the agency we hired them from is out of business, but my husband may have filed away some paperwork about them."

Elizabeth thought briefly about the state of the office file cabinet before adding, "My husband and my son kept a lot of old paperwork in the lowest drawer of the file cabinet that they should have sorted through and thrown out. I could never understand why they kept that old junk. If anything of use still exists, it would have to be in there."

"Please check."

"You'll just have to call back in a couple of hours. We're getting ready to have an early lunch."

"Will do," Harvey replied and then asked, "How are Marlena and Toby doing?"

"They're both doing fine. They belong here. I'm so glad they're home." Elizabeth was obviously still overjoyed.

Harvey understood.

"Okay," he replied. "Maybe I'd better call back in 3 hours - let's say at 2."

"Sure. I'll get to work on that filing cabinet as soon as I can."

Following lunch and having fed Toby, Elizabeth took a trash bag into the den. She was determined to clear the infamous bottom drawer of all unnecessary clutter. She didn't waste time. She glanced at each item and made a snap decision to retain it or dispose of it. Sadly, there seemed to be nothing of value. Then, with the drawer almost empty, she found something interesting. It was Molly's employment application. She read it over and found she had correctly given Harvey everything useful except for one thing, which was the emergency contact information. It was for Bernice Hurley, who lived at an address in Broad Creek, not Branchport. She couldn't at first imagine why she'd said Branchport. Then she remembered. Marlena had gone to Branchport for a job and the name must have stuck in her mind. At any rate, she hoped this news would help. When Harvey called, she gave him the town name.

Harvey was pleased. "Broad Creek is about 4 hours away from here, so I'm going straight to that address. If they're not there, whoever lives there now might be able to give me some kind of lead.

It was just after 6 p.m. when Harvey pulled up to the address in Broad Creek. Since it was around dinnertime, Harvey hoped he wasn't interrupting a meal. Nevertheless, he strode up to the door and rang the bell.

Inside the home, Molly had just put a pan of sweet rolls in the oven when she heard the bell. She glanced at the clock and thought, "Who could that be?"

She opened the door, and seeing Harvey asked, "Yes, may I help you?"

"I'm private detective Harvey Stevens, Ma'am. I'm looking for Molly Hurley."

"I'm Molly Hurley, what is it you want, Mr. Stevens?"

"You can call me Harvey, and how would you prefer to be called?"

"Molly is fine. What is it you want, Harvey?"

"It has to do with the Purlmens. May I come in?"

Molly knew immediately that this had to be about the heirlooms.

"Oh yes, you may come in," she said enthusiastically. "Have a seat and make yourself comfortable. I'm almost finished making dinner. I've got rolls in the oven and my grandson is on the way home. You might as well have some dinner with us."

Harvey was confused by this treatment. Molly seemed overly comfortable with him coming into her home immediately after he mentioned the Purlmens. It was as if the name automatically made him welcome. He found it hard to believe that two women he found to be extremely pleasant could have had a falling out. Then he remembered. Elizabeth had said she didn't like Sue, so *she* must have been the key issue. Back to the question at hand, he weighed Molly's demeanor and the savory aroma wafting from the home and decided to accept the dinner invitation.

"Having dinner sounds like a winner to me. It smells too good to turn down."

"Alright then, go wash up in that bathroom right there, and then we'll give Norman - that's my grandson - another few minutes to get here before we start eating."

Just after Harvey finished washing his hands and was leaving the bathroom, Norman walked through the door and went straight toward Harvey.

Harvey extended his right hand as Norman approached and said, "I'm Harvey Stevens."

Instead of taking Harvey's hand, Norman continued past him to the bathroom and said, "Let me wash my hands first."

Once the task was complete, Harvey rehashed the introduction as the men exchanged handshakes.

"I'm Harvey Stevens. You can call me Harvey."

Norman answered, "I'm Norman Hurley. Call me Norman."

Just then Molly called out, "Dinner's ready, come and get it."

Harvey was reluctant to delve into the subject of stolen items during the meal and was glad Molly had not asked him anything more about why he was there. Conversation over dinner consisted only of general small talk. He sincerely hoped Molly wasn't toying with him, or trying to butter him up to put some kind of slick slant on the heirloom mystery. He quickly eliminated that kind of thought. He figured Molly wanted to speak to him without her grandson present.

Then there was the Sue factor. Harvey was curious to discover her whereabouts. Where was she? Although Harvey was enjoying the meal and the conversation, that one question weighed heavily on his mind. It wasn't until Molly doled out ample servings of peach cobbler that he was able to convince himself to fully relax. He savored the cobbler while biding his time and maintained his patience. He figured all questions and answers would be ironed out after dinner.

After completing the meal, Molly announced, "Let's all go into the living room where we can talk."

The directive shocked Norman because his grandmother always cleaned the table and kitchen immediately after a meal. He knew something was up.

Once seated in the living room, Molly went to work on Harvey. Looking intently into his eyes, she asked authoritatively, "Alright, Mister Detective..." She stopped in mid-sentence to correct herself and slowed her speech to add additional fuel to her question. "Mister *Private* Detective Harvey Stevens, exactly what do you want?"

Molly's question and tone shocked both Harvey and Norman. The ball was certainly in Harvey's court.

Harvey retreated from his professional perch to the figurative position of someone trapped in a corner.

"Err... uh, Molly. Ms. Hurley - ma'am - I was hired by the Purlmens to look for their heirlooms."

Molly immediately dropped the formality and stature she'd saved over the years for the Purlmens and softened her tone. "I have the heirlooms," she said. "You wait right here."

When Molly left the room, Norman asked, "You're a detective? What's going on? What heirlooms?"

Harvey gave Norman the most prudent answer that came to mind. "I think we'd better wait for your grandmother to come back before we say anything else about this."

Norman nodded his head affirmatively and said, "Yeah, I think you're right."

The men sat transfixed as Molly returned with the lime-colored shoebox. She set it on the coffee table, opened it, and removed the little safe.

"This safe," she said while handing it to Harvey, "apparently holds the heirlooms. I've had it for over 20 years and it's never been opened."

Molly then turned to Norman and said, "Norman, your mother was sweet and kind, but she had a weakness for sometimes going overboard with wanting things. I wanted to tell you about the little safe years ago, but it never seemed like the right time."

To both men, she continued.

"Sue," Molly began, but then interjected an explanation to Harvey. "Sue is Norman's mother. She passed the day Norman was born. She and I worked for the Purlmens. At some point in time, she got a hold of their heirlooms."

Molly corrected herself. "I need to back up. At some point, Tom Purlmen and Sue began a relationship."

She paused to reach into the shoebox and retrieve a photo. While handing it to Harvey, she asked, "Who do you see in this photo?"

Studying it, Harvey answered, "Tom, a younger Elizabeth..."

Harvey glanced from the photo to Molly and continued, "You, that's Norman and I guess the other lady must be Sue."

"That's right about Sue, me and Mrs. Purlmen," Molly agreed, "But you have the men all wrong. That Tom you think you see is Tom's father Mr. Purlmen. The Norman you think you see is Tom Purlmen when he was around Norman's age. I'm a little surprised you didn't see the resemblance to Tom Purlmen when Norman first walked through the door today."

"Tom was pretty sick when I saw him so I didn't make the connection," Harvey said. "He looked like the older man in the picture, old and sick with graying and thinning hair and a mustache."

"Oh, okay, then I can understand it," said Molly. "You know, Mr. Purlmen died the same night we took the picture."

Molly turned to Norman and said, "I never told you all I knew about your father because I wanted the Purlmens to make the first move to find you. I didn't want to take the chance that you would go looking for someone who didn't want anything to do with you. Maybe I did wrong, but things were pretty bad between them and us when your mother and I left. I can't blame Mrs. Purlmen for her attitude. It was your mother and father who caused the problem. They were both so young and each one gave different stories about what went on. I really can't blame your father either. He had no idea that he and your mother were going to be parents. I did try to make contact once, but Mrs. Purlmen gave me so much grief that I didn't want to try again."

Molly took a deep breath before continuing. "Meeting Harvey and having him tell us the Purlmens think so highly of their heirlooms that after 20 years they sent him to contact your mother has given me the strength I need to discuss it."

Norman didn't know what to say. He sat there blocking negative thoughts about the two people who were responsible for his existence. He'd long ago ceased having an urge to brood about them. It was just that his grandmother had never before given as much information as she had that evening, and what she'd given was likely not as bad as things had actually been. He wasn't resentful to his grandmother because theirs' was a loving bond. She'd always gone out of her way to make sure he had a good life. If she believed his other grandmother was a good person, he felt he should jump at the opportunity to meet the part of his family he previously never knew existed. That is, should the opportunity arise.

Harvey spoke up. "I met Tom just about 2 weeks ago. He died shortly after that. He left a wife and son, Marlena and Toby. I met Elizabeth at the same time and she thinks highly of her daughter-in-law and grandson. I'm sure she would love to meet her oldest grandson, especially since he looks almost exactly like her son did at that age."

Molly interjected with an objection to the idea. "I'm sorry to hear he died, but the last time I spoke to his mother, she was quite nasty."

Harvey had an answer to the concern Molly posed.

"Any animosity Elizabeth had was towards Sue. She liked you Molly, and she told me so. She was really angry about the heirlooms, but she'll be getting them back."

Harvey thought about how hard Elizabeth worked to get Marlena and Toby back and was sure she would welcome Norman with open arms. He asked, "When can we make the trip?"

Norman broke free from his private thoughts and said, "I'm usually free on weekends, but I can always take time off, so tomorrow is fine with me. I work construction."

Molly wasn't as enthused. "You two are taking a lot for granted. You'd better call first to make sure it will be okay. I know how she is."

Harvey gave Molly a logical answer. "No, I know how she is. You know how she *was*. She'll probably welcome both of you into her home, especially since she'll be getting the heirlooms back."

Molly still wasn't convinced. "You wouldn't say that if you had been let go the way we were 20 years ago. I think you need to call her first and make sure."

"Right, that's fine," Harvey answered. "I'll call her and let her know I found the heirlooms and I'll be returning them to her tomorrow afternoon. I'll also tell her that you'll be coming along. I don't plan to let her know anything about Norman over the phone. We can let him be a surprise."

248

"Are you going to mention anything about Sue?" Molly asked.

"Hmm," mused Harvey. "I don't like giving any more information than necessary over the phone, but I do believe telling her about Sue would help soothe any bad feelings that might be lingering. What do you think?"

"Well, we did get along fine, but I know she didn't like Sue. You need to tell her Sue won't be coming along."

"Okay, if you think that's the best thing to do."

"There's no doubt about it."

"Alright, I'll call her right now."

"Use the phone in the kitchen."

When Harvey spoke to Elizabeth, he was direct and to the point.

"I'll be there tomorrow with the heirlooms, Elizabeth."

"You found them that fast? That's wonderful!"

"Yes, Molly had them tucked away in that tiny safe. She said she tried to reach you years ago, but it didn't work out."

Harvey had glossed over what Molly had said about the call she'd made to Elizabeth to hopefully get a decent conversation going. Then, to further his quest, he added, "I found out that Sue was the one who took it. She passed away over 20 years ago."

Elizabeth chose to not rekindle old wounds.

"Well now both of them are gone," she replied softly, more to herself than Harvey. She didn't want to bring Tom or Sue into any kind of extended conversation. She quickly added, "I liked Molly. She was a good housekeeper and cook. I don't hold any ill will toward her."

"I understand and I believe it would be good for you and Molly to see each other again. You know, for old time's sake. I'll drive her there, hand off the heirlooms, and give you two a chance to talk for a while before driving her back home."

Elizabeth had her doubts. "I don't know about that idea."

"Trust me, it will be worth your while." Stretching the truth, Harvey added, "She's looking forward to seeing you again. She has no hard feelings."

Elizabeth relented. "Alright, if you think so. What time do you think you'll arrive?"

"It'll be early afternoon. I'll give you a call before I get there."

"Fine. And thanks."

"My pleasure."

Harvey hung up the phone and reported back to Molly and Norman.

"We're all set. She's okay with seeing you, Molly."

Molly still harbored lingering doubts, but she hid them as best she could.

"It's alright with me. If both of you want to go, then we'll go."

"Good," said Harvey. "We'll leave bright and early. What's a good time?"

"You name it," said Norman. "Nana gets up early every day and I can set my alarm."

"I can be here at 9 AM," Harvey said

Molly had a better plan. "You can be here way earlier than that. You're welcome to stay here in the guest room."

Harvey immediately accepted the invitation. It allowed him to further gauge the people he had guaranteed Elizabeth would accept. The faith he already had in them was obvious as he handed the little safe back to Molly.

"Here," he told her. "I think you should continue to hold on to the heirlooms. You've been the safe keeper for over 20 years now, so I know you can be trusted overnight."

"Thanks," said Molly. Turning to Norman she handed the safe over to him and said, "Here, when we get there, you can give it to..." Catching herself midsentence, Molly corrected what she started to say and finished her sentence with, "you can give it to your other grandmother."

The following morning's 2-hour drive to the meeting with Elizabeth was populated with sporadic small talk as each mulled over their private thoughts about how things would go. All certainly hoped for the best, but each was poised for surprises.

Molly couldn't shake a feeling of foreboding that her old suppressed thoughts and tensions would resurface. She certainly didn't want to walk into a situation where she would have to defend herself verbally or physically. But for the fact the heirlooms had been safely stored and were being returned intact, she may not have agreed to the trip. After all, as Harvey had stated, Mrs. Purlmen had apparently spared no cost to get them back. On top of that, Harvey had personally guaranteed the return of the heirlooms coupled with meeting Norman would take care of any lingering ill will.

As she thought more about the Norman connection, a realization came to her. If Mrs. Purlmen wanted to see Norman at all, it would surely be to have him stay there and become a part of the family and family business. There would be no in between. She would grab ahold of him and never let go. That would probably be great for Norman. He'd be set for life in the Purlmen business world. Molly began to brace herself for the "loss" of her grandson. She couldn't shake the feeling, so she voiced her opinion.

"If your other grandmother does want to see you, she'll never want you to leave."

Not waiting for Norman to turn down the opportunity, she added, "She's an honest person. If you get a chance to be a part of the business, I want you to take it."

Norman was surprised at Molly's statement. It sounded like she had already decided he would be so overwhelmed by someone he had never met that he would just pack up his things and move.

In an attempt to allay her fears, he responded with, "I'll try to do what's best. You let me know how you feel about things when we get there, Nana."

Neither elaborated on the subject, but for Norman, the trip was filled with wonderment. Would this grandmother he'd never met accept him? Would he get along with his stepmother? How would he feel about meeting his half-brother? Harvey had said he knew his grandmother Elizabeth would welcome him with open arms, but how could Harvey be so sure if he'd only met her a couple of weeks ago? Yes, he understood he looked like his father, but would this new grandmother accept or regret the resemblance?

Harvey had a more pleasant trip as he continued to plan the meeting with Elizabeth. He digressed to think about a surprise birthday party he'd helped organize years ago. While the immediate instant the recipient experienced the surprise was rewarding, the build-up to the surprise moment had kept the planners on a mental high for weeks.

The difference here was that he was now the lone planner. He smiled to himself as he thought through the chronology of this planned meetup, but he decided not to share any details with the others until they were minutes from the home. He wanted this meeting to be a wonderful reunion of Elizabeth to her heirlooms, a reconciliation of sorts for Elizabeth and Molly, and to have the meeting capped off with the crown jewel of an added bonus. Elizabeth and Norman would be introduced to one another. Nothing he could think of topped the excitement he anticipated would result from the surprise he'd conceived.

Once they'd gotten close to the Purlmen home, Harvey finally began to let the others in on his plan.

"This is what's going to happen," Harvey stated. "I'll stop at the next phone booth I see and let Elizabeth know we'll be there in a few minutes. Once we get there, I'll get out of the car first and come around and open the door for you, Molly. We'll stand and shield Norman as he gets out of the car. Then we'll continue to hide him as much as possible as we begin to walk towards the door in case someone is watching."

"Are you going to the front door?" Molly asked.

"Yes."

"Then there's no need to worry about anyone seeing you unless they are staring out that one window on the left side of the porch and I'm sure she won't be sitting there waiting and watching. Just make sure you park as close to the house as possible."

"Will do, but we need to keep Norman hidden when she opens the door."

"That's fine, but are you sure it will be Mrs. Purlmen and not the daughter-in-law who opens the door?"

"Her name's Marlena. No, I'm not sure. Let me call and find out."

Harvey stopped and used a payphone to confirm the situation. Moments later he returned with good information.

"Elizabeth is in the den right now and Marlena just went upstairs to give the baby a bath. I told her we'd be there within 20 minutes, but we'll be there in fewer than 10. She'll be answering the door."

And answer the door she did. Harvey had positioned Molly in front of himself. Norman was close behind Harvey and hidden in the rear.

"Hello, Molly. How have you been?" Elizabeth gave a matter-of-fact greeting as if nothing had ever happened between the women, good or bad.

"I've been fine," Molly answered, uncharacteristically not returning the almost obligatory question about Elizabeth's health.

Harvey moved to put his plan into action. "Elizabeth, I'd like you to meet your other grandson, Norman." Harvey had spoken while stepping aside to bring Norman into Elizabeth's view.

Elizabeth's reaction when she saw Norman was priceless. She went from deadpan and distant to wide-eyed and joyful as she held out her arms and quickly walked past Molly and Harvey toward Norman. She immediately felt as if she'd been transported back more than two decades to where she would now have a do-over with her son. The difference here was this version of her son looked like he was far more alert and manly than Tom had ever been. She made up her mind immediately that she was not going to be denied this opportunity to have Norman be everything she'd wanted Tom to be.

Norman's reaction fit perfectly into what Elizabeth had in mind as he gave her a long embrace and heartfelt kiss on the cheek while clutching the safe in one hand.

"I'm happy to meet you," he said. "I wish we could have met years ago."

Unlike any of the half-hearted hugs she'd given Tom years ago, Elizabeth returned Norman's hug just as warmly and said, "Oh, I'm just so glad that we're together now."

Molly and Harvey stood transfixed as they watched the two embracing like it was a reunion of long-lost family members rather than a meeting of heretofore unknown relatives. It was apparent that Elizabeth's indifferent outer shell had been totally obliterated by meeting Norman. She then displayed a loss of composure with her next statement.

"Everyone, come in," she said. Then, realizing her mistake, she corrected herself with, "Oh, I'm sorry. I mean, let's all go inside."

Molly stepped inside while Harvey lingered to allow Elizabeth to enter, but she refused the gesture. She wouldn't release her hold on Norman and motioned for Harvey to enter.

"Go on in," she commanded.

Harvey did so, but he didn't go straight to the living room as Molly had. He felt he should explain the surprise now to get beyond the starting point for questions and answers that would likely surface before long.

"Maybe I should have told you about Norman over the phone, but something told me it would be better to wait to let you see him in person."

Elizabeth buried the thought. "Don't worry about any of that. The important thing is that he is here now. That's all I care about."

A bond had been formed and it was not one-sided. Norman was beaming and fully comfortable with his newly discovered grandmother.

"We should have met each other sooner," he said to Elizabeth, rephrasing and repeating his earlier wish.

"We won't worry about any of that. We'll just have to work extra hard to get you all caught up with the family business."

Harvey had expected Elizabeth to accept Norman, but not to this degree. He followed as they joined Molly in the living room.

Once there and seated, a beaming Elizabeth spoke. "Molly, he looks just like Tom did when he was younger."

Molly said nothing. She did manage to force a smile and slowly give her head an affirmative nod.

As a quick afterthought, Elizabeth looked at Norman and asked, "How old are you, Norman?"

"I'm 23."

"You're 23 and you look so much like my son did at that age. Of course, you should because you're his son."

Elizabeth still hadn't noticed the little safe and no one made any mention of it. She was still wrapped up in having met Norman. She smiled and continued.

"You know your father got married a couple of years ago to a young woman about your age. They have a son and that makes him your little brother. His name is Toby and he's less than a year old. He and his mother are upstairs. His mother's name is Marlena, and make sure that's how you say her name. Mar-LAY-nuh." Elizabeth spoke the name slowly and overemphasized each syllable.

Elizabeth had been hogging the conversation, although she now and then made statements and asked questions normally designed to trigger conversation from others. She did it again as she spoke directly to Molly.

"Molly, why did you keep Norman away from me all these years?"

Molly interpreted the question as more of an accusation than anything else and hesitated to answer, mainly because she was afraid that no matter what she said, the tone of her voice would reveal her displeasure at the remark.

Elizabeth didn't wait for Molly to reply. Instead, she answered her own question somewhat playfully to further her plan to become the main factor in Norman's life.

"I know, you just wanted to keep him all to yourself, but that's going to change," Elizabeth said.

Molly caught the drift of what Elizabeth was alluding to and felt like telling Harvey that it was time to go. She wanted the three of them to say goodbye right then and there. Even though she'd predicted Norman would become a fixture in the Purlmens' household, she wasn't ready for the transition to feel like it was being stealthily arranged. She'd also expected that it would be a swift occurrence, but watching it unfold at seemingly lightning speed was extremely shocking. However, rather than showing any kind of negativism, Molly reminded herself that establishing the Purlmen connection was likely in Norman's best interest. That fact was enough to allow her to continue to smile, although she was at a loss for a fitting reply.

Not that she needed to answer. Elizabeth was still on a roll and quickly spoke to Norman. She turned to him and said, "We have a lot of catching up to do, don't we Norman?"

"Yes..." Norman trailed off not knowing how to properly address this new grandmother.

Elizabeth had a remedy for that, but she wanted to discuss it with him in private. To the others, she said, "You two won't mind if I show Norman around a bit, do you? I especially want him to see the den because it will be his."

Neither Molly nor Harvey cared because they had been cut out of the conversation anyway.

As Elizabeth began to rise, Norman sprang to his feet to help her. Just then, Marlena came down the stairs.

Elizabeth offered quick introductions. "Marlena, this is Molly and this is Norman, Tom's eldest son. You already know Harvey."

Harvey rose, helping Molly to her feet so they could greet Marlena.

Molly said, 'Nice to meet you, Marlena. I'm Norman's other grandmother."

Marlena responded, "Nice to meet you too Molly," as they exchanged hugs.

Turning to Harvey she said, "Nice seeing you again Harvey."

Marlena's attention had primarily been focused on Molly and Harvey because she hadn't yet recognized Norman. However, when she did turn his way, she knew instantly that he recognized her as much as she recognized him.

"Nice to meet you too Norman," she said without making any attempt to move any closer. She gave a gentle and almost imperceptible head shake that indicated 'No' and hoped Norman recognized the meaning. Then she swiftly averted her eyes from him and turned back to Harvey and Molly.

Ordinarily, Norman would have gone over to Marlena to give a warm greeting, but two things held him back. The first was their obvious mutual recognition combined with the subtle 'No' signal he recognized, and the second thing was that his grandmother Elizabeth held onto him tightly. He looked at Marlena and did his best to refrain from showing his emotions as he responded to the greeting.

"Hello, nice to meet you," was all the response he could muster as he and Elizabeth had paused while the introductions were taking place.

"We'll be back everyone," Elizabeth announced to all.

To Norman, she continued with, "Come along Norman. Let's go to the den so the others can get better acquainted."

Once they reached the den, Elizabeth quickly began to get Norman acclimated.

"Go sit behind the desk so I can look at you."

As Norman did so, Elizabeth continued.

"How quickly and how well do you think you can learn all about a construction business and handling real estate?"

Norman's mind was still racing from having seen Marlene, who had been introduced as Marlena, but knew he had to get her out of his mind so he could converse with his grandmother.

"I have a business degree that included real estate courses and I've worked in construction. I'm sure I could pick it up without a problem."

"Good," Elizabeth replied. "I want you to start immediately, Norman. Where are you working now?"

"Well, I still do construction work, so I'm pretty much my own boss. It's like being a subcontractor because I work for hire."

To emphasize he could begin working immediately he added, "I'm between big jobs right now, so I've been working with a small-time contractor on a day to day basis. I don't need to do anything except call and let the major contractor know I won't be available for the next big job."

"Or any future jobs, Norman," Elizabeth added. "This is now your home."

"That's fine with me," he said enthusiastically. "I can just run back home to pick up my things and then come back and move in."

That didn't please Elizabeth.

"You won't have time to run back and forth. It will be better for you to get a whole new wardrobe and stay right here to concentrate on learning how to run our family business. You can get a few things today and use whatever you find in your new room. You don't have to worry about a car because there's one here that will be yours. Everything you need is already here."

Norman pondered the points Elizabeth had presented. After all, business management was what he studied for in college, and it's what he wanted to do. Still, he was torn between insisting that he needed to at least discuss things with his Nana, or succumbing to this rush to make an immediate move. But, before he could formulate what he considered a workable answer, Elizabeth had more to say.

"Also," Elizabeth told him authoritatively, "It would be pretty awkward for you to call me Grandmother while Marlena calls me

Mother. I think you and Marlena should both call me Mother."

The mention of the name of Marlena bought the other situation back to his mind and tipped the scales totally in his mind to remaining at the residence rather than going back home with his Nana. It was obvious that something really deep was going on and he wanted to discuss it with Marlene or Marlena or whatever her name was. He couldn't dare make any mention of his concerns to anyone. He figured it would be best to bide his time until he could be alone to discuss things fully with Marlene. For the time being, he'd pay attention to getting to know his newly-found grandmother whom he'd be calling Mother.

"Sure, Mother," he replied. "That would be a lot less confusing."

"Good, then it's settled."

Suddenly, Elizabeth noticed the tiny safe Norman was still holding.

"The heirlooms. You've got the heirlooms!" she exclaimed while taking the tiny safe from Norman.

"Yes, I just found out about the safe yesterday when I found out we're related."

"You mean you didn't know? Molly never mentioned anything about me?"

"No, she said she wanted the time to be right and I guess it took Harvey coming over to get the conversation started. The main thing she said about you was that you are a good person."

"Well, I always did like the way she took care of the house and cooked."

Elizabeth abruptly changed the subject to avoid discussing Sue.

"There are valuable heirlooms in this little safe. Let's talk about them and some other things before we go back out with the others."

In the living room, the conversation was pleasant but restrained. Harvey had anticipated the two women would be talking like magpies and he would be the odd person out of the conversation. Instead, the women acted as if there was a choppy undercurrent of issues brewing that neither wanted to delve into.

Harvey understood how Molly's longstanding trepidation regarding seeing Elizabeth would initially cause her to retreat into a shell. He could also understand how the way Elizabeth was trying to sweep Norman away would also hurt Molly's feelings. What he couldn't understand was why Marlena was acting standoffish. The relatively short time he'd spent with Marlena since he'd located her had been pleasant and he'd found her to be quite a conversationalist. Now, however, even any discussion about the baby seemed strained. Harvey had never before been around women who weren't ready to talk of babies and pregnancy seemingly ad infinitum. He knew he might have been misreading signs, but to him, there seemed to be a rough edge that needed to be smoothed and soothed.

When Elizabeth and Norman finally returned from the den, Elizabeth said, "Norman is going to fit right in. His education is perfect for the family business. He'll be moving into Tom's old room."

Molly understood what that meant. The prospect of a quick goodbye and having Harvey drive both her and Norman home that night had dissipated into nothingness. She was going to be the lone passenger in Harvey's car. Apparently, the decision for Norman to remain permanently at the Purlmen residence beginning immediately had already been made. Although she'd expected it, having it unceremoniously thrust at her was unpleasant. She masked her feelings by rendering a smile and doing her best to act as if the plan had been the product of discussion and consensus.

Norman reinforced Elizabeth's veiled proclamation far more directly as he said, "Oh, Nana, I won't be going home with you tonight. I'll be putting my college education to good use here by helping to run the business."

When no one else said anything, Harvey said, "Hey, that's great. Good for you."

Marlena used the announcement as the perfect time to break

away from the situation. She excused herself with, "I'll be right back after I check on Toby."

She went upstairs and saw that Toby was still asleep. While there, she quickly wrote this note:

We need to talk ALONE ASAP. I'll come to your room later once Mother is asleep.

She returned downstairs to find Elizabeth in the midst of coaxing Harvey and Molly to leave.

"You two should get on the road before it gets dark," Elizabeth said before adding, "Harvey, I know all that driving back and forth has to be tiring. Do you want me to fix you some coffee or something?"

Molly's initial lukewarm mood for this Purlmen meet and greet had been slowly descending into the pits of disgust, but now her feelings about the gathering hit rock bottom. She'd interpreted what she heard as a shameful way of ushering someone unceremoniously to the door. She didn't want to spend another minute in the home. She answered Elizabeth's coffee offer for Harvey with as much grace as she could muster with, "No, thanks. We're ready to leave now."

Norman knew his Nana was not her usual self, but he was determined to find out more about his newly discovered relatives quickly. He again spoke to her to hopefully give her confidence that she was still special to him and this Purlmen connection was more like a job than a wholesale departure from the home life they'd always shared.

"The work I'll be doing should be interesting, Nana," Norman told her. "I'll give you a call early next week to check on you and let you know how I'm doing."

Molly appreciated Norman's reassurance. Hearing it made it easier to endure the pain of the meeting coupled with the pain of parting. She answered with, "All right, give me a hug."

As everyone stood to bid one another goodbye, Marlena was able to slip the note to Norman.

Having the note in hand gave Norman some comfort. Though he was impressed with the knowledge that he'd be a part of the Purlmen business, there was a nagging worry about Marlene. He eased the note into his pocket to read later when he was alone.

As Harvey escorted Molly toward the front door, he had mixed feelings about the surprise meetup he'd arranged. Elizabeth and Norman had been ecstatic and they had fully connected with one another, but no one beside them seemed to fully welcome the new bond. The discontentment bothered him to the point where he had no desire to pursue Elizabeth for the additional funds he was owed for his work. The thousand dollars he'd received as a retainer fee had been surpassed by at least another thousand dollars. He untypically decided to simply tally expenses and not divulge what he'd spent for the discovery of things near and dear to Elizabeth.

Thinking ahead, Harvey decided that if Elizabeth did happen to bring up his fee in the future, he would refuse reimbursement and tell her his work was a gift to her. After all, he'd seen the anguish in Tom and Elizabeth before he'd found Marlena, Toby, and their lost heirlooms. He felt good at having been the catalyst to make things right in their world and he didn't need the money. He was satisfied because this was another job well done and the reward of his client's happiness would suffice for his payment.

As it happened, he couldn't possibly have anticipated his job was not yet complete and that many additional surprises awaited him.

12 Sunrise

Just as soon as Harvey pulled away from the front of the Purlmen residence, Molly turned to him and said, "I'm glad Norman is staying here. I think it's the best thing for him, don't you?"

"Yes, as long as he's happy. I know Elizabeth is happy with him."

After Harvey's statement, they drove in silence for a few minutes. Harvey realized Molly had gone through some emotional gyrations over the last 24 hours, so he didn't want to force her to speak about her feelings. He decided to wait for her to enter into further discussion.

Molly had indeed been on a roller coaster ride, but the way she was beginning to feel was a surprise to herself. Norman was now where she felt he rightfully belonged, so it was as if a weight she'd dutifully carried all these years had been lifted. While she wasn't pleased with any of the haughty inuendoes she felt she'd received while at the Purlmens' house, she was proud of the way Norman carried himself. She had no worries about him fitting in with them, nor did she think he would ever treat her with disdain. She truly believed the best thing that could have happened for Norman was to have him remain and learn to run the Purlmen business.

Molly's acceptance of Norman's new status wasn't the biggest surprise about her rekindled state of being. She saved that honor for herself. She realized that now, for the first time in her life, she was heading home to a house with only one resident - herself. Taking it a step further, she knew she hadn't even slept in a house alone more than a few times during her entire life. She felt a twinge of freedom after raising two children from childbirth to adulthood. Her journey from being a 14-year-old girl to this point in life had been well over 40 years in the making. She began to enjoy the ride as they traveled and, after those few minutes of silence, felt an urge to reopen the conversation with Harvey.

"You know," she began, "Going home today will be different for me. I'm not used to being alone."

"I know what you mean," replied Harvey. "Being alone is different for everyone, but it wasn't too bad for me. I lost my wife about 15 years ago, but since my work has always kept me away for long stretches, I was able to adjust without too much trouble."

Harvey sensed that Molly was relaxing more with every mile they traveled from the house. He felt more relaxed also. He'd completed all the tasks he'd been hired for and it was time to get back to doing whatever he wanted to do whenever he wanted to do it.

Then Harvey's thoughts drifted to the drudgery of having to drop Molly off and turning around to make the long drive home. He wondered if Molly might want to fix a meal and allow him to spend another night at her place. He planted a seed.

"Those sweet rolls you make, Molly, is it your own recipe or what? I've got a taste for them and I'd like to make some when I get back home."

Molly asked, "You're a cook?"

"When I don't eat out I am."

"Well, you won't have to cook or eat out tonight. We'll be back in plenty of time for me to put a meal on the table."

"That's perfect for tonight, but I need the recipe for when I'm by myself," Harvey told her before adding, "And if you have a recipe for homemade biscuits, I'd like it too."

"Regular homemade biscuits?" Molly asked. "They're easy. What you really should want is the recipe for sweet potato biscuits. That's the one to ask for."

Harvey liked the suggestion and let it be known. "Great, do you have a recipe?"

"I sure do."

"You know," Harvey mused, "I haven't had sweet potato biscuits since I was young enough to ask for them at my mother's knee. I thought making them was a lost art."

"Not lost on me - I love to cook. Listen, my grandparents came from Ireland, Wales, Africa, and right here in America. The one from America was a member of one of the Sioux tribes. My family has roots all over the place. Anyway, my mother and my aunt both loved to cook, and my grandmothers handed down recipes to both of them. They all taught me well. The only person in the family that didn't do me any favors was my father. I never got to know him. He and my mother got divorced before I was 2 years old."

Harvey had nothing to offer as a reply. He had zeroed in on Molly's references to Africa and the Sioux tribe. While he obviously had African connections, his father had once mentioned that some Cherokee blood also flowed in his veins. It made him feel like he and Molly shared a kinship. The fact that she readily admitted her mixed heritage gave rise to the likelihood that she viewed folks from the inside out rather than taking a prejudicial view based solely on a person's outward appearance. Harvey had admired the way Molly looked when he first saw her, but the more they conversed, the more he wanted to get to know her personally.

Very quickly, however, Harvey had a problem with his kinship train of thought. The issue was not because he found Molly attractive, but rather because he'd allowed old stereotypes to influence his way of thinking about her. He'd been fearful to even imagine that Molly might have also found him attractive until she'd mentioned her connection to Africa. That fear was a shortcoming he'd long since decided to eliminate from his way of thinking. He wanted to deal with others and be dealt with by others on an individual basis rather than ancestral connections.

Harvey had accomplished his equality goal professionally, but he'd fallen somewhat short of that mark on a personal level. He continued to maintain the habit of wanting to hear whomever he was dealing with mention some social thing that gave rise to the probability that they fully accepted him. That is, acceptance without first worrying about what he looked like or any kind of hang-up about things that may have happened somewhere to someone else in the past.

That some of his ancestors had been enslaved was something Harvey had accepted long ago an historical fact. He was able to temper that nefarious happening in his mind because those who had enslaved his ancestors were long gone. As his father once told him, "It doesn't matter now that some old master may have caught and forced himself on your great-great-great grandmother behind a barn or in some hayloft. Your job now is to deal with others with respect and expect the same respect from them. Those evil people from way back when have been long gone. Don't try to live your life as though you can change what happened in the past."

Harvey had never felt the need to justify himself beyond his abilities while he worked, so he decided to consciously apply that same posture here. He was attracted to Molly for whom she appeared to be as a person. If she found him attractive, he wanted it to be for the way she found him to be as a person as well. In a promise to himself to diminish the chance of immediately failing to keep his resolve, he told himself to keep his Cherokee heritage to himself, at least for now. Let whatever happens become a reality at face value, rather than have it progress as an offshoot of the memory of their ancestors' lives.

Molly found herself also putting out feelers, since she was also now a person who could do whatever she wanted to do whenever she felt like doing it. The first feeler *had* been the reference to her African heritage, although it had been done innocently with just a slight ulterior motive. She'd never before spoken of it to anyone outside of the family. Not that she had a problem with her racial mix – to her it was a not an issue. It was just that something about Harvey made her want him open up to her, and divulging that link seemed to be a quick way to do it. She'd admired the way Harvey looked and the way he carried himself from the start, so she decided to probe and get some answers.

Changing the main direction of the conversation, Molly was the first to resume the conversation.

"Now why would a man like you be worried about getting recipes and cooking for himself? she asked. You must have someone helping you with your needs."

"No, I'm all by myself. I was married for almost 20 years before my wife passed," Harvey told her. "We raised twin boys. Well, I should say that she raised them. I was mostly deployed overseas and she and the boys always remained stateside. Once they were old enough, both of them joined the military and both wound up eventually being deployed to Hawaii. They each found wives over there, and when they got out of the military, they stayed there. I rarely see them."

"That's too bad," Molly commented. "About not seeing them, I mean."

"Oh no, it's fine. You know what they say about a son being a son until they take a wife, but a daughter is a daughter for the rest of her life? Believe me, it's true. We just don't get together very often. My sons, my daughters-in-law, my grandchildren, and the rest of my family are all many miles away from me, but we still share family love."

Molly decided to expose some of her past.

"You were blessed. Me, I had gotten involved with an older guy when I was just 14. I got pregnant and he was lost in the second world war. We never had a family life because I never knew his family. Since then I've concentrated on surviving. First, I raised Sue, and when she died in childbirth, I raised Norman."

"You did a fine job. Norman has a great head on his shoulders."

Molly didn't consciously mean to make the next statement, but it opened the door for additional probing into the potential for romance.

"I've never even dated since that one man," she said.

Harvey was now thinking about the possibility of a close relationship with Molly, but he didn't want to move too fast or take advantage of the situation. Molly was an attractive woman and they were both around the same age. He decided to spend the remainder of the trip getting to know Molly and having her get to know him. She'd already invited him to dinner. Their next few hours of being together would dictate what would happen later that night.

* * *

Back at the Purlmen residence, Elizabeth monopolized Norman's time with talk while Marlena retreated upstairs with Toby. Dinner was a split affair. Marlena made herself something while Elizabeth and Norman planned to eat out. When it was time for them to leave, Elizabeth handed Norman the keys to Tom's car and let Norman do the driving. Following dinner, they visited clothing stores to get some clothes for Norman, with Elizabeth all the while tutoring him about things necessary to make Norman part of the family. It was clear that Elizabeth had fully inserted Norman into the void in her life.

When they returned home, all was quiet and Marlena was not in sight. Elizabeth was exhausted from the day's excitement and went straight to bed. Norman, however, was still on pins and needles as he retreated into what had been Tom's room. He was surprised by how well it was furnished, but he was shocked when he began to put away the new clothes that had just been purchased. The closet and drawers were already well stocked with Tom's things and the fit was perfect. So much for having to buy a new wardrobe. Then, after about an hour, he heard an almost imperceptible knock. He opened the door and was not surprised by who he saw standing there.

"Come on in, Marlene," he whispered without emotion. He'd already made up his mind he was going to call her Marlene no matter what anyone else said.

"I never thought we'd see each other again, Norman," Marlena answered softly.

Norman immediately wanted to make sure it was understood that the name Marlene was in and Marlena was out.

"Alright, first off, I'm going to be calling you Marlene. I had a teacher whose name was Mr. Marlayna and we had problems. And anyway, that's how you introduced yourself to me."

"That's fine. I never let anyone do it before, but it will be alright." Marlene breathed deeply and stated, "As a matter of fact, from now on, I'd prefer it."

"Good. So now, what's going on, Marlene? I've got about a thousand questions that need answers. I never would have..."

Marlene held up both hands to cut him short. "Please, please don't say anything. Just let me say what I need to say. You need to know my story, so please let me explain. I was born in Peru and don't remember my real parents at all. They were both killed in an earthquake when I was around two. I don't know how I got to America, but I wound up being adopted and raised by a wonderful couple who weren't able to give me very many details about my past. I don't even know if I was brought here legally or illegally. I just know

I have a social security number and a birth certificate that says I can celebrate my birthday every 4 years."

Norman almost smiled in acknowledgment of the leap year joke, but he instead remained stoic as Marlene continued.

"Your father and I met at the right time for me, but I think he was..." Marlene trailed off for a moment but then corrected herself.

"No, I *know* he was in desperation mode for a wife, probably because Mother wanted an heir for the family name. He tricked me into marrying him. Wait, I mean he tricked me into *thinking* I was marrying him. It was a sham. We were never married. The problem was he couldn't have children, at least not by the time I came along."

Marlene felt she now needed to reiterate the need for secrecy. "Please, whatever you do, don't let anyone know the part about not being married, especially Mother."

Norman was intently listening and only affirmatively nodded his head slightly to confirm his understanding.

Marlene then continued the discussion. "At some point, your father started with drugs and alcohol and maybe some other concoctions that caused him to become impotent and sterile. He hid this from your grandmother and me. I know he never told her because she would have gone through the roof. What he did was insist I get artificially inseminated, but I refused."

Marlene let the information sink in before resuming her explanation.

"Knowing so little about my past," she continued, "I didn't want to have my baby come from some anonymous donor. I wanted to know and love my baby's father. So, as an outlet from the confusion and nagging about artificial insemination your father kept giving me, I went out and got a job because I needed some space."

Marlene paused, took a deep breath, and let it out slowly, almost like a sigh before continuing.

"For the first 3 days of the job, they sent me to a class in Branchport. That's when we met."

She stopped to see if Norman's expression had changed, but it hadn't. She wanted him to speak and considered prompting him to say something but then remembered she'd asked him to listen while she spoke.

Norman, who had been more or less looking down and away from Marlene, understood her paradox, but he felt the best thing to do was to maintain his current posture and silence so she could continue when ready.

Finally, Marlene spoke again. "It was really strange. When I saw you at the gym, I couldn't help staring because you looked so much like your father. Staring at a man is something I never did before. I was brought up to be standoffish to men. Then, when we met at the restaurant, I at first thought it was just an incredible coincidence, but that feeling changed. Somehow, even though I didn't know what I was doing, my mind started racing. It was like, I don't know, divine intervention or something began to guide me along. You became the answer to my prayers for a solution to my problems at home. That night you and I were together was the first and only time I've ever been made love to."

Hearing the last statement, Norman turned his head and focused his eyes inquisitively into Marlene's eyes.

Answering his unspoken question, Marlene stated, "Yes, Toby is your son."

Ignoring the rule of silence, Norman asked for direct confirmation.

"Marlene, you mean I have a son that I never knew about that everyone thinks is my brother?"

"That's right. No one else knows and there's no way we can tell anyone else about it."

While Norman let the fact sink in, Marlene added emphatically, "We especially can't tell either one of your grandmothers. No one can ever know. Somehow your father found out I hadn't been artificially inseminated and he threw Toby and me out of the house."

271

Marlene decided she needed to correct her previous statement.

"I mean he made it look like I picked up and left and that's what he told Mother at first. Not long after that, he felt bad about what he'd done and he confessed to Mother it was his fault that I was gone. She wanted me back and she's the one who hired Harvey. When Harvey found me, he had to convince me your father had finally done the right thing and confessed to all his lies. Believe me, when he threw me out it was so bad that I wouldn't have come back except your father had written a letter that he gave to Harvey to give to me."

Marlene paused to consider whether she should include Tom's death as one of the things that convinced her to return. Knowing it was and wanting to get everything in the open, she added, "When Harvey told me your father had died, it became even easier to come back. I never wanted to see him again after all his lies. Now let me show you the letter."

Marlene retrieved the letter from her handbag. She let Norman read it before she began speaking again.

"See what I mean? We need to think things through and decide how we're going to handle everything."

Now upset after reading the contents of the letter, Norman mumbled, "You know, this kind of makes me glad I never got to know him."

Marlene tried to reel Norman back in so they could focus on the need for problem-solving.

"Listen, we have to make some decisions about how to handle things going forward. Right now, everyone thinks that your generation of the family never existed. It's like you got passed over and you're a member of the same generation as your son."

Norman was still thinking about the letter, so Marlene rephrased and expanded her statement.

"You know, I don't know anything about my past generation and I never will, because of the earthquake and being adopted, but you know a lot more about yours. It's just that, right now, the situation we're in makes you a member of the *passed* generation. That's P-A-S-S-E-D, as in passed over. It's not right for you, Toby, or me. We need to do something about it."

"That's crazy, really crazy," Norman answered. "Listen, I don't know where to start, but we need help from someone we can trust. I've never had to deal with this kind of problem before and I've never even heard of something like this happening to anyone."

Both paused to do some thinking. Norman spoke again after a few moments.

"The only professional person I've ever met that I would even begin to talk to is Harvey, but I don't think this kind of thing is something a private detective would know anything about."

Marlene agreed. "Probably not, but he would be a good person to ask. He knows how to keep personal business personal. Did he tell you about the soldier and the lady?"

"No."

"He had met a soldier in one place who told him things about a lady, but the soldier wouldn't give the lady's name. About 12 years later he met a lady who gave the same information from her point of view without giving the soldier's name. The meetings were thousands of miles apart, but from what each of them had said, he knew the soldier and the lady were talking about one another. He said that incident made him respect privacy more than most people ever do. We can trust him."

"We need to get his number. Do you have it or do you know his last name and where he lives?"

Marlene thought for a moment. "I saw his detective license, but I never got his number. I don't remember his last name and I don't know where his office is. I'm sure Mother knows."

"Right, but we can't ask Mother for his number, and by now he's probably already dropped my grandmother off. There's a good chance he's still driving or he's at his own house, wherever it is."

Marlene recognized that Norman had said 'Mother', so she asked for clarification.

"You said 'Mother'. You were talking about Mother Purlmen, right?"

"Oh yes. She let me know right from the start that I should refer to her that way. My mother died the day I was born."

"Sorry," Marlene answered. She then continued to digress with the same subject in mind. "You know, that means neither of us knew our parents."

"Right, but that's the way life and death can go," Norman reasoned.

Norman felt a twinge of sadness. He'd made his statement sound as matter-of-fact as he could, but this was the first time he'd ever heard it formally stated that both of his parents had passed. It was also the first time anyone had offered him condolences for their passing. He quickly recovered from the bit of sadness he'd felt, and felt he would likely never feel saddened about their having passed again. He let them go. Now was the time to concentrate on the predicament he found himself in as he journeyed through his own life. It was his turn to get the conversation back to the subject at hand.

"Alright, Marlene. Let's decide what do we need to do about what's going on here."

Marlene had a thought. "How about calling your grandmother? She might have Harvey's number. If she doesn't, get her to call Mother to get it. You could tell her the number is for me, but I don't want to go through Mother to get it. Something like that."

Norman agreed. "Good plan. It's too late to call tonight because Nana would think there's an emergency. I'll call in the morning, but I'll keep your name out of it. I'll just tell her I want to speak to Harvey man-to-man and ask her to get the number. She'll understand."

"Don't make the call from here in the house. You need to go to a phone booth."

"I will," Norman said before adding, "And now you need to go to your room before we get caught in here together."

Marlene didn't move right away. She nodded her head slowly in agreement as Norman stood and pulled her to her feet. They embraced, but neither made a move to kiss. Somehow both sensed that being more amorous than hugging would not be a good idea. Norman spoke softly as they broke the full embrace and he led her to the door.

"We're going to work this out. I can feel it," he told her.

"I hope so. Goodnight."

"Goodnight."

* * *

By the time Harvey and Molly arrived at Molly's house, they had given each other enough of a once over to have gotten well past the point of considering a relationship. Each wanted this to *be* their relationship.

Once inside the home, it was apparent that developing a closeness would come easy for them. Harvey was an eager kitchen helper, doing whatever task he could without ever getting in Molly's way, which made their dinner a joint effort. The same was true for clearing the table and washing the dishes. The closeness was such that they both knew Harvey would be spending the night and that it would only be awkward if they didn't share the same bed.

They did sleep together and their lovemaking went well beyond the physical pleasure both experienced. It was the affirmation of the achievement of oneness that only people who are truly congruent with each other ever reach. Afterward, both slept like contented babies.

Molly typically woke up at sunrise, but this morning found her and Harvey still sleeping at 9. That's when the phone rang. Molly answered sleepily.

"Hello."

Noman's excited voice crackled through the receiver. "Nana, I need for you to find out how I can get in touch with Harvey."

Molly let her guard down and asked somewhat loudly, "Not even a good morning?"

In the fog of being half-awake, Harvey heard the 'good morning' from Molly's statement and offered, "Good morning," in response.

Almost simultaneously Norman said, "I'm sorry. Good morning."

Molly knew Norman could have heard Harvey's voice, but she maintained her composure. She firmly placed her free hand on Harvey's arm and hoped he recognized it as a be still and be quiet command. He apparently did as she continued her conversation with Norman.

"Good morning, Norman. Now, what is it you need?"

"I need to get in touch with Harvey."

Realizing his grandmother would likely want him give her at least a little more information, Norman quickly added, "There's some man-to-man stuff I need some help with."

Molly was interested, but she needed to solve her own predicament first. She approached the issue head-on with a slight maneuver.

"You know, it was a little late when he was going to drop me off so I invited him in for dinner and let him stay overnight. Why don't I have him call you back in a few minutes?"

"That won't work. I'm in a phone booth and there's no number on the phone. I'll call back in about 10 minutes, but I'll have to call collect. I don't have any more change."

"That will be fine."

When she hung up the phone, Molly turned her attention to Harvey.

"Norman wants to speak to you. He'll be calling back in 10 minutes."

"Did he say what it's about?"

"All he said was something about man-to-man stuff. He called from a phone booth. I hope there's no trouble there."

276

"I wouldn't think so. As he said, he'd like to speak to a man about something. We'll find out when he calls back."

When the phone rang 10 minutes later, Molly was quick to answer. "Hello."

"I have a collect call from Norman. Will you accept the charges?"

"Yes," Molly answered.

The next thing Molly heard from the handset was Norman's voice.

"Hello. Nana?"

"Yes, Norman, Harvey is here. I'll put him right on." Handing the phone to Harvey, Molly said, "I'll go fix some breakfast. Ham and eggs?"

While taking the phone from Molly, Harvey said to her, "Perfect." Then he spoke into the receiver. "Hello, Norman. Are you okay? What's going on?"

Norman burst out with, "Harvey, I need some advice. I've got some stuff going on that you wouldn't believe. I found out that..."

"Hold on, Norman," Harvey cut him off in mid-sentence. "If you've got important personal things to discuss, it's best to do it in person, especially if it's something you're not comfortable discussing with your grandmother."

Norman understood the logic. "You're probably right," he admitted.

Doing some quick calculations, Harvey said, "I can be there in a couple or 3 hours. Do you want to meet somewhere or should I come to the house?"

"Uh..." Norman thought for a couple of seconds. "Yes, come to the house and then I'll offer to take you to lunch as a thank you for bringing the family together. Just the two of us, no women allowed."

"Good idea, I like it." Harvey quickly added, "Your grandmother might like to come too, so she can keep the other women and the baby company."

Norman hesitated only slightly before answering, "Uh, sure that would be okay. See you later."

"Okay," Harvey replied as he hung up the phone.

He walked into the kitchen and saw breakfast was on the table. He knew Molly was also ready, though probably more ready for answers than the meal, so he gave her what little information he could.

"I have no idea what Norman wants, but I told him I would be there in a few hours. He and I will be going out to lunch so we can talk and it would be nice if you would come along to keep the ladies and the baby company."

Molly responded with, "I'm surprised he didn't want to talk to me or at least tell you what he wanted over the phone. She paused for a moment before asking, "You don't think he heard you say good morning, do you?"

Harvey grinned at the reference, "Well, I'm sure he'll know and understand sooner or later."

He took her in his arms as a gesture of reassurance before adding, "But no, I think something else is going on. Let's have breakfast and get on the road."

Molly said softly," Okay, but I didn't say I wanted to go."

"You don't want me to drive all the way there and back by myself, do you?" Harvey asked in mocked astonishment.

"I'm kidding. Of course, I'll go. It's just that it would have been nice for us to have all day to relax together." Sighing, Molly then added wistfully, "Time flies when you're having fun."

Harvey quickly tacked on, "Or when you're under the gun to get something done."

"Ain't that the truth," replied Molly. Then, as if coaxed by some inner feeling, she added, "Before we come back, we should spend some time at your place."

The last statement surprised Harvey at first, but he quickly accepted it as Molly making a subtle but logical attempt to do a little detective work on her own. It made sense for her to make sure he did, in fact, live by himself in the neighborhood he'd described and the contents in his home would back up all information he'd divulged.

"That's perfect, I need to pick up my mail and check on things around the house." With a chuckle, he added, "While we're there you can try out some of *my* cooking."

"Yes, but let's eat my cooking now before it gets ice cold. Then I'll pack some things for a few nights so we can get on the road."

Molly had spoken in the most upbeat voice she could muster, but inside she felt weighed down by a foreboding that something ugly was going on at the Purlmens' house. If that was the case, it would be a crushing blow. She had come to grips fairly quickly about Norman's new life and his new job. She had also fallen in love. She certainly didn't need to have any rain begin to fall on her parade of happiness. Not now. At least, not so soon.

Meanwhile, two hours away, Norman left the phone booth and began to formulate his planned meeting with Harvey. He'd first let Mother know his grandmother and Harvey would be arriving in a couple of hours and then tell her he and Harvey would be going out to lunch. He'd have to describe it as a man-to-man thing as a thank you for getting the family together.

Another thing he needed to do was to have Marlene use an excuse to get out of the house by herself so she could join them for their discussion. He felt his grandmothers would happily volunteer to babysit for a couple of hours. He reasoned they should have more to talk about since they'd only seen each other for a short while the day before after being apart for more than 20 years.

Norman's thoughts then drifted toward the fact that his Nana would be thinking she would be visiting with his half-brother when in fact Toby was actually her great-grandson. That took some of the luster off the thought of this family gathering, but he had to keep his thoughts on track. He and Harvey needed a place to rendezvous. He'd find out from Marlene where she thought they could meet and have a private conversation.

Arriving home, Norman first encountered Marlene. "Where's Mother?" he asked

"Upstairs, I think she's in the shower."

"Good, I talked to Harvey and he's going to be here in a few hours."

"What did he tell you?"

"He didn't want to discuss it over the phone."

Marlene immediately understood and said knowingly, "The solider and the lady."

"Yeah, just like you told me, so we have to meet somewhere. What would be a good place?"

"Let's go to the MoreToEat Restaurant. Mother doesn't like it because so many young people are usually there. It's the first exit off the highway going north. You'll see the sign as soon as you make the turn. You can't miss it."

"Got it. You should probably wait 10 or 15 minutes after I leave with Harvey and then let mother and Nana know you need a couple of things from the store. Then ask them to watch Toby."

"Sounds like a plan."

Norman took his newspaper and walked toward the den. "Let mother know I'm in the den," he said as he left.

"All right."

Norman was 15 minutes into the newspaper when Elizabeth joined him.

"Good morning Norman, catching up on paperwork before breakfast?"

"No, just the newspaper for now. Listen, Harvey will be stopping by in a couple of hours and he and I are going out to celebrate bringing the family together."

"Oh, do you really think it's necessary?"

"I thought it would be a nice thing to do, Mother," Norman replied. "After all, he did a lot of work and he's bringing my grandmother along. You two didn't spend a lot of time talking yesterday."

Norman let his statements sink in for a moment before adding, "I don't know when I'll get another chance to see her again. I'll be really busy around here getting to know all about the business."

Those last two statements pacified Elizabeth to where she began to look forward to again seeing her former housekeeper. It would give her another opportunity to subtly convince Molly to relinquish more if not all the reins she had on Norman.

"Good," Elizabeth said. "Marlena and I will keep her company while you and Harvey have your lunch. I think it's a great idea."

With that, Norman was satisfied he'd done all he could to set the stage for the meeting. Glancing at his watch he figured Harvey and Nana would be there in another two hours or so. Time seemed to drag.

Once Harvey and Molly arrived at the house, the plan was executed like clockwork. Norman and Harvey left within 10 minutes and Marlene within the next 15. Elizabeth and Molly sat down and were able to converse freely about things in general, but each deliberately made no mention of anything that pertained to the names Sue or Tom. Both had gotten over the causes for their dissention and were able to retrieve the same type of feelings they'd had during their previous relationship.

However, while their conversation was pleasant, there was an inherent flaw. Each had unwittingly and unknowingly slipped back into the employer/employee mode they'd previously known. Elizabeth had no qualms about it, but Molly eventually began to feel slighted. She resolved, however, to keep any negative feelings hidden for Norman's sake. After all, Norman would be the head of this household and she would be...well, if things went the way they seemed to be going, she hoped she might soon be Mrs. Harvey Stevens.

At the restaurant, Harvey became the leader and organized the setting. With his expertise at displaying professionalism, he first asked the hostess if there was a room for private parties. There were two, but the smallest one was for up to 10 people with a minimum of 6. Harvey deftly got around the minimum person requirement by agreeing to a minimum tab of $200.

Once seated and served beverages, Norman began to inch his way into the matter at hand.

"I'm glad you're the kind of person who won't go around talking about other people's business," Norman began.

"I never divulge client information and I respect everyone's personal information," Harvey said. "I usually tell clients about how I keep things to myself by giving an example of a soldier I met and then a lady I met many years later. They didn't want anyone to know they had been together, but each independently gave enough information during casual conversations for me to figure it out."

"Yeah, and I'm glad about that because what I want to talk about can't ever get out."

The way Norman had acknowledged the abridged version of Harvey's episode with the soldier and the lady gave Harvey the impression he'd already told Norman the story, but he didn't think he had. After all, he'd only given an account of it to Molly during their drive back to her home. He couldn't believe she was so infatuated with him or tuned out that she would have allowed him to tell the same story twice in two days without reminding him he'd already said it. Curiosity got the best of him.

"Did I tell you that story before?" he asked.

The moment had come for Norman to let Harvey know the source of his knowledge as Marlene walked into the room.

"Nope. Marlene told me." Norman replied.

In a hushed whisper, Harvey corrected him. "You mean Marlena." Then in a full voice, he stood and said, "Marlena, how's it going?"

"Everything's fine, Harvey," she answered. Then she said to Norman, "You didn't tell him anything yet, have you?"

"No, I wanted to wait for you. I only let him know how I knew about the soldier and the lady."

Harvey was confused but patient. He asked no questions and instead motioned for the waiter to take their orders and later return with their food. Once they were alone and eating, he let them know the time was right to begin the conversation between bites.

"What's going on?" he asked.

Norman and Marlene exchanged glances before Norman began to explain.

"We knew each other before yesterday," he said. Realizing the statement went practically nowhere without further information, he pressed on.

"I mean we met once a year and a half ago in Branchport. We fell in love and..." Norman looked at Marlene. It was as if he was silently asking for permission to divulge what they'd previously agreed would remain a secret. He completed his statement with, "By some miracle, we now have a son that everyone thinks is my brother."

Harvey didn't have a quick answer to the unimaginable story he'd heard, but he felt a hasty reply would have been a mistake anyway. He said nothing and hoped one or both would expand on the statement.

It was Marlene's turn to speak.

"Tom wanted me to get artificially inseminated because he was sick and couldn't father a child. He only wanted a child for his mother. He was..., well, he was trying to use me."

She paused long enough to collect her thoughts before continuing. "I was in Branchport for the first and only time in my life when I saw Norman. I had been agonizing over threats Tom had been making, but I was firmly against going through with the test tube thing. So, when I saw Norman, who looked almost exactly like Tom did when I first met him, only younger, I was attracted. We got together almost by chance. There was no planning at first. Things just happened. As a matter of fact, we had seen each other earlier that day at a gym, but we didn't speak. We just happened to meet up at a restaurant later that evening and I wound up in his room."

Norman added, "I was glad that Mother took charge of me yesterday because seeing Marlene was a shock. I wanted to start asking questions, but Marlene gave me a little head shake not to. I didn't begin to relax yesterday until she came back into the living room just before you and Nana left and gave me a note telling me we needed to talk later in the evening. I waited in my room until she came to talk. She told me my father had done some sneaky things and they never really got married. He thought at first that Marlene had gone through with the artificial insemination to get pregnant, but he threw her out of the house when he found out that she didn't. He wouldn't let her use the family name for herself or Toby. He threatened to tell Mother about it, but he kept everything to himself and I'm glad of it. Mother wouldn't have gone for any shenanigans."

"Wow," Harvey said. "Most people wouldn't believe in coincidences like that, but I've always believed that anything that can possibly happen, *can* happen, no matter what the odds are against it. That's one of the reasons I tell people about the soldier and the lady. Other far-fetched things have happened to me, and probably most everyone else, if they stop to think about it."

Harvey stopped marveling at the story and finally asked a question. "So now, what are you two thinking about doing?"

"We need suggestions," Norman said. "I mean, at first we agreed we wouldn't tell anyone that I'm Toby's father, but I don't think we could tell the rest of the story without letting you know about the most important part. We're not sure what to do."

"Right," Marlene chimed in. "What would you do?"

"Well, first off, straighten me out about your name. I was told you only answer to Marlena."

Norman did the answering and purposely left Mr. Marlayna out of the story. "Marlene introduced herself to me as Marlene and the name stuck."

"Yes," Marlene agreed. "It wasn't until then that I accepted it and now Marlena is the name I don't want to use."

"Okay, Marlene it is," said Harvey. "I can understand that. Out with the old and in with the new. It's a good way to turn a page. From now on, it's Marlene. Now, what about this Mother thing, Norman? All of a sudden, you're referring to your grandmother as Mother. What's up with that?"

Norman replied, "She wanted me to call her Mother and told me so the first chance she got yesterday. She said it would be good for me to use that name since it's what Marlene calls her and Marlene and I are the exact same age."

"Right down to the day - February 29th," said Marlene. We're both leap day babies."

Harvey took a deep breath. "Okay, and now since we're getting so deep into this, I'm going to go against my principles."

Looking at Marlene he asked, "Would you mind telling me what was in that letter from Tom that I delivered to you?"

Marlene didn't hesitate. "It was pretty much about what we just told you. I know I was supposed to destroy it, but I never did. I let Norman see it."

"It's good that you let Norman see it. This way you both know what's going on," Harvey said. "Okay, my first bit of advice is actually in the form of a question. Are you in love with each other and do you want to live together as man and wife?"

Neither hesitated.

"I love Marlene and I want us to be together."

"I love Norman and I want us to be together with our son."

"Perfect. Now let's figure out the best way to make things happen."

Pulling a small note pad and pen from his pocket, he began.

"At the top of the list is for you to destroy that letter. Don't take the chance that someone might find it. It's good that Norman saw it, but that has to be the end of it. There's no reason to keep it any longer. Just think about how ugly it would be to have someone else read it."

"Okay," Marlene answered.

"Now we need to think about a few things, beginning with names. Turning his attention to Norman, Harvey said, "Norman, had your mother and father gone about things the traditional way, your last name would be Purlmen right now. Would you have any problem with that?"

The question took Norman by surprise. "I hadn't given it a thought."

"Well," Harvey told them, "you both need to think about it, unless 'being together' doesn't mean marriage to you. Does it?"

Norman and Marlene exchanged a look that meant neither had thought it through.

Harvey understood. "Listen, you both have to understand the head of the Purlmens' household is an extremely traditional woman who would probably be the last person you'd want to try to tiptoe past in the wee hours of the morning. Be honest – how do you feel?"

"Oh yeah, I want us to get married," said Norman, "But the problem is the situation. Marlene was married to my father."

"Not really though, remember?" Marlene spoke quickly. "We weren't married in the true sense of the word. As a matter of fact, we weren't married in any kind of way."

"Hold on, I was going to get to that," Harvey interjected. "Both of you know there was no legal marriage?"

"Yes. Actually, it was part of the letter, so Norman read about it," Marlene replied. "The letter also said not to tell anyone about anything in the letter, but..."

Marlene trailed off as she digested Harvey's question about knowledge of no marriage before impulsively stating and asking, "The way you asked about whether we both knew there was no marriage makes it seem like you knew. Did you?"

"I was told in private conversations, first by Tom and then by Elizabeth. Neither of them wanted me to mention that I knew about it to anyone except you, Marlene, but I was only supposed to mention it to convince you to come back. I never said anything to you because there was no need. Have either of you discussed it with her?"

"Not me," said Norman.

"Not me either," answered Marlene, adding, "I don't even like to *think* about any of the wrong things he did so I definitely don't want to talk about it."

"Okay, that's good. Make sure you keep it to yourselves. That's the best thing to do, all of us. We all need to treat it as if we never heard it before, right?"

Almost in unison, Norman and Marlene answered, "Right."

"Perfect," Harvey replied and then asked, "Marlene, do you want to marry Norman?"

Speaking directly to Harvey with dogged determination in her voice, she answered, "Yes, I want us to get married."

"Then I believe this thing is doable. The only potential roadblock is the head of the house, but unless I'm mistaken, she's already unknowingly swung the door wide open."

Harvey let the statement sink in before continuing.

"Listen, she was disappointed with her son. I mean, really disappointed. It showed and Tom pretty much told me so. Did you see it, Marlene?"

"Oh yes. I could tell."

"Then you come along Norman, and she wants you to call her Mother. She wants you to come right in and be part of the family and take the place of her son. She's making like your generation of the family never existed."

"That's the same thing I told Norman," Marlene chimed in. "It's like he's the passed generation of the family, as in passed over."

"Passed over generation – that's a good way to put it," Harvey agreed. "Now once you step up and let her know that the best thing that can happen for the family is for you and Marlene to get married, she'll go along with it. Do you follow what I'm saying?"

"I guess so," Norman answered, but his reluctant reply dripped with residual skepticism.

Marlene understood completely. "I know that's right, for sure. You can see she's treating Norman better than Tom. I know I can see it, and she only met Norman yesterday."

"Right. That means you're in the driver's seat, Norman. You need to tell her that for the good of the family and to reestablish pride in the hierarchy, you and Marlene should get married. Then, while you're at it, tell her you believe you should adopt Toby to get rid of the stigma of her son having fathered two half-brothers."

Norman stared blankly at Harvey for a moment before asking, "Do you think all that makes sense?"

"Yes, I do, but we need to fully work this out. I asked you about last names before. That would be one of the arguments. If you change your name to Purlmen, then you and Marlene get married, and then you adopt Toby, the name lineage will be preserved. To Elizabeth, legally and socially, she'll have the lineage intact. What she won't realize is that the lineage will be biologically intact as well. What she won't know won't hurt her, but if it ever came to light that Marlene was..."

Harvey stopped for a moment to rephrase what he was saying. He chose his next words carefully.

"I doubt she'd accept the fact that a chance meeting by you two was the catalyst for having created her great-grandson. I mean, who would believe it? I still find it hard to believe."

Neither Norman nor Marlene said anything, so Harvey began to organize.

"Alright," he said, glancing at his note pad. "All I have so far is 'destroy the letter'. Are we in agreement?"

"Yes," both answered simultaneously.

"As I said before Norman, you need to take Elizabeth aside and tell her you want to marry Marlene and adopt Toby. Once that's done, everything else will fall right into place. Do it as soon as we get back to the house. Don't tell her Marlene wants it too."

Harvey thought for a moment. "Let Elizabeth think she's the decision-maker. Tell her if she approves, you'll ask Marlene as soon as she gets home. Then add one stipulation – Marlene has to accept your request for her name to become Marlene. That way everyone can get used to it at the same time. Let me write this down."

Harvey's note looked like this:

Destroy letter

Ask Elizabeth about marrying Marlene

Change Marlena to Marlene

"Hmm. We need to find a reason to make the name change," Harvey said. "You can't just come out and make that demand."

"There is a good reason," Norman replied. "I had a teacher named Mr. Marlayna. He and I didn't get along at all."

"Cool," Harvey responded. "That takes care of that." Harvey completed the list.

Change surname to Purlmen

Adopt Toby

"This should give you more than enough ammunition to take to the battle," he said as he handed it to Norman.

"You're making this sound too easy," said an unconvinced Norman as he looked the note over.

"All you have to do is take charge. There's not a woman in the world who doesn't think a man is being noble for taking on and raising another man's child as his own. Now, if Elizabeth thought Toby was not a blood relative, I don't believe she'd be too enthusiastic about it, but for you to do it for the family's sake would be perfect. Trust me."

"I trust you," said Norman, "but what if she doesn't want us to get married?"

"I can't see that happening. Not with what Tom said before he died. He admitted to his mother that the marriage was bogus and that he had done Marlene wrong. He said he was sorry and it was all his fault. Also, the way Elizabeth accepted you was the exact opposite of the vibes I got for how she felt about Tom. Believe me, you are in charge, so take charge. What do you think, Marlene?"

"I agree. Mother loves you Norman. I can tell. She'll go along with it."

"Okay then," Norman said. "How are we going to stage it?"

Harvey continued to do the organizing. "Norman, you and I will go home first, and as soon as we get there, you take Elizabeth into the den for a private conversation. Immediately tell her you believe you and Marlene should get married. What you do next depends on her reaction. If she goes along with it, or even if she doesn't, tell her that you want Marlena to answer to the name Marlene. Then make the offer to change your name to Purlmen. Wait – tell her you want it to be cleared with Molly first. Finally, discuss adoption. Like I said, once she agrees to the marriage, everything else will begin to fall right into place."

"When do you want me to show up?" asked Marlene.

"Give us, I don't know, maybe 15 or 20 minutes. When you come in, peek to see if Norman and Elizabeth are back in the living room. Don't come in until they are in sight. It will be easier to keep things on track if there's no delay between each thing that gets accomplished. Any questions?"

"No, I'm ready," said Norman.

"Me too. I'll be there 15 minutes later than you."

"Perfect," said Harvey. "You know Marlene, what you said about the passed over generation is right, except once everything falls into place, it won't be about Norman being passed over anymore. In Elizabeth's eyes, it will be Tom and Sue that make up the passed generation. I mean, we have to accept the fact that they were who they were, Norman, and without them, you would never have been born.

No one can do anything about what that past generations did – and that's P-A-S-T generations. All any of us can do is take care of what we can reach out and touch and change, hopefully for the better. I have ancestors who were slaves. Molly told me you have some American Indian, African, Wales, and Irish blood, Norman. Probably some Hispanic blood, too. And Marlene, I remember that you told me you were adopted from Peru and you don't know anything more about your past. But we've all been living good lives because we look forward to doing the right things for ourselves and the people around us. It's like the part of the serenity prayer about having the courage to change the things we can. Changing, and in your case, actually fixing your family hierarchy makes a lot of sense."

"That's right," echoed Marlene. And I've always liked that serenity prayer."

"Yes, what you're saying does make sense," Norman said before pensively adding, "You know, the serenity prayer never really hit home with me until now. I never thought too much about it, but I guess I've been pretty much following it automatically anyway."

"That's good. We're in great shape with young folks like you. If more people looked toward making a better future and worked to fix past wrongs rather than to perpetuate the nonsense in the world, we'd all be better off." Harvey then added, "I guess we need to get going."

Glancing around, Harvey saw the waiter just outside the room. He beckoned for him to come closer before saying, "Check, please."

After paying the bill they stood to leave. Just as Harvey was about to take his first step away from the table, Norman had a thought.

"I'll bet you never heard of anything like this happening out of the clear blue before, have you, Harvey?"

"Probably no one has," added Marlene.

Harvey stopped dead in his tracks. He held up his hands and said to the others, "Whoa, Norman and Marlene, I'm glad one of you said that and the other one agreed. We need to sit down for a few more minutes."

Once seated he began to speak. "We've been so locked into your situation that I almost took another situation for granted."

To Norman, he said, "Your grandmother, Norman." Remembering that Norman had two he added, "Molly. How do you think she's going to feel about all this?"

Norman was slow to answer but finally said, "I think she'll be alright with it."

Seemingly off on a tangent, Harvey said, "All these things going on today have me divulging more inside information than I've ever done before, but I truly believe it's the right thing to do. Unless you two come up with a reason not to, I plan to let Molly in on everything that's going on. In the last couple of days, she and I have become close, and by that, I mean really close."

Looking directly into Norman's eyes Harvey added, "That's why I spent the night."

Harvey then stretched the truth slightly with, "She and I are probably going to get married, so I don't want to keep family things away from her. She deserves to know right away that she has a great-grandson and that you are a father. I want to be the one who has the pleasure of telling her."

Norman thought back to that early morning call and said, "I thought something was going on this morning, but I had other things on my mind so I ignored what I heard. Listen, all I ask is that you do right by her and I think you're the right kind of man."

Norman extended his hand and said, "Congratulations."

"Yes congratulations," Marlene repeated.

"Thanks, but I haven't quite popped the question yet. I just want you to know I'm going to," he said, shaking Norman's hand. "Speaking about incredible happenings though, it will only be incredible if she turns me down. She and I fell in love about as quickly as the two of you did, actually probably faster. Now let's get going so we can take care of what you two need to get done."

As soon as they were inside the house, it was apparent that Norman had taken Harvey's advice to heart. He made a beeline to Elizabeth and spoke to her in a hushed tone in an attempt to keep Molly from overhearing. He felt a little shy about calling one grandmother Mother and the other Nana.

"Mother, can I see you in the den? There are a few things we need to talk about." He held out his hand to help her to her feet.

Accepting his hand, Elizabeth spoke to the others. "We'll be right back," she said smiling.

Norman did not release Elizabeth's hand until they reached the den. He opened the door and guided her to the sofa. He remained standing while leaning back on the desk so he was above her in a position of authority. He elevated his pose one step further by crossing his arms as non-verbal punctuation to the seriousness of the matter.

"We need to straighten out the family legacy and it's up to me to take the first step," he began. "From what you've told me, we've got great family history, but right now it's in disarray, mainly because of things my father did."

"Well, Norman, just what do you think you can do about it?" asked Elizabeth.

Norman had the opening he needed so he sprang into action. "I believe Marlene and I should get married and that I should adopt Toby."

Elizabeth had never thought of the possibility so she sat and silently pondered the statement.

Norman was afraid he might have come on too strong too soon, but he couldn't back out now. All he could do was to try to support his statement.

"Just think about it. Rather than having me, whose mother was never married into the family, living here with you, my step-mother Marlene and my half-brother Toby, we'd have a traditional family setup."

Elizabeth was nodding her head slowly up and down affirmatively as the logic began to sink in. Norman interpreted this as a positive sign and decided to verbally test the water.

"What do you think, Mother?" he asked.

"Why, I hadn't thought about it before, but it might be a good idea." She began thinking about possible problems with the suggestion and the first issue she sited was off on the perfect tangent.

"You know, the first problem you might have is that you don't use Marlena's name the right way. Ever since I met her, she has insisted that everyone must call her Marlena."

For emphasis, Elizabeth pronounced it phonetically for Norman, slowly and deliberately while accenting the second syllable. "Mar-LAY-nuh. She won't accept Marlene."

With that, Norman knew the battle was over. All that he needed to do now was to put the rest of the cards on the table to get Elizabeth fully on his side. He eased back into the conversation with his rationale.

"Way back in junior high school I had this teacher named Mr. Marlayna. That guy had it in for me for some reason and he's the only teacher I ever had trouble with in any school I've ever attended. No way would I want to have to use that name every day, except in a negative way."

Elizabeth immediately accepted Norman's side of the story.

"Oh, I agree," she said. "In that case, I wouldn't want to use it either."

Then surprisingly, she doubled down on the name change. "I never did like the name Marlena. I don't understand why her parents would give her a Spanish sounding name anyway. I think you should insist on the name change."

"That I will. We'll work together on this. And speaking of names, don't you think I should first work on changing my last name to Purlmen? That way we can get the family straightened out."

"That's a marvelous idea!" Elizabeth had almost shouted her approval before asking "When do you plan on talking to Marlena – I mean Marlene?"

"I'll let her know as soon as she gets back."

"Do you think she might be back now?" Elizabeth wondered.

Elizabeth had gotten anxious, but Norman needed to slow the process. After all, they'd only been away from the others for a few minutes.

"I doubt it, and besides, I think we should take some time to maybe list things that need to be done for the family and the business. I want to start on whatever needs to get done bright and early tomorrow morning. Nana and Harvey will be alright out there."

"Alright. I like that you want to take charge and get things done."

"That's the way I am," Norman said as he left his perch and walked around to the desk chair. "Let's get busy."

"Wait, Norman," Elizabeth said. "Before we talk about work, there's more for us to discuss when it comes to you asking Marlene to marry you."

"Yes, Mother?" Norman was immediately afraid an issue had been discovered.

"There's something you need to know, and I don't ever want you to discuss it with anyone."

"Alright, Mother."

"It's about your father. Now, I don't want you to feel bad about him, but he did some things he never should have. One of the worst things was how he treated Marlene. I don't know what Harvey said to her to get her to come home, but just in case he told her everything your father did, I want you to be aware."

Norman just sat listening and hoping he wasn't going to hear bad news.

Elizabeth told him, "Your father never married Marlene. He did her wrong in the worst of ways. It made no sense and I'm ashamed of him. That's why I think it's so noble of you to take over the responsibility of raising Toby like he was your son. You've made me prouder of you by stepping up and asking to fix the family than you will ever know. And we only met yesterday."

Fighting back tears, she continued.

"Please don't ever bring it up to Marlene. She may not know how bad your father was to her. Only speak of it if she ever brings it up. Otherwise, leave it alone. It will be *our* secret. And if she does ever mention it, let her know that we don't need to discuss it. We'll leave all those negative and wrong things where they belong..." Elizabeth hesitated before uttering what she was going to say because she felt the words might be too harsh. Then, in the next instant, she realized what she started to say was exactly what she wanted to say, so she completed her statement with, "...dead and buried."

Norman could scarcely believe his ears. He now had to keep a secret that was already common knowledge to him, Marlene, Harvey, and by now probably his Nana. This was his chance to elevate the marriage question to an even more acceptable status and he made the most of the opportunity.

"I won't say a word to anyone about any of that, Mother. I'll do some research and make sure we can move forward without mentioning anything about it. But you know it's probably a good thing they weren't legally married. This way we can get married with both of us listed as single persons."

"That's right, that's right," Elizabeth agreed enthusiastically. "That would make it better."

Norman became pensive for a moment and then recited a potential chronology of things that needed to get done.

"I'll first talk to Marlene about calling her Marlene instead of Marlena. Then I'll discuss with her the pros and cons of our getting married and me adopting Toby. After that, I'll let her know that no matter what, I'm going to get my last name changed to Purlmen.

Neither spoke for a moment as they pondered Norman's plan. It was Norman who broke the silence with a previously unrecognized fact.

"You know," he said, "I said it was good, but actually it's great that they weren't legally married. That means I won't be marrying the widow of my own father."

"Why I hadn't considered that. Perfect. I'm glad you're taking charge, Norman." Elizabeth broke into a wide smile. "It's serendipity for sure that, so quickly after Tom passed, you came along and you've made me so happy."

Thinking about what she'd just said, Elizabeth added, "Serendipity was a favorite word of mine many years ago, but I haven't felt like using it for I don't know how long."

She inhaled and exhaled slowly and contentedly before adding, "Now let's go over a few business items that need to get done soon before we go back out with the others."

Norman created a task list, making sure everything they spoke of was not only listed but broken down into individual tasks. They wound up working together 10 minutes longer.

Earlier, in the living room after Norman and Elizabeth had left to go to the den, Harvey had turned to Molly so he could give her an update.

"Now that we're alone we can talk," he told her. "I'm going to bring you up to date on everything that's going on."

"Everything?"

"Everything. Keep in mind I'm going to tell you things that in any other situation, I would never tell. But this involves your family and you and I are close enough for me to share what I know."

"Uh-huh. That's right, so what's going on?"

"It's just hard to think about where to start."

"It doesn't matter. Just tell me."

"Okay. I'll start with the most important thing."

Harvey lowered his voice and leaned closer to Molly before giving her a build-up to the pronouncement he felt the news deserved.

"It's an incredible coincidence, but it's also a phenomenal, fantastic, who-da thought-it, you gotta be lyin', magnificent, lovely, wonderful miracle. Believe it or not, Norman and Marlene met about a year and a half ago and Toby is their son."

Molly just stared at Harvey expressionlessly so he expanded on what he'd said.

"Tom had gotten sick and couldn't have children. He wanted Marlene to get artificially inseminated, but she didn't want to. She had a meeting in Branchport at the same time Norman was there. They met by accident and one thing led to another. Marlene got pregnant from that one time they were together. When Tom found out, he threw her and the baby out of the house."

Molly was slowly catching up with what she'd heard. She asked incredulously, "You're telling me the baby is Norman's son?"

"He sure is."

"I don't believe it."

"Believe it. Wasn't Norman in Branchport a year and a half ago?"

"Yes."

"Right, and both of them told me the same thing. Oh yeah, when Norman and I were out to lunch Marlene walked in. They had set it up to discuss the whole thing with me to help them decide what to do. They chose me because they felt I would give good advice and not go running around talking about their situation."

"Exactly what did you tell them?"

"I asked them a couple of questions about how they felt and both answered that they were in love and wanted to be together. I told them they should get married and Norman should adopt Toby. That way the actual situation they were in would be made legal. The one stipulation is that no one can ever tell Elizabeth the whole truth. Only the 4 of us - you, me, Marlene, and Norman - will ever know everything that happened."

Molly's answer surprised Harvey.

"Why should we bend over backwards for her?" she asked. "Why can't we just let her know about everything so we can all deal with the truth?"

Harvey recovered quickly and gave an honest and heartfelt answer.

"Let's face it. Elizabeth wants to give the impression that the Purlmens are the type of people who are always in the right and have always had a history free from any kind of mistake or scandal. In short, she feels like she's upper class because of the family name and lineage. I don't believe anyone or anything will ever change her mind. She has to decide to make a change."

Harvey patted Molly's hand and continued.

"Folks like us are more down to earth. We know there's good and bad in varying degrees in everyone who has ever walked the face of the earth regardless of their name or where they come from."

"Right," Molly answered defiantly before rephrasing her question. "So why not just tell her the truth anyway and not cover anything up?"

"I believe the truth would cause her to not like or trust Marlene. The same with Norman. She wouldn't accept it. Right now, Norman is in line to be the head of the family business instead of doing construction work for who knows how much longer. Shouldn't he be allowed to pursue a ready-made career the way he told me he wants to?"

"Listen, I want him to take advantage of everything he rightfully should," answered Molly. "I'm just tired of the way she acts like she's better than everyone else."

"Some people have to live in a phony world and feel superior."

"Uh-huh," answered Molly, still not fully comfortable.

Harvey hoped Norman was doing better than he. Molly was giving him a run for the money. He tried another approach. "Listen, Molly, there are a few other things involved."

"Oh, like what?"

"Well, one of the things is the name. To appease any misgivings Elizabeth might have, Norman will be suggesting that his name gets changed to Purlmen."

Harvey readied himself for Molly's reply, which he assumed would be negative. This time, however, he wasn't worried. He was confident he had already prepared what he considered to be the perfect answer.

As expected, Molly answered with a question that dripped with repugnance. "Change his name from Hurley to Purlmen just to satisfy her?"

Harvey calmly stated his perfect answer, "Well, I'm hoping I can get you to change yours from Hurley to Stevens."

Molly's mood changed. It took a few moments for her to speak. Harvey waited patiently and was rewarded with Molly's sweet surrender.

"That sounds like a proposal," she said as her voice and attitude softened. "I think you already know I'm stuck on you. What else is going on?"

"Let's stick with my proposal to you for a minute. I want us to get married. I want us to leave here tonight, stay at my place and go ring shopping in the morning so I can propose to you the right way, if that works for you."

"That sounds wonderful. Hold me for a minute before we talk about anything else."

They shared an embrace before Harvey continued.

"Okay, here's the plan. Marlene should be coming home very soon."

Just then they heard Marlene approaching.

Hurriedly Harvey explained what he needed to tell Molly about Marlene.

"She was always Marlena until she met Norman, but from now on, she's Marlene. Call her that and congratulate her on their upcoming marriage when she comes in. But do it fast and quietly because Elizabeth doesn't know about it yet and Marlene can't be in here when they come out of the den. Come on."

Harvey rose from the sofa and helped Molly to her feet. They walked over to Marlene. Harvey spoke first to give the current status of things.

"They're still in the den Marlene, so it'll be a while before it's safe for you to come in. Meanwhile, I've been telling Molly what's going on."

"Congratulations," Molly said to Marlene. "Harvey told me that you and Norman are getting married and I'm a great-grandmother."

They embraced.

"Oh, thank you," Marlene answered. "It's not official yet, but we're hoping we don't run into any issues."

"We're making plans too because Molly said yes," Harvey said to Marlene. "We hope to make an announcement soon, but probably not today. We need to finish getting past your situation."

"That's great," Marlene said, hugging each one. "This has really been a great day."

"We'd better get back to the living room," Harvey said. "Marlene, you just relax and wait until they come out of the den. If all's well, Norman will ask you to come with him for a private conversation."

"Alright," she replied.

Harvey and Molly returned to the sofa and continued their conversation.

"Molly," Harvey began, "You know it makes sense for Norman's last name to be Purlmen, right?"

"Oh yes, I knew it from before he was born. Sue decided to make his last name Hurley so I went along with it. Like I said, my problem is that I don't like going along with things just to please the Purlmens."

"Well, there's more, Molly, and this is something else that can't ever be discussed. Tom Purlmen and Marlene were never married. Tom told me about it on the day I met him after Elizabeth left the room. He asked me to never let his mother know that I knew. He had already told her, but it hurt her so much that she kept it to herself until after Tom died. That's when she told me, but only in case I needed to use the information to get Marlene to come home. Are you following me so far?"

"Yes," Molly replied. "What else?"

"Well, I never had to mention it to Marlene, because she was ready to come home pretty quickly. The thing of it is, I found out today that Marlene already knew because Tom had told her when he kicked her out of the house. He had also put it in a letter that he'd written to Marlene. Norman found out when Marlene told him about it. What I'm getting to is that we all know, but Elizabeth doesn't know that we all know and it's something that she's ashamed of. That makes it another thing none of us can ever bring up. You're on board with everything in the plan now, right?"

"Oh, I understand. Don't talk about anything dealing with the mess they created. I get it," Molly replied. "But you know, it's a shame that she thinks having a child out of wedlock will stain her family. The most important thing about having a child is how the child is raised. And I still don't like her thinking she's better than anyone else, especially me. Once Norman changes his name it'll probably get worse."

"We can work together on that, but there is one more thing," Harvey said.

"My goodness, what's else?"

"Elizabeth wants both Norman and Marlene to call her Mother."

"Why?"

"I'm not sure, but if you think about it, it does make sense to her. She wants to live in a dream world of perfection. Let her have her utopia. The rest of us are fine being who we are and what we are."

"I know, Harvey. I just can't get past her acting like she's better than me," Molly proclaimed.

Harvey probed for additional information.

"You know, I can see where Elizabeth is proud of her family, or at least wants to be, but what about her makes you feel that she thinks she's better than you?"

"Because I used to work for her," Molly said.

"But that was what, over 20 years ago, right?"

"Yes, but..."

"But what?"

"I'm not sure." Molly trailed off with her answer and slowly shook her head. "I just don't know."

"Hmmm," Harvey mused. "Let me ask you this. What was her husband's name?"

"Mr. Purlmen? His name was Thomas."

"Uh-huh. And you called them Mr. and Mrs. Purlmen, right?"

"Yes, I always used Mr. or Mrs. with the people I worked for. We even called their son Tom Mr. Purlmen."

"Have you ever called Elizabeth by name since you first saw her again yesterday?"

"No, I haven't called her anything. We just talk."

"That's probably half if not pretty much all of the problem right there. Listen, when she comes out of the den she's should be at Norman's side. After Norman takes Marlene into the den, Elizabeth is supposed to mention the name change from Hurley to Purlmen. When she does, you need to say something like, 'Elizabeth, you know Thomas and Tom would be proud to know Norman was planning to carry on the family name'. Just put it out there that you know how to be big about things. As a matter of fact, after the first time, use her first name whenever you get the chance. I'll bet she's been saying Molly to you in just about every other sentence all day long."

"You know, I think you're right," Molly admitted. "She has been saying my name a lot. To tell you the truth, after a while I began to get tired of hearing it."

"Listen, I know it might seem ridiculous at first, but it would be a good idea to practice that line I gave you a few times before they come out here."

"Elizabeth, Thomas, and Tom would both be proud to know Norman was carrying on the family name," Molly recited. "I've got it and I'll do it."

"Good, and please don't stop using her name after that first time. Keep using it until you're both sick of hearing it."

"Yes, Elizabeth," mocked Molly with a smile before adding, "I'm practicing."

"You can practice on me any time, Baby," Harvey responded.

"Mm-hmm. I'm ready to leave and go to your place right now," Molly purred and then impatiently asked, "I wonder what they're doing in there?"

"Norman must be taking his time to make sure Marlene has gotten home," Harvey said. "I don't believe it's taking this long for Elizabeth to make up her mind."

About a minute later to everyone's relief, Norman and Elizabeth re-entered the living room. Marlene noticed them and also entered the living room. Norman was the first to speak.

"Marlene, I need to talk to you for a few minutes in the den," he said.

"Sure, I'll be right there," Marlene answered.

As soon as they shut the door behind them, Norman embraced Marlene and said, "Mother went along with the plan. We're all set. The only thing that came out of my conversation with Mother is that she told me you and my father were never married. She said don't tell you if you don't already know and she told me not to tell anyone else."

"Then the whole plan is perfect because I'd like to act as if I never knew," Marlene firmly answered. "We don't need to speak about it ever again."

"I agree. We'll give them about 10 minutes out there and then go out and make the marriage announcement. And the announcement about your name. And the announcement about adopting Toby."

Happily, with nothing else to do other than take some time before returning to the living room, they were able to embrace and share loving kisses.

Back in the living room during this time, no one had said anything until after the pair left and Norman closed the den door. Elizabeth opened the conversation.

"I'm glad Marlene didn't say anything about Norman calling her Marlene. Up until now, she would always say something, but for whatever reason, she didn't correct him. Norman told me he won't call her Marlena."

Harvey hesitated, hoping Molly would say something, but when she didn't, he spoke.

"She probably didn't want to be rude," Harvey offered.

"Well, that's good. I wouldn't want them to get off on the wrong foot." Elizabeth now focused on Molly. "I hope this isn't too big of a shock to you, Molly, but right now Norman is asking Marlene to marry him."

Elizabeth waited for Molly to say something, but all she got was a slight affirmative nod.

"Molly," Elizabeth repeated, "Norman wants to marry Marlene and change his last name to Purlmen."

Unbeknownst to Elizabeth, Molly had been waiting to hear what she considered to be the perfect statement from Elizabeth so she could recite the response she'd committed to memory. Now was the time.

"Elizabeth, Thomas, and Tom would both be proud to know Norman will be carrying on the family name," Molly said before adding, "and I will too."

Making that statement released Molly from the phantom oppression she'd been carrying, which freed her to expand her thoughts with a veiled dig.

"After all, Elizabeth," she continued, "had Tom and Sue done the right things 20 years ago, Norman would have been a Purlmen from day one."

Harvey figured he should get involved in the conversation to help keep things from getting out of hand in case Elizabeth took Molly's statement the wrong way.

"I'm hoping Marlene says yes and congratulations are in order when they come out. It shouldn't take too long to pop the question," he offered.

Elizabeth ignored Harvey and instead spoke her mind to Molly about Tom and Sue.

"Molly, I don't know what actually happened between those two and no one ever will. I believe it's best to consider ourselves fortunate to have a grandchild we can love and nurture. We need to get beyond talking about what that generation did. We're passed that now. Let's leave all the negatives behind."

Those statements satisfied Molly so much she didn't know what to say, but she felt the need to respond. All she could manage was, "Right, Elizabeth. Let's leave all the negatives behind."

Harvey stepped in and changed the subject, completely overriding all of his original thoughts about not divulging his and Molly's marriage plans.

"Love is in the air," he announced. "While you were in with Norman, I asked Molly to marry me."

"Really?" Elizabeth asked and looked at Molly quizzically.

"Yes, really." Harvey spoke quickly, still diplomatically acting as a buffer for Molly. "Taking this case was the best thing I ever could have done. It only took a couple of days with Molly to realize she's perfect for me."

Molly no longer needed Harvey to run interference by acting as an intermediary to shield her or Elizabeth from potential vocal darts. She'd been liberated by the simple act of respectfully dropping the class distinction she'd previously sustained through the years. Just before speaking, she was uplifted by thinking to herself, "Sue would have been proud of me."

"And Elizabeth, Harvey is perfect for me," added Molly, maintaining her resolve to use Elizabeth's name whenever she could for her own sake and in the memory of Sue.

Molly then doubled down on the statement by adding, "Harvey is the type of man I've always wanted, Elizabeth, and I'm glad you're the first one to know."

Both Harvey and Molly expected Elizabeth to have something to say by way of congratulations, so they waited patiently for her to speak.

A hush had come over the room as Elizabeth was at a loss for words. She was astounded by this marriage news and had been floored by Molly's shift from acting subordinate to suddenly behaving as an equal. The pause and her astonishment caused some of her long-suppressed and otherwise forgotten memories to rear their ugly head. In a panoramic flash, she remembered her mother once told her they were descendants of some shady characters and her grandmother was the first to finally put a halt to the dirty double-dealing. She'd had one child, a daughter. That daughter was Elizabeth's mother.

Elizabeth's mother was raised to be prim and proper in an overprotected environment. She became aloof, straitlaced, and prissy. As one would expect, she didn't get married until she was well into her twenties. She also had only one child. That child was Elizabeth.

As an only child, Elizabeth readily embraced being put on a pedestal. She developed the same aloof attitude her mother carried and steadfastly maintained that attitude throughout the years. Given her high and mighty frame of mind, she routinely rejected every negative connection to her past, unless she could somehow turn it into a positive. Her position was that she did not know anything about anyone in her family beyond her mother and grandmother. Never was there a mention of anyone else. Since there was no one around to reveal any of the sleaziness her ancestors had displayed, she simply acted as if nothing underhanded had ever been a part of her family. To portray herself as a know-it-all saint had always been easy, especially after she'd married into the wealthy Purlmen family.

However, there was one tangible thing that had been retained from darker days. It was the heirloom ring she wore, and she both loved and hated it. She proudly displayed it as a positive token to be passed down from mother to daughter, but in reality, it was tainted. Evidently, the ring had been stolen by one of Elizabeth's lady of the night ancestors during the Civil War. Neither Elizabeth nor her mother learned that fact until Elizabeth's grandmother revealed its true history on her death bed.

Elizabeth didn't know why at first, but she suddenly thought symbolically about her heirloom ring. She proudly possessed it, even though the method by which her family acquired it was tainted. She felt some shame that it had been the product of a theft, but accepted the fact that it was impossible to change what happened over a hundred years ago. The lofty status she attached to heirloom was proof that something imperfect can be rendered wonderful if held in high regard. In a larger sense, that was now happening within her family.

Elizabeth faced a hierarchical crossroad she had to come to terms with. Her elder grandson had decided to marry the wife of her son. That same grandson was planning to step up and treat his half-brother, who was her younger grandson, as a son to repair the social faux pas her son had created. On the heels of that, Harvey, a black man, was planning to marry her former housekeeper, Molly, who was her elder grandson's other grandmother. Her extended family was becoming a virtual calico conglomeration of persons from places unknown. That kind of setup mirrored the metaphoric description of the United States as being a melting pot, with its fusion of nationalities, cultures, and ethnicities.

To her credit, Elizabeth almost instantly believed she should take the high road. She would accept Molly's impending marriage and obvious attitude of equality as an example of her own earlier statement about leaving negatives behind. After all, she didn't honestly know her own family's full history, and she knew there had been problems and pitfalls along the way. The time was right to eliminate phony class distinction from her mindset.

Taking the thought a step further, she'd always admired the poetic phrase Dr. Martin Luther King Jr. used when he stated that he hoped to see his children 'not be judged by the color of their skin, but by the content of their character'. She surely admired it but had to admit to herself that she'd never before truly embraced it. Now she realized she needed to get beyond the phrase's beauty and delve into its spirit. She needed to apply the phrase's meaning to the family from this point on. After all, the strength of family relies on every generation working to build a positive relationship and philosophy for each succeeding generation. She also resolved to finally make a trip to the library to read and appreciate Dr. King's entire speech.

It had only taken Elizabeth a few seconds to breeze through her family's sordid past and determine it best to continue to hide the ugliness it contained. She despised ugly memories. However, a positive did come from those memories. She'd finally made a true and honest resolution and commitment to become a better person. The problem was she had to figure out how to go about it.

Fortunately, in another flashback, she thought about some of the things lawyer Rodney Stoner had once said of politicians. His point of view was that some politicians often don't do the right things, don't take action, don't want to compromise, and would sooner point fingers to confuse rather than coalesce to enhance.

Elizabeth's thoughts got her moving. She certainly didn't wish for her legacy to be stained by being compared to the practices of some misguided, ineffective, or do-nothing politician. She realized one of the first steps she needed to make was to fully accept Molly as her equal. However, she was not certain of the best procedure to go about getting done. She didn't think that she should go so far as to apologize to Molly. She correctly assumed such an act would appear condescending and patronizing. Instead, she resolved to live the right way in word and deed moving forward, which turned out to be a sound decision. Her resolution finally broke the silence created by her self-absorbed bout with her past. She was now able to respond.

Elizabeth's simple but honest reply to Molly and Harvey regarding their announced engagement was, "Molly, Harvey, I think you two will make a perfect pair."

"Thank you, Elizabeth," Molly answered.

Before Harvey could answer, the den door opened and they all heard Norman and Marlene approaching. None of them said anything as they waited for Norman and Marlene to arrive with the marriage decision. When the couple approached arm in arm, it was obvious that the answer was yes. Still, everyone wanted to hear the formal proclamation.

"Marlene and I are going to get married and I'm going to adopt Toby," Norman announced. "I'm also going to get my last name changed to Purlmen."

Harvey leaped to his feet and gave each a hug as he offered his congratulations. He helped Molly to her feet so she could do the same. He then helped Elizabeth to her feet and gave her a hug and congratulations. All now took their seats, and not surprisingly, Elizabeth had questions about the timetable.

"When will all this happen, Norman?" she asked.

"I'll begin with the name change first thing tomorrow morning. As soon as that's taken care of, we'll set the wedding date and get the adoption taken care of. Also, speaking about names, Marlene is Marlene from now on, not Marlena."

"That's right," Marlene chimed in. "Please call me Marlene from now on."

Harvey offered his assistance. "Name changes take a while, but I'll see to it that you get a good lawyer who will be able to push things along."

Harvey figured he should reiterate his and Molly's announcement so everyone would know that everyone else was aware of their upcoming marriage.

"Since those things will take some time it sounds like you two will be second in line to get married," Harvey announced. "Molly and I will beat you to it. We're getting married as soon as we can get it scheduled."

"That's for sure," echoed Molly.

Those statements triggered another series of congratulations and well wishes.

"Who would ever believe that my family's heirlooms were a big part of all this?" asked Elizabeth.

"It is hard to believe," agreed Harvey.

As an afterthought, Elizabeth added, "You know, it's funny. The heirlooms are still locked in the little safe after more than 20 years, and opening the safe to look at them doesn't seem to be too important right now. I mean, they're valuable and they represent some of my family's heritage, but what's really important is what has happened to us. It just seems almost unbelievable that it all happened because of a tiny little toy safe. Actually, it's not *almost* unbelievable. To most people, it would be *fully* unbelievable. I know it happened and I still find it hard to believe."

"You're right," said Harvey. "And there's another believe it or not. At first, I wasn't going to take the case because I'm retired."

Elizabeth suddenly thought about the payment. "How much do I owe you, Harvey? I'd forgotten about your expenses. They must have run pretty high."

"Not a dime," Harvey said. "What I've gotten out of this job is priceless. Money couldn't buy all the happiness I feel from the experience." He reached over and lovingly squeezed Molly's hand before adding, "And don't forget that after theses marriages, we'll all be dangling from somewhere on the branches of the same family tree."

"Yes, that's right, we will," agreed Elizabeth. She'd made the statement quickly, boldly, and evenly to show and convince herself and the others that she was in full agreement with the revelation.

"And you know," Harvey stated, "this has whole thing has unfolded like a storybook. In fact, I think you could call it a saga. Make that a compelling saga, full of pride and some upheaval, but I do believe the unity we're sharing today is perfect. All we have to do is work together to keep it forever. No more disarray."

"I agree, Harvey," said Elizabeth. "No more disarray."

Although her last statement was interpreted by the others as an agreement to Harvey's remark about the family in general, Elizabeth had actually directed her comment at herself. She felt she needed to clear the air and get things off her chest to wipe the slate clean for the betterment of the future.

"Everyone, listen to me," she began. "I've always tried to do the right things and lead a good life, but I realize now that I could have done a lot of things much better. I should have appreciated the people around me more and I should have done more to help my son become the man he finally became. What I'm trying to say is, I'm truly sorry for any of the wrongs toward anyone that I've committed, and I'm going to do all I can to be a better person in the future. Also, I'm ready to listen to suggestions. I really am."

Elizabeth softly clapped her hands together to interlace her fingers and asked, "Does anyone have anything to add?"

"No, what you just said is perfect, Elizabeth," Molly said. "We all need to follow your lead."

"Yes, that's right," agreed Marlene.

"Right on," Norman chimed in.

"I believe everyone should learn from past mistakes and strive to avoid making the same ones in the future," said Harvey. "We're going to be alright."

Then, with his keen sense for organization, Harvey had a suggestion.

"Those heirlooms that brought all this together deserve special recognition," Harvey reasoned. "As I understand it, the tradition has been to wait many years to bring them out and have a ceremony. I think the family should choose a reason to bring them out on occasions sooner than that."

"That's a good idea," Elizabeth said as she held up her hand to show her heirloom ring. "I wear mine every day." As an afterthought, she added, "I think maybe I'll give it to you Marlene, on your wedding day."

"Oh Mother, that would be wonderful," Marlene replied.

"Yes, I agree," said Norman. "And you know, I think we should hold a ceremony for the other heirlooms every 4 years on February 29th."

"I like that idea," said Elizabeth. "And I was thinking, it would be nice to honor my ring every year as part of your wedding anniversary celebration, once you get the wedding scheduled."

"That's good thinking," Harvey added before pausing for reflection. "You know, these last couple of weeks have been uplifting. I've gotten involved with a great family and I met Molly. This has been the biggest twist of fate that has ever happened to me. And just think, if the call had come in an hour later than it did, I probably would have been on the golf course. I don't think I ever would have met any of you."

"Yeah," Norman said. "It's hard to believe how all this happened..." He paused to measure his words before continuing. "...through just a lot of dumb luck."

Marlene looked at Norman lovingly as she added her opinion to bolster his.

"Yes," she said. "That luck was more like good karma. Good things happen to and for good people."

"It was both of those things – it was serendipity," Elizabeth stated.

Molly had the last word and she used the opportunity to both state her feelings and to punctuate her status as Elizabeth's equal. Looking directly at Elizabeth she said, "No, Elizabeth. This whole thing has been a blessing."

She then looked at each member of her soon-to-be extended family before declaring, "We've all been blessed with life, love, and a wonderful family."

* * *

Epilogue

Elizabeth took to heart the opportunity to virtually relive portions of her life. The admissions, revelations, and promises she'd made, although primarily to herself, became the mainstay of her way of thinking. She turned into a wonderful leader fully ready to pass the business along.

Norman and Marlene, along with Toby and his eventual siblings, prospered under Elizabeth's watchful and helpful eyes. They became the embodiment of the type of Purlmen family Elizabeth had always dreamed of.

Harvey and Molly continued to maintain the true love neither knew they'd been looking for. Rather than ever lamenting the fact that their life together didn't begin sooner, they grew closer and cherished their journey into a shared future.

The quartet of cohorts (don't worry about Elizabeth because you know she would never tell) kept their inside information under wraps. The bumps and bruises encountered to repair the family tree were never uttered by any of the players. Those ugly things remained "passed over" by all members of the immediate and extended family generation.

Metaphorically speaking, everything meant to be kept under wraps was squashed, squeezed, compressed and permanently buried inside impregnable fortresses of granite-like closed mouths.

Acknowledgements

Thanks to all of you who know you assisted me in my quest to write this book. My thanks also to those of you who had no idea you were helping me. I truly appreciate each and every contribution.

About the Author

Dave Echols has been aching to explore 'what if' questions through a novel for years, beginning with his successful penning of an impromptu newsletter during his 7th grade English class. Later, he accumulated a repertoire of potential 'what if' scenarios while serving overseas in the Army, completing his BSBA, working as a telephone technician, pursuing a career in the music entertainment field, and appreciating the many other twists and turns of personal and work life. He relishes situations, real or imagined, on screen or in print, where participants remain true to their character. The culmination of his passion is his novel, The *Passed* Generation. He has created a work that traces an extraordinary path toward an unusual conclusion.

9 781735 873220